THE GUMSHOE CHRONICLES
1920

Hope you enjoy Joey's journey as he deals with the realities of his time.

TJ Viola

a novel by TJ Viola

Outskirts Press, Inc.
Denver, Colorado

This is a work of fiction. The events described herein referring to actual places and/or historical characters are imaginary. All other events and characters described herein are also imaginary and are not intended to refer to specific places or living persons. The opinions expressed in this manuscript are solely the opinions of the author and do not represent the opinions or thoughts of the publisher.

Outskirts Press, Inc.
http://www.outskirtspress.com

ISBN: 978-1-4327-3691-0

Library of Congress Control Number: 2008939630

Outskirts Press and the "OP" logo are trademarks belonging to Outskirts Press, Inc.

PRINTED IN THE UNITED STATES OF AMERICA

This book is dedicated to our children, grandchildren and parents.

Every journey in life starts with a first step.

Dear Iris,

Thank you from the bottom of our hearts for taking such good care of our beloved sons Michael & Noah.

Happy Holidays! We hope that you enjoy their Grandpa's first novel.

Cheers!

Elle & Joe Power

Dec. 1, 2011

Acknowledgments

**Special thanks to Teresa R. Funke
for her unwavering support and
coaching during the writing of this novel.**

January

Growing up near the waterfront, you get used to the winter winds whipping off the Hudson and the overcast skies blanketing the city in a shroud of gloom. But a few days after returning home from the war, there was a chill in the neighborhood I'd never experienced before. It was the way Tony the Butcher tossed me a short nod rather than the warm embrace I'd expected. It was how the old folks, sitting on the steps of their brownstones, whispered as I approached and how the kids quit fighting in the streets to stare.

At first I thought it was my war instincts overreacting, slow to adjust to civilian life. But as I continued to walk down the street in my Italian neighborhood, the raucous sounds of commerce ground to a halt and mothers dragged their children indoors. Something was coming. I felt it; the neighborhood knew it.

Suddenly an explosion of eerie sounds erupted around me. Shrill whistles, rattling chains, and the clang of baseball bats beating garbage cans echoed off the stone buildings. Noises designed to instill fear. One by one my old gang emerged from alleyways, beneath stoops and open doorways. I'd seen and heard it all before. I'd given the same blank zombie stares that greeted me now. There was going to be a rumble—not with a rival street gang, but with me.

I took off, weaving between several fruit stands, brushing past bystanders as they screamed obscenities. My old gang was playing with me, just keeping pace. When I turned onto Front Street, I heard the familiar horn of a New York Ferry leaving its slip for Staten Island. Then, a quiet calm descended on the harbor as cranes ceased working and dockworkers dropped their cargo to watch five big lugs corner me, swinging their bats and chains. The workers knew us, all of us; we'd played and fought together growing up around the piers. My attackers were my closest friends. I wouldn't, couldn't let anything change that, even if it meant taking a beating for some unknown reason. As the five backed me up against a stack of crates, I fought to suppress the adrenaline rising in me as my survival instincts reacted to the threat. I was about to find out how much the war had truly changed me.

Vic had been our leader, but this wasn't the same guy I once knew. His face reflected the scars of war, and his words turned his sculptured features into a mask of rage. There was no doubt he wanted me dead; I'd seen that look many times fighting throughout Europe. The rest of the group stood back. They would brawl if for no other reason than to follow Vic, but they didn't share his depth of hatred.

"Joey, do you know what happened to my brother, Frankie?" The bat Vic held quivered inches from my face. "I was standing next to him in the trenches when a sniper blew his head apart. I had to wipe his brains from my face, but it didn't come off. It'll never come off. Where were you, Joey? We all swore an oath to fight and die together when we joined up, remember? Look around! We used to be ten, now there're five and *you*."

"Vic, I had every intention of shipping out with the gang."

"Yeah? How come you weren't in those filthy trenches eating dirt and spilling your blood like the rest of us?"

As Vic ranted, I removed my jacket. "I'm warning you," I said, "I'm not the person you remember. Back off; I don't want to hurt any of you."

Before they could respond, Mike O'Reilly's police car screeched to a stop.

"Stay out of this, O'Reilly," Vic shouted. "This ain't none of your damn business. You're not a flattie anymore."

"That's true, I'm off the streets. In homicide I don't have to deal with crap like this. I guess I could wait until all you wops kill each other."

"Watch it, O'Reilly, or you'll end up floating in the bay one of these nights. Only one of us *wops* is gonna get his today and that's Joey."

"Bats and chains are okay, fellas, but dump the blades," O'Reilly said, knowing he couldn't stop what was about to happen.

The switchblades all came out at the same time, but instead of hitting the pavement, they came hurling toward me. I went with my instincts and focused on Vic's chiv, hoping the others would miss by inches, like they had when we played chicken as kids.

I didn't flinch when the steel sliced through the palm of my outstretched hand. With the other knives still quivering in the wooden crates behind me, I put downward pressure on the dull side of Vic's blade, pulled it out of my palm, then used it to cut a piece of cloth from my shirt. Vic was unimpressed, but the others inched backward as I shoved the cloth through the gash in my hand.

When I finished, O'Reilly stepped aside as if to say *have at him.* Vic came first, swinging his bat. I snatched it away in one movement and instinctively moved to follow up with a palm thrust that would've shattered his sternum. At the last instant, I regained control, brought my forearm around, and smashed his jawbone with my elbow, knocking him to the ground. Out of the corner of my eye, I saw a glint of metal hurling toward my head. I raised the bat I'd taken from Vic and as the chain wrapped around the handle, I yanked Chris forward, dropping him with a knee to his groin and tossed the bat and chain into the bay. The dockworkers cheered then grew silent as the others charged. I dropped down, and as their bats and chains collided, I swept my legs around, knocking them to the ground. With my adrenaline pumping, I was ready for anything. Chris recovered, grabbed one of the knives, and took a swipe at my neck. Leaning back, the blade grazed my chin. I grabbed his wrist as the knife whisked by, twisted his arm behind his back, gripped the side of his face with my other hand, and was about to yank when O'Reilly shouted for me to stop. In another instant, Chris would've crumbled in a heap at my feet with a broken neck.

Vic sat up, rubbing his jaw while the others tried to stand, stumbling around in a daze. I turned to get my coat, thinking the fight was over. Suddenly they slammed me chest first into a stack of crates, holding my arms spread-eagle as Vic picked up a chain. Before O'Reilly could react, Vic ripped off my shirt to view the damage he was about to inflict and raised his chain.

"Holy shit!" Vic said.

The others let go and turned to Vic as he tossed the chain aside.

"What the hell happened to you?"

Everyone got a good look at the scars and burn marks that littered my back.

"The war, you assholes," I said as I grabbed my coat. "The war happened."

O'Reilly walked me over to his car, and we drove to my uncle's saloon. My uncle Luigi owns the four-story brownstone where I live with my parents and where Pop operates his custom men's shoe store. My uncle's bookie parlor and saloon are above us on the second floor.

Word traveled fast, and by the time Vic and the other guys got to the saloon, it was overflowing with locals. Even some of the dockworkers had taken off early and were already drinking and exaggerating the fight. A round of beers arrived at our table, and Vic raised a glass in memory of his brother.

"To Frankie."

"And the rest of the gang," I added.

Vic downed his drink and looked intently at the empty mug. "What happened that day? Why didn't you ship out with us?"

I didn't want to relive the war, but I owed him an explanation.

"When we were waiting to board the bus, two of the camp orderlies came and took me to the Commander's office."

"Yeah, we saw that. What I want to know is why."

"I had some skills he needed."

"Like what?"

"Look, Vic, Frankie died because it was his time. There wasn't anything you or anyone else could've done. So quit blaming me or yourself. The Commander assigned me to another unit. I had no choice; it's as simple as that. Early the next morning, I shipped out to another training base for three months, then overseas."

"What unit? Where? What kind of training? What about all those scars? How'd ya get 'em?"

"That's my business. The war's over."

"It'll never be over," Vic said, drawing back another drink.

Chris's girl, Rosalie, brought over another round, a few ice packs for our bruises, and some medical supplies. She gently held my wrist and inspected my bloody palm.

"I'm gonna take that cloth out and clean the wound with some peroxide. Hopefully it won't get infected. Sorry, Joey, but this is gonna hurt like hell."

I didn't recoil when she poured the peroxide into the wound, and the guys noticed.

"Joey, how can you take that much pain? You didn't even flinch when Vic's knife went through your hand," Chris said.

"It was part of my training."

"Bullshit! Why the hell would they train you to take pain? If you got shot in the trenches, chances were you died. End of story."

"Believe what you want, Vic. I'm done trying to explain myself to you."

Rosalie finished wrapping my hand and was about to leave when I caught her arm. "You did a nice job, thanks."

"I patched up my share of wounds over there."

"Where were you stationed?"

"Lyon, Verdun, I don't know. All the field hospitals seemed the same after a few months. You should have that looked at by a doctor. You're lucky you didn't damage any tendons."

As I watched her walk back to the bar, I silently envied Chris. I turned my attention back to the guys. An hour ago they were ready to crack my skull open, and now it felt like old times again. That's the way things are growing up in the city; one minute you're friends, the next you're fighting for your life. I was beginning to think nothing had changed after all.

My uncle Luigi and several of the dockworkers came over to listen to the guys telling war stories. "Wait a minute," Luigi said to Vic and the group. "You guys are all bullshitters. You want you should see a real war hero, I'll show ya one." He walked behind the bar and returned with a beat-up old metal box and dropped it on the table.

"How the hell did you get that, Uncle Luigi? You had no right going through my stuff."

"Joey, I didn't ..."

"Since I've been home, you've treated me like a leper, along with everyone else in this damn neighborhood."

I fought to calm myself but lost it when the guys opened the box and passed around my medals.

"Jesus, Joey. You're a damn' hero," Vic said.

I leaned forward on the end of the table and would have yanked Vic out of his seat if I hadn't seen the terror in his eyes. Before I knew what I was doing, the end of the table was several feet off the ground and dropped with a thunderous force. Some of the guys stood to avoid the spilt beer and fell over backwards, landing on the floor.

"You all disgust me. I left as Joey Batista and came back as Joey Batista. When did I ever show you, any of you, I was a coward? When did I even once give you cause to doubt my friendship?"

I looked around and most everyone held their head down. "These medals mean shit to me. They remind me of death, unbelievable pain, and a piece of me that's lost forever."

I got the hell out of there and walked down Market Street, across Front and sat between two piers on top of the retaining wall, trying to decide if I should leave town and set up my PI business on Staten Island or Jersey. I'd made my decision when Mike O'Reilly joined me.

"That was quite a display you put on," he said.

"You weren't much help."

"I'm not talking about the fight. I knew you could handle those bums, but then again, I didn't expect Vic to try to kill ya."

"I saw it in his eyes."

"I'm talkin' about the mess you made at Luigi's. It's not like you to lose your temper, especially with your uncle."

"Are you the same after the war?"

"No, guess not," O'Reilly said. "Want to talk?"

"Not really."

O'Reilly got up to leave then sat back down. "You know, I heard rumors about a special unit formed to operate behind enemy lines and infiltrate the enemy's upper echelon. I believe they called themselves the *Death Squad* because they weren't expected to make it through the war."

If O'Reilly wasn't such a good friend, I would've simply walked away, but instead I sat there looking across the bay, watching seagulls swoop down behind some tugboats searching for tasty morsels as I remembered the day Shawn, his kid brother, died during a street fight. A gang from another part of town came into our territory; one thing led to another and the stilettos came out. I was there when it happened. As soon as Shawn hit the ground, everyone scattered. He withered in pain as blood poured from his side. I couldn't leave him. There wasn't anything I could do but cradle him and helplessly watch him die.

O'Reilly had been a beat cop at the time. He'd heard about the brawl and came running around the corner, waving his nightstick. He stopped when he saw us, gently took Shawn from my arms, and cried. Even though O'Reilly is six years older, that day created a bond between us most people never experience.

I don't know why I told him. I guess some things have a way of coming out.

"After Anita's disappearance, I wanted to kill myself but didn't have the guts. When the war broke out, enlisting in the service presented an easy solution and the Commander's offer to join a suicide squadron seemed to seal my fate. I volunteered. I guess Vic and the guys were right; I did leave them."

"Why did you come back?" O'Reilly asked.

"For Anita. I returned home because I realized I'd learned skills that might help me discover what happened to her."

"What type of skills?"

"I held back today. I could've killed every one of them in a matter of minutes and almost did. I thank God I didn't."

"What did you actually do during the war?"

"I killed people. Anyone who got in my way died. There was only one focus in my life and that was to complete my missions."

"People die in wars. I try not to think about the number I killed," O'Reilly said.

"There's a difference. I targeted specific people. I knew who they were. In some cases I befriended them, deceived them, betrayed their trust."

"Are you saying you were an assassin?"

I turned and looked at my good friend and told him the truth. "I was worse than an assassin."

O'Reilly didn't say anything for a few moments. "Were lives saved because of your missions?"

"That's what they always told us."

"Did you believe them?"

"Yes."

"That's all that matters."

"I wish it was that simple. Certain memories are hard to shut away."

"You still didn't say how your training will help find the truth about Anita," O'Reilly said.

"In some ways it's hard to explain. To stay alive I had to know what people were thinking and not just rely on their words. I had to see things that others might miss; I had to trust my instincts."

"Have you decided what you're gonna do now that you're back?"

"I'm thinking of leaving and setting up my business on the Island or Jersey."

O'Reilly looked at me oddly, and that's when I realized I hadn't told him about my PI license.

"Did you ever wonder why I came home so late after the war ended?"

"The army sent your folks a letter telling them you were recovering from some wounds."

I almost laughed. "Out of twenty who joined the Death Squad, three survived. The army didn't know what to do with us. They hadn't planned on any of us returning home and didn't know if we were fit to re-enter civilized society. They put us in a sanitarium and ran all sorts of tests. As part of our rehabilitation, we had to learn a profession. I guess they figured if we could earn a living, we wouldn't turn to crime. I chose to become a private investigator. At first they tried to talk me out of such a violent career, but in the end, I convinced them all three of us were uniquely qualified."

When I finished telling my tale, I looked over at O'Reilly and saw his eyes glazing over. He understood. The Joey Batista he knew no longer existed.

"Why are you thinking of leaving?"

"How can you ask that after what happened today? Even my family had doubts about me."

"Ya know, Joey, it's been tough on your family. They defended you the best they could, and their businesses suffered. Not for a moment did they doubt your courage."

"Then why didn't they tell me what people were saying? Why didn't you?"

"I guess we figured you'd tell us what happened when you were ready."

I still wasn't convinced until O'Reilly gave me a glimpse of how he dealt with Shawn's death.

"We all lost a lot of friends and relatives from the war and the damn Spanish flu. Everyone is still bitter and grieving. I suggest you find a way to forgive them, even Vic. This neighborhood is in your blood; it's your home. You have family and friends here and you need to take it as it is. I did. We live in a dangerous place, but leaving after my brother died would have been a mistake. My father and brother spilt their blood on these streets, and someday I will too. I wouldn't have it any other way."

* * * * *

It'd been a little over a week since the *big fight,* as it became known in the neighborhood, and most everyone treated me with respect again. But there was something I still needed to do.

I found Uncle Luigi tending bar, horsing around with his favorite customers, joking about the Prohibition Act that was about to go into effect in a few days. It seemed everyone in town was using the Act as an excuse to drink until they had to be carried home, even though they knew the booze would keep flowing. In fact, Uncle Luigi already had his suppliers lined up.

I walked behind the bar and got my uncle's attention. "Uncle Luigi, I want to apologize for showing such disrespect the other day, especially in your place. You've been good to me and my folks, and I had no right to say the things I did."

The guys around the bar pounded their mugs on the counter, and Uncle Luigi responded by giving out a free round of drinks. I expected one of his bear hugs, but instead he led me out of the saloon.

"Don't worry 'bout it kid. If I had to apologize every time I did something stupid, I wouldn't have time to do anything else. On the other hand, now that you're back in my good graces, I have a surprise for you." We walked up to the third floor, and at the top of the stairs, the office door on the left had a frosted glass panel painted with a sign, *Joey Batista, Private Investigator*. Luigi opened the door and showed me around. "You're all set. You can live here and run ya business. You got a hideaway bed, bathroom, and closet, everything you need."

I walked behind the desk and looked out the window. There was a fire escape that led to Market Street.

"How did you know?" I asked.

"Some big shot from the army came to see us before you arrived home. He said the country owed you a debt of gratitude and while you recuperated from your injuries, you were studying to be a PI."

"That's all he said?"

"If you ask me, the guy was nuts. He said we should try not to get you upset because you might have a bad temper." Luigi looked down and laughed. "Maybe he wasn't so crazy after all."

I turned back toward the window so he couldn't see my face. I didn't want my family to know what I'd become during the war.

"Uncle Luigi, I can't afford this place. I don't even have my first case."

"Not a problem. When you get some dough, give me a slice."

"How much of a slice?" I knew enough about my uncle

to nail down a firm agreement.

He rubbed his chin then gave me a slap on the back. "Ten percent."

"Ten percent after expenses and I get to renegotiate whenever I want."

"Now you're sounding like your pop. He's always trying to lower the rent. Okay, it's a deal." We shook hands.

"I'll tell Ma and Pop and move in right away."

"They know. It was gonna be a surprise. We were boxing up your stuff the other day, that's when I found your medals."

This time I gave *him* a bear hug.

* * * * *

My first case came a few days later from Tony the Butcher. His shop's a few buildings down the street from ours, away from the waterfront. I've known Tony all my life. He and his wife are good, honest folk. They work twelve to fourteen hours a day, except Sundays.

I went in to buy a roast for Ma when Tony asked me to step into the backroom. I knew right away something was wrong. He wasn't smiling.

"Joey," he said. "The Missus, she tells me you're a private eye now. No?"

"That's right, Tony. You got a problem I can help with?"

He handed me a subpoena that ordered him to appear in court on February 16, 1920, to face charges of criminal neglect, accused by somebody named Tommy Stefano. The subpoena alleges that on the night of December 17, 1919, Stefano sustained extensive bodily injuries when he slipped and fell on a patch of ice in front of 1252 Market Street. According to the document, Stefano was unable to work and sought two thousand dollars in damages.

I knew Tony didn't have that kind of jack because he gave away most of his profits. He always had a special price for families down on their luck.

"Tony, that's more than you make in a year. Did this really happen?"

He struggled to find the right words, so I suggested he speak Italian.

"Hey, I'm American now. I can speaka English," he said. "Yeah, he falls, but there was a no ice. I clean my sidewalk every day. When I help him up, he says to me he's okay and walks away. Now this!"

I asked Tony a few more questions and suggested he hire a lawyer. This didn't go over too well.

"Joey, I come to you for help and you say get a lawyer. I don't want no lawyer. I want you to fix this."

"Tony, you have to go to court, and you can't do this without a lawyer. I tell you what I'll do. I'll hire a lawyer and find out more about this Stefano guy. All you have to do is answer the lawyer's questions and show up for the court date."

"Okay, but Joey, don't trust no lawyer. I'm surprised your pop don't tell you this."

I borrowed the subpoena and told him I'd take his advice. When I left, Tony had a big smile, and I had a free roast. As I walked home, I couldn't help but wonder how I was going to tell my uncle he could only eat ten percent of the roast.

The next afternoon I went to see Frank Galvano, the lawyer who had the office next to mine. I've known him since before the war but was never in his office. Immediately upon entering, I realized I'd chosen the wrong profession. Frank sat behind a large redwood desk in a pinstriped suit, with floor-to-ceiling bookcases lining the walls of his office and an inlaid parquet floor with a striking octagonal design. I stood in the doorway like a kid in a candy shop, not knowing where to look first. Frank got up and grabbed my hand.

"Joey, great to see you. Congratulations! I would have come by, but I knew you were busy setting up shop."

"Thanks, Mr. Galvano."

"Hey, we're both professionals now. Drop the mister and call me Frank."

"Thanks, Frank. Mind if I come in? I have a case I could use your help on."

"Sure thing, take a seat. What can I do for you?"

As I entered the room, I was thinking I needed to get a couple of these high-back leather chairs. "Mr. Galvano, I mean Frank, Tony the Butcher is being sued, and I think the whole deal stinks."

I gave him the details and mentioned Tony didn't have a lawyer. It didn't take Frank long to assess the case.

"I agree with you, kid. This whole setup sounds like a con. Probably Stefano's lawyer is some low-life scraping the barrel, and there must be a crooked doctor involved. I'm sure this Stefano character is living the life of an invalid, so he'll have plenty of honest neighbors testifying on his behalf."

We agreed to work on the case together.

"I'll tell Tony to expect a visit from you to discuss his defense. Oh, just so you know, he doesn't trust lawyers."

"Who does?" Frank chuckled.

I was about to leave when Frank gave me some advice. "What you need is to snap a picture of this Stefano guy in the act of being normal, and make sure you can prove the date the picture was taken. If you bust this scam, I may have some work for you."

I left his office with mixed feelings. I was hoping my

first case would be a murder or jewelry heist, something with a little more pizzazz. Get a picture. How obvious was that? Frank left out the important part. What was I supposed to do, follow Stefano around with a camera under my coat? What the hell, only my second week as a PI and I had a case with the possibility of more to come.

I got back to Tony and we agreed on a fee: three dollars a day plus expenses. Now all I needed was a plan. I already had quite a bit of information; the subpoena indicated Stefano lived near the theater district around West 42nd Street and 8th Avenue and, according to Tony, Stefano was in his mid-twenties, about five-seven, five-eight, with a good build. I just had to prove he wasn't really injured.

Even though Stefano didn't live far from my office, I figured I'd stake out his place around the clock for about a week. I asked Ma to keep an eye out for any customers on the slim chance I got some walk-in traffic.

It wasn't hard to find Stefano; he lived in an apartment building in an upscale neighborhood. I was lucky enough to locate a room for rent by the week a few blocks over. I positioned myself to watch Stefano's place by taking on a new profession, that of a beggar. The trick to this disguise was to be able to change back into an ordinary bird in a few seconds, so I could follow my target without raising suspicion. I brought the essential items with me: an old, dirty, worn-out cap; a double-sided army coat, with one side torn and dirty and the other like new; two pairs of gloves and shoes, old and new; and hair grease, so my hair could look disheveled or fashionably slicked back.

By five the next morning, I was begging on a corner where I had a great view of Stefano's building. I was actually picking up some loose change, and for a brief instant the thought crossed my mind if the PI business didn't pan out, I might have another option for making a living. Standing on a street corner, however, under a perpetually overcast sky, enduring the damp, bitter cold winds blowing off the bay in winter and the sweltering humid days of summer, didn't seem appealing.

The day passed agonizingly slow until early afternoon, when Stefano lumbered down the stairs with the help of a private nurse, who was quite a knockout. She guided him into a wheelchair, and they visited a few of the local shops before stopping at a small park where Stefano proceeded to feed a family of pigeons.

I hobbled over to the park to get a good look at my adversary. As I approached, Stefano became agitated.

"Get out of here, you bum."

I persisted and inched closer, begging for money. Stefano went into a rage. If it wasn't for his nurse, I'm certain he would have launched himself out of the wheelchair to attack me. His nurse placed a calming but firm hand on his shoulder, brushed her lips against his ear as she whispered something, reached into his jacket pocket and gave me a dime. I blessed her for her kindness and shuffled away. I now knew a little more about my new friend; Tommy Stefano had quite a temper and the nurse was more than his private nurse. She knew exactly what was going on.

I figured they needed to keep up the act during the day, but would eventually go stir crazy, sneak out after dark and return before sunrise. I took the chance that my reasoning was correct and rested during the day and continued my watch at night.

The first night I almost froze to death. The temperature dropped to minus five as the wind whipped relentlessly between and around the buildings, making it difficult to find protection. I spent most of the night huddled inside a doorway and occasionally walked up and down the street to keep up the pretense of begging, but in reality, I was trying to keep my circulation moving. The evening passed uneventfully; their lights went out around eleven and all was quiet except for the howling wind.

On the third night, I hit pay dirt. A Checker Cab drove up around one in the morning and the two of them, dressed to the hilt, slipped out of the brownstone and melted into the cab. I wrote down the license and cab number and waited for their return. Around five in the morning a cab drove up with its lights out.

I now had more to go on. They were gone approximately four hours, probably to one of the new, illegal upscale saloons that popped up around town as the Prohibition Act went into effect. I estimated this mysterious speakeasy, as the illegal saloons have become known, was at least twenty to thirty minutes away or they would run the risk of being recognized.

At this point in the investigation, it seemed I could proceed in a few directions: follow them in a cab the next time they went out, which wasn't practical since cabs didn't typically hang out in the neighborhoods, or try to discover where they had gone and stake out the joint. The last choice seemed the best option; it would be easier to avoid detection and a lot warmer. But first, I needed to find out where the taxi had taken them.

* * * * *

Once back at my office, I took a long, hot shower, ate a huge breakfast to the delight of Ma, gave both Tony and Frank an update, and then waited until mid-afternoon to call the Checker Cab Company, impersonating my friend O'Reilly.

"This is Sergeant O'Reilly from the 14th Precinct. I'm

calling about a hit and run involving one of your cabs last night in Queens...

"Well, there probably wasn't any noticeable damage to the cab. The cabbie sideswiped a couple at an intersection around one-fifteen in the morning. The guy has a broken hip now…

"Cab number 17, license YC482…

"That's not possible? Why not?

"Okay, slow down I'm taking notes…

"You say number 17 had a pick-up at one o'clock near the Theater District at West 48th and 8th Avenue and dropped the customer off in the Lexon Hill area at 15 East 61st Street at one-twenty…

"Yeah, I agree, nowhere near the accident. I might come by in a few days though to check your books…

"That's right. Sergeant O'Reilly's the name, 14th Precinct."

A little past midnight, I took a cab to the drop-off point and arrived at what looked like a deserted warehouse. Fortunately, another cab pulled up and a young couple got out and walked to a side door. I caught up with them as they gave the password to a mountain of a man: "Rocco sent us." When the big bruiser opened the door, I was conversing with the couple and we walked in together.

We entered a short, narrow hallway that led to a massive steel door with a five-inch square peephole about six feet from the floor. This door didn't open until the outer door closed, a precaution against a federal or local police raid. As I followed the pair into a small alcove, it took a few seconds to adjust to the bright lights and raucous sounds coming from an adjacent room. I hung back and let them check their coats before I approached the counter. I was a little reluctant to remove mine since all the racks were full and the counter overflowed with coats. A young hostess saw my hesitation and assured me she had a system, even though things looked chaotic.

"Guess I'm a latecomer," I said.

"Yeah, most everyone arrives between ten and midnight. You look kinda lonely. There ain't many singles around tonight."

"Actually, I'm working a case." She backed away. "I'm not a cop, I'm a private eye," I quickly added.

"I never met a shamus before. You must lead an exciting life."

"Don't know yet, this is my first case."

"A rookie PI, now that's interesting," she said.

Looking around, I noticed a concession carrier with cigarettes, trinkets, and a stack of newspapers on a chair, along with a camera behind the counter.

"It appears you have more than one job."

She followed my glance.

"There are three of us, and we rotate jobs during the night, as well as share tips. We used to have lots of arguments over who should man the coatroom at close, since that's when the big dough rolls in. This way it's fairer."

"Whose idea was that?" I asked.

"Mine."

I could tell she was a sharp dame, and she had everything I needed to nail Stefano.

"How'd you and your friends like to help me out and make a few extra bucks?" Her eyes lit up as she leaned forward to hear what I had to say.

"I tell you what, why don't we meet after close and I'll go over the details?" She readily agreed.

Upon entering the main dance hall, the noise melted into the background as I watched a talented jazz band play "Sweet Georgia Brown" on a small stage directly opposite the entrance. I took a moment to survey the room. The dance floor appeared to comfortably hold twenty-five to thirty couples, but at least fifty were dancing. Seventy to eighty tables encircled the dance area and each could accommodate six customers. At first glance, it looked like most of the tables were occupied. On my right and left were identical semicircular bars made of mahogany with brass foot rails. Three bartenders manned each bar, and the booze flowed nonstop; clearly Prohibition was gonna be good for the underground economy. The dance hall was lavishly decorated with large chandeliers and velvet drapes over nonexistent windows. There were additional rooms behind the stage, guarded by two burly giants who obviously weren't standing there to enjoy the music.

To my left, a spot opened at the bar, and I took up my position for the night. I stood between two heavy drinkers who weren't interested in small talk. I tried to break the ice with Sam, the bartender. From his appearance it looked as though Sam had been through some rough years; his face reminded me of an old, worn-out punching bag, and the size of his belly indicated he sampled the merchandise more than a few times a night.

Sam liked to talk, which made the time pass quickly. In a previous life he'd been a boxer who never quite made it to the top. He'd been bartending all over town for the last ten years. Sam seemed like a nice guy, no family to speak of—just a lonely soul trying to stay out of trouble and make an honest living.

As time dragged on, I figured Stefano was staying home to nurse his imaginary injuries. I asked Sam if any of the dames at the bar might consider dancing with a stranger. He walked down a ways and leaned over to talk to a tall blonde. I had noticed her during the evening, sipping from the same drink. Sam came back and said Sally could use a friend and would enjoy a few dances. As I got up to introduce myself,

Sam grabbed my arm.

"I like Sally. Treat her right. She's not what you might think. She's a nice kid, educated too, just down on her luck."

"Don't worry, pal. I'm not looking for a good time, just some company."

He let go, but not before letting me know he meant business. For an old guy, Sam had one hell of a grip.

I reached between Sally and the guy next to her and placed my drink on the bar. "Sam tells me you might like to take a few spins around the dance floor. I'm Joey Batista."

Sally turned and I found myself gazing into the saddest eyes I've ever seen—not exactly what I had expected. Maybe Sam was wiser than he looked; Sally needed company more than I did. I suggested we grab a table and spend a few minutes getting acquainted and signaled Sam to refresh our drinks. As I watched her walk to a table, I could tell she had class. I wished I wasn't working a case; beauty, class and brains were not exactly a combination easy to find these days.

We spent the next hour getting to know each other, including some time on the dance floor. After the third dance, she relaxed and opened up. She came from a wealthy family, her dad being a successful banker. She left home a few weeks ago with a boyfriend, against her family's wishes. It turned out her parents were right; her friend spent what money she had and walked out. Even though she had an education, she'd never held down a job and couldn't bear going home to face her father. She looked about my age, twenty-four, a real looker, and seemed like a sweet kid who'd hit some hard times. Sally didn't have much money left, so she spent her days looking for work and her evenings in this joint, to be around people.

Near closing time, I wished her luck in finding a job

and went back to the bar to help Sam clean up so I'd be the last to leave.

The three hostesses, who were all smiles and giggles, greeted me at the coat counter ready to leave. The hostess I originally spoke with was Martha, a brunette, and the other two were Dorothy, a redhead, and Ginger, a blonde. As we walked out arm-in-arm, Rocky, the doorman, looked at me with envy. I gave him a wink and a big tip so he'd remember me when I returned the next night. Martha handed me the speakeasy's private card in case someone else was on duty when I returned.

Martha lived within walking distance and invited us up for a drink to talk about the case. Within five minutes we were beyond the warehouses and into a well-kept neighborhood with six-story apartment buildings. Fortunately, Martha lived on the second floor; I'm not sure I could have climbed six flights of stairs after a night of dancing and drinking. Each floor had four apartments, two midway down the hall opposite the stairwell as you came onto the landing, and one on either end of the hall. The hallway was dimly lit, narrow and had a mild mildew odor. Martha's place was at the end of the hall, on the right as you walked up the stairs. The apartment itself was fairly spacious. As we entered, we stood in the main living area that had four corner windows overlooking the intersection below. To the right of the entrance was a small kitchen with all the latest conveniences. It was clear from the furniture and other details in the apartment that the hostess business provided a reasonable income, and even though I'm no expert, Martha had good taste and an eye for decorating.

After several drinks, we got down to business. I gave them a complete rundown, including how I had disguised myself and tracked Stefano to the speakeasy. They were fairly impressed with the PI business and certainly felt sorry for Tony, but to my dismay, were hesitant to get involved.

"What seems to be the problem? A few minutes ago you were excited, and now you all want to pull out?"

Martha was the one who spoke up. "Do you know who Stefano is?"

"What's there to know? He's running a small-time scam."

"I don't think so," she said. "Maybe next time you should do a little investigative work before you take on a job."

"What are ya talking about? He's a nobody."

"Joey, he's a mean son-of-a-bitch, and he's trying to prove himself to people you don't wanna mess with. Do yourself and us a favor. Go home and find a new case."

"That's not an option. Sometimes people need to take a stand against animals like Stefano. Ya gonna help or not?" I said with some disgust.

I went into the kitchen to give the girls time to talk things over and poured myself a shot of whiskey. After ten minutes, they joined me, and Martha mixed up an extra strong batch of drinks. The girls didn't have to say a word: they were in. I understood their concerns. They were afraid of Stefano and of losing their jobs. I would do what I could to keep them safe, but I couldn't promise anything more. That wasn't enough for Martha.

"I don't know how you think we can help, but whatever it is, Stefano must never know we were involved. Is that clear?" she demanded.

I was beginning to like this dame; she had real moxie.

"I'll tell you what, we'll figure everything out together." That seemed to ease some of their concerns.

It took us about an hour to put together a reasonably

straightforward plan. The fact that Martha had been extremely generous with the booze probably made the plan look easier on paper than it would be in reality. At the time, it sounded foolproof, and the girls were looking forward to the excitement. Before leaving, I offered to pay for their help. They laughed, saying I probably needed the scratch more than they did.

The next night I filled Sam and Sally in on the details, and they both agreed to help, Sally because of the relationship we were developing and Sam because he hated Stefano's guts. They had some prior run-ins at the club, and Sam had to rough him up a bit.

We agreed that when I spotted Stefano, Sally would leave our table and let Sam know the sting was about to begin. She'd then stay at the bar so she wouldn't get caught in the middle of the action, and Sam would be ready to break up the fight I hoped would occur between Stefano and myself. I felt comfortable with the overall details and realized if the unexpected happened, I would have to react and rely on my military training.

When it became evident Stefano wasn't going to show that evening, Sally and I relaxed and enjoyed each other's company. As we parted, I asked her to come by my office when this was all behind us to discuss the possibility of a job with my family's business. Both of us realized I wouldn't be able to return to the speakeasy after I tangled with Stefano. I scribbled directions to my office on a napkin.

It had been three days, and I was beginning to second-guess myself about staking out the saloon when Stefano and his nurse arrived and sat at a table not far from ours. I caught Martha's attention; she soon came by and asked if we wanted our picture taken. As we talked, I indicated where Stefano was sitting. She took a quick look around, walked over to Dorothy, who was hawking cigarettes and the *Daily News*. Sally left the table and blended into the bar crowd to let Sam know everything was set to go.

I sat by myself downing several diluted drinks, pretending to be blotto. I leaned forward, leered at Stefano's nurse, trying to get her attention. She spoke softly to Stefano, who then turned in his chair and gave me a vicious shove, knocking me to the floor. Stefano purposely stepped on my ankle as they got up to dance. After a few seconds, I slowly stood up and gave everyone the go signal by clumsily spilling my drink. Martha and Dorothy rushed to get into position while I walked up behind Stefano.

I tapped Stefano on the shoulder and slid in between him and the nurse. Once he realized what was happening, Stefano grabbed my shoulder with one hand, twirled me around and then came forward with a right hook, cursing like a longshoreman. As his fist came toward me, I backed away, just as the flash from the camera exploded, catching all the action—including Dorothy holding the front page of the *Daily News* overhead in the background.

The music stopped as people backed away. Sam pushed us apart, but not before I landed a punch that from the sound of the blow had broken Stefano's nose. In the excitement I almost forgot I was supposed to be drunk. I stumbled backwards, headed toward the door, then glanced over my shoulder to make sure Sam still had Stefano restrained. Martha, already at the coat counter, handed me the photographic plate. I gave both her and Ginger a peck on the cheek and quickly left the speakeasy. I found out later that Martha raised the alarm that someone stole her photographs just as Stefano came running out of the dance hall with Sam not far behind. Apparently Stefano didn't suspect a setup. He was more concerned about finding "the bum" than why Martha was yelling.

It wasn't until two in the afternoon the next day that I gave Frank Galvano the photographic plate and explained what it contained and how I obtained it. He sat behind his big desk, listening intently. When I finished, he stood up, enthusiastically shook my hand, and said he would take it from there. Next, I went to see Ma and Pop and agreed to have supper with them that evening.

* * * * *

The instant we finished saying grace, Ma launched into her Italian mother routine.

"Joey, where have you been? You look so thin. What are you doing to yourself? This private eye stuff is no good, here, eat, eat!"

Pop shrugged his shoulders and gave me a look that said, "What can I say? You better eat and keep your mouth shut."

In between the antipasti and the chicken parmesan, I suggested to my folks they should think about expanding their shoe business by trying to attract new customers. Pop almost choked on a hot pepper.

"My son, the private investigator, he gets one case and now he's a business expert."

"Papa, listen to your son. He went into the army and got educated. Joey," Ma said, "what you mean?"

I learned over the years the best way to deal with my folks was to be brutally honest. "How many young women do you have as customers? None! How many new customers have you added in the last six months? None! And I bet you're selling fewer shoes than last year because a lot of your old customers are dying."

"Joey, your father, he works hard. Can he help it if people die?"

"That's exactly my point," I said. "We need to attract new, younger customers. I think you should sell shoes to men and women."

Pop's neck turned several shades of red. "Okay, what should I do? Get duded up and smile at all the young girls as they walk by the store?"

Ma gave him a stare that could have melted an iceberg. He sat down and tried to calm himself.

"Pop, I know you work hard and you're the best shoemaker in town, but times are changing fast since the war. All you have to do is hire a young woman who understands today's fashions."

Just then, Uncle Luigi came down and the conversation immediately changed.

"Hey what's all the fuss about? Are you two arguing over politics or religion?"

Uncle Luigi ran the Democratic Ward in our part of town and had already put the machine in motion to elect the next mayor, even though the election was months away and the candidates undeclared. Pop knew a lot of people in the community, and my uncle wanted to make sure he would support the right candidate: his. I actually appreciated the interruption, since my discussion with Ma and Pop was getting out of hand. All I really wanted to do was plant a seed. I think I succeeded.

After dinner, I went up to my office to put the final changes on a report for Tony and Frank. I also wrote out a bill for my services but crumbled it up and tossed it into the wastebasket. I needed to wait until the trial and see if Frank got the charges dropped against Tony.

I refocused my attention on the report when all of a sudden, it sounded like someone knocked down the door. As I looked up, the largest person I've ever seen ducked under the doorframe. I thought he was going to rip the seams of his suit as he maneuvered into the room.

"Are you Joey Batista?"

"Yeah, that's right. What can I do for you?"

My uncle came rushing into my office as I slowly reached for my gun.

"Hey, Butch, it's been a long time. Ya mind telling me what business you have with my nephew?"

"The Boss wants to see him."

My uncle turned to me. "You'd better go with Butch. He'll take you to see Mr. Castellano."

Mr. Castellano ran the waterfront and supplied all the speakeasies with booze; he also had many other questionable enterprises. As a kid, I'd actually worked for him for a few years. My uncle had made the arrangements for the job; I ran a numbers route and, fortunately for both of us, my parents never found out.

Butch had his car parked in front of Pop's shop with the motor running, and both my parents were looking out the window as I got in. I saw Luigi run over to reassure them as the car pulled into traffic.

No one ever said being a PI would be dull; it was only my first month and already some Neanderthal was taking me for a ride. Butch wasn't much of a conversationalist; I guess when you're his size, you don't need to say much. I sat quietly in the back seat and made mental notes of where we were going. We headed down Market Street toward the waterfront and drove into one of the many pier warehouses that lined New York's harbor along Front Street. As we drove into the structure, some of which could be as long as a city block, I could see several tugboats moored along the outside. Most of the open storage bays we passed were stacked high with cargo from freighters the tugs had guided into the harbor. As we continued to drive toward the end of the pier, I couldn't help but remember the times when I had skinny-dipped off the pilings during hot, muggy summer days with my friends Shawn O'Reilly and Bobby Balcone. Reality came rushing back when we stopped a few feet behind a black car. Butch and I got out, then he came over and gave me a hard shove. As I stumbled toward the car, its back door swung open. I gingerly bent forward to look inside.

"Joey, come in. It's been a long time."

"Hello, Mr. Castellano. It's good to see you again. Your man Butch said you wanted to see me."

As I sat down, he put his hand on my knee, "Not so fast, first tell me about your mom and pop. How they doin'? How's the shoe business?"

"They're fine. The business is a little slow, but they're in good health and Uncle Luigi keeps an eye on them."

"Now there's a real hustler. If I didn't already know, it would be hard to tell your father and Luigi are brothers. It wasn't like that when we grew up together in the old country."

"What do ya mean? Pop was different back in Italy?"

"Nah, forget I said anything. You know your old man; he minds his business and makes great shoes. They never wear out, but I guess that could be both good and bad for business."

We laughed, and I felt a little more at ease.

"I hear you're now a private investigator. How's it going?"

"I'm about to wrap up my first case, and I have a few others in the fire," I lied.

"That's great! Good honest work, and right now I need someone like you, someone I can trust."

"Sure, Mr. Castellano, whatever I can do for you."

"Ah, you remember the old days, when you were little and running numbers for me? I always liked you—very dependable, very loyal, and very observant. You always knew when someone was skimming money, trying to pull a Chinese squeeze."

Castellano turned and looked out the window; for a moment, I thought he had gone into some kind of trance. I sat quietly, feeling uncomfortable, until he broke the silence that had engulfed the car.

"You remember my kid brother, Angelo? Sure you do, he liked you."

"He always asked me if I did my schoolwork before letting me begin my rounds."

"That's right. He didn't want you to become one of us wise guys."

As Castellano turned toward me, I suddenly saw a tired man, not the energetic boss who seemed larger than life.

"My brother, he turned out okay. He became a doctor, wanted no part of the business or me. He even changed his name."

I didn't know where any of this was going. "How can I help, Mr. Castellano? Is Angelo is some sorta trouble?"

"He's dead, Joey. My kid brother's dead."

The silence that followed was screaming all around us as the noises normally in the background suddenly came roaring into the car. I could hear the seagulls circling the boats in the harbor, tugboats rubbing their hulls against the pilings, pigeons nesting in the rafters, but most of all, I could hear Mr. Castellano's memories rushing through the night.

"They say he committed suicide. My brother, he would never commit suicide. No decent Catholic would. No, he was murdered, and I want you to find out who did it."

"Sure, Mr. Castellano, sure. But if I were you, I'd hire an experienced investigator."

"Joey, I don't want anyone to know I'm looking into

Angelo's death. Since he changed his name and left the neighborhood, most people don't know he's my brother, not even his wife. I need someone I can trust and that's you. I want whoever killed him to think I buy into this suicide crap."

The pupils of his eyes became small and penetrating. "Joey, you understand what I'm asking? I want you to tell me who killed my brother and why!"

"I understand."

"Good. Butch will pick you up every Saturday night, so we can have a little chat."

He handed me an envelope. "Here's some dough. I have a lot of enemies, and I must know if they're going after my family."

"I'll get right on it, Mr. Castellano."

"I knew I could depend on you. There's some information about Angelo in the envelope as well. Good luck, Joey."

The ride home was uneventful and without conversation, except for a comment Butch made when I got back into his car.

"Good to see you're still alive, kid."

* * * * *

The last thing I wanted after meeting with Castellano was to face my uncle. He would drill me relentlessly to squeeze out every detail about my conversation with the Boss—a conversation I swore I wouldn't reveal. As I got to the second floor on the way to my office, I squatted down on my hands and knees, trying to cross below the speakeasy peephole, but to no avail. My uncle flung open the door, pulled me up by my armpits, and greeted me with a bear hug.

"Joey, glad you're still in one piece. I've been lookin' out this damn hole for over an hour. What's the matter, you lose somethin'?"

I had to catch my breath before I could respond. My uncle is an ox of a man who doesn't know his own strength, and one of his hugs can do serious damage.

"Just dropped a few coins," I said.

"Come with me. We need to talk," he said as he grabbed hold of my arm.

He practically dragged me to his back office through a throng of bodies that lined the bar, who ignored us as they drank and argued over Prohibition and women getting the right to vote.

As we got to his office, my uncle hurled questions at me even before the door closed.

"Now tell me, what's this all about? Are you in trouble? Why didn't you tell me if you were in trouble with the Boss?"

"I'm not in trouble."

"Then why would he want to see you? Are you doin' a job for him?"

"Uncle Luigi, slow down, I'll tell you what I can. There's no reason to worry. Everything's fine."

"Okay, here, I'm sitting down. Don't leave nothin' out."

I took a second to gather my thoughts and get my story straight since I couldn't tell him about Angelo.

"Butch took me to meet Castellano at the end of Pier 17. We talked privately in his car."

As soon as I mentioned Pier 17, Luigi clenched his fists and had trouble staying seated. He clearly didn't like the fact the Boss had arranged a clandestine meeting.

"I swear I had no idea what was going on."

"Just tell me what he wanted."

"I can't. All I can say is he gave me a job."

Luigi propelled himself out of his chair and paced back and forth, cussing and waving his arms.

"No! You are not getting mixed up with the Boss. Running numbers as a kid, no harm, but working for Castellano now is serious business. I'll tell him myself, don't you worry!"

"You don't need to get upset. He asked me to do him a personal favor as a private investigator. That's it."

He grabbed the back of my head, pulled it down, and looked up so we were eye-to-eye.

"This so-called favor has nothing to do with his business, you're sure?"

"I'm sure. Ma would kill me if I became a gangster."

Before letting go, he broke out into one of his huge grins.

"Yeah, she'd kill me too. Don't you ever tell her you ran numbers for him."

I took the opportunity to head for the door, hoping to avoid any more questions, but he got to the door as I pulled it open, slammed it shut, and pinned me against the wall, with his huge hand pressed against my chest.

"Joey, you listen to me. The Boss, you give him a finger and he takes an arm; you give him your arm and he takes your soul. You remember that!"

"I will. If I need help, I'll ask. I promise."

Satisfied, he insisted we have a couple of drinks together. One thing led to another, and it was after three before I finally got to bed.

Even though I was beyond tired, my mind wouldn't stop racing: reviewing all the details of Tony's case; thinking about Sally; seeing Butch ducking through the doorframe; reliving the ride to Pier 17; recalling the look on Castellano's face when he told me about Angelo's death.

All these thoughts, combined with the sounds of the waterfront and the smell of diesel fuel mixed with the odor of seawater still in my nostrils, stimulated my senses, making sleep impossible. My mind had accelerated into high gear, and there wasn't anything I could do to control my thoughts. I just stared at the ceiling and waited for sunrise.

February

At the break of dawn, still in a stupor, I dragged myself out of bed, made my way to the shower and managed to get dressed with great effort. I put my feet up on the desk and sipped a hot cup of coffee, thinking I should take the day off, when I remembered the envelope Castellano handed me the night before. Inside was a letter, and when I unfolded it, ten one-hundred dollar bills tumbled onto my desk.

I stared down in disbelief just as someone gently knocked at the door. I swept the letter and the money into the top drawer. The sun, piercing through the window behind my back, reflected off the door's glass panel into my eyes as it opened. I couldn't make out all the features of the person entering; however, it was definitely a woman with long, shapely legs. Putting down her suitcase, she asked in a timid voice if she could come in. The voice sounded familiar.

"I hope I'm not bothering you, but you said I should stop by."

I couldn't believe how stupid I was; all I can say in my defense is that I'd had a rough night. "Sally, sorry. I couldn't see who came in because of the sun's reflection."

As I came around the desk to greet her, she collapsed in my arms. I carried her to my bed, unbuttoned the top of her blouse, and placed a wet towel on her forehead. A few minutes later she sat up and explained what happened since we'd last met.

The day after my confrontation with Tommy Stefano, her landlord threw Sally out and took what money she had for back rent, leaving her with only some small change. She wandered the streets and rode the subway for shelter. It wasn't until last night that she found the napkin I had given her with directions to my office in her coat pocket.

"Oh, Joey." She rested her head against my shoulder and cried. "When you didn't seem glad to see me, I lost all hope."

I did my best to reassure her everything would be fine, laid her back down, and covered her with a blanket. In no time she fell asleep. I heard Ma coming up the stairs so I ran to meet her halfway.

"Morning, Ma."

"Whatsa matter with you? I always have to wake you up. You gotta no sleep?"

"I'm fine. What's for breakfast?"

Just then Uncle Luigi came down, pulled me aside before entering the dining area, and whispered in my ear. "Who's the dame?"

I was sure the jig was up, but Luigi didn't let on during breakfast.

"So your pop tells me you want him to hire some female help," he said fighting to keep a straight face. I could've killed him.

"Yeah, we talked about it. We need new customers and I think the best way is to hire a young woman to sell women's shoes."

"Sounds like a great idea!" my uncle said as he gave me a wink.

Pop still wasn't buying it. "I make men's shoes and they sell. I don't need women customers."

"Vito," my uncle said, "your son's right. If I didn't react to Prohibition, we would all be looking for a place to live because I wouldn't be able to make the payments on my bank loan. Time is passing you by, your old customers are dying off and your sales are down. I suggest you listen to Joey. This time, he knows what he's talking about."

Ma didn't say much, but after my uncle's comments, she walked around Pop's chair, bent over gently, putting her arms around his neck and whispered in his ear.

"Okay," he says, "looks like I don't have a choice."

Uncle Luigi leaned back and gave me a nod.

"Great, Pop. I know someone who's looking for work, and she has real class."

"Ah! Now the truth comes out. When can I meet her?"

"How about I bring her over for lunch, and we can talk her into taking the job."

After breakfast, I went back to my office to straighten up the place and get Sally ready to meet Ma and Pop. As I picked up my dirty underwear, I saw Ma glaring at me from the doorway with folded arms across her ample breasts, shaking her head.

"Ma, I can explain. It's not what it looks like."

"Don't worry. I saw her come up this morning. Besides, you're not a boy anymore. Poor child, she looks a mess."

"I met her during my investigation. She helped me, and now she's down on her luck."

Ma gave me a stern look. "Did you create a problem for her?"

I told Ma the whole story, and she immediately became overwhelmed with affection for the 'poor girl', as she put it.

"Don't worry, I'll handle Papa. When she wakes, bring her down. Poor thing is probably starving," she said. "And don't forget to shave," she added without looking back as she left the room.

Without thinking I rubbed my face, feeling the stubble.

I knew I had forgotten to do something. I had to laugh. I may not be a boy anymore, but I'd always be her son.

I gently woke Sally at eleven and explained my idea about helping with Pop's shoe business. She gave me a friendly kiss, which I responded to more aggressively than she expected or desired. A half-hour later, after a hot shower, she looked like a new woman, with a knockout smile, rosy cheeks, and dressed to impress. She was ready, but first I needed to prepare her to meet Pop, since he could be tough on people when he felt put upon.

"Sally, I need to warn you that my pop can seem unfriendly at first, but really, he's a nice guy when you get to know him."

"Sounds like my father. Came to America with a few pennies and had to fight for everything, but underneath his tough exterior, he's a pussycat."

"I'm not sure I'd call Pop a pussycat, but you look like you're ready to tame anything that comes your way. Let's meet the family."

Uncle Luigi was waiting on the second floor landing, casually leaning against the wall. "So, this is the wonder girl. Wow! What a looker, and you're right, she does have class."

Sally's cheeks flushed.

"Sally, this is my uncle Luigi. He always says what's on his mind, and he has extremely good taste in women."

"It's nice to meet you. Joey speaks fondly of you," Sally said.

"Call me Uncle Luigi, but don't believe anything he says. I have a reputation to uphold. Now, let's go face the old man and don't worry, I'll be right behind you."

My uncle kept laughing all the way to the first floor, and any chance of making a quiet entrance quickly evaporated.

Ma and Pop were waiting in the hallway outside their apartment. Ma embraced Sally, and as we all entered the kitchen, Pop muttered something about being the last to know what the hell was going on.

Ma had really outdone herself; there was enough food to feed the entire neighborhood. She served antipasti, followed by homemade minestrone soup. Next she brought out stuffed shells with ricotta and homemade sausage hot from the oven. When we finished the stuffed shells, the main dish of chicken cacciatore arrived, and if that wasn't enough, Ma topped the meal off with freshly baked apple strudel. As a kid, I suspected a German lurked somewhere in her family tree, but the reality was she was raised near the Italian-Swiss border, which is why she spoke several languages and was one hell of a cook.

"Sally," Uncle Luigi said, "you've got my vote for the job if Mama makes this type of meal every day."

"Luigi," Ma said. "If you ate like this every day, you wouldn't be able to fit through the door."

Pop had had enough small talk and got right to the point. "My son tells me you wanna work in my shop. Tell me why."

Sally had a mouth full of food and had to swallow fast.

"Sorry, Mr. Batista. Joey said you would like to expand your business to include shoes for women, and I believe I can help. I understand ladies fashions and have a head for business. More importantly, I need the job, and from what Joey has told me, you need my help."

"An honest girl. I like that. You live around here?" Pop asked.

"No, I have to find a place."

"I'll tell you what. You can live in the back, in Joey's old room, and join us for meals, but as far as pay is concerned, that's more difficult."

"I realize I need to earn my wages. Why don't we agree on a percentage of your increased sales?" Sally suggested.

Pop liked her proposal, since he couldn't lose. "So, it's settled, five percent of the profits from the sales to women."

Pop put out his hand to seal the deal, but she didn't take it.

"Actually, I was thinking more like fifteen percent."

I could see a smile reappear on my uncle's face and a look of horror on Ma's as she waited for Pop to explode.

"Okay, ten percent," Pop said.

Once again Pop put out his hand and this time Sally shook it and expressed appreciation for his generous offer.

Pop became more relaxed after the negotiations, and we had a good time talking. Of course my uncle had to bring up politics, speculating on who the Democratic nominee for mayor would be. Eventually Pop got around to asking Sally more questions, and she didn't hesitate to explain all that had happened to her since leaving home, which immediately brought tears again to Ma's eyes. I noticed Pop looking away, so I suspected he still had a soft spot he didn't like to reveal.

After lunch, I showed Sally my old room, and as I was about to leave, she caught my arm and pulled me close.

"How can I ever repay you? Your family seems nice, and the job is perfect."

"I'm just glad things worked out. To be honest, you had me worried when you asked Pop for more money."

"He reminded me so much of my father that I took a gamble. I figured he likes to barter, so I gave him the chance."

As I turned again to leave, she held on, bringing us even closer together. I tried not to respond without embarrassing her. I didn't want to get seriously involved with anyone at this point in my life. I had a business to establish and still needed to discover what happened to Anita.

"Sally, I don't think either of us is ready for a serious relationship. We should just enjoy each other's company."

She gave me a hug and a warm kiss. "Sure, Joey, I understand. I just thought from the way you responded upstairs that things were different. But you're right. We both need time."

"Can you blame me? You're an attractive woman, but I was out of line." I wished her luck with Pop and explained I'd be working on a new case that would consume me for a few weeks, but I would come by before taking off.

I left Sally in Ma's capable hands and went back to my office to read Castellano's letter. I was about to open my desk drawer to admire the money when Frank Galvano popped in unexpectedly.

"Joey, I hope I'm not barging in at a bad time. I stopped by to remind you that Tony's preliminary hearing is in a few days. I need you in the courtroom because I might call you as a witness against Tommy Stefano."

"Nothing could keep me away. How did the photograph turn out?"

"Great! I thought since it's your first case, you'd want a copy. But do me a favor, don't hang it up yet. I'm a little superstitious."

I expressed concern that I couldn't read the date on the newspaper Dorothy held over Stefano's head in the background of the picture.

"Don't worry, it's a great shot. I'm sure the judge will throw out the case. Oh, one small detail, I'll need a copy of your bill to Tony. I intend to ask the judge to order Stefano to pay all expenses."

I wrote up a charge for twenty dollars, just to cover my out-of-pocket costs. Frank laughed and handed it back.

"Save this in case we lose. I figure fifty dollars a day, plus twenty dollars for daily expenses; make out a bill for seven hundred."

"I can't bill Tony that much!"

"You got a lot to learn, kid. Trust me, I know it sounds like a lot of dough, but you've earned it, and if we win, it won't cost Tony a cent."

Before he left, Frank asked me to get photographs of Tony's butcher shop, a few shots of where Stefano lives, and interview some of his neighbors.

* * * * *

Once I completed Frank's assignments, I concentrated on my new case. The letter from Castellano contained the details I needed to launch my investigation.

Castellano's brother, Angelo, had established a clinic about ten years ago on Staten Island, not far from the ferry terminal in Tompkinsville, under the name of Dr. Vincent Taglio. The clinic specialized in drug rehabilitation for young women, mostly from wealthy families who valued discretion. Angelo had a successful practice, a wife named Maria, and no children. The wife found him dead in his office around ten at night. It was getting late, and he had skipped dinner. Concerned, Maria knocked on his office door, with no response. She was about to knock again when his office phone rang. She heard him pick it up, so she returned to the kitchen thinking he'd get something to eat when hungry. A short time later there were two gunshots. Members of the nursing staff came running down from the second floor, and after several attempts, they were able to break in the door.

The preliminary police report, which Castellano somehow gained access to, indicated his brother died of a bullet wound to the head. There wasn't any sign of a struggle, and the police found the door and all windows locked from the inside. An inquest, scheduled in three weeks, most likely would go along with the police recommendation: death by suicide.

Based on the facts in the case, I figured there were only two logical explanations. Either he committed suicide, as the police believed, or his wife killed him and figured a way to lock the door from the inside after leaving the room.

My immediate concern was how to obtain access to the crime scene and become part of the investigation. I knew it wouldn't be easy, since I didn't have connections on Staten Island. In fact, I didn't have many connections anywhere. I was about to call Castellano to see if he could help when I thought of O'Reilly.

O'Reilly greeted me on the phone with a warning. "Hey, I hear you're tangling with Tommy Stefano. If he's anything like his brother, I'd watch my back."

"Thanks for the advice, but I'm not worried. It's a small-time beef, and Frank Galvano tells me Stefano will only get a few months, if that.

"Just be careful. You're lucky his brother's in the slammer. So, what's on your mind?"

"First, I need to tell ya, I used your name the other night to get information."

"Ah, now I understand. The other day I got a weird call from the Checker Cab Company. Some guy wanted to know when I'd be coming in to check his records. Was that your doin'?" he asked

"Hope you don't mind."

"Not a problem, just don't make it a habit."

I explained I had a new client who wanted me to look into the death of a Dr. Vincent Taglio, and I needed a contact on the Staten Island police force.

"As it turns out," O'Reilly said, "you're in luck. That's if you pay for drinks the next time we get together."

"If you can get me involved in this case, it'll be worth it."

"A good friend of mine, Lieutenant Sullivan, runs the homicide division over there. I'll give him a call."

"Thanks, Mike. I'll keep in touch."

"Just don't forget about the drinks, and if this does become a habit, I'll expect a cut of your take." We agreed to meet at my uncle's when I wrapped up my investigation.

The next morning I headed out to the Island. I always found the ferryboat ride from Manhattan to Staten Island enjoyable. As a kid, my parents would take me to the Island about once a month to visit an old friend of theirs, who had come over with them from Italy and settled on a small farm. As I got older, Luigi took me to their farm almost every weekend to hunt for pheasant and quail. My uncle had a passion for firearms, and by the time I turned fourteen, I'd become quite the marksman. Ironically, it was my skills with a rifle that first caught the eye of the camp commander, and when he learned I was fluent in Italian and German, my military fate was sealed.

The ferry rides and shooting lessons weren't the only reasons I looked forward to those visits. Their daughter, Anita, was a beauty, and by the time we were fourteen, we secretly agreed to get married as soon as we were old enough. Four years later, she disappeared without a trace. The search for her lasted weeks, but in the end, the police assumed she'd run off with some drifter. But I knew differently. If she were alive, she would've found a way to contact me or her father. Something terrible had happened to her, and it was my fault.

I stood in the bow of the boat, with the cold wind stirring the embers of wonderful memories of the good times we did have together. It was difficult, but I did my best to push the thoughts of Anita back where they belonged until the time was right for me to discover what really happened to her. I still had a lot to learn about the PI business. As I walked to the front of the boat, the cold air brought my thoughts back to the present, and I marveled at how this huge boat was going to dock into that speck of a pier.

Just as in the past, the ferry gently slid between the pilings, and the deckhands, in their blue jeans and leather jackets, emerged from the bowels of the boat to secure the ferry and direct passengers onto Staten Island, an island that still had an innocence lost to the other boroughs of New York City.

It was time to get down to business. I drove out of the ferry terminal and turned right onto Richmond Terrace, looking for the Dr. Vincent Taglio Sanitarium for Young Ladies. It was located on a lush estate adjacent to Sailor Snug Harbor, a retirement community for sailors from a different era. In the center of the estate stood a majestic Victorian mansion reminiscent of a home you would find on a southern plantation. Its wide, sweeping veranda welcomed all to enjoy a promise of tranquility and to enter a portal of a more peaceful time. The grounds contained several small, lily-white cottages and a barn freshly painted in the traditional red with black trim. As I drove along the long, semicircular, pebbled driveway to the entrance of the mansion, it became evident that something unusual was taking place; it seemed more of a carnival atmosphere than a murder scene.

I parked away from the crowd, and as I approached, I saw an all-too-familiar sight: reporters jostling each other to get a scoop, harassing anyone they could find with relentless questions and bright flashbulbs, hoping to get the picture that would appear on the front pages of tomorrow's newspapers.

Realizing it would be nearly impossible to get through the throng of reporters, I made my way around the house and entered from the back-porch door that opened into a large kitchen area. I quickly passed through the kitchen into a long hall with several rooms on either side. The hall flowed into a majestic parlor with a sweeping staircase on the left spiraling up to the second floor. On the right was an inviting sitting area with a grand piano off to one side. These images flashed by as I exited the house and put my arm around Mrs. Taglio's shoulder.

"Okay, that's enough questions for today. Mrs. Taglio gave her statement to the police, so move on and let her mourn in peace." I gently turned the woman around and directed her toward the entrance to her home. Shouts of outrage followed us into the sitting area as I closed the door behind us.

"I don't know who you are, but I owe you a debt of gratitude for rescuing me from that pack of animals."

"You're welcome, Mrs. Taglio. I'm Joey Batista, a private detective working for an old friend of your husband's."

"Please call me Maria. Now tell me who hired you, and what exactly do they expect you to accomplish?"

"My employer wishes to remain anonymous and wants to know who murdered your husband. He's known your husband since they were children and refuses to believe he committed suicide."

"I don't want to believe he killed himself either, but there's no other possible explanation." I could tell she hoped I would come up with some other answer.

Before I responded, a police sergeant came in the front door. "Sorry, Mrs. Taglio, for arriving late. I got rid of those scavengers. Is this one of their lot?"

"I'm a private investigator. The name's Joey Batista," I

said as I offered my hand.

"Okay, Mr. Batista, if that's your real name. Get out of here. There's still an investigation going on."

Maria held onto my arm and told the sergeant I was her guest and would be looking into Vincent's death.

"Sergeant, if you'll call your lieutenant, I'm sure he'll give me clearance to investigate the crime scene and assist Mrs. Taglio," I said.

"I'll do just that. Don't touch nothin' till I get back."

Maria and I walked down the hall to the kitchen. She poured us both a hot cup of coffee and then simply collapsed into her chair, holding the cup with both hands as if trying to absorb some strength from its warmth.

"This must be a difficult time for you. Do you have any family in the area to help?" I asked.

"I've been an orphan all my life. The only family I had was Vincent, and now he's gone. To be honest, I don't know what to do."

I reached out and gently touched her arm. "Maria, I'm here to help, and my employer will do his best to assist in any way possible. But first, I need to know more about your husband's work and the circumstances of his death."

Strangely enough, my words had the opposite effect from what I expected. Maria sat upright, withdrew her arm, wiped away a few tears and gave me a look of total distrust.

"How do I know you're telling the truth? As the sergeant said, you could be an extremely clever reporter."

"I'm not a reporter."

"You say you represent an old friend of my husband's. My husband had no old friends; he didn't even have a past or any family. He never talked about himself. It's as if his life began when we met."

It was clear that my response would determine if Maria would allow me into her life, and without her cooperation, there was no way I could solve this mystery. I took my time, showed her my PI ticket, and chose my words carefully.

"Maria, right now you need to trust someone. As you can see, I'm not a reporter, I'm a private investigator, and Vincent did have a past. We all do. Vincent helped me when I was a kid, and I'd like to repay my debt by helping you. To be honest, I'm also getting a large retainer to find out what happened the night he died."

"You knew Vincent when you were young?"

"Yes, but unfortunately I can't give you any more details without exposing the identity of my employer."

"What do you want to know?" Maria asked.

"Why don't you tell me about the clinic? When did it first open?

"We built the house about ten years ago as a live-in dorm for young ladies with addiction problems."

"Did Vincent have any other businesses or activities?"

"He didn't have time for anything else. Vincent was totally devoted to his work and spent many late nights counseling his patients, trying to provide some comfort as he withdrew them slowly from their addictions."

"Did he have a successful practice?"

"Oh, yes. You would be surprised what wealthy people will pay to have their daughters' problems solved in a discreet manner."

"As far as you're aware, there were no financial worries. How about your personal relationship? Did you have any marital issues?" I boldly asked.

"Vincent was a caring and attentive husband, and I was faithful to him. I'm not aware of any reason for him to commit suicide."

I noted she didn't indicate he was faithful to her. "Sorry to ask such delicate questions, but I need as much background information as possible to put my investigation into some kind of context."

Maria appeared stoic. She never looked away, sitting upright with her hands folded on the table, but underneath that exterior, there was a woman trying to come to grips with her loss.

"I understand," she said. "I can assure you, you haven't asked anything that hasn't already been addressed by the police."

"Can you tell me about the night he died?"

Maria took a long, hard drink from her coffee mug. I had the impression she wished it contained something stronger.

"It was around ten at night, and Vincent had worked past dinner. I went to his office to check on him when I heard his phone ring. I hesitated, not wanting to disturb him. He answered the phone, so I went back to the kitchen. Prior to reaching the table, I heard a gunshot. I momentarily froze, and before I could reach the office door, I heard a second shot."

"Was there anyone with you at the time the shots were fired?"

"Yes, I was having tea with Margaret, the head nurse."

"How about the other staff members and patients… where were they?"

"We have fifteen girls living upstairs, and they had all retired for the night. There is also a staff of three nurses, who were making their final rounds when the shots were heard."

"Did anyone see or hear anything unusual that night?"

"To my knowledge, no one saw anything out of the ordinary."

The sergeant returned with a smirk on his face. "You must have some clout. The lieutenant said to treat you like one of the boys."

I was careful not to show my satisfaction; I would need his cooperation.

"Thanks, Sergeant. If you don't mind, I need a few more minutes, and then I can join you to review the crime scene."

As he walked away, he swore under his breath. I made a mental note to get on his good side as quickly as possible. I turned my attention back to Maria.

"What about the patients? Are they going to be transferred to some other treatment center?" I asked.

"I called the parents and reassured them it would be best for everyone to stay together to console each other. Vincent was very close to his patients. I also explained I had hired a specialist to join our staff to continue Vincent's delicate work. They all agreed with my proposal, since there aren't many places for their children to go besides the public sanitariums."

I understood her meaning. The parents were more concerned with avoiding a scandal and would tolerate a brief interruption in their daughters' treatment.

"Thanks for being so open with your answers. I may want to talk to you later if you don't mind."

Maria grabbed my hand and squeezed with incredible strength. "Mr. Batista, I also want to understand what happened that night. If he killed himself, I need to know."

"That's why I'm here."

"I'll inform the staff you were a friend of Vincent's and ask them to cooperate fully. We do have an extra room if you would like to stay during your investigation," she said.

"Thank you, I might take you up on that offer."

The sergeant stood outside the office door, reading his handwritten notes with a scowl on his face.

"Sergeant, if you don't mind, tell me in your own words the official opinion concerning this case."

"I can do better than that, Joey. You don't mind if I call you Joey?"

I didn't blame him for being sarcastic. I noticed his nametag, James Rafferty.

"Sure, Jim, Joey's just fine."

He smiled, then his expression abruptly changed.

"Have we met before?" he asked.

"Not that I'm aware of. Why?"

"You look familiar and so is your name. Hey, I know you. You were that guy who was a real pain in the ass during an investigation I worked on."

"Was it the disappearance of a young woman?" My knees suddenly felt weak. I reached my arm out and placed it on the wall to steady myself.

"That's right. Never did find out what happened to her. At one point we suspected you, since you constantly hung around getting in the way."

Luckily, Maria came over and asked if we needed anything before she prepared dinner. When she left, I repeated my question to the sergeant, asking him to give me his take on what happened the night Vincent died. At that point in time, I wasn't ready to relive Anita's disappearance.

"I was on duty when the call came in, so me and another officer got here in no time, probably took less than ten minutes. We were down by the ferry terminal. You wouldn't believe the confusion around this place, but the missus there is a pretty strong woman and got the girls and nursing staff back upstairs and made sure everyone stayed out of our way. I checked to make certain the doc was dead, which wasn't difficult since the back of his head was scattered all over the bookcase. I secured the scene and waited for the coroner to arrive."

It was evident that the sergeant was experienced and had a tendency to be blunt.

"I understand everyone's conclusion is that it's a clear case of suicide, clean and simple," I said.

"That's right. The doc gets a disturbing phone call, pulls out his gun and tries to shoot himself in the head but misses because he has the shakes. You know, lost his nerve. He then sticks the gun in his mouth and pulls the trigger, can't miss. Happens all the time."

I had to admit it sounded plausible. But I agreed with Castellano, if Angelo had a problem, he would've dealt with it head on. Someone might die, but it wouldn't be Angelo.

"Just sounds too simple," I said. "My understanding is the door and all the windows were locked. What about the wife? She must have a key to the office. She could've walked in, blown his brains out, locked the door and nobody's the wiser."

"We thought of that. She has an airtight alibi. The head nurse was having tea with her, and they both heard the shots together. Unless they're in cahoots, it looks like suicide. Besides, the door was bolted from the inside."

I stood in the doorway of Angelo's office and slowly took in the whole scene. The room was fairly large, with a ten-foot ceiling. The one thing that struck me as unusual was how few windows there were. Everything else looked normal enough.

Floor-to-ceiling bookcases lined the back wall, and a large antique oak desk faced the entrance to the room, positioned a few feet in front of the bookcases. There were two comfortable looking chairs opposite the desk, and to the left of the desk was a row of file cabinets along the entire wall. To the right of the entrance, in the middle of the room, six more leather armchairs appeared scattered in a poorly formed semicircle. The right wall, opposite the semicircle of chairs, had two picture windows with an old roll-top desk situated between them. Antique hutches lined the walls adjacent to the door. The floor consisted of highly polished oak planks with an occasional rug.

As we entered the room, Rafferty pointed to the chalk outline where the body had fallen. It appeared Angelo stood behind his desk when the bullet shattered his skull. He collapsed on the floor to the left side of his desk; blood and gray matter splattered several shelves of the bookcase, as well as the floor behind the desk. I crouched next to the outline to get a better view of the pattern of blood and to look for any marks on the wooden floor that might indicate a struggle.

"Where did the gun come from?" I asked the sergeant.

"According to his wife, one's in his desk drawer and another gun was in his bed nightstand."

"You said 'was.' What do ya mean?"

"A few months ago, she noticed the gun missing from the bedroom and asked him about it; he was fairly non-committal. He said something about moving it for safety reasons."

"Which gun did he use?"

"The one from the bedroom."

I looked at the chalk outline. "It's hard to tell if the gun fell by his right hand or if he's gripping it."

"It's clear from the crime photos that the gun is in his hand."

"What about powder residue and prints?" I asked.

"Everything fits. Like I said, an open and shut case."

"Did you find the first bullet fired?"

"We found it lodged in a medieval reference book behind the desk. You can see for yourself," the sergeant said as he reached for the book and handed it to me.

The bullet was missing, presumably taken for ballistics tests. "How was the book positioned, on the floor or still on the shelf?" I asked.

"It had fallen forward on the shelf. As you can see, Dr. Taglio stood some books up flat to take up more space, probably because he didn't have enough material to fill the shelves. We believe the bullet slammed the book against the back of the shelf and then fell forward."

Looking around the room, everything seemed in order, no sign of a struggle, except for the desk chair out of position, which was understandable given the circumstances theorized by the police. The desk was uncluttered. A few pencils on the left side, a fountain pen and ink well at the head of the desk, and a desk lamp—as far as I could tell, nothing out of the ordinary.

The sergeant stood back and watched as I tried to take in the entire scene and didn't volunteer any information.

"I have a few more questions if you don't mind."

"The lieutenant ordered me to treat you like one of our own. Besides, it's interesting to see how a private dick works."

I smiled and wondered how he would react if he knew this was my second case.

"Did you get anything from the staff or patient interviews?"

"They all gave the same story. The staff was about to leave, all the girls were locked down, Mrs. Taglio was having tea with the head nurse. Everyone heard the shots, no one saw anything."

"Any of the staff members have a police record?"

"Whenever the doc hired anyone, he asked us to check, and as far as we could tell, all the help are law-abiding citizens."

"Thanks for taking the time to give me your perspective. Sure look like a suicide."

"Smells like it too. It's always hard for the family to

accept, but it happens ya know. It happens a lot."

I asked the sergeant to have someone drop off a copy of the crime scene photos and the case report in the morning, since I intended to stay over in order to interview the staff the next day.

"Sure thing, and if you have any more questions, just give a holler."

"If I uncover anything new, I'll pass it on to you. I don't want anyone knowing I'm working the case." The sergeant seemed to like that idea and shook my hand.

"Sounds good. I could always use a boost to my image."

When he left, I told Maria I would take her up on her offer to stay the night. She seemed pleased. I think she truly believed her husband was murdered, and having a man around provided some sense of security.

"The spare room is just opposite Vincent's office. We often have last-minute guests, so you should find everything you need. We're going to have dinner in about an hour if you would like to join us."

"I noticed you have a rather large kitchen. Does everyone eat together?"

"Oh, yes, Vincent insisted we have as much normalcy as possible and included the girls and staff as family. As he often said, there's no better way to build trust and friendship than sitting down together and breaking bread."

Dinner presented an opportunity to meet everyone present on the night of Angelo's death. Besides Margaret and the three nurses, there were a groundskeeper and fifteen young ladies ranging in age from sixteen to their mid-twenties. The clinic was full, since there were sixteen rooms on the second floor, fifteen for patients and one for Margaret, the head nurse. The groundskeeper had a small bungalow on the premises, and the nursing staff had the option of living off property or in a three-bedroom house on the grounds. All the nurses lived elsewhere on Staten Island, but chose to stay at the clinic during the week.

When I entered the kitchen, the room fell silent as everyone turned in my direction. Fortunately, Maria came to my rescue and made the appropriate introductions. Immediately the girls bombarded me with questions.

"Do you know who did it or did he kill himself?"

"Have you ever shot anyone?"

"Is it dangerous being a private investigator?"

I did notice a few things from the chaos caused by my presence. Most of the young ladies were animated and firing questions, except for one young girl who tightly held the arm of an older patient, and a few other girls who looked almost catatonic and were dependent on the nurses for their nutrition.

After dinner, as was their normal routine, everyone except Ron, the groundskeeper, sat in the living room and socialized for a few hours before retiring. This gave me the opportunity to continue talking with Maria.

"Do you mind if we stay in the kitchen?" I asked. "I would like to know more about the clinic and your future plans."

"I haven't given the future much thought. My priority is to make sure the girls get the care they need," she said.

"I'm certain one of your options is to open a restaurant. I've had some great Italian food, but your cooking is exceptional. Just don't ever tell my ma I said that."

It was good to hear Maria laugh. Slowly she was adjusting, and I sincerely hoped my presence helped.

"I do love to cook," she said. "It's always been something I've enjoyed, and having the clinic gave me the opportunity to expand my culinary skills and at the same time contribute to Vincent's work."

"Would you mind explaining the clinic's daily routine?

It'll help me ask the right questions tomorrow during my interviews."

"Breakfast is from eight to nine, so the girls usually wake between seven and seven-thirty."

"How do you maintain discipline? Everyone appears to be well-behaved, yet some of them must be under tremendous stress."

"The one thing my husband insisted upon was having a precise schedule for each day. His theory was if the girls could count on consistency, it would reduce anxiety and increase the effectiveness of his counseling."

"What do you mean? How precise?"

"Each patient knows what to expect every day, especially when they will receive their medication."

"When the girls aren't in counseling, how do they spend their time?"

"They are free to walk the grounds, participate is some cooking classes that I teach, and have the opportunity to further their formal education. We retain several retired teachers who structure programs for them as needed."

"Tell me more about your husband's routine."

"He classified his patients into two groups depending on the severity of their addiction. Vincent would see each patient from the more addicted group every day, personally administer their medication, and provide one-on-one counseling. He would counsel the less severe group every other day."

"I noticed the chairs in his office are positioned in a semicircle. Did Vincent do all his counseling in groups?"

"No, the girls in the more difficult group, as I mentioned, had a private session every day; the other patients had three group sessions a week."

"I wouldn't think his patients would talk about their problems openly with other girls around. Isn't that an unusual approach?"

"Yes, and at first I didn't think it would work either. But Vincent was very successful. He believed by living together, the girls became friends and realized they shared many of the same problems."

"It sounds like Vincent had a pretty heavy load. He must have worked long hours."

"Often he would come to bed around one or two at night due to writing reports, conducting independent research, and studying new literature."

It was late, so I said goodnight to Maria and thanked her again for her hospitality. As I entered my room, I looked back down the hall toward the kitchen and noticed Maria sitting where I had left her, with her head resting on her folded arms, quietly crying.

Early the next morning, I found the groundskeeper scraping a section of the wrought iron fence that enclosed the property, getting it ready for a fresh coat of paint.

"Morning, Ron. I was hoping to talk to you after dinner last night," I said.

"I don't much hanker hanging around all them females."

"Understandable. Mind if I ask some questions now?"

"That's up to you. I got work to do."

"Did you get to spend much time with the doctor, being the only two men on the estate?"

"I get my orders from the missus. Doc was always busy. No time for the likes of me."

"Did you hear the shots the other night?"

"We don't get a lot of traffic on this road at night, but it's not unusual to hear the cars backfiring as they go by, so I didn't think much about the noise until I heard yelling coming from the house."

"Did you see anyone, possibly a stranger, on the

grounds before or during the commotion?"

"Nope. As you can see, the fence is fairly high, and we don't get many visitors on weekdays."

During our exchange, Ron kept on working, never really acknowledging my presence. Suddenly, he stopped, leaned on the fence for support, and stood holding a metal scraper.

"How about answering a question for me? What's going to happen to this place now that Doc's gone?"

"From what I can see, Mrs. Taglio has everything under control. A new doctor will be taking over soon, until more permanent arrangements can be made."

"Ha, sounds to me like things are already changing fast."

"I guess that's to be expected given what's happened. How about taking a few minutes and showing me the grounds?"

There were plenty of mature trees and benches where patients could sit and read or just enjoy the solitude and sounds of nature. A few of the larger oak trees had homemade swings close to a small pond occupied by a family of ducks. All in all, a nice park-like setting, but I'm sure the girls got bored having to adhere to Angelo's rigorous routine.

After breakfast, one of the more outgoing young ladies, Roseanna, took me for a quick tour of the upstairs dormitory. She looked about twenty-one, somewhat plain in appearance and extremely friendly. She had recently completed her therapy and was scheduled to leave the clinic in two weeks, back to her folks in Syracuse, New York. She thought the world of the doctor and was sincerely upset over his death. She credited him with curing her addiction and looked forward to a new life, free of drugs. By the way she was hanging onto me, I suspect Angelo wasn't able to solve all her problems.

We went up a spiral staircase located in the living room to the second floor, which opened into a sitting area. In the center of the back wall, opposite the stairs, were two French doors leading to a wide corridor with eight rooms on both sides. None of the rooms had windows, but they received ample light and fresh air from adjustable skylights. Roseanna apparently noticed my dismay at the lack of windows and explained that patients arrived in various stages of addiction; it was necessary to prevent them from escaping. Without windows, the rooms felt like prison cells.

All of the patient rooms were identical. Bookcases lined the back wall, and each had a single bed, nightstand, a small desk with a reading light and an armchair. Off the living quarters was a bathroom with a shower. No one left their room for any reason after lockdown.

Roseanna eagerly answered my questions, deepening my understanding of how Angelo ran the clinic.

"I understand from Mrs. Taglio the patients are separated into two groups depending on the severity of their addiction."

"That's right," responded Roseanna. "The girls who occupy the rooms on the left side of the hall received more intensive treatment, and Dr. Vincent controlled their medication. Margaret, the head nurse, dispensed the medication for those on the right side, and they spent less time with the doctor."

"Has the difference between groups ever created problems?"

"Not that I'm aware of. We try to help one another; we've all been down pretty low and understand each other's needs."

As we walked down the hallway, I noticed the two women who were fairly withdrawn the night before talking in one of the rooms to the left. After the tour, I thanked Roseanna for her help and went back and rapped on their door. The door was ajar and opened further from the force of my knock. I saw the younger of the two rocking on the bed holding her knees to her chest, as the other tried to comfort her.

The older one reacted to my presence.

"What do ya want, Mr. Detective?"

"I was hoping I could ask a few questions. I'm sorry but I don't remember your names."

"I'm Shirley, this here's Mary, and as ya can see, she doesn't feel like talkin'."

"Do you want me to get Margaret?" I asked.

"Don't waste ya time. I've already tried. She goes strictly by the book. Mary gets her medication in half an hour."

"Shirley, if you don't mind my asking, you sound like you're from Brooklyn."

"That's right. What of it? I'm a charity case. There are two of us. The doc did his bit for society."

I thought it best to back off, but I still had basic questions about how Angelo operated the clinic.

"Can you tell me why Dr. Taglio administered your medications personally rather than letting Margaret manage all the patients?"

"The doc changed our medication level based on how we felt; that's the problem with Mary here. Margaret's been givin' her the last dose the doc wrote down, but she needs more, much more."

Just then a policeman arrived with a package. I thanked Shirley and told her I would talk to Mrs. Taglio about Mary's medications.

It was getting close to noon, and I needed to leave. After receiving the case file from the officer, I thanked Maria for her hospitality and indicated I'd be back on the following Monday to continue my investigation.

On the ride back to Manhattan, I tried putting all the pieces together. On the surface it appeared Angelo had been a dedicated, hardworking professional, committed to his wife and patients. But for some reason, I had a bad feeling in my gut.

* * * * *

I spent the next few days in my office going through the police report, examining the crime-scene photos and documenting my own observations, looking for any indication that Angelo didn't commit suicide. I found a few inconsistencies that pointed to murder, but I couldn't get around the fact that Angelo had locked himself inside the room. If I didn't have Castellano to deal with, I would've found it amusing that one of my first cases mirrored a Sherlock Holmes mystery.

I got to the point where the same thoughts kept swirling around in my head and realized I needed a break. I went downstairs to get some lunch and noticed Sally rearranging a display. She jumped when I grabbed her hand and led her out of the shop toward the waterfront. Pop came running after us with a mallet in his hand.

"Hey, what are you doing? She has work to do."

"Don't worry, Pop; I'll bring her back before dinner," I said as we ran down the street laughing.

We sat on a couple of empty crates by one of the deserted piers.

"I thought you threw me into the lion's den and left to see if I would survive," Sally said as she caught her breath.

"I told you Pop is set in his ways."

"You weren't exaggerating."

"Just don't back down if you think you're right, and try to get Ma on your side. Works every time," I said.

"I'll give it a try."

"So, tell me. Have you made any progress?"

"Your father has agreed to sell women's shoes, but he wants to custom make them."

"What are you concerned about? You've already accomplished the impossible."

"You don't understand. Custom shoes would be too expensive and not in fashion. I want him to sell a line of factory-made shoes."

"Oh!" I groaned.

"Exactly. He's been avoiding me for the last few days."

We visited some of the shops on the way back to the apartment building, and that's when I remembered Sally didn't have any money. I gave her a small loan, since it didn't sound like she would be getting any pay from Pop for some time.

Next I dropped in on Frank Galvano.

"I was hoping you'd stop by before the trial tomorrow."

"Like I said, I wouldn't miss it. Do you need help with any last-minute details? I'm off for the night."

"Only one thing left," he said. "Your services are worth a lot more than what we agreed to last time. Write out a new bill for an extra three hundred. We have Stefano in a death hold, so let's make him pay," he said with a nasty grin.

I wrote out a new bill for an even grand and he handed me two passes for the upstairs gallery reserved for special guests of the court. I asked Sally to come along.

* * * * *

We were the only ones in the gallery since this was a preliminary hearing and not a controversial or sensational lawsuit. Just before the judge entered the courtroom, however, a junior member of the *Daily News*, who had gotten a tip from Frank, joined us. Frank had assured him he could get a front-page story if he hung around for the hearing.

Tommy Stefano was playing his part like a real trooper, sitting in a wheelchair, bandages on his nose and around his head, arm in a sling and a blanket covering his legs. His private nurse looked impressive, decked out in full uniform, hat and all, with plenty of leg showing. His lawyer sat behind two large law books on their table and a stack of official-looking documents.

The bailiff called the session to order, and the Honorable Judge Jeremiah O'Dell of the First District Court of New York entered the courtroom. Without delay, the judge asked the prosecuting attorney to make his case as succinctly as possible. Tommy's lawyer, who wore a blue suit with a bright yellow bowtie and two-tone shoes, addressed the judge in a booming baritone.

"Your Honor, my client has been incapacitated for the past two months due to the negligence of the defendant, who violated city ordinance 375 that requires all businesses to keep their sidewalks clean of obstacles and to remove snow and ice within twenty-four hours of a storm. My client, on December 17, 1919, slipped on a large patch of ice and sustained serious injuries resulting in intolerable pain that turned a once-vibrant young man into this weak and feeble person you see before you today. I put into evidence, Your Honor, his medical records, which contain documented proof of his injuries from a respected physician. I also have signed affidavits from many of his neighbors, who will testify to the seriousness of his injuries and his incapacitation. But most damaging of all, I put into evidence notes from Officer Mulvaney's incident report he took during his investigation. You will see from his notes, the defendant confirmed my client did indeed fall on his premises on the night of December 17, 1919."

He rested his case and sat down with an air of self-confidence, as if to say to the judge that the verdict should be self-evident. The newspaper reporter leaned over to us with a puzzled look.

"Sounds like an open and shut case. I don't see a news story," he said.

I told him to hold tight until Galvano presented his defense. Frank slowly rose and walked to the front of the bench to address the judge.

"Your Honor, I would agree with the prosecutor that my client, an honest, hardworking immigrant, should pay dearly for such a blatant act of negligence that injured Mr. Stefano so grievously." Frank waited a moment to increase the surprise of his opening statement.

"That is," he continued, "if any aspect of this tale were true. I intend to show, Your Honor, that every bit of the evidence against my client is pure fabrication, and, therefore, I will request the dismissal of all charges. In fact, there is such collusion to deceive this court, I would request Tommy Stefano be cited for contempt and liable for all court and legal fees as well as damages to my client's reputation as a result of this outrageous attempt at deceit."

Tommy's lawyer was instantly on his feet, objecting loudly to Galvano's accusations. Judge O'Dell pounded his gavel, demanding order.

"I will have no more outbursts of this nature, and as for you, Mr. Galvano, I hope you can substantiate such serious charges, or I will hold you in contempt and liable for slandering Mr. Stefano."

"Thank you, Your Honor. First, let me point out that my client did come to the plaintiff's assistance on the night in question, as indicated in Officer Mulvaney's report.

Please note, however, the report states my client didn't actually see Mr. Stefano fall, nor did he see any snow or ice on the sidewalk. It is documented my client asked the plaintiff if he was injured, to which the plaintiff answered that he was fine and walked away without assistance." Frank walked over to his table and picked up a copy of Officer Mulvaney's report.

"It is also important to note that Mr. Stefano filed his complaint several days after the alleged incident. I have to wonder why. Was it possibly because there was no ice on the sidewalk on the night of December 17?"

Frank returned to his table and dropped the police report down with enough force to break the silence in the courtroom.

"Your Honor," he continued, "it is obvious from the plaintiff's pitiful condition, on display before us today, that he is incapable of any meaningful physical activity. However, I place in evidence before you a picture of the plaintiff on January 25, 1920, at a well- known speakeasy, not only dancing but in such fine physical condition he participated in a brawl. I might add he has a pretty good left hook." There was slight laughter from those in the courtroom, which the judge quickly silenced.

"I believe, Your Honor," continued Frank, "the plaintiff claims his left arm has been in a cast since the alleged accident."

Tommy leaned over to talk to his lawyer and then looked around the courtroom. At the same time, his nurse quietly slipped into the background.

"Mr. Galvano, I would agree this is potentially damaging evidence; however, this picture could have been taken any time before the accident," the judge stated.

"If you take this magnifying glass, Your Honor, you will see a young lady in the background holding up a copy of the *Daily News* that she sells to the patrons of the establishment where this photo was taken."

The judge looked carefully for several minutes and concluded that he couldn't make out the date of the paper. He refused, therefore, to accept the picture into evidence. Frank looked dejected as he meandered back to his seat. Suddenly, he stopped and turned toward Tommy and then to the judge.

"Your Honor, I realize that the date isn't visible; however, can you read the headline?"

"Yes, quite easily. It takes up the whole front page: "Mayor Will Run for Third Term." I still don't see how this helps to prove your serious accusations."

"Allow me, Your Honor, to submit a copy of the *Daily News* dated January 25, 1920. As you can see, it has the exact same headline, and I have a signed affidavit from the editor stating that January 25, 1920, was the only day this particular headline appeared on the front page."

Tommy knew he was in trouble when his lawyer shouted at the judge he had no idea his client was faking his injuries. Still looking around the courtroom, Tommy noticed me leaning over the banister. He jumped out of his wheelchair, hurling threats in my direction. "You're that bum. You're a dead man, you hear me? A goddamn walking corpse."

At this point, the judge wildly banged his gavel, demanding order in his court. The reporter took my picture and ran downstairs to get more photos of the confusion and of Tommy wildly flinging his cast around. It took quite some time for the judge to regain control of the courtroom.

"Mr. Stefano, you have committed a serious offense against this court and the defendant. I hereby find you in contempt and order you to spend no less than four weeks in jail, to pay all fees associated with this case and an additional two thousand dollars in damages to the defendant.

You will stay incarcerated until all monies are forthcoming. All charges against the defendant are hereby dismissed. Next case!"

Tommy left the court in handcuffs, dragged by two guards, as he continued hurling death threats in my direction. I finally understood why Galvano wanted me to provide him with an outrageous bill for my services. The judge never questioned the fees.

* * * * *

The next day the cover story of the *Daily News* boasted of their involvement: "Daily News and Joey Batista, Private Detective, Uncover Scam!"

I couldn't walk down the street without someone either slapping me on the back or hugging me by way of congratulations.

That night, right on schedule, Butch arrived, and I slid into his car hoping to avoid giving Ma a heart attack. Just like last time, Butch was a man of few words.

"I hope ya making good, kid! The Boss, he's not happy, and when da Boss isn't happy, bad things happen."

"What's the problem?" I asked.

Butch tossed a copy of the paper onto the backseat. "He's not happy!"

The rest of the ride passed in silence. It was like watching a movie reel over again, except this time, "the Boss, he wasn't happy."

As soon as I got in his car, Castellano snarled.

"Didn't you take my money to do a job for me? You tell me why you're on the front page of the paper when I told you I wanted an unknown private dick working my case. Besides, when I hire somebody, I expect an honest day's work. What are you doin' working another job?"

From past interactions with Castellano, I knew it was best to stand firm, but at the same time, be respectful. At least it worked when I was a kid.

"Mr. Castellano, in my profession you need to take what you can, when you can. Sometimes, I'll have two, maybe three jobs, at different stages and sometimes I'm sitting around twiddling my thumbs."

"Listen, kid. When you work for me, you work for me and nobody else. *Capiche*?"

Clearly I was walking on thin ice, but I remembered what my uncle said: "Give him a finger and he'll take an arm."

"There's no recipe for solving crimes," I said. "It takes hard work, imagination, time, and a great deal of luck. Sometimes the best ideas come when you're working on a different case. It gives your subconscious time to think."

"Joey, I like you, that's why I picked you for this job, and I trust you, but you're bullshitting me. I'm gonna tell you somethin' and I'm gonna tell you only once. When my employees push back on me, they don't last long. You understand my meaning?"

"I understand, but let me assure you we both want the same thing, to find out how your brother died. If you're not satisfied with my results, I'll drop my other jobs."

"If I'm not happy with your results, you won't be around to drop your other jobs. It'll be too late. Now tell me, what's going on?"

"I think Angelo was murdered. I don't know how or why. On the surface it looks like suicide: no way into the room, no way out, and no motive."

"You listen to me. I don't pay you for feelings. I want facts, why, and who, especially who."

I'd never seen the Boss so agitated.

"I think what you really want to know is if Angelo was

hit by a rival mob. So let me ask you a question: Do you know of any mob killings staged to look like suicide? Your brother was unarmed, a private citizen with a legit business, no planning necessary, an easy target. No, this wasn't a hit."

"Okay, so tell me why you got this feeling he was murdered. I know what I just said, now tell me."

"Angelo was successful, confident, respected in his field, and had a loving wife."

"That's it? That's all you got?"

"I believe your brother was left-handed, and the gun was found in his right hand."

"How can you remember if he was right or left-handed?"

"He kept his office very neat, especially his desk. His pencils were on the left side of the desk and all his important papers were in the left-hand drawer."

"So, you have more than feelings. Angelo was like me, left-handed and good with a gun, taught him myself. You got anything else?"

"Just one more thing. According to the police report he stood behind his desk, put the gun in his mouth, pulled the trigger, and then collapsed to the floor. If that's what happened, then why was the gun still in his hand? You'd think it would have fallen out when he hit the floor."

I gave Castellano a complete update, all the details about the crime scene and the whole business setup. When I was done, he seemed more concerned about Maria than who killed his brother. What's she like? What's she gonna do now? Does she need anything?

"Next time you bring me more facts and tell me how to help my brother's wife. She's family," he said.

"Mr. Castellano, once a week is too often. A case like this could take months. I would prefer we met every other week."

He thought about my suggestion for a minute.

"Okay, next week you tell me how to help Maria, and the following week you tell me who killed my brother."

I took that as a sign it was time to leave. I opened the door, but before I moved, he put his hand on my shoulder and turned me toward him.

"Anybody else who talked to me like you just did would be dead. If we're ever around my men, you remember that. You got guts and brains, tough to find people like you in my line of work. I'd hate to lose you."

I contemplated asking for more money when he handed me another envelope. The PI business certainly had its financial rewards but was potentially short-lived. Still working my second case and I already had two death threats. I just hoped Tommy Stefano would find more important pursuits than exacting revenge after getting out of the jug. As for the Boss, he likes to talk tough, but I thought it wise to take his advice and show him the respect he deserved, especially around his crew.

* * * * *

I needed a break from being harassed, so Sally and I went to Coney Island and took a leisurely stroll along the boardwalk. During the winter months, most of the amusement rides and arcades are closed, but we did accomplish our primary objective for taking such a long trip on a cold, blistery day. Just as we had hoped, Nathan's hot dog stand on Surf Avenue was as busy as ever. If you've never had a Nathan's hot dog, take my word for it, you're missing one of the simpler pleasures in life. I wouldn't be surprised if in a few years his business expanded all over New York.

We sat on a bench and ate our dogs in blissful silence. Once finished, we simply enjoyed listening to the soothing sounds of the ocean waves breaking against the pilings and the sea wall. As in the past, we found it easy to share our thoughts.

"Joey, I'm so grateful you entered my life when you did. I don't know what I would have done."

"To be honest, I think in time it will be us who owe you a debt of gratitude. I never thought I would see the day Pop would sell factory shoes. Without your influence, my guess is he would be out of business in a few years."

"Oh I don't think so; he's a talented man."

"How did you ever convince him to change his mind?" I asked.

"I took your advice."

"Ma?"

"You were right," Sally said and then changed the subject. "Tell me more about your new case. Have you determined if it's murder or suicide?"

"I'm pretty sure he was murdered, but I don't have hard proof. The unfortunate reality is if I'm correct, it was probably an inside job, and I like everyone I've met. I'm beginning to think that to be a good private investigator, I should remain more detached."

"I'm not sure I agree. The more feelings you have for others, the better you'll understand their motives."

"Maybe. I guess only time will give me the experience I need to know for sure. Enough about me. What have you been up to besides trying to reshape an old man's thinking?"

"Actually, I'm dealing with two old men," she said. "As you know, I left home against my father's wishes. He was so angry, he disowned me and forbade me from ever returning."

"That's a heavy burden to carry around; without family we have no roots. Have you tried contacting him?"

"That's one of the things I wanted to tell you. I sent him several letters with all the details of my experiences since leaving home. I even asked for his forgiveness. I didn't think he'd ever respond, but yesterday I received a letter."

Sally pulled out an envelope from her handbag and handed it to me.

"I'm not sure I should read this. It's really between you and your father."

"I want you to see the good you and your father are doing. Your father helped me find the right words to touch my dad's heart."

As I finished reading, I looked up and saw tears rolling down Sally's cheeks. I think we both knew she'd be returning home soon.

* * * * *

The thought of riding the ferry every day to and from the clinic wasn't appealing, as March fast approached, bringing with it bone-chilling weather. It would be best to stay at Maria's until I managed to solve the mystery of the locked room. I also had the compelling motive of getting back into Castellano's good graces.

A cleaning crew, who were in the process of emptying their truck of supplies, occupied my usual parking spot at the clinic. I raced past them to the entrance and called out for Maria. I noticed she glanced down and moved closer to the opposite wall as she passed Angelo's office.

"Maria, what's going on? Isn't this still considered a crime scene?"

"The police said they've completed their investigation, so I'm having Vincent's office cleaned."

"Would you mind if the cleaning crew comes back tomorrow? I need more time to determine what really happened the night Vincent died."

"The new doctor arrives today."

"If I were him, I'd want to spend my first day meeting the patients and staff, not setting up my office," I said.

"Alright, but I must get everything back to normal. We already had one parent pull their child out of the clinic this weekend."

"One more favor, then I'll get to work. I'd like to stay until I complete my investigation."

"That's not possible. The doctor will be using the guest room!"

I had to think fast. "That's fine. I'll use the room vacated by the patient who just left. Scouts honor, I'll be on my best behavior."

She laughed, which helped release some of the tension building between us.

"Of course you can stay. Sorry I was being short with you. I simply want this nightmare over."

I created quite a stir when the girls realized I had moved into one of the rooms. Shirley was particularly unhappy I was her new neighbor.

"Are we goin' coed, or are you still snooping around?" she sniped.

"That's what private eyes do."

"Sometimes it's best to leave sleeping dogs lie. The police are gone; maybe you should also pack up and fade away," Shirley said as she walked into her room and slammed the door.

Once in Angelo's office, I locked myself in so I wouldn't be disturbed. Standing with my back to the door, I slowly scanned the room trying to see, trying to sense, trying to hear what really happened to him. Sometimes there's a simple clue, some sign that ultimately points to a solution, at least that's what my instruction manual had emphasized over and over again.

After a few minutes, I sat at Angelo's desk and once again flipped through the police report. The pictures were graphic; I only hoped Maria hadn't seen the gruesome scene. The back of Angelo's head had literally exploded. I couldn't blame Maria for wanting to clean everything; the stench of death was becoming unbearable.

As I turned each page, probably for the tenth time since receiving the file, I came across a close-up of the book cover with the bullet hole from the first shot fired. Turning the chair around, I saw the book again, lying face down on the second shelf from the top. I was surprised that such a crucial piece of evidence still remained in the office. I figured the cops felt the bullet was the only item of importance. It would have been a fairly interesting book cover even without the bullet hole squarely in the middle of the pyramid. The book had 627 pages, and the bullet almost pierced through the entire book. Page 598 had a small dimple but was otherwise intact.

I was idly flipping through the book when I realized something didn't seem right. I rippled the pages again, paying closer attention to the movement of the bullet hole as the pages flew past. Sure enough, I had just found the missing clue. The bullet the police had removed wasn't the first shot fired; it was the second. Angelo was already dead when the bullet struck the book.

I grabbed a pencil from the desk and rummaged through the drawers until I found a wooden ruler. I measured the distance from the top of the book cover to the center of the bullet hole: five and a quarter inches. On page 598, the distance from the top of the page was three and a half inches to the indentation. The bullet clearly entered the cover at an angle from the direction of the floor. I placed the book back on the shelf, as described by Maria in the police report, and stuck the pencil into the bullet hole; the line of sight pointed to the floor just slightly to the left of the desk. Not what I'd expected. Angelo's right hand had come to rest at least three feet from the desk.

Whoever killed Angelo put the gun in his hand after he had fallen dead and fired at the bookcase to leave powder burns on Angelo's hand. The only explanation for why the pencil didn't point to the gun was that the book sat on the shelf at a forty-five degree angle. I determined the angle by turning the book until the pencil pointed at the outline of Angelo's right hand.

Maria knocked on the office door, breaking my concentration. Dinner was ready. I took a few minutes to calm myself and joined the household for another one of Maria's fantastic meals. The new doctor had already arrived.

"Joey, I would like you to meet Dr. Swartz. He has agreed to continue Vincent's work until I can find a physician interested in buying Vincent's practice.

"Dr. Swartz, this is Joey Batista. He's a private investigator and was a friend of my husband's." As we shook hands, I had a good feeling about Dr. Swartz.

"Nice to meet you, Doctor. I know everyone is grateful for your help during this difficult time."

"Yes, I've been made to feel quite welcome, but to be honest, I'm a little confused as to why you're still investigating Dr. Taglio's death. My understanding is the police have come to a definitive conclusion."

I didn't answer.

"Ah yes, maybe we should discuss this matter some other time. Now we must enjoy what looks to be a delicious meal."

After dinner, Dr. Swartz visited with the nursing staff and a few of the patients, while Maria and I spent a pleasant evening on the front porch, each with a glass of lemonade.

"Now that the investigation is over and life is settling back into some semblance of a routine, have you had a chance to make any plans?" I asked.

"Actually, I've been giving your suggestion some thought," she said. "Working in the restaurant business seems to make sense, and I do have enough money to go back to school to get some management training. It will be difficult being on my own again, especially since I don't have family or know many people. I never realized how isolated I'd become since meeting Vincent."

"You're not as alone as you think. Vincent actually had a large family, and they are looking forward to meeting you." I didn't think she was ready to face what I truly meant by *family*.

"I always assumed Vincent had a falling-out with his relatives," she said.

"Maybe I can help bridge that gap. In the meantime, don't worry about the future, just keep this place running."

When we parted for the night, she caught me off guard as she held my hands, pulled me down to her height, and planted a kiss on my cheek.

"Thanks, Joey. Even though we still don't know what really happened the night Vincent died, you've been a great help."

She went inside, and I stayed on the veranda trying to figure out how someone entered Angelo's office, shot him, and left undetected with every exit locked from the inside.

* * * * *

The next morning I took an early walk around the estate, trying to piece together the facts I had uncovered since I arrived at the clinic. When I reached the pond,

Shirley jumped off a swing and met me halfway.

"I figured you for an early riser. I didn't think entering your room last night would've been a good idea," she said.

"No, I guess not."

"Maria told me you were a friend of Angelo's." I did my best to hide my surprise when she used his real name.

"That's right," I said. "You might say he tried to be a positive influence in an otherwise corrupt environment when I was a kid."

"Sounds like you didn't *really* know Angelo. He was a creep."

"Could be; I was young and only saw a big shot in the neighborhood being nice to me. No one had heard from him in over ten years, and to be honest, I was surprised to find he'd become a respected psychiatrist."

"He just hung up a damn shingle."

I had expected as much. Money in the right hands could buy any type of credential, and Angelo certainly had the contacts.

"You seem to know a great deal about Angelo. Care to tell me how?"

"Sure, why not. Your friend Angelo turned me into a hooker when I was twelve." I turned away, hoping she wouldn't see my reaction, but she didn't miss a stride and continued talking, reliving her past.

"I was alone, afraid, barely staying alive. At first he brought me food and then gave me a place to stay not far from where he lived. Soon after, the bastard got me hooked on drugs and brought some of his friends around. I was one of his favorite bitches for a long time, and one day he just disappeared. I continued doin' what he taught me. We met again two years ago, of all places, on a ferry ride. I was heading to Staten Island for a private party; he was returning from a medical conference. He talked about his practice and made me an offer I couldn't refuse. A place to live, all the drugs I needed, and three square meals a day, just for a few private sexual encounters a week. All those late nights in his office had little to do with work."

She didn't resist when I put my arm around her shoulder and gently pulled her closer as we continued to stroll through the garden. Words simply seemed meaningless. I wondered what else I didn't know about the Castellano family.

"What now?" I asked.

"I'll probably hang on here as long as possible. Eventually I'll end up on the streets again. At least Angelo did me one favor. I had asked him to get me off drugs and he did."

"How about the other girls…are they all legitimate patients?"

"After about a year, Angelo asked me if I had a friend who would agree to our arrangement. I did. Except for her, the others girls are real patients," she said walking away. I gently grabbed her arm.

She smiled as she looked up at me. "No more questions. You're the PI, I'm sure you can find your own answers."

She shook loose from my grip.

"Shirley, I know he was murdered."

She stopped, slowly turned, and gave me a blank stare. "Well then, you're one up on the coppers."

I had to let her go since the cleaners were due to arrive mid-afternoon, giving me only a few more hours to continue my examination of Angelo's office. Maria had given me the key to Angelo's file cabinets and, in a relatively short period of time, I got a good feeling for the results Angelo had actually achieved. Amazingly, he was extremely successful and had a greater than ninety percent drug addiction cure rate. I guess a little common sense *can* go a long way. Angelo maintained a meticulous filing system, and if files were missing or returned improperly, it would have been obvious. I hoped a missing file would point to a potential killer.

Next, I methodically walked around the room, doing my best to avoid the stains behind Angelo's desk. After about half an hour, I sat in one of the chairs positioned in the semicircle and tried to picture the murder scene within my mind's eye. I slowly reviewed all I had seen since arriving at the crime scene: the scarcity of windows; the chalk outline of his body; splattered bloodstains; book-shelves covered in death; and the mysterious bullet hole in a lone book. The only thing I knew with some degree of certainty was that everything that night had happened in a flash, in a small section of the room by his desk.

Blurry images kept flashing through my mind each time I went through the sequence of everything I had heard and observed. My subconscious was screaming to bring something to the surface. I knew I had missed a vital clue. I sat there going through everything again and again. Then I saw it: the final piece of the puzzle I needed to unlock its complexity.

It was just a small drop of blood floating inconspicuously in a sea of red. I got up from the chair and squatted down next to the chalk outline. There it was, a perfect semicircle of blood on the floor at the base of the bookcase, looking normal under the circumstances. But where was the other half of the bloodstain? The baseboard lining the bottom of the bookcase didn't have a corresponding mark of blood. The only logical explanation was that the bloodstain continued under the bookcase. There had to be a secret door behind Angelo's desk, and it must have been open the night Angelo died.

I frantically moved books and pushed every inch of the bookcase's wooden frame, looking for a hidden mechanism, but nothing happened. I sat in the desk chair and took several deep breaths, trying to slow down my heart rate and clear my mind. I asked myself, where would I put the latch for a hidden door? The answer finally came to me. He couldn't take a chance of someone accidentally hitting the mechanism, so it wouldn't be part of the bookcase. I reached inside each desk drawer and felt around the edges of the desktop. Nothing. I pulled out the center drawer and ran my hand along the inside surface and felt a metal latch with a finger loop. I gave it a strong tug, and a section of bookcase directly behind me swung open into a darkened room.

Maria knocked on the office door, informing me the cleaning crew had arrived. Since her husband's death, she had never entered the office, so I had time to close all the desk drawers, slip through the hidden door, and secure it gently before the cleaners came into the room.

I found myself standing in pitch darkness, totally disoriented, not daring to move for fear of alerting someone. Maria gave instructions to the person in charge of the clean up, and I heard her wonder aloud where I could have gone. After a few tense moments, the cleaning crew turned on their equipment, creating enough noise to drown out any sounds I might make. I slid my hand along the wall and switched on a light.

It took a moment to adjust to the glare from a bare bulb inserted into a ceiling fixture. Looking around, I began to see Angelo for who he really was. The room was about seven feet wide and ran the entire length of the house. At the far end there was a narrow staircase leading to a second level. The room was bare, except for a bed and a floor-standing glass cabinet that contained hypodermic needles and a fortune in heroin. I had a feeling I knew what I would find upstairs. Sure enough, he could enter each of the patient's room through a similar hidden bookcase door and could also spy on the girls through peepholes. I was trying to locate my room when I heard Shirley talking to Mary, who was still having serious withdrawal symptoms, even though the nurse had upped her dosage.

"Shirley, I gotta have more medication, my insides are coming apart. Let's tell them what really happened. They'll understand. I gotta get more, please."

"Okay, baby. I know where Vincent kept some extra medication. Just hold on a bit longer, I'll get some. The police have closed the case, and when the new doc sees your condition, he'll fix you right up. I promise I'll be back soon and you'll feel better."

Clearly Shirley knew about the hidden room and the stash of drugs, but she wouldn't be able to get access to the room due to the cleaning crew. I made a quick decision that could cost me my license, but sometimes you have to go with your gut. I entered my room from the passageway, ran out into the hall, and knocked on Mary's door. Shirley answered, standing in the doorway looking anxious.

"What the hell do you want now?" she sneered.

"Believe it or not, I want to help. I have a pretty good idea why Angelo was murdered." She led me into her room and closed the door behind us. As she defiantly turned to face me, I saw the inner strength that had sustained her for so many years.

"He deserved to die!" she said.

"I agree, but that's for a higher authority to judge. The important thing right now is to protect Maria and to get Mary what she needs."

I told her I knew about the drugs and the hidden door in the bookcase and suggested she use her entrance to the hidden room.

"You can only open the door to these rooms from the other side of the bookcase. Angelo always came for me."

I walked over to the bookcase and pushed open the entrance. "I shoved some paper in the latch hole. I suggest you take enough drugs to help Mary for a few days and trust me to handle everything else." She looked at me in disbelief.

"I have no doubt he deserved to die," I said.

She understood my meaning; we agreed to meet again in the garden after breakfast the next day.

* * * * *

A cold front had moved in during the night, and I'm sure we made a strange sight huddled together on the garden bench.

"Are you going to turn me in?" Shirley asked.

That was the question I'd wrestled with all night. The police had closed the case, Maria was trying to move on with her life, and Shirley had pulled herself halfway out of hell.

"It would help if I knew why and how you managed to almost pull off the perfect murder."

"You already know about our arrangement. As I said, it was better than working all night and turning most of the money over to my handler. Besides, Angelo was definitely skilled at helping his patients through some difficult times. As far as I was concerned, I had the good life. Then Mary came along, a confused kid who had experimented with drugs, but far from addicted.

"I could tell Angelo wanted her the moment she arrived. I saw that hungry look in his eyes so many times when I was young. After a few weeks, I noticed her condition deteriorated rapidly, too rapidly. He moved her to the intensive side of the dorm, and at that point, I knew what was going on. He was making her more dependent on heroin and him. The outrage I felt was uncontrollable; he was doing to her what he had done to me. I could only wonder how many other girls he had corrupted over the years."

As I gently pulled her closer, she put her head on my shoulder and quietly wept. We stood together for a few minutes, then I asked her the one question I didn't have an answer to. "How did you manage to shoot him at such close range?"

"I never intended to kill him; I just wanted to get him to leave Mary alone. The night before, when he returned me to my room, I fixed it so the door in my bookcase stayed ajar. The next evening I heard him enter Mary's room. I waited a little bit then crept down the hidden stairs and saw everything. When he finished having his way with her, he gave Mary the heroin she so desperately craved. She was almost unconscious when the phone rang in Angelo's office. He had to answer it quickly because Maria had knocked on his office door and would wonder why he didn't pick up the call.

"He kept one of his guns in the drug cabinet, and I took it. I crept into his office through the opening in the bookcase. He stood off to the side of the desk looking toward the windows and didn't notice me. He appeared to be angry with the caller. Apparently someone threatened to expose his false credentials. I crouched down and hid by the front of his desk. When he hung up the phone, I surprised him, demanding that he stop what he was doing to Mary. He just laughed and went for his other gun, which he kept in his desk. The rest is hard to remember, it happened so quickly. He stood there laughing and slowly pulled out the gun, probably thinking I would back down. He was still laughing when I shoved my gun into his mouth and blew his brains out. The rest you probably figured out. I got Mary back to her room and then all hell broke loose."

Shirley wiped a few tears from her face and suddenly

turned rigid.

"Are you able to handle all that's happened?" I asked.

"He deserved to die, and I have no regrets. But don't worry, I'm not going to fix all my problems by killing people." After a brief pause, she asked again, "Are you going to rat on me?"

At that point I knew exactly what I wanted to do.

"No, the case is solved. Everyone's satisfied, so let's keep it that way," I said.

She was obviously relieved, but streetwise enough to know her future remained uncertain.

"What about Angelo's brother?" she asked.

"I'll take care of Castellano. What I want you to do is sit tight, continue to care for Mary, and stay off drugs. Whatever you do, don't panic."

We walked back to the house in silence, lost in our own thoughts. Later I said my goodbyes, wished Doc Swartz good luck, and told Maria I would be in touch sometime next week. I asked her not to make any major decisions until I returned.

* * * * *

The ride back to Manhattan seemed exceptionally long, as did the whole month of February. Standing on the bow of the ferry, I could feel the March winds blowing across the bay, sending a shiver down my spine. I had a similar feeling many times during the war, and it was never a good sign.

March

The disgusting odor of bile filled my nostrils as I yanked my head out of the toilet bowl, wiping my naked arm across my mouth. I don't remember getting out of bed, but when I walked through the open bathroom door, images from my past struck again, and I lunged back for the bowl. I hoped the nightmares were behind me. But how could they be? My nightmares are my reality, my memories. The sights, the sounds, the smells, the feel of cold steel on my flesh as I pulled the trigger, the veil of death passing over so many eyes as I muffled their screams with one hand and drove my knife deep into their flesh with the other. These things will never, can never, go away. Standing again in the doorframe, looking at the sight before me, I realized there are too many nightmares to face, too many sleepless nights waiting in my future.

My mattress, wedged in a corner covered over with blankets to create a "blind," a place to hide until my target arrived, was a stark reminder of how I had served my country. Again my muscles ached as I remembered sitting motionless for days, waiting. My mission had been simple—make it look like an accident. One shot, the tire exploded, and the Pierce-Arrow luxury car crashed through the safety barrier as it made a sharp turn along a Swiss mountain road. Mission accomplished. But where did his kids come from? He always traveled alone. I didn't see them when I took the shot. Their screams echoed along the canyon walls as the car spiraled off through the air into a ravine. I watched the horror on their faces through the riflescope, until the car burst into flames and their flesh melted away, searing their agonizing death into my memory. My first mission and all I had to do was kill one person, a banker, a financier of the war—but three died that day.

As time went on and the complexity of my assignments increased, I began to crave the tension, the suspense, the feeling of not knowing if I would survive. I became an addict, not to drugs, booze or even violence. I crave adrenaline, that extra rush when faced with danger, the possibility of death, the unknown. It's what kept me alive behind enemy lines, enabled me to sense when to act and when to retreat. Even near death, beaten beyond consciousness, I could summon its power simply by thinking of Anita. The thought of never knowing what happened to her would trigger a surge, giving me strength to continue, to endure the unbearable.

My need for excitement, for living on the edge, was probably the real reason I became a PI. Like a true addict, I wanted more. My need for adrenaline was greater than the terror of my nightmares.

So far I haven't been disappointed. I was about to explain to a Mafia boss that his brother didn't commit suicide but got knocked off by some broad and deserved to die. I also had some nutcase lurking in the shadows of my life, ready to put a bullet in my head.

I tried to go back to sleep, but it was useless, so I went for an early morning walk.

A few hours before my weekly drive with Butch, I still didn't have a clue how to explain Angelo's death to Castellano. I leaned back in my chair and put my feet on the desk to gather my thoughts when Frank Galvano entered without knocking.

"Payday has arrived," he said, slamming his palm down

on my desk, leaving behind a thousand dollars. Just a few months ago I was nearly broke, and now it was raining hundred-dollar bills.

"Thanks, Frank. Sure looks like we took Stefano to the laundry."

"We did. That's the good news. The bad news is Stefano's still ranting about getting revenge, and he sounds like one demented, mean son-of-a-bitch."

I opened my coat and showed Frank my piece.

"Smart move," he said. "He'll be out in a few weeks, possibly earlier because money talks in this town." As Frank opened the door to leave, he made a suggestion. "If you spruce this joint up, you could charge a lot more."

Before I could respond with a wisecrack, he continued, "I'm working with someone who could use your help. When the time's right, I'll send her over. One more thing, she's a real looker!" he said with a wink as he closed the door.

That's all I needed, another broad in my life. I decided to avoid Frank for a few days, at least until I tied up the loose ends from my first two cases. After he left, I was trying once again to play out in my mind how the hell I was gonna explain to Castellano the circumstances surrounding his brother's death when Butch barged into my office two hours early.

"Ready, kid?" he said, holding open the door to conceal the fact that one of the hinges had just ripped from the frame. The hinge didn't bother me, but his attitude did.

"No, Butch, I'm not ready! And don't call me kid; the name's Joey."

"Okay...*kid*! The Boss, he's waiting. Let's go."

* * * * *

"My boys tell me you've been taking life easy the last few days. That can only mean one of two things: you're either a lousy PI and only interested in milking me or you know who killed my brother. Which is it?"

Castellano spit his words out with clenched teeth.

"Your brother didn't commit suicide."

"I know that! I paid you to find out who killed him."

"Some dame blew his brains out."

"Was it a hit?"

"No."

The muscles in his face relaxed then quickly contorted his features into a snarl.

"Who is she?"

I knew from my earlier experiences with the Boss that he was a man of honor, with a strict Sicilian code of conduct, and I believed Castellano would never betray a trust. He also held others to the same high standard. Shirley's life now depended on that code.

"Before I answer, I want you to know he was killed in self-defense and, in my opinion, deserved what he got."

"No, Joey. You tell me the details—all the details—and I will be the judge and jury. Don't leave anything out," he said as he leaned back in his seat and stared straight ahead.

I had the eerie sense of being in a confessional, trying to tell just enough to get absolution but not the whole truth. I told Castellano's profile the sordid facts of his brother's actions. When I was done, he turned and looked deep into my eyes.

"You're not going to tell me who killed Angelo, are you?"

"No."

"You've told me enough. I can find her!"

"*I know,* but I hope you won't. Your brother ruined her life. She's suffered enough."

"You're asking me not to avenge my brother's death?"

"I'm asking you to make atonement for his actions by letting her live."

"Is Maria involved in any way?"

"Maria is one of Angelo's victims. She had no idea of his background or the activities he engaged in at the clinic. In her mind, she had the perfect marriage."

"She must have been naïve or deeply in love," he said.

There were other possibilities as well; most Mafia wives chose to ignore the truth about their husbands, but in Maria's case, I believe she was indeed ignorant.

"If possible, I'd like to spare Maria the truth about Angelo," I said.

"What are you thinking?"

"Buy the clinic, send in a construction crew to remodel the house to eliminate the hidden room and passageway."

"Would she consider selling?"

"She'd like to leave the clinic behind her."

"I know you, Joey. You've thought everything through already, so spit it out. What can I do for her?"

"Maria's an excellent Italian cook and would enjoy being a chef or manager of a restaurant."

"Not a problem," Castellano said. "Angelo owned La Cucina Restaurant. A close friend of the family took over the management when he left town."

"When can she begin?" I asked.

"Anytime. She can be an assistant chef until she learns the business."

We spent the next hour working out the details of the clinic's reconstruction. We agreed I'd be the middleman and make the necessary arrangements and that it would be best not to reveal Angelo's real identity to Maria until she had settled into her new life. As I was about to leave the car, Castellano pulled me back.

"We're not finished. You tell the young girl who killed Angelo that I will not exact my right of blood. As you said, she has suffered enough at the hands of my family." Castellano had given her absolution.

He paused, removed an envelope from his jacket. "Here's your final payment. Hope I can call on you again if needed."

"It's gotta be legit. I have no desire to get involved in the organization's business."

"I understand, and I'll respect your wishes. There is, however, another matter, Tommy Stefano." This got my attention.

"Tommy has family connections and has been trying to earn a position in the organization. You're lucky his brother is serving time for a bank job, but he still controls part of Jersey and has asked the area bosses to authorize a hit. You've made a powerful enemy."

I knew Tommy was dangerous, but this I didn't expect.

"Fortunately, you also have friends in high places, so his request got turned down, but Tommy's crazy enough to do something on his own. Be careful. No matter what happens you better be looking over your shoulder until this matter is resolved," Castellano counseled.

"How does it get resolved?" I asked.

"You have a lot to learn about my world," Castellano said. "Either they kill you or you kill them, and even then it might not stop."

What Castellano said about my having friends in high places made no sense. Castellano and his family were the only connections I had to the mob.

"What friends?" I asked.

"I don't have time to explain. Ask your uncle. In the meantime, watch your back, and I'll do what I can to keep you safe."

In the military I never had to look back and worry about the carnage I caused. All I had to do was infiltrate enemy lines, complete my mission, get out alive, then train for the next assignment. The PI business wasn't as straightforward.

Cleaning up my first two cases turned out to be more complicated than I expected and took valuable time away from finding a new client. Going almost two weeks without dough flowing into my coffers could become a problem in the future. Thanks to Castellano's generosity, this wasn't an issue yet.

I figured it was time to give Luigi his percentage of my take from both jobs and maybe have some fun doing it. I carried a brown paper bag under my arm into my uncle's private office at the back of his speakeasy.

"Hey, Uncle Luigi, looks like you're having a good night."

"Business is booming since Prohibition. You know how it is—everyone wants the forbidden fruit."

"I guess some things never change."

"Thank God for that. So what brings you back here? You need somethin'?"

"I thought I should give you your cut of my earnings before I come home some night and find I've been evicted for not paying the rent."

"You never have to worry about that. We're family! Pay me when you can," he said with a serious expression.

At that point, I dumped four hundred and fifty dollar bills on his desk. As he tried to jump out of his chair, he stumbled and landed back into his seat. I laughed and soon found myself in one of his famous bear hugs.

Letting go, he said, "Joey, I thought you were a private eye, not a bank robber."

"Take it when you can, Uncle Luigi. I could have a couple of dry months."

"That's true, but the Boss has been singing your praises, and that can't be bad for business, not to mention having your picture on the front page of the *Daily News.* So, tell me, you want to change our arrangement and pay a regular rent or keep things as they are?" he said as he stuffed the bills back into the bag.

"Like I said, I'm not sure when the next case will pop up, so let's keep things as they are for a few more months. I would, however, like some things in return."

"I knew there had to be a catch to all this loot. Whaddya want?" he asked with some hesitation.

"Not much, just another apartment. It's not professional to be sleeping in my office."

"Okay, the place above you is empty. What else?"

"The bathroom needs fixing up."

"Like what?"

"Everything, but I'd be happy with new fixtures for now, and hot water."

Luigi looked at me, then the money. "I'll get a plumber on the job next week. Just make sure you keep the rent coming." We shook hands and sealed the deal. "I hear Tommy Stefano is getting out soon. You packing that piece I gave you?" he asked, as he patted me down.

"Castellano's also warned me so I'm being extra cautious. That reminds me, the Boss mentioned I had friends in high places but didn't explain what he meant. He said to ask you."

Luigi looked away for a moment. "Some other time. I'm busy now. Come by in a few nights. We'll have a couple of drinks, and I'll tell you a little something about your ma and pop."

Before I could insist, he ushered me out of his office and locked the door.

* * * * *

A few nights later, I hopped a cab over to Stefano's favorite saloon to check on Martha and the girls. When Rocky, the bouncer, saw me, his face turned to stone as he pushed me away to let some patrons inside. Once we were alone, he grabbed my lapels and hoisted me several inches off the ground.

"Are you crazy? If Tommy or his pals see you here, you're a goner."

"I just want to make sure the girls are okay, and then I'm outta here."

He let go and I stumbled against a wall. "What ya talking about? They got dumped. Lucky they didn't get knocked off."

It never occurred to me that I was putting the girls in real danger. I tried to get more details, but Rocky shoved me away again. "Get outta here before I get mine. I got hell for letting you in the joint in the first place." I could smell his fear, so I quietly left.

I ran to Martha's flat. Needless to say, I wasn't welcome. She opened the door, and spewed forth a string of obscenities. Before I could respond, the door slammed shut. I heard her talking to Dorothy and Ginger, then they all began yelling. I waited a few minutes and knocked again. Ginger opened the door and blocked the entrance with an evil stare.

"Look," I said. "I didn't mean for any of this to happen. I just found out tonight and came right over to see how you all are doin'."

"Doin'? How do ya think we're doin'? We all moved in here, and in a few days, we'll be walking the streets, thanks to you."

"Come on, give me a break; maybe I can help."

Ginger turned to the other girls, and I could hear Martha in the background. "Let the creep in and hear what he has to say."

I sat on the sofa and the girls all stood around, looking down with their arms folded. I should have kept my mouth shut and let them continue to rant, but I didn't.

"Honestly, I don't know how this happened," I said.

Before I could say another word, Martha let me have it.

"You dumb-ass. You show up at the trial, get your ugly face plastered all over the paper, and you don't know what happened? What? You think Tommy's stupid? He's not the brightest guy in town, but he can add two plus two."

I felt like a heel. I never gave their safety a second thought. "Listen, you gals have a right to be angry. My only defense is inexperience. It was my first job, and I didn't think everything through."

I said something right for a change because they finally calmed down. Ginger sat next to me and gently touched my arm, as if to say, "you'll learn." Dorothy still stood over me, but with her arms at her sides, shaking her head, and Martha retreated to the kitchen, pacing back and forth.

"Why don't you tell me everything?" I asked.

Martha stormed out of the kitchen. "Stefano came straight to the speakeasy after getting out of the slammer and accused us of setting him up. He slapped us around, but fortunately Sam and Rocky got him corralled before he did any real damage. Next thing we know, he's talking to the owner and comes out of the office all smiles. As he walks by us, he says, 'First I'm gonna get that bum, and then you bitches.'"

Ginger continued, "Before he left, he turned, pulled his hand out of his jacket as if he had a gun, and pretended to shoot us. I was never so scared."

"A few minutes later the owner told us we were fired,"

Dorothy said. "We tried to find work, but the word's out. There ain't nothin' in this town for us; we have to leave."

That was it, end of story. Ginger cried, Martha and Dorothy looked downtrodden, and I felt like shit. To make matters worse, they had an eviction notice tacked to the door of the apartment.

After a few awkward moments, I realized it was my mess to deal with.

"Okay, girls, I'm gonna set things straight, but you need to work with me."

"Forget it," Martha said with a look of disgust. "You're worse than having Typhoid Mary as a friend."

"Listen to me, you all need to move out of this place—tonight!"

Martha was about to object when Dorothy brushed her aside.

"He's right. Stefano probably has the lowdown on us by now and knows where we are."

"We gotta act fast," I said. "My uncle owns an apartment house across town, and there's a great flat that's vacant. I want you all to move in tonight, right now. I'll arrange to have your stuff picked up tomorrow."

Martha still didn't like the idea of hooking up with me again. "Are you nuts?" she shouted. "First of all, I owe back rent, and my landlord is watching every move we make, and if you think I'm leaving my things behind, you're even crazier than I thought."

As I walked over to her, she backed away. "How come you're behind on the rent?" I asked

"What, you think we got paid when we got fired?"

"Here's two hundred bucks to pay your rent and some spending money until I can find you all work. As far as your belongings, I'll have a moving crew here first thing in the morning. It might take a few days to arrive because they'll need to make sure no one can trace the delivery," I said.

They all stared at the money. It finally sunk in that they needed to do something, and my offer was an option, probably their only one.

"What kind of work?" Martha challenged.

"I see a few possibilities. I need to work out the details. A job in my uncle's speakeasy, possibly a hostess at an Italian restaurant and working as my secretary."

"Great! A secretary to a loser. I'm not taking *that* job," Martha said.

"What about Stefano?" Dorothy asked.

"Let me worry about that jerk. He'll come after me first, and if he's successful, my uncle will take things from there."

Martha threw her hands up. "Are you connected too? Is that what you're saying?"

I looked at her for a few seconds before answering as it dawned on me that I really didn't know the answer to her question. "Look, I'm giving you ladies a chance to get out of this mess. I'm sorry for what happened, but I can't undo the damage I've caused. Right now you need to take my offer and get the hell out of this place." I turned to Martha. "And you need to pay your back rent."

Martha snatched the money out of my hand, and I watched helplessly as she walked out the door without saying a word. My wad of cash was dwindling fast: first Sally, then Luigi, and now Martha. As if that wasn't enough, I just gave up my new apartment and would be back sleeping in my office.

By the time we got to my uncle's place, the girls looked beat. We grabbed a table, and I ordered a round of drinks to keep them occupied. I then went in search of my uncle.

"Looks like ya have the makings of a harem. What's

goin' on?" Luigi asked.

"They're the dames who helped me nail Stefano. He figured out they were in on the deal and got them fired."

"They need a place to hang out?" he asked.

"Yeah, I thought you could let them use the flat you promised me."

"Sure, you gonna give me another ten percent?" he said smiling.

"You gotta be kidding. They also need work. How about taking one on? They have real class and experience."

"They wanna work the back room or out front?"

"Not *that* kind of experience. How about it? You gonna help?"

"Sure, which one?" he asked, looking past my shoulder at the girls.

"They need to talk it over. One more thing, I need a moving crew for tomorrow morning to get their belongings."

"Not a problem. Anything else you want now that you got me in such a generous mood? Come on, you got that look. What is it?"

"It's Stefano; he also threatened them, so I'm putting you at some risk."

"Are you kidding? In this business, every day is a risk. Besides, we got Stefano covered. We have his picture from the paper, and everyone is watching for him. Not to worry," he said.

"Thanks, Uncle. You wouldn't know how to get hold of Castellano, would ya?"

"Sure, tonight he has his poker game over at La Cucina. You want I should give him a call?"

"Yeah, I need to get the girls settled."

It took only a few minutes to explain the situation to Castellano before he offered up a position. Everything was working out, and I was about to share the good news with the girls when I noticed my neighbor, Frank Galvano, sitting at the bar. We chatted a few minutes, and he agreed to split the expenses for a secretary; his only requirement was she could type. I was finally ready to face the girls, and none too soon.

"About time! Every drunk in the joint has been hitting on us." I ignored Martha and laid out their options.

I wasn't sure I got the best end of the bargain. Martha reluctantly agreed to be my new "office manager," since she was the only one with typing experience. She came up with the fancy title. Ginger agreed to work for Uncle Luigi, and Dorothy opted for the restaurant job. Next, I showed them their apartment, and as I said goodnight, Martha thanked me for my efforts but couldn't quite let go of her anger.

"Of course, none of this would've been necessary if you didn't get us involved in your crazy case."

"That's one way to look at how things turned out," I said.

"Oh yeah, how would you look at the mess you got us into?"

"Your lives have taken a new direction. Who knows what might happen. For instance, it looks really crowded in there with only one bed, and there's plenty of room in mine."

"What? Are you suggesting we draw straws?"

"Works for me."

"Men!" she said in disgust as she slammed the door.

* * * * *

I had a couple of rough nights in a row, waking every few hours in a cold sweat. These nightmarish attacks seemed to be taking place more frequently, bringing with them vivid images of the war. Memories I wanted to suppress. I was about to finally fall asleep when someone pounded on the door. At first I thought it was part of my dream but then realized it was Luigi's voice yelling as the sun pierced through the window.

"Hey, Joey, get up. Your pop and I need you downstairs."

As soon as I opened the door, he slipped into the room.

"Where are the dames?" he asked looking around.

"What dames?"

"Ya know, the ones from the other night. What was it like? Oh, to be young again."

"What are you talking about? They're in their own apartment. You gave us the key, remember?"

"Joey, are you my nephew or not? Do you have my guinea blood running through those veins? I'm not so sure anymore."

"Uncle, quit the crap and tell me what's going on?"

"Get dressed and your ass downstairs. We've got to go to the Island."

"What's going on?"

"Just do what I said and come down for breakfast. I don't know why you've been so damn tired lately. You're not even sleeping with one of them."

Luigi left as suddenly as he came, shaking his head.

As I was dressing, Martha came down to my office. "What's the racket about?" she asked. "Don't forget you have people sleeping upstairs."

"Sorry, but I don't know what's going on. My uncle and Pop want to go to the Island for some reason."

"Do you need me to come along?" she asked.

For a moment I forgot our new arrangement. "No, I don't think so. Why don't you work for Frank for a few more days, and then we can figure out how you can help me." She put her hands on her hips, smirked, then turned to leave. "Hey, since you're up, come down for breakfast. It might be good for you to know what's happening."

The kitchen was packed, and Ma was busy cooking and serving bacon and eggs. When I walked in, she put down the plates she carried, came over, and smothered me with a hug.

"Oh, Joey, I'm so sorry," she said weeping.

I looked around the room and saw Sally standing in the corner with her head down, Pop aimlessly moving food around his plate, and my uncle and Castellano smoking stogies, stinking up the place. No one said a word.

"Pop, what's goin' on?"

"It's Tom Sgarlata. He's dying and has asked for you. We need to leave; he doesn't have long to live."

I couldn't believe it. Anita's dad had never missed a day working his farm. I suddenly felt overwhelmed with remorse; I hadn't visited him since returning home. I thought about it but couldn't bring myself to go back to the place where Anita and I had spent most of our time together.

"Why didn't someone tell me earlier?" I shouted.

"Joey, don't be angry," Ma said. "Anita's been gone for over six years. Digging up the past is no good."

I couldn't stay mad at Ma. I knew she meant well. "Ma, I will never forget Anita, nor do I want to. Until I know what happened to her, she'll be a ghost at my side."

Martha barged into the kitchen, shattering the tension hanging over the room. "Mornin' everyone." She noticed Castellano and immediately introduced herself as my new office manager.

"What does an office manager do?" Castellano asked.

"I don't really know. We're still working on that," she said.

Once Martha and Sally sat down, I turned to the Boss.

"Mr. Castellano, I didn't know you knew the Sgarlatas. I don't mean to be disrespectful, but I never saw you there or ever remember Anita or her father mention you. Why are you coming with us?"

He was about to answer when Pop spoke up. "Joey, we all grew up together in the old country. Me, your uncle, Castellano, Sgarlata, and a few others you haven't met. We took an oath. We knew we would go different ways once in America, and we swore whatever happened to one, happened to us all. We are family through blood and friendship, and nothing will ever separate us."

I was beginning to realize there were parts of my family history, especially in Italy, that I wasn't fully aware of and probably would never know. And I wasn't sure I wanted to. If Castellano was such a close friend, why was this the first time I saw him in our house?

* * * * *

The others left me alone on the front porch of the farmhouse as they paid their respects to Mr. Sgarlata. Leaning against the railing, looking out over the acres of land, I could see row upon row of cornstalks rippling in the wind and remembered how Anita could always find me no matter how hard I tried to hide in the tall maze. The haystack by the gnarled oak tree looked larger than I recalled, and when the swing swayed in the wind, I saw Anita launch herself off the seat, land on top of a stack, and roll down to the ground covered in hay and full of laughter. The pigpen smelled worse than ever, and I recalled how Anita and I would run around in the muck trying to catch Herman, her favorite pig.

As I was still remembering, Pop came out of the house

and put his hand on my shoulder. "He wants to see you now. Son, he doesn't look the same. I thought you should know before going inside."

I turned back and took one last look over the property and began to see beyond my memories. Weeds had overgrown the fields that now lay barren. The barn doors swayed in the wind, and two plows and a wagon were rotting outside near a mud hole. There were no manure piles or pigs rutting around in their pens. The oak tree, split by lightning, died years ago but still held onto a frayed rope that dangled to the ground. Death's shadow had encroached, ever so slowly, from all sides onto the farmhouse, and now a dark cloud preceded it, drenching everything in its wake.

"I know, Pop. I know he's not the same."

I don't remember walking past the kitchen to the main bedroom. Upon entering the room, I saw three figures dressed in black attending an old man encased in his bed covers. As I came forward, an elderly neighbor stepped back with her head down. A priest, anointing Mr. Sgarlata's forehead, whispered some ancient Latin prayer, made the sign of the cross, and moved away. A doctor holding onto a skeletal hand tried to find a pulse, then gently placed the hand back by Mr. Sgarlata's side and receded into the shadows. Then I saw her again: Anita sitting on the edge of the bed, beckoning me forward, wearing her favorite dress, with her long black hair pulled back in a braid, revealing the beauty of her radiant face.

"Joey, come closer," said a raspy voice. The image of Anita faded, replaced by a sinewy arm reaching out to me.

"Mr. Sgarlata, I'm sorry. I didn't know."

"Joey, take this." He pulled out an old envelope from under the bedcovers and handed it to me. "I sold the farm; I have no family. You were to be my family. Anita told me, she told me she loved you."

"Mr. Sgarlata, you need to rest."

"Joey, I'm dying. I'll get plenty of rest," he said with a weary smile. "I want you to find Anita, find out what happened to her. You can do this. I know you can."

"Mr. Sgarlata, I tried years ago, and so did the police. You can't ask this of me. I'm not ready."

"Joey, you need to know or it will eat your insides rotten, like it did mine. The only way to find peace is to know. Trying to forget doesn't work."

Before I could respond, the figures of death reemerged from the shadows to administer their comfort and pushed me aside.

I found myself on the porch again with Pop, Uncle Luigi, and Castellano. They apparently were in the room when I spoke to Mr. Sgarlata.

"What's in the envelope?" my uncle asked as he took it from my hand and read its contents. "It's his will. He left you everything. If you find her alive, you're to give her what's left. If she's dead, give her a Christian burial and any remaining money to the church. When he dies, the developers who own this land will bulldoze the house. Take what you want and give the rest to his neighbors. He says he wants justice for her and peace for you."

"Tom Sgarlata hasn't seen you in years, but he knows how you feel," Pop said. "You need to find out what happened to Anita, but if I were you, I'd treat this just like you would any other case. It will take time, but someday, you'll learn the truth."

"You need anything, no matter what, you come to me," Castellano added.

When I returned from the Sgarlata farm, I told Martha to shut down the business. I explained I needed to focus all my energy on finding what happened to Anita. She hadn't run away with some drifter. I knew that and so did Mr. Sgarlata. He wasn't asking me to find Anita; he wanted revenge, and I wanted the same. I always did.

Martha was in no mood to accept more changes in her life. "Are you telling me I'm out of a job again because you want to solve a murder case that may or may not have happened years ago? Let me tell you some reasons why that's a really stupid idea. First, I need this job. You wanna know why? I'll tell you, because you got me fired from my last one. Remember? Second, you're not a real PI just because you read a few books and have a fancy piece of paper hanging on your wall. You need experience. You said you tried before to find out what happened to Anita. Do you have any new leads? I didn't think so. Third, you need to deal with Tommy Stefano. Do you at least remember him?"

She was still listing reasons as I left the office and walked downstairs to my uncle's joint.

O'Reilly occupied his usual table, talking to Rosalie as she brought over two new drinks. I sat down uninvited and ordered. "I'll have two of the same and keep them coming till my uncle drags me upstairs to my room."

Rosalie sat down next to O'Reilly. "Joey, you got a problem? I can tell ya, booze ain't gonna help," she said.

I resisted making a nasty remark about how women should mind their own business and instead found myself sharing what happened. When I finished unburdening myself, Rosalie wiped away a tear, and O'Reilly waved for another waitress to bring more drinks.

"Joey," Rosalie said, "I know you don't want me telling you what to do, but I think Martha's right."

"And so do I," O'Reilly added. "All you're gonna accomplish is to run around aimlessly, getting frustrated and ending up here every night trying to drown away memories that need to stay inside. A case this old is tough to solve even for an experienced detective. I agree with what ya pop said. Work on the case, but don't stop living."

"How do you know what my pop said?" I asked.

"Oh, he and Luigi left a short time ago and told me everything."

I didn't notice Rosalie had gotten up to go back to work until I felt her arms around my neck and a gentle kiss.

As the night wore on, I became more canned and told O'Reilly some of the things I'd been keeping twisted up inside.

"I once told you I agreed to join the so-called Death Squad because I wanted to die, I didn't want to live without Anita. The truth is I couldn't live with my own guilt. I should have been with her. She had asked her father if she could marry me, and when she told me we had his blessing, I chickened out. I wasn't ready, and that was the last time I ever saw her. I'll never forget the look on her face as I walked away. Mike, I need to find out what happened to her. That's the only reason I'm alive today. I should have died more than once in the war but I didn't. I didn't because I wanted revenge, and I knew that if I stayed alive, someday I'd get it. I did whatever it took to survive, no matter who I had to kill or how much pain I had to endure."

"Why do you think I spend every night drinking this rotgut?" O'Reilly asked. "I know who killed my kid brother, and I'm torn between letting the law do its job and doing it myself. I know the son of a bitch will never fry for killing Shawn, but I've brought him in for other murders, and every time some judge lets him off. I care about nothing else. I'm telling ya, take your time, work on other cases, and build your skills, as Martha said. Live your life, and one day you'll come face-to-face with Anita's reality and then you'll know what to do."

"Sounds like you're not taking your own advice," I said.

"I'm not. That's why you should. You don't want to end up like me."

"Who killed Shawn?"

"You think I'm gonna tell you, knowing what you did during the war? I don't want to arrest my best friend."

The next morning I woke up with a horrendous headache and a resolve to take everyone's advice. When I finally got the strength to get out of bed, I was surprised to find Martha sitting at my desk, hard at work.

"I thought we'd agreed you'd work for Frank until another apartment became available so I could move my bed out of the office. Besides, we haven't discussed how best to use your time," I said.

"Frank felt I should help you. He's running out of things for me to do."

"If we're going to work together in my bedroom, why don't you just move in?" I said, half-joking, half-hoping.

"That's not necessary. All you have to do is get up early and take a cold shower," she said without a hint of humor in her voice. "I asked O'Reilly to get the police file on Anita's disappearance. I didn't think you'd mind, and I'm going to the *Daily Post* archives building this afternoon to search for some of the old news reports. I also took the liberty of calling Maria. I told her you had some news for her and you'd be by sometime during the week."

It occurred to me Martha had a pretty good idea what her job entailed. In short order she had me focused again. It did take a few days to make the financial arrangements to buy the clinic and organize a construction crew, but when I had the details worked out, all I had left was to convince

Maria to accept Castellano's offer.

* * * * *

As usual, I thoroughly enjoyed the ferry ride to Staten Island and found myself eager to give Maria the good news when I realized I had forgotten about Shirley. She was safe from Castellano and the cops but unemployed, and it would be impossible for her to work anywhere in our neighborhood. Her former clients would recognize her, the word would spread, and she'd be treated as a common tramp. I looked at the problem from every conceivable angle and still didn't have a solution when I arrived at the clinic.

As I drove up to the house, Maria waved and then continued talking with Ron, the groundskeeper. Before I could park, Shirley came running down the stairs of the veranda and walked alongside the car, shooting questions at me.

"Where the hell have you been? I almost went back on that junk; my nerves are shot. What's goin' on?"

Maria and Ron turned to see what the commotion was about.

"Take it easy. Didn't I say everything would be okay?" I was hoping I sounded more confident than I felt, but then again, I did have some good news.

"Sure, two simple words: trust me. How often have I heard that from the men in my life?" she said through clenched teeth. "Shit Joey, I killed a Mafia boss's brother. Did you forget?"

I parked the car, grabbed her by the arm, and walked over to the veranda, where we could talk without drawing attention.

"Shirley, calm down. I talked to Castellano, and you needn't worry. I think if Angelo were alive today, he'd kill him himself." She stopped walking and yanked me down off two of the stairs leading up to the veranda.

"What are you saying?"

"What you have to understand," I continued, "is Castellano has high moral standards, but at the same time, he's a Mafia boss. Somehow he's blended the two; in fact, they all do. He would never condone how Angelo used his power to corrupt a young girl, nor would he stomach how he abused his position at the clinic."

Tears filled Shirley's eyes. I wanted to pull her close but had to settle for holding her hand, since some of the other girls were approaching the front of the clinic. We went for a walk around the grounds and ended up sitting on a bench, watching three mallard ducks waddling back to the pond. After a few minutes, she regained her composure.

"What now?" she asked.

"I don't have all the answers. We need to find you a job so you can stay off the streets. To be honest, I haven't been able to come up with a good idea. You can't work anywhere in our old neighborhood because you'll be recognized. I need more time to think of a solution."

"Why can't I work here?" she asked.

I thought she was kidding. I should've known better.

"What do you mean? What type of work?"

"What I've been doing for the past year: working with the girls; holding group meetings; being there when they need someone who knows what they're going through."

I must have looked skeptical because she rushed on. "I know Angelo's methods, and they work. I'll just continue doing what I've been doing, but this time I'll get paid."

I realized at that moment Shirley would be fine; she knew how to get herself out of a jam.

"I'll talk to Maria and include you as part of the deal

I'm going to offer her tonight."

"What deal?"

"Nothing you need to be concerned about. In the meantime, don't worry about Castellano, and make yourself useful to the new doc."

"What are you going to tell Maria about me?"

"Nothing, the official report is that her husband committed suicide. She doesn't need to know about how Angelo abused his position."

As it turned out, Maria had always suspected her husband was running away from his past and wasn't surprised to find out he had family in New York. She apparently wasn't as naïve as Castellano and I believed. Maria agreed to sell the clinic and eagerly looked forward to her new job as one of the assistant chefs of an established Italian restaurant. Before leaving, I met with Dr. Swartz and made arrangements to have the clinic shut down for a few weeks for renovations and secured Shirley an attractive, paid position on his staff.

The ride back to Manhattan felt good until I realized I was the one out of work. I hoped I'd be able to aggressively dig into what happened to Anita when I had put my first two cases behind me, but Martha's and O'Reilly's efforts to find more information hadn't panned out. The Staten Island police misplaced Anita's case file and needed to search their entire archives, which were scattered over three buildings. They didn't see my urgency and wouldn't commit to when they might locate her file. Martha's research at the *Daily Post*, although useful, didn't turn up anything new. I had already read every news article at the time of Anita's disappearance, and reading them again only increased my frustration.

By the time the ferry captain gave three blasts from the horn signaling he had successfully docked the ferry into its slip, I felt completely down. I had to face Martha's sarcasm on a daily basis, constantly watch my back for Stefano, and was stymied by my own inexperience to discover the truth about Anita.

Since I couldn't think of a good reason to go back to the office, I never made it past my uncle's saloon, where I sought out O'Reilly.

April

I awoke later than usual and didn't bother to close the hideaway, since today an army of carpenters, plumbers, and electricians were descending upon my world to fix up the office. An apartment had become vacant on the fourth floor, and Martha was having improvements made before she moved. Everything had to be timed perfectly because I was moving into her old apartment. Martha gave me strict orders to vacate the office no later than ten, which meant I had fifteen minutes to get my ass out of there.

I was fumbling with the strap on my shoulder holster when I heard a gentle knock, and as I looked up, a gorgeous redhead entered, bringing with her the aroma of lilacs. As I walked over to greet her, a commotion erupted on the stairwell outside my office. My uncle and some of his men were running up the stairs yelling something about Stefano. As their warnings registered, I lunged at the redhead, hitting her hard in the midsection, driving us both toward the bed. We landed on the mattress and rolled over the edge, as a barrage of bullets from a tommy gun shredded my window and riddled the room. My uncle returned fire from behind the solid brick wall of the doorframe, keeping Stefano from entering through the window.

I found myself underneath the redhead, who had her face buried in the nape of my neck. Unable to move, I gave her a gentle nudge. She slid off, amazingly calm under the circumstances. The noise was deafening. Stefano screamed my name, firing haphazardly, frustrated that my uncle's bullets were preventing him from moving across the fire escape landing so he could get a clear shot at me. I didn't have to say a word. The redhead saw the situation, and together we inched backwards toward the opposite wall, where the only way Stefano's bullets could get us would be for him to step through the shattered window and expose himself to my uncle.

I pulled out my .45 and crept toward the window to get into the action when I realized the redhead didn't have a chance if Stefano took me out. He wouldn't leave behind any witnesses. I moved back and signaled for her to come toward me. I gave her my .45 and was about to show her how to use it, when she flipped open the barrel and spun it around to make sure it was fully loaded, then kissed me hard on the lips. My uncle saw what I had done and slid one of his guns along the floor as his bodyguard ran across the doorway firing. Stefano caught the man in mid-flight. The sound of gunfire suddenly ceased as everyone watched the bloody body stagger and fall into the room.

My uncle's gun stopped under my desk, out of reach. I inched along the floor with my arm outstretched, and as I felt the cold steel on my fingertips, Stefano leaped across the window to the other side of the fire escape and saw what I was doing. In his excitement, he leaned into the room and was about to blast me to hell when my uncle exposed himself to get off a shot. Stefano let loose a burst of lead that caught Luigi in the shoulder. He spiraled across the hall and down the stairs. Suddenly, Stefano's tommy gun flew out of his hands and he stumbled backwards out the window, hitting the fire escape railing hard, nearly going over the side of the building. The redhead had fired at just the right moment.

I grabbed the gun from the floor, stood directly in front of Stefano, and aimed at his chest. He desperately reached for the revolvers in his shoulder holsters. The sound of the hammer of my gun falling onto an empty chamber engulfed us both. The fear on Stefano's face melted away when he realized I was out of bullets. I was staring down both barrels when Stefano's chest exploded, spewing forth blood and bone fragments in my direction. It took a moment for me to realize I was still alive.

I ran to the window, trying to see who had fired the fatal shot. Sirens blared as police cars converged on the building. People emerged from every nook and cranny in the neighborhood and crowded around our stoop to get a better view, preventing the police from entering. The sweat dripping off my forehead, mixed with Stefano's blood, blurred my vision. I wiped my sleeve across my face, and then I saw him; our eyes locked as Butch turned the corner to get away from the scene. The Boss had kept his promise to protect my back.

It's hard to recall all that occurred during the next few hours. I do remember Frank making sure the redhead was okay and then washing some of the blood from my face.

"I'm not hit, Frank. How's my uncle?"

"Your dad's patching him up. Looks like he'll be fine, but I can't say the same for his bodyguard."

The police were making their way up the stairs. "Frank, take my client to your office. I don't want her involved." The redhead handed my gun back with a steady hand. She was good looking, could handle a gun like a pro and had nerves of steel. At that moment I should've known she was about to alter the course of my life.

* * * * *

I spent several hours at police headquarters, explaining the mayhem that destroyed my office. Fortunately, Mike

O'Reilly led the investigation.

Mike leaned in close and sneered for the benefit of the DA who stood in the corner. "Tell us again, Batista. Why was Stefano gunning for you?"

I played along. "How many times I gotta repeat myself? He was pissed because I got him busted. The whole thing was front-page news two months ago. Don't you guys read the newspaper? You got snitches all over town, and the word was on the street. He wanted to get even and you know it. I should be asking *you* why I didn't get police protection."

"Let me get this straight. Stefano opens up with a tommy gun, and you hold him off with your peashooter. Is that what you want us to believe?"

"Yeah, that's right."

"That's a load of crap! What about your uncle and the dead guy?"

"They came up to see what was happening, and Stefano nailed them both. That's when I got the chance to shoot the gun out of his hand. They had nothing to do with this."

"You still expect us to believe it wasn't you who shot Stefano in the back," O'Reilly growled into my face with a *wink*.

"Look, Sergeant, you were there. I looked like a damn vampire covered in Stefano's blood and guts. Now you tell me, how the hell did that happen if I shot him in the back? I'm not going to say it again, he was shot from outside just as he was about to nail me."

"Your guardian angel, I suppose," O'Reilly snapped.

The DA pulled O'Reilly aside then left without saying a word.

"Okay, Joey, get out of here. The DA doesn't believe he has a case against you, but if I were you, I'd be more careful in the future. He doesn't like having gun battles in his town, especially in broad daylight. It makes us good guys look bad." O'Reilly opened the door to the interrogation room. "Why don't we talk tonight at your uncle's place? I want to know what really happened."

"Give me some time. I need to check out a few things first. I'll catch you during the week. By the way, thanks for the wink. For a minute there I thought you were bucking for a promotion," I said, smiling.

"Nah, just a show for the DA. He's always looking to make a name for himself, so he's trolling for cases he can sensationalize. A word of advice, don't get on his bad side. He can be a real son-of-a-bitch."

"I'll keep that in mind," I said as I left the room.

It took a while for life to got back to normal. Ma, Martha, and Sally joined forces to ride herd over the tradesmen remodeling my office, but now it was more of a reconstruction job. My uncle Luigi was recovering nicely, but as ornery as ever, and he had a few choice words for me when I went to see him.

"Tell me somethin'. What the hell kind of PI are you?" he asked as I walked into his hospital room.

"What's that supposed to mean?"

"You don't act like a PI. You should become a lawyer, maybe a doctor, better yet a dentist."

"Hey, I came in here to thank you, and you give me grief. What's the problem?"

"I'll tell you what the problem is. You'd better toughen up. This Stefano guy advertises all over the place that he's gonna blow you away, and what do you do? Nothin'! I want you to listen and listen good to what I'm about to say. The next time someone threatens you, don't wait, hit him first. You need to build one helluva reputation, or the punks in this town will put you in the ground before the year's out. Do you understand what I'm tellin' you?"

There wasn't much I could say; he was right. I put everyone around me at risk. I should've confronted Stefano as soon as I found out he tried to put out a contract. He had declared war. I knew how to respond and I didn't.

"I hear ya, and it won't happen again."

"It better not!"

I grabbed his hand with both of mine and squeezed hard. "It won't, but I can't help wonder why I didn't get this sage advice sooner? You knew Stefano was out to get me."

Luigi grinned. "You got me there, kid. Guess I'm getting old. Now, tell me, who was that dame? I never saw a broad handle herself like that."

"I don't know. Stefano went berserk before we had a chance to talk, and then Frank took her to his office when the cops came. I'm having dinner with her tonight at La Cucina. Hopefully, I'll get the lowdown."

"She must be desperate to still want to hire you after everything she went through."

"She doesn't seem like the desperate type," I said.

"I know what you mean. Wish I were a few years younger. She's my kinda woman."

I got up to leave after a few more minutes of bantering. "Uncle Luigi, what happened the other day will never happen again. I appreciate what you did, and I'm sorry about Joe. He was a nice guy."

"And one helluva bodyguard," I heard my uncle say as I closed the door behind me.

* * * * *

The redhead arrived at the restaurant right on time. When we entered, Dorothy gave me a nod of approval as she led us to a table in a secluded corner. Before we had a chance to sit, Maria came rushing over, creating an awkward moment since I wasn't able to properly introduce my date. Seeing my discomfort, the redhead handled it beautifully. "Maria, how nice to meet you. Joey was just telling me how much he respects you. I'm Mrs. Jacqueline Forsythe."

"Then you know I owe Joey a great debt of gratitude. I hope you enjoy your meal, and if there's anything you need, just let me know." Maria turned and gave me a brief kiss on the cheek, then walked over to a few of the other tables to greet her regular customers.

Finally, I knew who my mystery woman was, the wife of the managing editor of the *Daily News*, one of the most influential men in the city.

"Mrs. Forsythe, the phone book's full of reputable private investigators. Why choose me?" I asked as we sat down.

"Don't you think we should have a drink before we talk business?"

Once the drinks arrived and we ordered dinner, she told her story. "You were front page news and my husband was impressed with your ingenuity. You see, he's being blackmailed about my past."

"I don't understand. If you've had past indiscretions, why is your husband being blackmailed?"

She simply smiled at my naiveté. "My husband is aware of my 'past indiscretions,' as you so gently put it. If the blackmailer made public certain information, it would certainly ruin my husband's aspirations of becoming mayor, to say nothing of leading to my possible demise."

She certainly had my full attention. "How did this information get into the hands of the blackmailer?"

"I kept some papers in our safe, along with my jewelry.

We were robbed recently; these documents were also taken."

"Are you sure the thief was after the jewels and not the documents?"

"Sure? One can never be sure, but I believe it unlikely. You see, only one man knew of their existence, and he thinks they were destroyed when I supposedly died in a fire. You might say these documents were my insurance policy in case he ever discovered I was still alive."

I needed a moment to digest what she had just said, so I lit a cigarette, a bad habit I picked up during the war. Whenever I went on a new assignment behind enemy lines, I always had one final smoke, just in case it was my last. I took a long drag and slowly let the smoke drift around us. I thought if I asked any questions or made any comments, she might not continue. I needn't have worried. For whatever reason—she wanted to tell her story.

"I grew up in Chicago, and for the most part, I was on my own. My mother died at an early age, and my father was a worthless drunk who didn't come home one day. I spent most of my youth on the streets, begging, stealing, and enticing men looking for a good time, setting them up to be robbed by the group of boys I roamed the neighborhood with.

"As time went on, petty theft turned into bank robbery, beatings into murder, a small-time gang into a syndicate, and I belonged to the boss of the outfit. After a few years, I wanted out, so I stole some incriminating evidence, along with a stash of cash, skipped town, changed my name, and here I am, Mrs. Alfred Forsythe."

"You left out the part about being burned to death," I said.

"We'd converted an old warehouse into a pretty nice hangout. I had just gotten back from a late night with a few girlfriends, and the guys were out on a job. I was alone, the safe was sitting there, and I knew the combination. I took everything I could carry and torched the place, not knowing some floozy had fallen dead drunk onto my bed earlier in the evening. The rest is history. The place burned to the ground, and they found a charred body."

I couldn't believe what I'd just heard. She confessed to an accidental homicide as casually as some hood might brag about knocking off a bank. I'd never met anyone quite like her. She was certainly right about one thing: If any of her past got into the press, it would destroy her husband's career.

"Why are you telling me any of this? All you had to do was give me some facts and send me on my way."

"You risked your life by giving me your gun. I saved yours," she said as she reached for my hand. "I would say we already have a unique relationship. Then, there's always the fact that if you ever want to work again in this town, you'll keep what I said confidential."

I pulled my hand back and downed my drink. "I'll need a cover, a reason to be around you and your husband."

"I take it that means you'll accept my case. I hope, Mr. Batista, I've made it clear there could be an element of significant danger involved."

"Danger comes with the territory. Besides, I got a taste of living on the edge during the war, and in a strange way, I enjoy it."

She smiled and then slid an envelope across the table. "I already know that about you. Not many men would have done what you did. You knowingly left yourself defenseless by giving me your gun. I think we have a lot in common.

"The envelope contains five thousand dollars and your so-called cover," she continued. "You're now an investigative reporter for the *Daily News,* Mr. Batista. When you return my documents, the position becomes permanent and it pays handsomely. Don't worry; it won't interfere with your business. My husband simply wants any news scoops you can provide; he may also assign you to work a specific story from time to time, at a significant bonus, of course."

"If we're going to work together, Jacqueline, the name's Joey." Before she could respond, dinner arrived, and our conversation took on a lighter tone. We had a pleasant evening and enjoyed several specialty dishes Maria prepared. As I walked Jacqueline to her car, I asked one last question. "You haven't said much about the jewelry that was stolen along with the documents. I'll need a description of each piece and pictures if you have any. The stuff has probably hit the streets already and might lead me to the blackmailer."

After getting into her car, she looked up at me with incredible green eyes. "I'm not as interested in the jewelry as I am the documents, but I'll give you a description of each piece when we meet with my husband for lunch tomorrow in his office. Goodnight, Joey, and thanks for a nice evening."

* * * * *

The next few days were anything but dull. First, I got the bad news from Frank that sharing Martha's time wasn't working out. She couldn't just sit and take notes; she had to add her opinion as he counseled clients.

To make things worse, he gave me the job of telling her.

"Martha, Frank talked to me, and it turns out he doesn't need an office manager. I agreed to take you on full time," I said.

"I always knew you were crazy! What am I supposed to

do all day while you're out playing detective?"

"Get a PI ticket."

"Now I know you're nuts? Why do *I* need a license?"

"You saw what happened last week with Stefano. If you're going to be my secretary, you need to carry a gun. You can take a mail order course, and I'll teach you to shoot. I'll even help you with the tests. In this line of work you need to be good at gathering information and defend yourself in a tight spot."

She looked as though she was going to object, but then accepted the idea. "Well, at least I finally have a nice office to work in, and besides, your mom is one hell of a cook."

That's when I told her I was taking on a new case and would be gone for a few days, possibly more. Before she could explode, I handed her the five grand I had received from Jacqueline Forsythe and told her to take out her pay and deposit the rest in the company account. I guess knowing there was money in the bank helped overcome any further objections.

I showed up a few minutes late for lunch, but Jacqueline's husband didn't seem to mind. Alfred Forsythe seemed like a nice guy who got himself caught up in an unfamiliar world. Sure, he'd witnessed firsthand the underbelly of the city, but he'd never walked in it, smelled it up close, or bent down and picked up the slimy muck. He was an observer, a narrator, or more simply put, he reported on other people's triumphs and tragedies. Now, for the first time, he could become the story others would write about.

I wasn't surprised he was much older than Jackie, given she never really had a father figure in her life.

"Alfred, Jacqueline tells me you're having a bad month. How much are they asking?"

He hesitated. "Fifty thousand."

"Can you raise that kind of money without questions

being asked?"

"I have the money."

"How and where are you supposed to make the drop?"

"I don't know. The note said to have fifty grand in one hundred dollar bills ready by Thursday. That's all." I could tell I made him uneasy. I gave Jacqueline a quick look. She smiled and tactfully informed me of my blunder.

"Joey, no one who works for the paper calls my husband Alfred." Alfred squirmed in his seat, but she was enjoying herself.

"Sure thing, not a problem," I said.

"So, Al, are you still going to run for mayor?" They both looked at each other, and I laughed.

"Don't worry," I said. "I'll watch my Ps and Qs. I'll need a copy of the blackmail note, a look at your apartment setup, and the safe that was broken into."

Al had the note with him, and Jacqueline agreed to take me by their apartment after lunch. The blackmailer was a man of few words: *Give me the money or I'll expose your wife for who she really is.*

"Call me as soon as you get further instructions," I said.

"Why would the blackmailer risk a second letter? Why not include everything in one?" Al asked.

"My guess is you're being watched to see how you react. If you bring in the cops, the drop-off gets more complicated. If you handle things on your own, it makes things simpler for the blackmailer. In my opinion, the blackmailer is someone fairly close to you, probably an employee."

Al bolted out of his chair and looked through the glass panels enclosing his office at the mass of people sitting behind desks, banging away at their typewriters. "I don't believe you."

I didn't feel like debating the matter. Either he was going to listen to me or find himself another PI. "I'll need a sample from every typewriter in the building by morning—all of them, even those not in use."

"That's impossible. Everyone will want to know why," Al said.

"Maintenance. Send out a memo explaining you're initiating a typewriter maintenance program and get someone on it right away. I'll need the entire alphabet, including numbers, along with the location of each machine."

That put a real damper on lunch, but I did get a good description of the stolen jewelry and a chance to call Martha before Jacqueline and I left to inspect their apartment. I figured making a list of all the hockshops in Manhattan would keep Martha busy for a few days.

I hitched a ride with Jacqueline to her uptown apartment, thinking it would give me a chance to inquire about parts of the case that didn't seem to fit together.

"I don't understand why your husband would still consider running for mayor, knowing it might expose you to danger. As his wife, you would be front page stuff, especially with your looks."

She gave me one of those expressions most men would die for, held my hand, and didn't say a word until we got out of the car and the chauffer drove off. "I think it's best we talk where we're assured of privacy."

She introduced me to the doorman as a good friend of the family. "Jonathan, this is Mr. Batista, a dear friend of ours. He will be visiting from time to time, and I would appreciate you allowing him free access to our apartment."

In the main lobby, I suggested she go ahead as I looked around and talked to some of the staff.

"Don't be long," she said. "Tenth floor."

"What number?"

She turned with a sweeping motion and brushed aside

her long, red hair. "The tenth floor."

The clerk at the front desk was of no help since he was fairly new, but Jonathan, an old-timer, would sell out his grandmother for a fin. I got some good information.

I'm not going to waste time describing the Forsythe's tenth-floor apartment. Let's just say they have money and don't mind spending it. Jacqueline had changed into something more comfortable, which apparently in women's lingo means more revealing. Al was a lucky guy.

She made drinks and sat next to me on a sofa. It was obvious where all this was heading, and I wasn't about to ruin a good thing with Al. Solve this case and I was on easy street, with a steady income to cushion the rough times that would certainly come.

"Jackie, how about answering my question now," I said as I put my glass down.

She stiffened and put her drink next to mine. "No one's called me that in years."

"I didn't think you'd mind."

"I don't, it just reminds me of who I really am."

"I like the person I saw in my office, and that person was Jackie," I said.

She moved a little closer. "As you correctly deduced, my husband doesn't know everything. In fact, he knows very little about me. I told him I had a past I wasn't proud of and I did whatever was necessary to survive. He doesn't know about the fire or my relationship with the Chicago underworld."

"So, he thinks the blackmailer is threatening to reveal your history as a common whore?"

"Just for the record, I was never a whore. I told him I had a few indiscretions when I was younger."

"That explains a great deal. How about showing me the safe?"

As Jackie rose, her loosely tied satin robe rippled open, revealing perfectly formed legs. Taking my hand, she led me down a long hallway.

"Is this Al's office?" I asked as we passed an open door.

"Yes, but the bedroom is straight ahead." She corrected herself with a laugh. "I mean the safe is in the bedroom."

"That may be true, but I'm not sure the bedroom is safe."

"That depends on what you're afraid of," she said with a gentle tug as she continued to move down the hall.

"I'd like to inspect Al's office first. The fire escape is on this side of the building, and I want to see if the window has been tampered with."

She stood in the doorway with her arms crossed, watching me as I inspected the windowsill and the wooden floor for any telltale marks. Everything looked normal, and the window had a double-locking mechanism. Before leaving the room, I wandered by Al's desk and looked at an incomplete letter still in his typewriter. He probably received the blackmail note as he was composing his response to the Democratic Nominating Committee for Mayor.

I noticed a few rough drafts of future editorials neatly arranged on the right side of his desk. Al appeared to be critical of his own work. Each draft looked heavily edited, with notes in the margins and crossed-out sections. As I stood by Al's desk scanning a few of the articles, Jackie became impatient.

"Why the interest? Are you thinking of taking up a new profession?"

"No, I'm still trying to learn the one I have. There are a couple of editorials here that aren't as marked up. Are they yours?"

"How in the world would you know that?"

"Al appears to pound the keys as he types. You, on the other hand, have a gentler stroke. The print isn't as dark. How about showing me that safe now?"

Jackie held onto my arm as we walked through two curtained French doors that opened into a bedroom suite tastefully decorated with early nineteenth century furniture. Every aspect of the room exuded sexuality, from the plush lily carpet to an array of mirrors strategically positioned to draw your attention, to a large canopy bed draped with whispery sheer netting.

Jackie sat on the bed, laughing at my failed attempts to locate the safe.

"Give up? It really is cleverly hidden," she said.

She pulled a small lever behind one of the bedposts, walked over to the wall of mirrors, and easily pushed two of them inward. They swiveled on center pins, revealing a large stand-up safe.

I stood for a moment looking at the safe and knew the theory I had been entertaining since inspecting Al's editorials was correct. The safe was an exact duplicate of my uncle's, and without the combination, no ordinary can-opener could crack that safe. It would take a soup job, and the safe was in one piece.

"Have you had much luck hocking the jewelry?" I asked without turning around. I didn't give her time to protest. "I'm familiar with this type of safe, and only an exceptional safecracker could open it. I suggest you put on more suitable clothes and join me back at the bar for a good stiff drink. I know I could use one." When I turned around, the door to the bathroom slammed shut.

"How did you know?" she asked as she joined me in the living room.

"Several things gave you away. Your flirtation during dinner the other night didn't fit the woman I saw in my office. That woman would be less subtle and much more direct. I checked with the doorman before coming up and, according to him, you're the only dame in this building who doesn't have something going on the side, which told me you're either discreet or faithful to your husband."

"That's it?"

"Not concerned about your jewelry."

"I never cared about such things. Al enjoys showing off his wealth."

"Then there's the blackmail note."

"What about it? There's nothing in it to indicate I wrote it."

"The note has the same two defects as your editorials; the letters r and m have distinguishing characteristics. Al wouldn't notice this because when he types, these defects disappear due to the extra ink that gets applied from his pounding the keys."

"Why would I steal from my own husband? Anyone could have broken into the apartment and typed that letter. The person who cracked open the safe could have done it."

"Once Al announces his bid for mayor, your past life would be exposed. You only had two choices: tell Al the truth or skip town. For whatever reason, you chose to run out on Al. You needed money, thus the robbery that never happened, the blackmail note and your phony act with me. You wanted me to believe you were unfaithful to Al, and there were plenty of possible suspects who knew where the safe was hidden." I held back a few other clues. No sense humiliating her more than necessary.

"You gonna tell Al?" she asked, slipping into her old vernacular.

"No, but I think you should, and then we'll square things with this old beau of yours so you can get on with your life."

"You don't know Sal; he's ruthless. If he knew I was still alive, he'd go berserk."

"How much money did you take, and how long ago was it?" I asked.

"It's been five years and I walked off with twenty grand. But he won't care about the money. He'll just want me dead."

"You said you also took some documents as insurance. What were they?"

"One of my jobs was to case the banks. Sal would then make detailed floor plans from my descriptions and sketch out everyone's position and timetable. He was so proud of his work he actually signed each drawing. There was one heist that didn't go right. Two cops got shot. I took the plans from that job."

We both downed another drink. I stared at my empty glass and remembered my uncle's advice: *When being hunted, become the hunter*. I was uniquely qualified to do just that.

"Jackie, if I were you, I'd go on the offensive. Tell your husband the truth. Right now he thinks you were a hooker; he might be relieved to find out you were only a bank robber.

"As for Sal, let me take care of him. I'll need thirty thousand to pay him back with interest and a picture of the bank's floor plan. Keep the original in a safe place. Now, call your chauffer. If I stay much longer, all bets are off. When you and Al decide what to do, stop by the office and let me know."

"Thanks, Joey. I don't know how I'll ever be able to repay you."

"As far as I'm concerned, you already have. If you weren't so handy with a gun, Stefano would have made Swiss cheese of me the other day. When I get this Sal creep off your back, we're even."

* * * * *

Martha and I had a slow week, which didn't do a lot to convince her that working with a private eye was a good idea. She had signed up for the mail-order course and was making real progress with a handgun, but she wasn't interested in learning self-defense.

"Who needs all that fancy stuff? I know where to kick a guy," she said.

I don't know how long Jackie was standing in the doorway listening to our chatter, but she had a good response to Martha's argument.

"If a guy's holding you from behind with a gun to your head, you'd be dead with that strategy."

Martha snapped back. "Who asked for your two bits, and who the hell are you anyway?"

I walked over to Jackie and took her coat. "Martha, this is Jacqueline Forsythe, a client of ours." I directed Jackie to my new inner office, which was basically a floor-to-ceiling partition separating the original room into two halves. During the reconstruction, we also added two more windows, so each office would have access to an extended fire escape landing.

"I like what you've done with your office. Quite an improvement over my last visit," Jackie remarked.

"I'm sure this isn't a social call, although I wouldn't mind if it was. I've been waiting to hear from you. How did your talk go with Al?"

"You were right; he took it much better than I thought. Angry I planned on leaving him and for the deception, but at the same time relieved." She handed over a valise containing thirty thousand dollars and said, "We both want to take you up on your offer."

"I'll need more details."

"His full name is Salvatore Santangelo. When I knew him, he was ruthless, and I'm sure time hasn't improved his temperament. Don't trust anything he says, and whatever you do, don't get close to him. He's very good with a knife and always carries a Derringer." She looked down as she spoke, and when she lifted her head, her eyes filled with tears. "Joey, he's a madman. Once he finds out I'm still alive, nothing will stop him from finding me. If you do this, chances are we'll both end up in the bay."

"There's only one way to find out."

"I don't understand. How you can be so confident?" she asked.

"There's a lot you don't know about me."

* * * * *

It turned out Castellano knew Santangelo by reputation. Several of Santangelo's peers had conveniently disappeared, allowing him to rapidly expand his territory. He owned a number of high-end speakeasies in the Chicago downtown area and controlled the drug traffic. The Chicago syndicate was getting nervous about Santangelo's tactics and questioned his loyalty to the organization. I didn't give Castellano many details, just that I needed to have a private conversation with Santangelo on behalf of a client. He suggested I convince Santangelo one of the higher-ups wanted him to do a special job for a sizeable amount of smack and I needed to talk with him in a secure location. I liked his suggestion.

Needing to look the part, I ordered two tailor-made suits that included some unique requirements for concealing several specialty knives I had used in the army. Once I had my train tickets, hotel reservations, and clothes, I was ready to go. Martha booked rooms in two hotels, so I could move between locations if things heated up.

I drove into town a few days later around midnight, and by the time I checked into both hotels, it was past one, a good hour to go saloon hopping. I hit all three of Sal's joints on the first night. I was confident word would reach Sal that some out-of-town hood was asking questions. Just as I suspected, I had a tail when I left the hotel the following morning. It wasn't hard to lose him as I toured some of the city sights. By three in the afternoon, I sat in my room at the other hotel. I had expected someone would eventually search my original room, so I left items behind that would pique Sal's interest: some hardware and a personal letter from Al Capone that was a brilliant forgery. All I had to do was wait until dark, and then enter the lion's den.

Two days after arriving in town, I sat at a table in Sal's home base, keeping an eye on traffic and watching two half-naked dames doing a dance routine that didn't leave much to the imagination. Suddenly, four torpedoes with iron bulging from their suits surrounded me.

"You boys want a drink," I said, "then sit down. Otherwise, move on; you're blocking my view." When I pushed my chair back, they moved aside and Sal sat down, chomping on a cigar.

"I'm told you've been asking about me. Such behavior can be dangerous, especially for strangers. You might find yourself wearing a wooden kimono if you keep it up."

"I take it you're Sal. I got a message from Capone."

Just as Castellano said, this got Sal's attention.

"What's in the satchel?" he asked, pointing with his cigar.

"Money."

"Let's see."

I opened the case and shut it before he could reach for some of the bills.

"So, what's the message, errand boy?" He was salivating but had to keep up the tough guy image for his goons.

"It's private. You got an office in the back, I suggest we use it." I got up and walked toward his office, and that's when I discovered Sal was crazier than Jackie said. He turned over the table, pushed two of his bodyguards aside and charged after me. Before he could say a word, I spun him around, grabbed the Derringer from under his coat jacket, and held it to his head.

"Let's get something straight, Sal; I'm not an errand boy. You want this job from Capone or not?" I took a chance and gave him back the gun. He waved for his boys to put their pieces away, and we all walked together to his office. Two of his guys stayed outside; the rest of us went in after they frisked me for a concealed heater.

Sal's so-called office looked more like a huge luxury hotel suite. His desk was directly opposite the door, about five feet away from the bottom of six steps. The two bodyguards and I waited at the top of the stairs. When Sal got settled behind his desk, he waved us down.

I didn't budge. "I said this was private. The hired help can stay here, guarding the door." He told them to wait at the top of the stairs.

I placed the valise on the front of his desk, slowly opened the locks, and rotated the case so he could see the dough. "Capone wants a hit put on the district attorney."

"What? The man's gotta be off his rocker," he said.

"This is just a down-payment. I suggest if you want the job, you take the jack and put it in your safe. Otherwise, I'll take his business elsewhere. In which case, you might find yourself on the wrong side of a contract. Capone doesn't like leaving loose ends."

He took the valise and opened his safe. "No need to bring in any competition. I can handle the job."

"Sal, I have something else you might want to put away." He turned toward me as I put the picture of the bank layout in the center of his desk. He placed the valise on the floor by the open safe and came over to take a look.

"I suggest you keep your mouth shut and listen to what I have to say." He looked confused as he stared at the picture. "The money and the picture are from Jackie. She sends her regards. The money is for restitution; the picture is an insurance policy. If anything happens to her, the floor plan goes to the police." It took a few seconds before he connected all the pieces. He flung his chair against the back wall, yelling like a madman.

"You tellin' me that bitch is still alive? You're not from Capone!"

I stood erect with my hands folded in front of me and smiled.

"Get this jerk and skin him alive until he tells me where that whore is," he yelled to his two bodyguards, who still stood at the top of the stairs.

Sal reached for his Derringer, but this time I wasn't as gentle. I pulled a thin blade out from under my sleeve and sliced open the back of his hand. He dropped the gun on his desk and grabbed his hand, screeching like a banshee. I knocked the Derringer onto the floor and turned in time to face the two bodyguards rushing down the stairs. In the excitement, they didn't pull their guns but tried to overpower me with their superior size. I caught one with a vicious chop to the trachea, crushing his windpipe; he grabbed his neck and crumbled to the floor gasping for air. I ducked just in time to avoid a blow from the other torpedo and buried my knife deep behind his kneecap. I caught him in the face with my knee when he bent over in excruciating pain.

As his face came up from the blow, I drove my palm hard into the bridge of his nose. He died before hitting the ground. I retrieved my knife as he fell backwards.

I turned toward Sal just as he reached his bloodied hand for the knife Jackie warned me about. He was fast but I was more accurate. My right side burned as his blade sliced through my flesh. Fortunately it missed any organs, but it bled profusely when I removed the knife. Sal, on the other hand, had my chiv buried deep in his heart. I cut a swath of cloth from a curtain and wrapped a makeshift bandage around my waist to stop the bleeding. I took the valise I had given Sal and filled it to the brim with additional stacks of hundreds from his safe. I then pulled my army-issued knife out of Sal's chest. Just never know when it might come in handy again. Besides, the blade was so unique it could be traced. Next, I took the photo off his desk, strapped on a shoulder holster I took off one of the dead bodyguards, and casually opened the office door. The noise from the band was so loud that as I closed the door behind me, I had to shout for the two thugs guarding the office to hear me. "Sal doesn't want to be disturbed."

* * * * *

As soon as I got back to New York, I went to see Castellano. The Chicago slaughter was front-page news, and I owed him an explanation. I walked into his office and gave it to him straight. When I finished, he wanted to make sure I didn't leave evidence of my identity behind. He didn't want any connection with a mob hit. As it turned out, the powers-to-be in Chicago were relieved Sal met such a premature death but still needed to at least try to avenge his murder. So far the mob didn't have any leads on the stranger who came to town and then vanished.

Castellano finally asked the one question I didn't want to answer. "How the hell did you do so much damage without firing a shot, by yourself, against such odds?"

"I got lucky."

Castellano knew I was lying. "Bullshit, luck had nothing to do with it. I heard how you handled yourself against your old gang. You're not the Joey I knew. You're more complex, more deadly."

"War and life have a way of changing people. You should know that."

He understood my meaning, walked me to the door, and gave me a kiss on both cheeks as a sign of deep respect.

* * * * *

As I entered Jackie and Al's apartment, I noticed the newspaper lying on the sofa.

"I'm afraid Sal didn't listen to reason." There wasn't anything more to say, so I returned their money and walked out.

Two days after returning the Forsythe's money, I received a signed contract from the *Daily News* as Jackie had promised. I was now an investigative reporter with a monthly retainer of five hundred dollars, about twice the going rate. More importantly, payment for specific assignments would be negotiable.

* * * * *

Martha walked into my inner office and dropped Anita's case file on my desk. It had taken the Staten Island police almost four weeks to find the lost file. Martha announced she cancelled all my appointments and would make sure no one disturbed me, then quietly closed the door.

Every four or five hours, she brought in food and drinks and left shaking her head. By the time I called it quits, it was past two in the morning, and the office was a mess, with dirty dishes piled high on a chair and crumpled papers littering the floor. Exhausted mentally, physically, and emotionally, I hoped some insight would strike me during the night and point me in a direction, any direction.

The next morning I read Anita's file over and over again. No matter how many times I flipped through the pages, the information remained the same. The investtigation didn't get assigned to anyone until three days after Anita's father had reported her missing. The police had assumed she was just another runaway. Once on the case, they seemed to do a thorough job. They interviewed all the surrounding neighbors, the local farmhands and two drifters, who made the rounds doing odd jobs for food, lodging, and a little cash. They formed a small investigative team, but no leads developed.

No one saw anything, and everyone who might be a suspect had an alibi. Practically half the residents of the Island joined in the search and, as I remembered, we covered several square miles looking for her body. Not a damn thing, not one piece of evidence ever showed up. She just disappeared.

I was about to put the file in my desk drawer when I noticed the name of the lead investigator. Sullivan. Sergeant Jimmy Sullivan. I wondered if he could be Lieutenant Sullivan, O'Reilly's friend who gave me the okay to get involved with Angelo's case. If so, maybe he could help.

May

The newspaper Martha carried flew into the air, and the pages descended around us and down the stairwell outside my uncle's speakeasy.

"Where the hell are you going in such a hurry?" she asked as I helped her off her butt.

"Sullivan hasn't returned my phone calls, so I'm going to the Island and plant myself outside his office until he agrees to see me."

"I think you're wasting your time. Take a look at this," she said as she searched the stairs for the front page of the *Daily News*.

Unflattering pictures of Sullivan appeared under attention-grabbing headlines: "Killer on the Loose," "Three Victims in Ten Days," "Police Baffled." According to the news story, all the murdered girls were white, in their teens to mid-twenties, and sexually disfigured. An elderly couple on an early morning stroll found the latest victim stretched out on a park bench not far from the ferry terminal. Given the circumstances, I knew the only person Sullivan would take a call from was O'Reilly. His father was one of the top homicide detectives in the city before he died, and O'Reilly had trained under him.

My hunch paid off, and in return for O'Reilly's assistance, Sullivan agreed to review his old notes from Anita's case. They scheduled a meeting for a week from Sunday, Sullivan's day off.

Since I had time to kill before the meeting, I took care

of some domestic business. I felt the time was right to change my rent agreement with Uncle Luigi. Ten percent seemed like a rip-off now that I realized the PI business could be lucrative.

Renegotiating anything with Luigi can be one heck of an ordeal, especially when he believes he already has the advantage. That's why I didn't give him his cut from the Chicago job until we sealed a new deal. It took a few rounds of drinks and a lively, sometimes animated debate.

"Hey, Uncle Luigi, if you're not busy, I'd like to buy you a few drinks."

He was standing behind the bar drying a beer glass that he dropped when he looked up. "Jesus, look what you made me do."

"You're kidding. Are you now blaming me for everything that goes wrong?"

"When's the last time you bought *me* a drink? I'll tell you, never. So you must want something. Let me guess. You have another dame that needs a place to live?"

"Look, I just want to buy you a drink."

"Okay, I'm sorry. You're right, we should talk more. You're a good nephew."

Now I felt like a real heel and debated whether I should talk about the rent some other time. He brought over a bottle of whiskey, sat back in his chair, and lit up a stogie.

"So, how's the PI business? I haven't seen you around lately," he said.

"I had to leave town for a few days to work on a problem for the redhead, and when I returned, Anita's case file was waiting for me."

"Did you find anything interesting?"

"It turns out O'Reilly knows the lead investigator and has set up a meeting for next week. I'm hoping he'll be able to give me some insights."

"Sounds like you're making progress. That's a good thing."

We both took a shot of whiskey, and when we put our glasses down, Luigi leaned across the table, and for some strange reason, I found myself doing the same. We were practically eye-to-eye, nose-to-nose, when he said. "Are you trying to tell me you're moving your business out of my building?"

I leaned back. "No."

"Good."

"Why would you think that?"

"Because I'm losing too many tenants; they didn't mind the saloon, but apparently an illegal speakeasy is a different story."

"Sorry to hear that. Things must be getting tight," I said.

"Nah, they don't want to live here, but they sure as hell don't mind my booze. This place is a goldmine. I hope Prohibition lasts until I'm dead and buried."

He gave me the perfect opening. "Maybe I should pay you a fixed amount for rent so you can depend on the income."

"You wanna pay rent! I kinda like the deal we have. If you take in a big haul, I get my share. Whatever you make, no matter how you make it, I get ten percent. Right?"

"Yeah, sure, but if I focus my time on Anita's case, you get nothing. You'd be better off with a steady income."

"You really think so? I'm not so sure. How much you wanna pay?"

"Oh, I don't know. What do you get now for a flat?"

"Twenty-five dollars a month is a good rate," he said, leaning back with a slight smile.

"That sounds fair."

"Nephew, you gotta remember, you're special. You

have an office that requires more upkeep. You remember the new fixtures and guaranteed hot water? All that cost money. Then there's your personal harem. They don't pay twenty-five dollars a month because they're friends of my favorite nephew."

"I'm your only nephew," I said, realizing I was losing control of the conversation.

"Exactly, that's why for you I'll give a special rate of a hundred a month."

"You're kidding."

"No. For that low rent, look at all you're getting. A business where people might get shot up at any time, an apartment with a great view, places for all your friends to stay at bargain basement prices. Actually, I think I should charge two hundred."

"You're right, a hundred a month is fair."

"Good, I thought you'd see it that way. Now tell me, what did you want to talk about?" he said, puffing away on his cigar as we shook hands.

He looked so smug I couldn't resist. "I wanted to pay you my back rent." I took an envelope out of my pocket and slid it across the table.

Luigi smashed out the stogie on the table and opened the envelope. "Five hundred bucks, are you kidding me?" At first he was excited but then realized he'd been conned. "You dirty little sneak. You held back, took advantage of my generosity, and screwed me out of the great deal I had. You're making money faster than the damn government. What a deceiving SOB; I was much better off with ten percent." He took the money and put it in his pocket. "About time you learned something from me. Sure took you long enough," he said, smiling.

After we had another drink, he asked some tough questions. "Are you telling me that redhead gave you five Gs to do a job for her? What kinda job pays that much dough?" He furrowed his brow then walked over to the bar, picked up an old newspaper, and threw it down on the table, pointing to the headlines. "Was that you? I know ya went to Chicago a few days back."

He had me cold, but I didn't admit to anything.

"Uncle Luigi, be serious. Some guy walks into a Mafia stronghold, kills a high-level boss and two of his goons without firing a shot, then walks out and disappears. Do you seriously think I could do that? Why, just a few weeks ago you gave me a lecture on how I needed to toughen up."

He looked at me hard, grabbed my shoulders, and gently swatted my cheek.

"Yeah, what was I thinking? That would take a real professional."

We had a good laugh. As I got up to leave, I spotted O'Reilly.

"He came in just before you screwed me out of my ten percent. If ya ask me, he's having some problems. You can always tell," my uncle said.

Mike didn't notice me until I slid into the seat opposite him.

"Hey, Joey, let me buy ya a drink. You're gonna need it." He slurred his words as he downed what looked like his fourth boilermaker.

"Don't you think you should lighten up on the booze, Mike?"

"Lighten up? I still have a ways to go. You remember Bobby Balcone?"

"BB, sure. He liked to bust everybody's balls, always pulling a prank on someone."

"Not anymore."

"Whaddya mean?

"He's dead, tortured."

I grabbed Mike's whiskey bottle and took a long swig, hoping to dull the feelings welling up inside.

"We found what was left of him in an abandoned warehouse this afternoon, in Little Italy of all places."

"Why would anyone kill BB?"

"How the hell do I know? Probably someone trying to get information he didn't have or didn't want to give up. Stupid bastard."

I reached again for the whiskey. "I'm not done yet," O'Reilly said as he grabbed it from my hand.

Listening to Mike and recalling the pictures of the dead girl from the Island, I realized we lived in a hellhole filled with despair, crime, and degenerates waiting to ambush the weak. No wonder everyone wanted their booze; they needed something to help them tolerate all the shit that surrounds them every day.

"I have some boys tracking down BB's movements, but I'm not hopeful. He just bummed around picking up odd jobs, mainly keeping to himself," O'Reilly said.

"I know it was tough seeing BB like that, but Luigi tells me you've been hitting the bottle pretty hard lately. This isn't just about BB."

About to drop a shot of whisky into his beer mug, he stopped, stared at the shot glass, and then downed it.

"It's my old lady. She's been giving me hell. It seems I'm the only honest cop left in the city. Everyone else is living high on the take."

"Let me get this straight. She's mad because you're an honest cop?"

"You got it!"

The last thing I wanted was for O'Reilly to become like the rest of the bums on the force, but his wife had a point. He could make more money being a garbage collector than a cop in this town.

"Did you tell your wife why you won't take bribes?"

"It's not something I like to talk about."

I couldn't help but think back to the day his kid brother died. Shawn was only fifteen, and word got out that he was collecting from some local businesses for one of the beat cops. Shawn had just finished his rounds and joined a bunch of us when another gang from uptown showed up. When Shawn took a shaft in the gut, his killer grabbed his collection money. Mike always suspected the fight was a setup to get at the dough. Ever since, O'Reilly's never taken a bribe.

"Mike, I'll tell you what. Why don't we work together? I could give you a cut of my take."

"Work together?"

"Yeah, you know, help each other out."

"Joey, I'm a cop and you're a PI, remember? Not a great combination. I'll probably have to bust you someday for breaking the law. That's what PIs do isn't it? Do whatever they damn well please and to hell with the law."

"Maybe, but we can still help each other. You need money, and I can always use information. It's simple: I crack a case, give you a cut, and if possible, you get the publicity. The more visibility, the better your chances for a promotion, and in the meantime, you make some jack on the side without dirtying your hands."

Dumping a shot of whiskey into his beer, O'Reilly said, "I'll think about it."

"Do me a favor and lay off the whiskey. You might think a little clearer."

I rose to leave. He motioned me back, pointing at a copy of the *Daily News*. "I've been saving this. Was that your work?" he asked with a smirk.

"What makes you think I had anything to do with that?"

"Martha told me you were in Chicago last week and had her book ya two hotels for the same nights. Now tell me, why would ya do a dumb thing like that?"

"I had my reasons; one of the tricks of the trade when you're tailing someone. Tell you what, Mike, I'm gonna call it a night. Think about my offer."

As I left the bar, I looked back and saw O'Reilly draw back another shot of whiskey. I swore I'd find a way to help him. But first, I had more immediate problems to deal with. Martha and I needed to have a long talk about keeping her trap shut.

I waited a few days before confronting Martha, which was wise, since it gave me time to calm down and realize I shared in some of the fault. I never did lay down office rules or give her anything meaningful to do besides waiting for new clients. When I felt I was ready, I called her into my office.

"Martha, we need to talk about some issues." I was about to learn the hard way to choose my words more carefully around women.

"You're damn right we have issues. You see this steno pad, there's nothing in it. Why? I'll tell you why, because my boss, the wannabe private detective, never has anything to say. My typewriter collects dust, and the phone never rings. You don't need a secretary; you need an office maid. Even that wouldn't be a decent job because you're never around." She was just warming up when Ma walked in carrying a package.

"Joey, why you mail this box to yourself? My son, I don't understand him. Do you?" she asked Martha without looking at her or giving her a chance to answer.

"Where you been, Joey? Why don't you spend more time with Sally? She likes you, and *she's* a nice girl." Ma put the package on my desk and left without even a sideways glance at Martha.

"What? What am I? Just because I worked in a speak-easy, I'm not a 'nice girl?' Maybe I should remind your ma that her brother-in-law owns one."

I walked around the desk, took the pad from her hand, and gently guided her into my arms. "She didn't mean it that way, and I'm sorry for not realizing how boring the job is."

Martha responded to my embrace, and as she looked up, we gently kissed, just as Sally happened to walk into the office. Sally left before I could react.

"Well, any chance you had with her just vanished. I'm sure your ma will be disappointed," Martha said with a hint of satisfaction.

I ran to the stairwell and called, but Sally was already out of sight. Halfway down the stairs I remembered Martha. I returned to the office thinking I had way too many dames in my life. Martha still stood leaning against my desk, but with her arms folded across her chest. As I walked into the office, she said, "Don't worry about me. I'll still be here when you get back. But I'm gonna give you some advice. You better decide and decide fast what kind of relationship you want with Sally, or you're going to end up hurting her, and I know you don't want that to happen. Now get out of here and do what you have to do."

I had a sudden urge to grab Martha and take her upstairs to my apartment. "I'll be back. Put the package away, and we'll open it later."

When I got to the bottom of the stairs, Ma stood there with a look of scorn. "Joey, what did you do to Sally? She's crying like a little child."

"Ma, I don't need this right now. What's going on is our business, don't interfere."

"Interfere? When do I interfere with your life? You do

whatever you like; all I'm good for is cooking and cleaning and praying that you don't get killed doing whatever it is you do as a PI."

Before I knocked on Sally's door, I turned to Ma and waved her back into her apartment.

As I entered Sally's room, she came over and we held each other as she continued crying. She clung to me for several minutes before separating. I gently wiped away her tears. "Sally, there's nothing going on between Martha and me. We were having a small argument before you came in and made-up with a hug. That's all."

"And a kiss," she added.

"It just happened. There isn't more to say."

She stepped back and took a long, hard look at me. "How do I know you're telling the truth? You've been so busy lately. I'd hoped we'd be spending more time together, and when I do see you, you're in the arms of another woman."

"Sally, I've tried to tell you I'm not ready for a relationship. I still have Anita and the damn war haunting me and a business to establish. I can't get seriously involved with anyone."

"Anyone. I'm just anyone. Well, then, I guess you'd better get back to work. I wouldn't want to hamper your career," she said, pushing me away.

"Sally, you're not being honest with yourself or with me. If I took advantage of our relationship, I'd be no better than the guy who left you stranded. You want more than I can give right now, and even though you're everything a man could possibly want, the time's not right for us."

She surprised me with her answer. "You make it sound like I want to get married and raise a bunch of kids. Isn't there anything between friendship and marriage?"

I thought it best Sally have some time to think. We

agreed to go for a walk after dinner, and when I left to go upstairs, I promised myself I would spend more time with her. But somehow I knew I wouldn't. It wasn't just my career; I needed to move beyond Anita before I could get serious about someone again, and no matter what she said, my gut told me to keep my distance for both our sakes.

When I returned to the office, Martha was reading Anita's case file and didn't ask any questions about Sally. I got the package Ma had brought up earlier and put it on Martha's desk.

Sure enough, as Ma said, it looked as though I'd mailed the package to myself. Martha looked over my shoulder as I opened the box and almost fainted when she saw its contents. The box overflowed with cash, and on top of the money, BB had placed a hand-written note.

Hey, Joey, I finally got a break. A couple of bozos were running from the cops and hid a suitcase full of loot not two feet from where I was sleeping. I'm gonna skip town before the heat comes down, but if it does, I don't wanna be caught with all this dough. Will ya take care of it till I get in touch? If somethin' happens to me, keep the dough and find the bastards. I know I can trust you. You're the only guy in our gang that didn't make fun of my gimp, BB.

I was speechless, but Martha wouldn't shut up. "Who's BB? How much money is there? Where do you think it came from? I bet it's mob money."

I gently put my hand over her mouth. "Slow down and give me a chance to answer. BB was a friend of mine; we grew up together. He's dead. The cops found him a few days ago in a warehouse, tortured. Right now I'm gonna give the money to Uncle Luigi to keep in his safe, and then I'm gonna do what BB asked: find the bastards."

When we finished counting, there were five stacks of hundreds totaling ten grand each, neatly arranged on my desk. "You know," I said more to myself than Martha, "the last time I saw BB was when the guys and I shipped out for base camp. He came down to the train station to wish me luck. He'd tried to enlist with the rest of the gang, but the army rejected him. I remember he took it pretty hard; having a bum foot never seemed to bother him until he couldn't fight for his country. I tried to look him up when I got stateside, but it seemed he'd dropped out of sight."

I was heading for my uncle's joint with the box when I heard Martha toss her steno pad in the wastebasket.

"Sorry, Martha. I got sidetracked. There's plenty you can do to help. We could use a filing system containing everything you can find about the rich, the famous, and the infamous in this town. I also want you to run some advertisements in local papers. We need new clients."

Her shorthand was rusty, so for kicks I picked up the pace. "And don't forget your number one priority is to get your PI license. Someday I'm gonna need backup or you'll find yourself in a jam because you work for me. You gotta have a piece and be willing to use it."

"Listen," she said, "I can find a job now that Stefano's dead. I don't need you to make work for me."

"If I didn't need you, I'd tell ya. But there's one thing we must get straight. What happens in this office is our business. Where I go, who our clients are, how much we take in, everything is confidential." Her face flushed as she went back to her desk without saying a word.

* * * * *

O'Reilly and I met at BB's crime scene. It was a typical, deserted warehouse with shattered windows, rusting machinery, and rats scurrying from one rubbish pile to another. The one exception was a lone chair in the center of the cavernous building, surrounded by a puddle of dried blood. As we approached, a swarm of flies dislodged themselves, giving the illusion the chair had moved.

"Got anything yet?" I asked O'Reilly.

"Same old story. No one saw or heard a damn thing."

A sense of rage and guilt flowed over me as the flies returned to the chair. BB had just reached out to me from the grave, but I'd only made one feeble attempt to get in touch with him after returning home. Looking at the solitary symbol of his death, I had flashbacks of him always trying to keep up, always in the background because he was different.

"I'm not letting this one go, Mike. He didn't deserve to die like this. I want everything you have."

"Like I said, we don't have much. Looks like BB lived here for some time. There's an alcove behind that half-wall where he slept. Most everyone we talked to liked him. He could always get a meal in a pinch, but mostly he worked around town cleaning up after the joints closed down. All we can deduce is some street punks wanted to have a little fun and went too far."

I walked around the wall into the alcove.

"You're not going to find anything, Joey. My boys went through the whole building," O'Reilly said.

They didn't know what to search for. I did. After five minutes of sifting through BB's junk that O'Reilly's men had tossed around, I moved aside a mattress wedged in a corner. I found a small suitcase with a train ticket hidden in the inside lining and a few pieces of new clothing scattered among the rest of BB's clothes. I brought all the items over to O'Reilly.

"I think we just found the motive for BB's death.

Looks like Bobby came into some money and planned to skip town."

"Where the hell did he get the dough to buy such nice clothes?" O'Reilly asked, scratching his head.

"You tell me. Did anything unusual happen around this neighborhood a few days before BB's death?" I already knew part of the answer, but I didn't want O'Reilly asking uncomfortable questions, especially about money.

"There was a raid on a whorehouse about three blocks over. The place was a cover for a drug operation run out of the basement. We made a good haul, a couple of hired goons and enough heroin to supply the whole lower east side for a week."

"What about cash? How much did you get?"

"Only a few grand, but two of the drug dealers got away. We had the neighborhood cordoned off but never did find them." I didn't have to give O'Reilly any more hints. "Shit, they must have stashed this suitcase full of drug money somewhere in here thinking they could come back later when the heat cooled off. BB probably saw the whole thing. Poor schmuck, he shoulda left the money and got the hell out. My guess is the thugs came back, tortured BB until he told them where he hid the dough, and then finished him off."

"Mike, I'm gonna get these bums. I need to know right now if we're working together to nail these bastards."

"Sure, Joey, but no vigilante stuff. Based on what you told me and what took place in Chicago, I know what you're capable of doing. We're talking about mob money and not your little neighborhood-type bosses. This is Little Italy, and these boys play tough. You go after one of them, and they'll take out your whole family and anyone else who gets in the way."

I didn't answer, but he was right. I couldn't go after

these guys like I did Sal Santangelo. I was too close to home. "Who controls the drug traffic in this part of town?" I asked.

"Moralli. Nothing moves without his okay."

"Where does he hang out?"

"The Brown Pig, a restaurant across town that fronts for a gambling hall."

"If you know so much, why don't you bust him?"

"I've been on this guy for years and even brought him in for murder once; turned out to be a waste of time. These thugs have half the judges and the rest of city hall on their payroll. All we can do is kick in a few doors every now and then to make the public think we're doing somethin'; other than that, we're stymied."

"I'm not… As you said, I don't have to play by your rules or worry about corrupt politicians. I'll figure out a way to get this Moralli character and the guys who did this to BB."

"Just heed my warning, and let me know how I can help."

* * * * *

Sullivan waited for us at the ferry terminal. As we shook hands, a reporter, hiding behind a newsstand, jumped out and took a picture. O'Reilly made an attempt to catch the guy, but he vanished among the crowd exiting a ferry.

"Don't worry about it, Mike. These days I can't take a piss without some crazy reporter following me into the john," Sullivan said.

"How the hell are ya supposed to solve a case when your every move shows up in the morning paper?" O'Reilly asked.

"It's a problem. I spend more time dodging reporters

than tracking some crazed killer."

"Take control," I said.

"What are ya talking about? Take control of what?" Sullivan snapped.

"The reporters, the newspapers."

"How?"

"Have a meeting everyday with the press and give them the latest information and answer questions."

"How's that going to stop what just happened?"

"Ban any paper from the meeting that interferes with your investigation."

Sullivan didn't respond but instead suggested we continue our discussion over coffee at a small diner.

"O'Reilly tells me you're investigating the Sgarlata girl's disappearance. I imagine you read the case file by now and have questions," Sullivan said.

"I'm interested in what's not in the report. Did you have any hunches as to what happened to Anita? What about suspects? The report said everyone close to her had an alibi. Did you believe them all?"

"You have to understand, Joey, that the lieutenant has had hundreds of investigations since then. Don't expect too much," O'Reilly said.

"It's okay, Mike," Sullivan said. "I had a chance to review the file myself and I remember the case, mainly because of Joey."

"What do ya mean?" I asked.

"Well, at one time you were our chief suspect. In general, you were a big pain in the ass. I'm not surprised you turned out to be a private dick. Every chance you got, you were underfoot, searching for clues. I thought you were overdoing the grief."

"Anita and I were close."

"I know, kid. But why dig up old memories? Sometimes

it's better to move on."

"Her old man is dying and asked me to find out what happened to her. I tried to forget, but now I no longer have that option. I never really did."

We talked for an hour about the investigation and some of the insights the police gathered that never made it into the report. The official conclusion was that Anita got tired of farm life and ran off. The lieutenant had his own theory at the time, but his superiors wanted the case closed so he could move on to more pressing matters. Sullivan had suspected that a couple of drifters who were working the local farms may have killed her, especially when they disappeared a few weeks after Anita. Every attempt to find them failed; the investigation shut down a short time later.

After discussing Anita's case, O'Reilly inquired about the recent murders and offered to lend Sullivan some experienced homicide investigators.

"Thanks, Mike, but if the press discovers I'm getting help from across the bay, it'll be all over the front page of every paper. My department can't afford to lose the confidence of the residents of the Island, especially now."

As it turned out, Sullivan and his team had made little progress: no fingerprints, no murder weapon, no witnesses, no clues whatsoever, which is why he was eager for O'Reilly to help in some capacity. Sullivan's superiors were running out of patience, along with the public.

"I have a copy of what we have so far from all three cases tucked inside this newspaper," he said as he stood to go, leaving the paper on the table. We shook hands, and O'Reilly casually picked up the paper.

"How about we meet once a week in the city and have dinner?" O'Reilly suggested. "It'll give you a chance to get away from the reporters, and if Joey and some of my guys show up to talk about the cases, who will know?"

Sullivan agreed.

Before O'Reilly and I boarded a ferry back to Manhattan, the lieutenant suggested I let him know if I developed any new leads on Anita's disappearance. He said he'd do what he could to help.

On the ride back, O'Reilly expressed his doubts about finding the truth about Anita. "Sorry, Joey, I thought Sullivan might be able to give you some new insights."

"He did. He made it clear he believed the drifters were involved or one or more of her neighbors. Remember he said the Ruffalo boys acted suspiciously when questioned, but they couldn't shake their alibi. I knew them both. Louie was a follower, did whatever his brother Ralph wanted. Ralph enjoyed taking chances and was constantly in trouble. He was a real sick son-of-a-bitch and took pleasure in hurting others, including small animals."

"Why didn't you suspect him at the time?" O'Reilly asked.

"I was just a kid, and even though I didn't like Ralph, he always treated Anita like a sister. All the neighbor boys did."

Before we parted, O'Reilly handed me the newspaper with the case files. "If anyone discovers I have these files, Sullivan will be in a mess. Let me know if you find anything interesting. I'll come by your office when I can and look them over.

* * * * *

Life at the office with Martha had improved considerably since our brief show of affection. Even though it was an awkward development, it demonstrated she had forgiven me for causing her to lose her previous job, which I'm sure she would never admit outright. In return, I showed her she meant more to me than someone I owed a debt to. But the underlying issue still remained; I didn't have enough work to keep her busy. The only solution I could come up with was to get her out of the office and more involved with my cases.

"Get your things. We're taking a trip to Staten Island."

"Why do you need me to come along?"

"You might pick up on something I miss, and I'm tired of hearing you bitch about having nothing to do."

Before I could put on my coat, she was by my side, ready to go. First we visited Anita's father to uncover information about his neighbors at the time of Anita's disappearance and to pay my respects again before he passed on. He confirmed my memories about the Ruffalo boys. After a short stay with Mr. Sgarlata, we drove over to what remained of the Ruffalo farm. Martha had already tried to track down both boys and unfortunately, Louie had died in the war, and she wasn't able to locate Ralph.

Developers had bought most of the Ruffalo land and built cheap-looking, wooden-framed houses along the dirt road that led to their farmhouse. At the entrance to their remaining ten to fifteen acres stood a roadside stand used for selling vegetables. I found the sight depressing, because it symbolized how much Staten Island had changed since Anita and I were kids.

As my car traveled over the dirt road, it created a huge dust cloud, giving the Ruffalo's ample warning that they were about to have company. I pulled the car up to the front porch, where Rose stood in an apron, waiting to greet her unexpected guests.

"Hello, Mrs. Ruffalo, I'm Joey Batista. Maybe you remember me. My folks used to take me to visit the Sgarlata family. Anita and I would come over to visit with you from time to time."

It took her a few moments, but then she came down the steps and engulfed me in her arms. "Oh my God, Joey, you look so different. Why the last time I saw you, you were a scrawny little kid."

Martha got out of the car and introduced herself. "Hello, Mrs. Ruffalo, I'm Martha Peone, a friend of Joey's."

"Nice to meetcha. Please come in and have some lemonade." As we walked up the steps, she called to her husband. "Aldo, Aldo, you'll never guess who stopped by."

Aldo had a heavily bandaged foot and stayed seated in a rocker. "Sorry, I can't get up to greet you folks proper. You'd think after all these years I'd be able to chop firewood without getting my foot in the way. Made a damn fool outta myself is what I did."

We all pulled chairs near Aldo, drank our lemonade, and talked about the weather, how farming doesn't pay anymore, the war, and the great sickness that came from overseas. We talked about everything but Mr. Sgarlata's health, which I found surprising. After Rose served us hot apple pie, I brought up the subject.

"We just paid our respects to Mr. Sgarlata. It's been a real shock to see him so close to death; he always seemed indestructible to me."

"Oh my God, yes. Poor man, he's never been the same since Anita left him," Rose said.

"Has anyone ever heard from her? Ya know, in all these years, he never mentioned her, not even once," Aldo said.

"No one knows what really happened. Even now it's difficult to think about," I said.

"Of course, you two were close, I know," Rose whispered.

Martha got the hint and picked up the conversation as we had planned.

"Joey tells me you have two boys who are a few years older than him. How are they doing? Are they helping you with the farm?"

"That was always our hope, but then the war came along and changed everything. Our son, Louie, died in the war; he's a hero you know. We got all kinds of medals when they brought him home for burial. Ralphie, we don't know where he is. He went off to enlist with his brother, but the government says they have no record of him," Rose said.

"I'm sorry to hear about Louie, but I'm sure you're proud of what he did. Ralph will show up someday; he was always a loner," I said.

Rose nodded her head in agreement, and her husband looked out the window. An awkward silence followed, so I probed in another direction. "We also wanted to stop by the Cognetta's to see how their boys are doing, but it's getting late, and we need to leave for the city soon. Did they also enlist?"

"Oh yes, all three. It's very sad what happened. Michael Cognetta, the young one, died somewhere in Germany, Carmine came home unharmed but passed soon after of the sickness, and Andy is working the farm with his dad. Andy got shot in the leg and has a bad limp, but he manages," Rose said.

We were about to leave when Mr. Ruffalo stopped us with a question. "What about you, Joey? Did you enlist to fight like my boys, and what are you doin' now?"

"I signed up with the rest of the guys in my neighborhood. Now I'm a private investigator," I said, looking directly at him.

"A private detective, that's interesting. You never did believe Anita ran away from home. So I take it this wasn't a social call."

"It was both, Mr. Ruffalo. It was both," I said as I held the screen door open for Martha.

Giving Martha a glimpse into the complexity of investigating a case helped her realize she has a critical role to play in our business. In addition to setting up our filing system, Martha redoubled her efforts to locate Ralph Ruffalo's whereabouts and obtaining the details of Louie Ruffalo's service record. She reasoned Louie may have spoken to an army buddy about his brother, Ralph. She also spent more time reviewing the police report on Anita's disappearance. As *she* increased her workload, Martha's attitude toward her job improved.

With Martha focusing her efforts on Anita's case, it allowed me to spend the next few days saloon hopping, trying to get information on Moralli's illegal businesses and review the information Lieutenant Sullivan provided about the Island murders.

* * * * *

One afternoon, after returning from a meeting with O'Reilly, I found Martha hard at work cutting out news clippings for the filing system.

"You had a visitor today. Some kid left a box on your desk," she said without looking up.

"Did he say what he wanted?"

"Nah, I don't think he could speak. He kept pointing to your office, grunting guttural sounds. I watched him put the box on your desk, and then he ran out."

I glanced into the room and saw a small wooden box placed on the center of my desk. It looked like it belonged at the bottom of a trash pile, but I took great care not to damage it because the kids who lived off the streets had precious few possessions. The press-fit lid was tough to pry open, and when it finally came off, the box flipped out of my hands. Martha came in when she heard it bounce on the desk. She picked up a news clipping that had fallen out, as I inspected what looked like a bracelet made from electrical wire.

"What's the article about?" I asked as I turned the bracelet over in my hand.

"It's a photo of the Bryson girl."

"Who?"

"Geez, Joey, you need to read the papers and stay on top of what's happening around town."

"Quit the wisecracks and tell me what you know."

She pointed to the picture. "This guy here is Charles Bryson. He's a Wall Street big-shot; his niece was kid-napped."

"When?"

"And here I was thinking setting up a filing system of the town's rich, famous, and corrupt was just a trick to keep me busy and off your back." She stepped into the outer office and returned with a folder marked "Bryson Kidnapping."

As she flipped through the file and read a few news stories, I tried to make the connection between some rich kid, a street urchin, and a cheap piece of wire. It made no sense. How did the street kid fit into the picture? Martha was still spewing facts when I cut her off.

"Okay, I get it. This Bryson guy is floating in dough, some rich relative of his dies years ago, and he gets stuck raising the now-kidnapped girl, what's her name, Rachel, who's about seventeen today."

"Right."

"Shit! Look at this," I said pointing to the photo. "The girl has on the same bracelet or one just like it." It was tough to see because of the poor quality of the printed photo, but she definitely had something similar on her wrist.

I looked up from the clipping and said, "Dig deeper. I want to know all about Bryson, his family, the kidnapping, and especially if there's a reward."

"Are you telling me that scrawny kid is somehow connected to the girl's kidnapping?" Martha asked.

"I don't know what to think. Tell me everything you can remember about him. How old did he look? How tall? What did he look like? Are you sure he couldn't speak?"

Martha shook her head in disbelief. "Do you really think I can't tell if some kid can't speak? Well, it turns out he can speak, but not with his mouth. He used gestures and he's damn good at it. He's somewhere between sixteen and eighteen, about five-foot-four or -five. I don't know for sure. He's white with black hair and poor as dirt."

Just then Ma came in and said everyone was waiting on us for dinner.

* * * * *

I intended to sit next to Sally, so I could get a feel for how she was doing, but Uncle Luigi had already finagled his way between Sally and Martha, and I ended up sandwiched between Ma and Pop. Uncle Luigi appeared to be in an exceptionally good mood. He gave me one of his knowing smiles and dove right into the antipasti.

"Vito," he said. "Your son here is doing okay. Pretty soon he'll own the whole damn building. No, I take that back, the whole damn street, and I'll be renting from him. Best deal I ever made was charging him ten percent of his profits for rent."

It sounded like he was salivating over the fifty grand I had gotten from BB. Apparently he had conveniently forgotten we had recently renegotiated my rent.

"That's right, Pop. Business is great, and just last week Uncle Luigi and I agreed to a new rent arrangement. Ain't that right, Uncle?" He couldn't answer with a mouth stuffed with food, but I think he got my point—don't expect ten percent, especially from the fifty grand.

Pop suddenly became irritated. "Sure, my son, the great detective, runs around all day solving other people's problems. What about mine?"

"What are you talking about, Pop?"

"Of course you don't know. You're never around. Okay, hotshot detective, I'll give you a problem and you solve it. Women don't want handmade shoes. They want *style*. So, we're selling factory-made shoes to them. Now, most of my old-time customers are asking about factory shoes, cheap factory men's shoes. Pretty soon no one will want handcrafted shoes, and I'll be sitting in the park feeding pigeons."

"You're right, Pop; you have a serious issue, but don't blame Sally. If she wasn't here, you'd already be feeding pigeons, and you wouldn't be making any money. What you need to do is open a new business."

Everyone stopped eating. "Joey." Ma was pissed. "Your papa is not so young anymore. How can he do that? Look what you've done. You make him feel bad. Papa, don't listen to Joey. He knows nothing about making shoes."

I was getting the evil eye from everyone, and if I didn't quickly explain what I meant, I would soon be getting the silent treatment as well.

"Pop, here's my point. If you don't sell factory shoes, someone else will. So why don't you sell and fix them?"

"Fix what?"

"The shoes! When they break or wear out, repair them. That's your new business, Vito's Shoe Repair."

My uncle liked it; he stood, pounded on the table, and

pointed at me. "What did I tell you, Vito? Your son is smart, a money machine. You can have the vacant shop on the other side of the stoop, and Sally can run the shoe store. I'll give you the same deal I gave Joey; I get ten percent of the profits."

Pop didn't say anything, but he was thinking about it. We had a great meal, and for the first time in many months, we were all enjoying each other's company and having fun.

After dinner my uncle and I walked upstairs, and before we parted, I asked him to let me know when O'Reilly came by the speakeasy.

"I have a new case, and I could use both of your help," I told him.

Word of O'Reilly's arrival reached me a little past midnight. When my uncle saw me approach, he jerked out of his chair and pushed me aside into a corner. O'Reilly had filled him in on the gory details of BB's murder.

"Why didn't you tell me about BB? I want to be there when you find those maggots. You understand me? They don't deserve to live, and they don't deserve to die fast. This is what I meant when I said you needed to toughen up. Everybody knows Bobby was your friend, and in this city, in this neighborhood, in this family, we take revenge. Don't you ever forget that. Now, let's talk to your cop friend, and you tell me how I can help get those bastards." He put his arm around my shoulder and practically dragged me over to the table.

"Sorry, Joey," O'Reilly said. "Guess I was too graphic. I forgot how hot-blooded your uncle can be."

"Don't worry, he's not going to cause any trouble. We're doing this my way. Moralli probably didn't kill BB himself, but some of his men did. If we do this right, we'll get him and he'll lead us to the murderers and the evidence we need to send them away." Before I could continue,

Luigi smashed his beer glass down on the table.

"What did I just tell you? There is no justice in this town. Everyone is corrupt. Moralli will have his goons back on the streets before the judge's gavel makes a sound. My way is best; my justice is best. Joey, didn't he tell you what they did to BB? Why would they do that? He was nothing, a nobody."

"He had their drug money. If they didn't get it back, Moralli would think they stole it, and that would've been the end of them," I said.

Luigi quickly made the connection to the money in his safe and settled down. When we finished explaining O'Reilly's theory as to why BB got bumped off, Luigi realized O'Reilly wasn't aware of the fifty grand and kept his trap shut.

Once my uncle regained control of his emotions, I got a chance to go over my plan for dealing with Moralli.

"What do you want us to do?" Luigi asked.

"I need you to spread the word that a professional hit man from Detroit, a relative of BB's, arrived in town looking for revenge. Make him sound like the Grim Reaper."

"What relative? BB had no brothers, and both his parents are dead," Luigi said.

"I don't know. He must have had some extended family. Make it a cousin on his mother's side. Use your imagination."

"Okay, I'll think of somethin'."

"O'Reilly, I need everything you have on Moralli. The size of his gang, details about where he hangs out, where he lives, his girlfriends, his habits, everything. I tried to get some information, but it was difficult without raising suspicion. I'm going to put pressure on this guy, and when I need backup, you both better be there."

Up to this point, O'Reilly hadn't said much. He seemed

more thoughtful and depressed than usual. He downed another drink and twirled the glass in his hand.

"You know, Joey, your uncle's right about somethin'. I've been tryin' to get the goods on Moralli for years, and he just walks. The law can't touch him, not in this town."

This was the second time O'Reilly mentioned he'd been personally trying to nail Moralli, which didn't make a lot of sense. There were cheap hoods like Moralli all over the city. Why focus on him? I wondered.

I called Ginger over and ordered another round of drinks. When she left, I tried to appease both my uncle and O'Reilly. "I'll tell you what, do this my way, and if he and his torpedoes walk, I'll personally settle the score for BB."

My uncle still wasn't satisfied. "How are you gonna do that, and if you can, why not do it now?"

O'Reilly answered before I could. "I agree with Joey. Let's give the law one more shot at Moralli. If it doesn't work, Joey and I will *both* take care of matters."

Luigi seemed satisfied, so I brought up my new case. "I'm looking for a kid; he probably lives off the streets. He's sixteen, maybe eighteen, around five-foot-four, has black hair, scrawny, and doesn't speak. He can't live too far from here because he came by my office and dropped an interesting mystery on my desk."

"What kind of mystery can a kid like that have?" Luigi asked.

"I'm not ready to say. I just need to find him. What about it, Mike?

"I have a friend over in patrol. I'm sure the beat cops can find him."

* * * * *

Working through the details of how to deal with

Moralli wasn't easy, but I had enough experience now to realize that in the PI business, the best strategy was to act then deal with the consequences. Using that philosophy, I ended up with a simple plan: apply more and more pressure on Moralli until he did my bidding, then move in with O'Reilly and his boys.

My uncle did a great job spreading false stories of a hit man who came to town looking to avenge the brutal murder of his cousin, BB. After a week of hearing rumors about the atrocities this fictional character committed in Chicago, Detroit, Philly, and Jersey, even I looked over my shoulder at night.

The time seemed right to ratchet up the pressure. I gave Al Forsythe a call and told him about the buzz around town and suggested that if he ran a story on the drug trade, he might scoop the other papers before dead bodies littered the streets. He agreed to do a front-page exposé on the city's illegal drug traffic, highlighting BB's murder and hinting that a major syndicate hit was about to take place as rival gangs fought for control of the city's lucrative, illicit business.

"Al, I appreciate your willingness to run such an explosive story on short notice."

"Are you kidding? Stuff like this sells papers. What about some follow-up copy?"

"Don't worry. If I hear anything else, I'll keep you informed. I suggest you dig up as much dirt as you can on a small-time hood named Moralli and be ready to go to print with little notice. Based on what I'm hearing, there's a good chance he's gonna get whacked."

"Not a problem, but don't kid yourself about Moralli. He's anything but small-time. He has half the city in his pocket, and the other half's waiting in line."

"Now I know why you're such a successful editor—you

have a way with words. How about a favor in return for the information I just gave you? I want to be assigned to investigate the Bryson kidnapping," I said.

"Why? That's old news. The case is on ice, and the unofficial word is the girl's dead."

Al's hesitation didn't feel right. "Al, according to the contract we have, I'm an investigative reporter for your paper. I want to investigate this kid's disappearance, and if I don't turn up a story, it'll cost you nothing."

I thought the line went dead, but then heard what sounded like Al tapping his fingers. When he finally spoke, his voice was at a slightly higher pitch.

"I'll tell you what, Joey. Why don't you talk to Jacqueline about the Bryson case? She knows Bryson and can probably get you connected better than I can. If the paper reopens an official investigation at this point, that in itself would be news and draw unwanted attention back onto the family and the paper. The family has suffered enough, and everyone will want to know why we're investigating a closed case. Before I take on that gorilla, I need a good reason."

I still sensed there was something else going on but didn't push the issue.

* * * * *

I wanted the rumors and news stories to have the desired effect on Moralli before I actively disrupted his business dealings. This gave me time to get everything I needed and learn more about the Bryson kidnapping.

Before leaving the office to visit Jackie Forsythe to see what she knew about the Bryson kid, I asked Martha to run a few errands. Martha was really digging into Bryson's life and didn't appreciate my interruption.

"I'll get to it next week. I'm right in the middle of some interesting dirt," she said as she turned to get back to her reading.

I knew a firestorm was about to erupt, but I didn't mind because Martha looked sexy when she got upset.

"Sorry kid, I want the stuff by tomorrow. You need to be able to work on more than one case at a time if you're going to make it in this business." I walked back into my office, leaned back in my chair, and waited for her reaction. I wasn't disappointed.

She stormed in and let me have it.

"I'm finally working on some interesting stuff, and you want me to drop what I'm doing, go to Chinatown, and buy smoke bombs for God knows what reason. Not only that, you expect me to pack some heat, and before long you'll probably have me doing something illegal in the dead of night."

"Well, actually…" She didn't give me a chance to finish, slamming the door on her way out.

Something was still bothering Martha, and it wasn't just work. She actually looked like she was enjoying setting up the filing system and doing research. I made a mental note to have another talk, maybe under better circumstances.

Jonathan, the doorman at Jackie's building, recognized me from a few weeks ago and gave me one of those all-knowing looks that I couldn't let pass. "Strictly business, pal."

I didn't expect a maid to open the door, but given the size of their apartment and Al's position, it seemed to make sense. I only had to wait a few minutes until Jackie made her appearance. Just like the first time I'd laid eyes on her, it seemed we were the only two people on the planet. She wore her hair long, not following the latest craze, and had on a black satin dress that accented every contour of her body. Fortunately, the formal tone in her voice broke the grip of her spell.

"Joey, I didn't expect you so soon. Al mentioned you might stop by someday to discuss the Bryson kidnapping."

"Things are a little slow right now, so I thought I'd take Al up on his offer. He tells me you know this Bryson guy and might be able to give me some details about the kidnapping and set up a meeting. I thought I'd do a little snooping on my own. It seems Al doesn't want to resurrect a dead story." By the look she gave me, not a good choice of words.

"Charles is a major benefactor at the orphanage where I volunteer. His niece, Rachel, spent every chance she could with the children. Over the last two years, she and I became close."

"I got the impression from Al that the case was closed, which seems strange. It's only been a few weeks since Rachel was taken."

Jackie's facial expression changed, and she tried to hide her feelings by asking the maid to bring some drinks as she turned her back and walked over to the couch. I gave her a chance to regain her composure and then sat down.

"The kidnappers never made contact with Charles; there were no demands of any kind. The police believe the girl died accidentally during the abduction and the kidnappers disposed of her body and skipped town."

"Do you believe that's what happened?"

"I don't know what to believe. I'm deeply saddened she's gone. Why this sudden interest? And if Charles didn't hire you, who did?" she asked.

"Just call it professional curiosity." I wasn't ready to reveal too much until I located the mystery boy who couldn't talk. Jackie was street smart and sensed I was holding back, but knew not to probe further. "Once I know more, I'll fill you in, but for now I might want to meet this Bryson guy. You think you could arrange a meeting when I ask?"

"Sure," she answered. "He comes to the orphanage every couple of weeks, and I could introduce you as a friend, or I could arrange a meeting at his home."

"That would be great."

Jackie walked me to the door without saying a word; she seemed to be struggling with something.

"What's on your mind?"

"You're constantly surprising me with your talents. Now you can read my thoughts," she said. "I wanted to ask you to give me a call sometime if you need help on a case. Since meeting you, I've come to realize how dull my life has become. I'm really not the high-society type but have to play the role because of Al's position."

"I might take you up on that offer, sooner than you think," I said.

"That would be great, and let me know when you want to meet Charles Bryson. I hope you can help find out what happened to his niece."

I assured her that when I needed to meet Bryson, I'd get in contact with her. As we said good-bye, she gently squeezed my hand, and as the door closed, I could still feel the warmth of her touch. My uncle had it right when he said she was some kinda dame.

* * * * *

The next day I got a call from O'Reilly. They found the street kid hanging out in the Bowery around Chrystie and Delancey Streets, not exactly a great neighborhood.

It didn't take me long to track him down. He was on the street corner holding a small baby and begging for money.

My first thought was to advise the kid to move to a different part of town; half the residents of the Bowery were professional beggars. I dropped the bracelet into his little pot that contained a few coins, not even enough for a decent meal.

The kid made guttural sounds, got up, and ran down a flight of stairs into what looked like an abandoned brownstone. I didn't follow, figuring he'd be back to get his pot of money. He soon did, no longer holding the baby, and gestured for me to follow him. I wasn't about to enter that hellhole until I knew a little more. For all I knew, the kid took the bracelet off the girl, and the kidnappers were holed up inside.

I sat on the ground and took the bracelet out of the pot and put it back into the wooden box. Then, I took out the news clipping of the kidnapped girl.

He took the box back, put the bracelet on his wrist, pointed to the picture, and patted his chest. Maybe Martha could figure out what his gestures meant, but I sure as hell couldn't. He became frustrated, making louder and louder noises. He took off the bracelet, unraveled the wires, and made two bracelets, then pointed again at the picture. I finally understood; he'd made the bracelet in the picture. So the question now was, how did the Bryson girl get it? I followed him into the dilapidated building.

As we entered, the only light came streaming in through broken windows, making it difficult to avoid the mounds of discarded trash. If it wasn't for a gentle breeze meandering through the abandoned rooms, the stench would've been unbearable. A baby cried, and the sounds of others moving around in the darkness made me feel uneasy. At the end of the hallway, the mystery kid opened a door and waved me in. It took a few seconds for my eyes to adjust to the darkened interior. In a corner, an old-looking woman was nursing a baby, and three other kids were horsing around on a tattered mattress.

"What do you want?" the woman asked without looking up.

"This kid wanted me to come in. What's his name?" I asked.

"Stanley."

"I'm a private eye, and Stanley came to my office and left behind this newspaper clipping." I handed her the picture. "Do you know her?" I was hoping she could give me a lead.

"She's my daughter, Stanley's sister."

I didn't know what to say. None of this made any sense. "That's not possible. She's the niece of a rich business man, Charles Bryson."

She peered up at me with disgust. "Don't you think I would knows me own daughter? This Bryson guy, is he tall, with a big belly and talks funny?"

"I don't know, I've never met him," I said.

"Some PI you are. He paid for her."

I wasn't sure I heard her correctly. "Are you telling me you sold your daughter? You sold her to a complete stranger?"

"Look around ya mister. What does ya see? I have all them kids and more, a bum for a husband, no money, no food, and somebody comes along years ago and gives me five hundred dollars to take one of them off me hands. You're damn right I sold her, and good thing I did or we'd all be dead bys now."

There wasn't much more I could say. As I followed Stanley out, I noticed a neat pile of old newspapers in a corner, conspicuously out of place. I touched Stanley's shoulder and pointed to the papers. He handed one to me. Tommy Stefano's picture was on the front page. I looked over to his mom for an explanation. "Yah, he can read, about the only thing he can do. Don't ask me how, never spent a day in school."

That cleared up one mystery. I had wondered why he picked me to find his sister.

"He has no money, he can't pay ya. But you already knows that, right, mister PI?"

When we got back outside, I asked Stanley to put the bracelet back together. When he handed it to me, I gave him ten bucks.

It took me a long time to get back to the office. I just walked around trying to make sense of what Stanley's mother had said. She looked old but was probably only in her late thirties, and in those short years, had lived a lifetime of despair. When I finally got home, I was tired and disgusted with myself. I'd never asked what the girl's real name was. Well, I would soon find out.

June

On humid, hot summer nights, the neighborhood comes alive in different ways than during daylight, when everyone is rushing and hustling for a buck. After the shops are closed and dinner is a pleasant memory, chairs come out onto the fire escapes and in front of the brownstones; the steps become crowded with neighbors spreading the day's gossip, listening, and giving encouragement. The street pulsates with laughter and friendly shouts of disagreements. It's during these times a neighborhood's character is forged and a unique bond builds among neighbors that lasts a lifetime.

On such a night I should've been out with Sally or Martha, trying to make some sense of the lives we shared, but instead, I was huddled in a corner with my uncle and O'Reilly, drinking and explaining how I intended to finger BB's murderers and bring down Moralli at the same time.

"Joey, you're taking too damn long. I don't give a rat's ass about Moralli. I want the creeps who tortured BB."

As usual, my uncle overreacted, but O'Reilly showed restraint and liked the idea of finally getting the goods on Moralli. "Listen, Luigi, let's give Joey's plan a chance to work like we agreed. He gets Moralli to flush out the killers, and we get him on attempted murder and who knows what else. Remember what we said: if the courts let them off, then Joey and I will even the score."

"I think ya both gone soft, but you can count me in," Luigi said. Then he leaned forward and added, "I better see some action soon, Joey, and I mean soon!"

O'Reilly broke the tension by handing over a list of Moralli's business enterprises as promised, and it was clear Al Forsythe had been right. Moralli wasn't a small-time hood. He owned a piece of the action in nearly every criminal activity that existed in the city.

"Moralli is taking the rumors about a Detroit button-man seriously," O'Reilly said. "He's doubled his personal bodyguards and increased security around his money-laundering operations. To be honest, Joey, I don't see how these rumors will help. It'll be harder than ever to get to Moralli."

"See, I told you. We're not making progress," my uncle said.

Sometimes my uncle can be pretty thick, and I was running out of patience. "Uncle, imagine you're Moralli, and you just surrounded yourself with extra protection, and all of a sudden, you realize this 'hit man' can still get at you any damn time he wants. What then?"

"Okay, but you tell me, Nephew, how the hell are you gonna pull that off?"

"That's my job. You two just make sure you're ready."

"Ready for what?" Luigi asked with outstretched hands.

I downed my drink and got up to leave. "You'll know soon enough. All I need is another couple of weeks, and then we'll be able to put BB to rest."

Just before leaving the speakeasy, I turned and saw Luigi and O'Reilly deep in discussion. My uncle was more animated than usual, as he seemed to agree with whatever O'Reilly was saying. I was tempted to go back and hear what they were talking about, but I had to organize the next phase of my attack on Moralli.

The next evening, Jackie, Sally, Martha, Dorothy, and Ginger stood around my desk staring at the smoke bombs, looking nervous—except for Jackie. To her what we were discussing seemed like child's play.

"Joey, I don't know if I can do this," Sally said.

"That's okay. Now's the time to pull out, but you'll miss the opportunity to bring down one of the biggest criminals in the city."

Martha gave me a look. "Oh, well that's comforting. The last time we helped you with one of your exploits, we only brought down a small-time hood, lost our jobs, and you almost got killed."

She had a point, and I didn't have a good response. Luckily Jackie stepped in. "You ladies need to relax. If we do exactly what Joey explained, I don't see how anyone's going to know we were involved. Joey, why don't you run through the setup again?"

"Jackie's right. Remember, these bombs are not dangerous. They'll make a loud noise and a hell of a lot of smoke and that's all. If they go off close to someone, they won't get hurt, but they might shit their pants." It was good to see the girls laugh. "At approximately five minutes after eight this Saturday night, we're going to hit three speakeasies and two of Moralli's restaurants at the same time. You will each carry a smoke bomb in your handbag and enter a bathroom stall at exactly eight. Once in the stall, light up a cigarette, insert the fuse halfway down the cigarette, and place the bomb back in your bag. If you don't notice a good spot to place the handbag outside the bathroom, simply leave it in the stall and put one of these out-of-order signs on the stall door. You'll have about two minutes before the fuse ignites. When the bomb goes off, run out with everyone else and disappear into the night. This is important. Make sure the handbag can't be traced back to you.

"Jackie, your job is a little more complex. You'll need to convince Al to take you to the restaurant Saturday night.

Hopefully he won't notice you don't have your handbag when you return to the table. Make sure you keep him in the dark about this job. It'll be a big news story, and I don't want him to know we're involved. Right now the *Daily News* is doing a great job making everyone believe a drug war is about to erupt. If Al finds out I've been using him, he might expose the truth."

"What about you? What's your role in all this while we're out creating panic?" Martha asked.

"I have a little extra surprise in store for Moralli at his main hangout, one that will definitely get his attention."

"So why do you need our help?" Sally whispered.

"I want him to think BB's cousin isn't working alone."

"I'm confused," Dorothy said. "Why do we have to do any of this? Let the guy from Detroit everyone's talking about avenge his cousin's death. Why do we need to get involved?"

Jackie saw the frustration on my face, leaned against the wall, and grinned.

"There is no hit man from Detroit," I said. "BB doesn't have a cousin who's in the mob. I made that whole story up to make Moralli think his life's in danger."

"But it's in the papers, and everyone's talking about him," Sally said.

"Ladies, I made it all up! I gave Jackie's husband a line of bull. That's why I don't want him to know she's involved. There is no hit man. I wanted Moralli to think there is so when we're done creating havoc on Saturday night, he'll be so scared he'd turn over his own…"

Jackie caught my mistake before I finished and interrupted my explanation. "You all need to understand what Joey just told you could get him killed. If Moralli finds out he's being conned and that Joey is responsible, he'll be fish bait."

The girls all swore they would keep their mouths shut and agreed to follow through with their assignments.

* * * * *

My part of the job worked as planned, with one not-so-minor exception. I successfully planted a large smoke bomb on the intake fan located on the roof of the Brown Pig restaurant, where Moralli had his headquarters. As I expected, when the smoke poured out of the air vents, Moralli ran from his office in a panic like everyone else. I slithered along the back wall of the restaurant, past the wave of people, into his office, holding a wet cloth over my mouth, and skewered a bloody pig's heart to Moralli's leather chair with a note attached. I had one leg out the back window when a cough and a soft moan came from somewhere inside the room. I followed the sounds and blindly reached out through the thick smoke and touched a dame stretched out on a couch. I tried to get her up but without success; I had no choice but to take her with me. My smoke bomb wasn't as harmless as I told the girls. If the dame stayed where she was, she would probably die from smoke inhalation.

She didn't weigh much and was half-naked, something I couldn't worry about. By some miracle I got her out the back window and into my car just before the fire trucks arrived. I drove down the first deserted alley I came to, pulled over, and put my jacket around her. To my amazement, she was just a kid, no more than eighteen, and completely oblivious to her surroundings. My hatred for Moralli intensified with each sleazy detail I uncovered.

I had a real dilemma about what to do next; I couldn't drop her off at a hospital without giving away my identity, but I knew from O'Reilly that Moralli used doped-up street kids to push his drugs. The girl needed immediate help.

Sirens were wailing all around the area, making it difficult to think. I had to move. I drove toward home thinking Ma would know how to help the girl when I heard the echoing horn blast from a ferryboat, signaling it had successfully docked. That's when I knew what to do. It would take a few hours, but it was the best solution to my predicament.

It was past eleven when I got to the locked gates of Angelo's old clinic on Staten Island. It took Ron, the groundskeeper, about ten minutes to respond to the racket I made. At first he didn't recognize me, but as soon as he did, he helped carry the girl into the doctor's waiting room. I asked him to wake the doc and also get Shirley, thinking she could help calm the girl once she regained awareness of what was happening around her.

"Joey, what's going on? It's almost midnight," Doctor Swartz said as he tried to suppress a yawn.

"It's a long story, Doc. I need you to keep her here until I can find out who she is. I'm sure she's been drugged and inhaled quite a bit of dense smoke."

"Was she in a fire?"

"Doc, I don't have all night. Will you help her?"

Just then Shirley walked in. "Of course he will."

She came over and gave me a hug. "What kind of mess are you in now?" she asked.

"It's complicated. Let's just say I found her in a place she shouldn'a been."

Shirley looked down at the girl, stepped back, then collapsed at the girl's side, pulling her close and sobbing into her hair. Shirley looked up at me with tears streaming down her face. "Who the hell did this to her? Joey, answer me. What bastard did this to my kid sister?"

After the doc got the girl stabilized, Shirley and I spent

several hours talking about her sister and how I happened to find her at the Brown Pig. To my surprise, Shirley knew more about Moralli and his organization than I did. She had been one of his private hookers. He used her to entertain some of his best customers and closest business associates. Shirley had tried to hide what she did for a living from her sister, but one night the girl followed Shirley to the Brown Pig restaurant and boldly sat down next to her, just as Moralli introduced Shirley to her evening's date. Shirley figured Moralli later purposely recruited her sister as a way of getting even with her for dropping out of sight when she accepted Angelo's offer to live at the clinic.

By the time Shirley and I finished talking and I got back to the office, it was past four in the morning. The girls were sound asleep on various chairs, so I tried to quietly slip back out, but I never did oil the hinges on the door.

"Where the hell have you been?" Martha demanded.

Sally flew off the office couch and gave me a crushing hug, half-crying, half-smiling. "We thought something happened to you. Oh Joey, it was so scary. I almost got caught."

"Let's give Joey a chance to tell us what he's been up to, and then we can fill him in on our little adventures," Jackie said.

I was about to sit down, thinking to myself how nice it would be to have a woman like Jackie around, when I noticed Ginger curled up in a chair with her arms wrapped tightly around her knees.

"Hey, kid, what's the matter? You look like you've had a rough night."

"Joey, things went the way we planned, but everyone was so scared. I never want to do anything like that again. Please don't ask."

"Don't worry, I won't. That goes for the rest of you. It

was too risky." Martha and Jackie didn't say anything, but from their expressions, I knew they had enjoyed the excitement. I tried to gloss over what happened, but the girls wouldn't have it. An hour later I finally pushed them out the door, and when I got to my apartment, I hit the bed hard.

I didn't wake up Sunday until after lunch. Wanting to avoid questions from Ma about why I missed so many meals, I stopped by my uncle's joint to get something to eat. Before I could order food, O'Reilly and my uncle escorted me into Luigi's office.

"Joey, when you said you had a little surprise for Moralli, we didn't expect you to panic the whole damn city. How the hell did you hit so many of his joints at once?" O'Reilly asked.

I hadn't seen the morning papers yet. I walked over to my uncle's desk and picked up the *Daily News*. "City Under Siege" read the headline. There was a picture of Moralli outside the Brown Pig, watching helplessly as smoke billowed from his building. The news story repeated the street rumors that an underworld hit squad was stalking Moralli for the brutal murder of a homeless cripple, who happened to be a cousin of a notorious Mafia assassin.

I dropped the paper back on the desk and turned to my uncle. "Is that enough action for you?" I asked.

"Not bad," my uncle said, "but what's next? We still don't know who killed BB."

I explained everything that happened the night before, except for the part about Shirley's sister. "My guess is when Moralli sees the heart dripping with blood, he'll take the attached note seriously."

O'Reilly and Luigi looked at each other. "Okay, I'll bite, what did the note say?" Luigi asked.

"Bring the bastards who killed my cousin to Pier 21 at

midnight, Friday, or the next time it won't be a pig's heart. I want to hear them confess to killing my cousin, then you can deal with the bastards. I'll be watching, and remember, it's them or you!"

"Jesus, Joey, that's brilliant. We get a confession, and Moralli has to do the job himself because his crew would never trust him again if they knew he gave in to your demands. We'll get him on attempted murder and the Sullivan Act for carrying a weapon." O'Reilly sounded excited.

"How the hell do you expect Moralli to pull this off without help? Remember these guys are killers," Luigi said.

"He'll need help for sure," O'Reilly said. "My guess is he'll use his brother, who's also been untouchable. This is getting better all the time. I'll have a couple of my men with us just in case something goes wrong. Joey, are you going to keep up the pressure on Moralli or wait and see what happens on Friday?"

"Nah, I'll just let him stew and see if he buckles. If he doesn't show up at the pier with the goons that killed BB, then I'll get serious. In the meantime, I have this other case to work on."

"You talking about that kid I found for you?" O'Reilly asked.

"Yeah."

"What's that all about anyway?"

"It's not important. Just doing the kid a favor."

I went to get something to eat, leaving O'Reilly and my uncle huddled together deep in conversation. It seemed to me they were becoming pretty chummy lately.

* * * * *

The next morning I got up early to see if Martha wanted to go out for breakfast. There was something still bothering her, and if we were going to have any kind of civil working relationship, we needed to get things out in the open.

I knocked a few times before she opened her apartment door wearing a bathrobe and a towel wrapped around her head.

"Joey, what a surprise. Come on in. I was just in the shower."

"Maybe this isn't a good time. I'll come back later."

She reached out and pulled me into her apartment. "Sit down, I was just about to pour myself a cup of coffee."

Before I could say anything, she disappeared into the kitchen. I wandered aimlessly around the room, waiting for her to return. The apartment was stylish, just like her last one. She came back with two cups and sat on the sofa, revealing her incredible legs still moist from her shower. It must have been obvious that I was staring.

"Joey, if you look any harder, I'll feel naked."

"Sorry, it's just that you're one gorgeous dame." I couldn't believe I said that.

"I never thought you took much notice." She moved closer and handed me my coffee and then removed the towel from her head, letting her wet hair fall around her face.

The next thing I knew the both of us were clawing at each other like animals. Martha's aggressiveness wiped out any hesitation I might've had. I didn't care about anything else, and facing each other at work Monday morning seemed a long way off.

When we'd finished, Martha slipped back into her robe, took out a pack of smokes, and lit two cigarettes as I dressed.

"So, tell me, Joey, why did you really come by?" she asked as we sat on the couch sipping our cold coffee as if nothing had happened.

"You were happier when I first met you. Now you seem angry most of the time. I guess I wanted to ask if there was anything more I could do to make up for getting you involved in the Stefano case. You lost your job and had to move; your whole life changed because of me. I honestly didn't intend for this to happen today."

Martha took a long drag on her cigarette. "I guess you might say this little trist solved part of my problem." I could feel my face turning red as she reached over and held my hand. "Don't worry, these things happen, and I know you're not interested in being tied down with a woman. I don't have any problem with us working together. Besides, the job is getting more interesting. The other night was wild and exciting, almost as fulfilling as this morning." She leaned over, exposing her breast as we embraced, and we shared a warm, moist kiss, arousing our passions once again.

This time, exhausted, we laid naked in each other's arms on the rug by the sofa. The coffee table had overturned, spilling our drinks, and a lamp had crashed to the floor. I gently moved Martha aside and dressed again. "We better straighten up this place before Dorothy and Ginger come home," I said.

"No need to worry about them; they both had to work today. Besides, they're going to move out soon."

"I thought you all were getting along great. What happened?"

"Nothing happened. I'm going to tell them tonight," Martha said as she slipped into my arms.

"I guess that means you don't mind if I come by again."

She looked at me with a radiant smile. "Joey, you look like a cat that just swallowed a canary. Maybe focusing less on work and more on the people around you will help you see the obvious. I'm attracted to you and I'm lonely. So until I find someone to settle down with, it would be nice if we were more than friends."

We talked for a little longer before I left. We both had forgotten about breakfast.

I entered the office Monday afternoon a little unsure of what to expect. I peeked in and saw Martha hard at work. When she saw me, she immediately walked over, closed the door with one hand, placed the other on my neck, stood on her toes, and gave me a kiss without saying a word, and then went back to her reading.

Feeling foolish just standing there, I walked to my office door and then looked back. "Don't worry," she said. "I'll behave myself."

After thirty minutes, she came into my inner office. "Joey, I've finished my research on the Bryson guy and the kidnapping. You wanna go over it now?"

"Sure," I said, still a little uncertain how to behave or what to expect from her. Thankfully, she acted professionally.

"You already know bits and pieces, but for you to get the full picture, I'll need to go back a few years. Bryson's younger sister married a rich guy, and they had a kid named Rachel. Bryson has never been married, and at that time was fairly successful with a small financial business. He apparently made a fortune in railroad stocks and got a reputation as a shrewd, hard-nosed, but sometimes reckless investor. He experienced several wild swings in his financial fortune over the years but always seemed to find a way of coming back.

"About fifteen years ago, his sister's husband got himself killed in a bank robbery. The crooks took him as a hostage, and he died during an exchange of gunfire with the cops. The sister inherited a fortune and passed away of natural causes two years later, leaving Bryson with a four-year-old girl and as the executor of her estate."

"Do you know the details of the will?"

"That's the interesting part. When the girl reached fifteen, Bryson inherited half the money in the estate. Up to that time, he only received expense money to raise the girl. Speculation at the time was the sister realized her brother tended to take financial risks and was concerned he would lose the kid's inheritance if he had complete control. She basically gave her brother some incentive to invest wisely and increase the kid's fortune, since he would eventually get half of it free and clear."

"Did her strategy work?"

"Apparently it did. He tripled the total inheritance in thirteen years."

"What would've happened to the money if the girl died before turning sixteen?"

"All the money would go to a local orphanage where the sister had volunteered her time."

"When would the girl inherit her remaining estate?"

"When she turned twenty-five or got married, whichever came first. If she died after sixteen and before either of those two events, Bryson got everything," Martha looked up from her notes. "My guess is this Bryson guy bumped the kid off to get the rest of the money."

I realized then there was a price to pay for our newfound intimacy. She was going to inject herself deeper into my cases, but I didn't mind. After all, Martha was smart, liked the excitement, wanted to meet people, and didn't expect more than I could give out of our relationship.

After putting all the pieces together, it did seem like a simple case, but why was Bryson being so generous to the orphanage where his sister had volunteered if he was the monster we both suspected? I needed more information, and Jackie was the one who could fill in the blanks. She had first met Bryson at the orphanage.

* * * * *

Jackie had a few days to herself since Al was traveling to upstate New York to convince the Democratic bosses, who controlled the city's local political wards, to support his run for mayor.

We met again at La Cucina for dinner, and this time Maria gave us a quiet booth in the back. I suspected she thought we needed to be discreet since she now knew Jackie was married. Jackie had the same impression.

"If we keep on meeting here, I'm afraid rumors will fly. Maybe we should vary restaurants," she suggested.

"I think that would seem more suspicious. Besides, I like the food here," I said. Jackie's smile was contagious, probably because her eyes radiated her sexuality. "You never did tell me how you met Al," I said. "To be honest, he seems a bit old for someone with your youthful experience."

"Youthful experience, now that's an interesting choice of words. I have to admit it's an intriguing story. When I arrived in the city after escaping the clutches of Sal Santangelo and his gang, I landed a job at a paper as a copy boy."

I was about to ask a question when she cut me off in mid-sentence. "I don't know why, but for some strange reason they wouldn't call us copy girls. Anyway, I would take the copy from the reporters and run the stories to the editors. We had to maintain an incredible pace since there were always deadlines to meet. After the editor made his changes, I would rush the copy down to the pressroom.

"One day, about a year after I left the *New York Post* for the *Daily News*, there was an article about a bank robbery, and I read the story as I ran up the stairs. When I got to the editor's office, I thought to myself the story really stunk, but to my horror, I said so aloud. The editor was Al, and he immediately stopped reading and looked up. I think it was the first time he ever took notice of me. He asked how I would change the copy. I basically told him the story would be more interesting if it included the bank robber's point of view. I still remember the look on his face. He was dumbfounded, sat me down in his huge chair, and asked me to rewrite the story, which I did. He had to correct my spelling and grammar, but went with my changes and the story was a hit.

"The rest is history. I reviewed all his crime-related stories, made changes, and then he would reword my comments and go to print. We developed into a good team. I learned from his rewrites and became a pretty good editor in my own right. One thing led to another, and we got married. End of story."

"Wow, talk about rags to riches. You and Al seem to be doing okay financially. I'm surprised the paper pays so well," I said.

"Actually, he has another source of income. I'm not really sure, but I believe he has family money. That's enough about me. How did you get into the detective business?"

"I made the decision during the war and stuck with it. I really didn't have many attractive options when I came home. My father's business was quickly becoming obsolete, running a bar didn't seem exciting, and getting more involved in the local Mafia was out of the question because Ma would have killed me. I once thought about being a cop, but O'Reilly talked me out of that idea. The rest, as you say, is history."

Our food arrived, giving me a chance to change the conversation to the real reason for our meeting. "Tell me how you met Bryson. Was it through the orphanage?"

"Actually, Al introduced me to Charles. They've

known each other for many years. In fact, Bryson committed a large contribution to Al's fundraising efforts for mayor, but unfortunately, he recently suffered a serious setback in some of his investments."

I hid my surprise by shoving a forkful of lasagna into my mouth. Al had lied to me about his relationship with Bryson. I probed a little more into Al's life.

"Why is Al so interested in being mayor? He seems to have everything a man could want: a beautiful wife, wealth, an influential job, and the respect of the community. Now that he knows more about your past, I would think he'd be worried that such a scandal would kill his election chances."

"I think it goes back to basic human nature, the desire to have more, never being satisfied, and thinking that you're invincible. Isn't that what drives progress?" she said.

"I'm afraid you're getting too philosophical for me. In my way of thinking, it comes down to greed and the lust for power."

"I think you just agreed with me. It's probably one of the reasons I was attracted to Al. I like aggressive men."

I'm not an expert on women, but the look she gave me when she made that comment had invitation written all over it. It seemed like bits and pieces of the old Jackie from Chicago emerged the more she became involved in my life. If she knew I was curious about why Al tried to discourage me from investigating the Bryson kidnapping and that he also lied about his relationship with Bryson, the transformation might become complete.

Our conversation drifted back into areas unrelated to work, and before we knew it, we were eating dessert.

"It's getting late and I'm sure your chauffer is suffering from leg cramps waiting for us."

Jackie looked up from her chocolate cake with a whimsical, guilty look. "I didn't think you would mind driving me home, so I gave him the night off."

I knew where this was leading, and I didn't think I would have the willpower to resist. The feelings between us were building way beyond my limit of self-control.

"We should leave; otherwise, it'll be late when I get back to the office," I said.

She picked up her purse and offered me her coat to hold open for her. "You know, Joey, Al and I have an interesting relationship, one of convenience. He craves power, and having a much younger, attractive wife adds to his mystique. I needed to clutch onto stability or end up with another jerk like Santangelo. Like I said, I tend to gravitate toward aggressive men."

Distracted by the scent of Jackie's perfume, as I drove her home I didn't notice a car rapidly coming up behind us. The jolt that followed sent Jackie headfirst into the dashboard. I stepped on the gas and turned toward her to see how badly she was hurt. That's when I saw car lights heading directly for us. I figured Moralli somehow fingered me as the source of his sudden problems and sent his goons to end his nightmare. I only had a few seconds to react before lead filled our car. There wasn't anyplace to turn except for an open space in front of Tony the Butcher's store.

I shoved my gun into Jackie's hand. "Shoot the glass panel in the front door and run to the end of the butcher counter. I'll be right behind you."

She didn't say a word but held onto the door handle and braced herself as the car jumped the curb, crashing into the display window wall at an angle to the front door. Bullets were flying in all directions when the occupants of the other two cars realized what we were doing. I reached down, grabbed my ankle gun, and propelled myself through the shattered glass seconds behind Jackie. We didn't have a lot of ammunition; I knew where Tony kept his knives and grabbed a handful from the countertop as I shoved Jackie behind the end support. Just then, Tony came running down the back stairs from his apartment.

"Tony, it's Joey Batista. Get back upstairs and call my uncle. Go!" I shouted. He turned around as bullets riddled the front of the store, sending glass fragments in every direction. Two men stood in the showcase windows and continued shooting. I signaled to Jackie I was going to move along the backside of the counter and try to distract one of the bastards by throwing a cleaver. She understood and picked up a large carving knife and checked her ammunition.

The carnage that followed almost rivaled what I saw during the war.

As the shooter closest to me prepared to jump from the window platform, he looked down. At that instant I stood and threw the cleaver. He leaned backwards to avoid the blow, which caused his tommy gun to lift up, firing wildly into the ceiling. I then hit him in the chest with three shots centered on his heart. Jackie kept the other gunman pinned down with her remaining shots. When he realized she was out of bullets, he turned in my direction before I could swing my gun around to fire. Nothing I could do would save me, my life was in the hands of providence, and once again those hands belonged to Jackie. With my gun pointed at his chest, the man stood there with his eyes bulging, blood squirting from his neck. He swayed and then collapsed. Jackie pulled me down as the sound of gunfire erupted outside the store. We made it back behind the counter support when a shockwave, followed by a fireball, came roaring through the store. The blast apparently knocked us unconscious, since what happened next is still a blur. I awoke first. Jackie and I were clutching each other, huddled hard against the steel end of the counter, fire trucks were pouring water over the entire building, and the reality of what just happened didn't come back until O'Reilly helped us to our feet.

"Jesus, Joey. What the hell happened?" O'Reilly said looking from me to Jackie.

"I think Moralli discovered who I am and moved in to eliminate his problem. You need to let us go, Mike. My family and others could be in danger."

"Your uncle can protect them. He just about destroyed half the block fighting those goons outside who attacked you."

"What happened?

"Four gunmen used the three smashed cars for cover as your uncle started shooting. Luigi, outgunned, went for the gas tanks and blew everybody to hell. You two had better go out the back before the DA arrives. Your uncle and two of his boys are waiting for you.

"Check on Tony and his family. Some bullets hit the ceiling. And Mike, tell him I'll make good on the damages."

He nodded and turned, shouting orders, giving us an opportunity to slip out the back.

My uncle agreed to get Ma, Pop, and all the girls out to Castellano's compound. They would be safer there until I took care of Moralli.

Jackie refused to go with the others. "We're going to finish this together," was all she said, and I wasn't about to argue with her. I told her to clean up in Martha's place and change into a sexy outfit, Martha had plenty of them. As she came into my room, she put a hand over her mouth to suppress a gasp. She'd seen my scars as I slipped on a black, knit pullover shirt. Jackie put her arms around me and held on tight without saying a word.

"We both have our scars. Some of mine are visible. Now tell me how the hell did you ever learn to throw a carving knife like that?" I asked.

"That's not important. I want to know your plan for dealing with Moralli. Are you going to kill him tonight?"

"If I have to. I want to get the guys who murdered BB and only he can lead me to them. Things, however, just got a lot more complicated than I'd planned. I'll need you to distract Moralli's bodyguards, so I can get to him before he has a chance to raise an alarm. According to O'Reilly's report, Moralli's brother usually sends one of his hookers over to spend the night. That's where you come into the picture. When you enter Moralli's room, I'll make my move. I want him to know I'm still alive, and he has one more chance to deliver the goods before I kill him, and kill him I will."

I gave Jackie my stiletto and a thigh gun, courtesy of my uncle's personal arsenal, and I took my army duffle bag filled with what I would need.

For a guy who thought he had wiped out all his troubles, Moralli still had a heavy guard in place. I told Jackie to give me twenty minutes before going into her act, but after seeing the situation, I wished I'd given myself more time. Moralli lived on the top floor of the building, and I planned to scale the building, take out any guards on the roof, repel down, silently enter his room, and surprise Moralli before he could sound an alarm. Scoping out the building, I noticed a fire escape on the opposite side; it was easier than scaling up the back of the building and would take less time.

I caught the first guard taking a smoke break, and before he knew what happened, I had him gagged and bound. I was about to straighten up and go find the second guard when he appeared out of the shadows.

"Hey, Marco, you got a light?" he said, slowly walking towards me, fumbling with a pack of cigarettes, trying to knock one free.

I picked up the cigarette butt lying on the ground, took a deep drag, and held my hand out, drawing his attention to the hot ashes. As he bent forward with the unlit cigarette in his mouth and reached for my hand, I saw the sudden fear in his eyes, but it was too late. I pulled his head down with my free hand and simultaneously brought up my knee. Within seconds I had him hog-tied alongside his friend.

I prepared my grappling rig to rappel down to Moralli's window, when I heard someone walking up the stairs to the roof from the stairwell.

"Hey Marco, it's time for your break," another guard said as he emerged through the heavy metal door to the roof.

I came up behind him and pulled the gun from his shoulder holster. He turned violently, and then froze, looking down the barrel of his own .45. Surprisingly, he stood there smiling.

"We were wondering when you would show up. All the guys are saying you're crazy, but I doubt you're stupid. You pull that trigger, twenty of Moralli's thugs will be all over ya, and that would be bad for both of us. Why don't you consider a little hand-to-hand combat? You win and walk away; I win and get the dough Moralli put on your head."

He had a point. Actually, he had two, as he pulled out the largest knife I'd ever seen. I could have killed him with one of my throwing knives, but there'd been enough killing tonight, and he seemed like a likable guy—until he caught me across the chest with a vicious swing that sliced through my shirt and drew blood. He made a fundamental mistake by not shifting his weight before swinging the knife back. In two swift moves, I had him disarmed and the knife at his throat. "I didn't come here to kill anyone tonight. I just want a little chat with your boss. So let's go join your buddies over there."

Once he realized I wasn't going to kill him, he cooperated as I gagged and tied him to the other two guards.

I steadied myself on Moralli's windowsill and was about to enter when the door to his bedroom opened slightly. "Hey boss, your brother sent over an especially nice present for ya tonight." Jackie entered the room and quickly moved into the shadows.

When Moralli turned to face the door, I noticed he had someone in bed with him. "Hey, doll, come on over and join the fun before this one passes out." When Jackie didn't move or say anything, he shifted to get out of bed. Before he stood up, I held a knife to his throat.

"You're a little short-handed tonight, Moralli. Six of your guys are no longer with us," I said.

"What? Who the hell are you?"

"Keep your voice down. If your bodyguards come in, I'll get my revenge right now. My note was bloody clear. Nothing has changed. I want BB's killers."

"I got your message. My brother and I will deliver the package on time."

"So why did you try to take me out tonight?"

"Listen pal, I don't know what the hell you're talkin' about. My boys went to put a hit on some broad as a favor for a business associate."

It never occurred to me Jackie was the target. "Tell your friend to hire a professional next time."

"Wait a minute, are you telling me you wiped out six of my best men? What do you have to do with this broad anyway?"

I had to think fast. "I was keeping watch over your place when I noticed your torpedoes pile into two cars. Curious, I followed. To tell you the truth, I didn't like the odds, especially against a woman, so I took the opportunity to get some practice."

Jackie came out of the shadows, stepping into the moonlight that streamed through the open window, and pointed to herself. I nodded, and she quietly moved back. She had just realized she was the intended target tonight and not me.

Moralli started to say something, so I jerked his head back hard and pressed the knife deeper into his neck, drawing a trickle of blood. "I said keep your voice down."

"Take it easy. We have a deal; you'll get what you want," he whispered.

"Just making sure we don't have any misunderstandings."

"Don't worry!" he said. "I know when I'm beat."

"Good, I'm glad we understand each other. I'm going to tie you to the bedpost so you can't call the cavalry. You, by the door," I said to Jackie, "pick up that sock and shove it in his mouth."

I was concerned Moralli might recognize Jackie so I covered his eyes with my free hand as she approached. When she finished, I had her blindfold him from behind.

Jackie and I were about to leave when the girl in the bed moaned and rolled over. That's when I saw the bracelet. At that moment, all the pieces of the Bryson kidnapping fell into place. I motioned for Jackie to come over.

"It's Rachel." Jackie knelt down by the bed and moved the hair from the girl's face and then pulled out her stiletto. I caught her in mid-flight and grabbed her wrist as she lunged for Moralli. "Calm down, I need him alive."

I turned to Moralli and held my knife to his neck again,

drawing more blood as I pulled out the sock.

"What's she doing here? Every copper in town is looking for her."

"Just having a little fun before doing another job for my friend. Don't tell me you don't do the same when you have a chance, especially in your line of work." I didn't say anything and shoved the sock deeper down his throat.

"What are we going to do? I could try to take her out the front door," Jackie suggested.

"That will never work. The thugs outside must know about the girl and would suspect something. We all have to leave by the window." Jackie looked at me as if I was nuts then noticed the blood on my shirt.

"It's nothing, just another scar to add to my collection. We don't have much time. Get her dressed."

I went to the window and pulled on the rope. I was confident it would hold the three of us, but the challenge was how to get us all down at the same time. I didn't think I could hold both girls' weight.

"Jackie, have you ever rappelled down a rope before?"

"No, but I'm willing to try."

"It's too dangerous at this height." Making two trips wasn't really a practical option, but it was looking like the only one available to us when I remembered a film I'd viewed during my military training. "This is what we're gonna do. I'll carry her over my shoulder and get positioned on the rope. When I move down even with the windowsill, you grab hold of the rope and step on my other shoulder. As I descend, try to put as little weight on me as possible by using your arm strength as we move down."

I expected an alarm to sound at any time, but we made it to the street without incident. Jackie wanted to take the girl to her place, but I convinced her she would be safer at Castellano's with everyone else. I had my suspicions about

Al, and now they were even stronger. I was almost certain; Al, Bryson and Moralli were somehow connected, but I didn't know how.

Jackie realized from what Moralli had said that she was the target of tonight's onslaught at Tony's, but assumed it was the Chicago mob trying to avenge Sal Santangelo's death. I wasn't ready to share my suspicions about her husband until I had more proof.

Once Rachel was safe, Jackie insisted we tell Bryson and let him make the appropriate arrangements to bring his niece back to health. I disagreed, and before Ma or anyone else at Castellano's compound could take her side, I grabbed Jackie's arm and shoved her up the stairs to one of the bedrooms. Surprisingly, she didn't lash out as I pushed her into a chair.

"Did you see the cheap bracelet on Rachel's wrist?" I didn't give her a chance to answer before handing her the one I had in my pocket.

She gingerly held the bracelet, looked up, and questioned me with her beautiful, emerald-green eyes.

"Rachel is not Bryson's niece." I told her about the street kid who gave me the box, the kid's mother, and her story. I didn't mention to Jackie I suspected her husband was somehow part of the puzzle. Jackie agreed to keep the girl under wraps until we could get the truth out of Bryson. Before leaving the bedroom, I asked for a favor.

"This is going to seem strange, but I need you to trust me and not ask any more questions. I don't want you to mention anything that's happened yesterday or today to your husband when he returns from his trip," I said.

She walked over to me, put her arms around my waist, and rested her head on my shoulder. "You're not telling me everything. Is Al somehow involved in all of this?"

"I'm not sure, but I suspect he is. If we can get Bryson

to tell the truth, we'll know. In the meantime, don't say anything and be careful. If Al begins to act strange, get the hell out of your apartment and come to my place. And don't worry about Rachel. As soon as she's fit to travel, I'll take her to the clinic on Staten Island."

* * * * *

Friday night finally came, and we were in position waiting for Moralli to drive down the deserted pier with his henchmen responsible for BB's death. I was on one side near the end of the pier, and my uncle, O'Reilly, and two others, who looked like plain clothes detectives, were waiting on the opposite side, hiding behind some large, wooden shipping crates. I knew I was playing a dangerous game with the lives of the hoods who killed BB, but I really didn't give a damn. If all went according to plan, I expected O'Reilly to step in at the right moment to get Moralli on attempted murder and arrest the other two for BB's death. O'Reilly would finally get Moralli and his brother off the streets. If Moralli killed the two bums before O'Reilly could react, so be it.

A black sedan drifted out of the shadows with its lights off and stopped about twenty feet from the end of the pier. The pulse of the waterfront seemed to halt with the car as I prepared myself to deal with the unexpected. The driver's-side door creaked open, and Moralli stepped out into the moonlight holding a pearl-handled revolver.

"Hey, Mr. Detroit, I got your boys. I'm holding up my part of the bargain, so you'd better do the same and go back to the slime pit you came from." He looked around, trying to find where I was hiding, and then gave the okay to his brother, who got out and dragged two men from the back seat with their hands tied behind them and heavy chains wrapped about their bodies. It looked like they were going for a one-way swim.

"Okay boys, it's time to sing. Tell my new friend what you did to his cousin," ordered Moralli. His brother didn't say a word; he kept looking around, probably hoping to get off a shot.

"Boss, what ya doin'? We didn't take no money, honest. We told the truth. This bum was livin' where we stashed the dough, and he wouldn't talk," one of them said as the other whimpered.

"Look," Moralli said. "I believed you, or you'd be dead already. Just tell my new friend, who's hiding somewhere in the shadows, what you did."

"We didn't mean to kill him. We was scared you'd think we took the dough. He wouldn't talk and things got messy. You know how it is."

"Sure I do. You enjoyed yourselves and went too far. Ain't that right, boys?"

The whimperer finally spoke up. "Boss, whaddya doin'? We've been with ya for years. Just kill this guy. We didn't take the money, honest."

"You gotta understand something. Guys like you come cheap; there are hundreds roaming the streets wanting to be tough guys. Sorry, boys, it comes down to you or me and you lose," Moralli said.

I expected O'Reilly to step in, but I didn't see any movement, and then Moralli made his move and all hell broke loose.

His brother was shoving the two goons closer to the edge of the pier when Moralli stopped him. "You're right, boys. You've been loyal and don't deserve to drown, not a nice way to go." He looked them straight in the eyes and unloaded his gun, which had a silencer. They hit the ground like dead weights as the metal chains echoed their death along the waterfront.

I tried to react, but was too late. Moralli's brother saw me moving toward them and took aim when O'Reilly's boys came running from behind the crates and opened fire, killing both Moralli and his brother. They then turned on me and fired wildly. I ducked behind some crates, not knowing what to do. I couldn't shoot at police officers. When they realized they missed, they ran to Moralli's car, spun it around, smashing into boxes, and peeled out down the pier.

My uncle and O'Reilly came out from the shadows and stood over the dead bodies. "I think we'd better get the hell out of here before the cops come," O'Reilly said.

I didn't understand. "Weren't they your boys, Mike? What the hell did they have to kill Moralli for, and why shoot at me?" I shouted.

"They were members of Moralli's gang. I guess they didn't like how he treated their friends," O'Reilly said.

"Jesus, Mike, you never intended to arrest Moralli. You and Luigi had this planned all along, using his own men. You just killed four people."

"Joey, get this through your skull," Luigi said. "We didn't kill nobody. The Bryson kid is safe from those bastards, and BB got revenged."

I ignored Luigi's ranting and looked over at O'Reilly. "Mike, what the hell just happened? You won't take a goddamn bribe, but you plan a gangland massacre." Before he could answer, sirens blared in the distance.

"Let's get outta here. We can talk at your uncle's," he said calmly.

I got there first and downed several stiff drinks in a row. I didn't know if I was more pissed because I couldn't get additional information out of Moralli about the Bryson case or because I felt betrayed by my uncle and O'Reilly.

When they sat down, I didn't look up.

Luigi spoke first. "Joey, I don't need to explain anything to you. You knew how I felt about BB's murderers. They were scum and got what they deserved. I'm only sorry I didn't get to pull the trigger myself."

It wasn't my uncle who bothered me. He believed in an eye-for-an-eye and would never change, but O'Reilly? What would drive him to take the law into his own hands? He waited for his three drinks to arrive and drank two of them before speaking.

"I knew if I told you what we were planning, you'd call the whole thing off. You asked how I could do this. It's simple. Moralli is the one who killed my kid brother, and I've been trying to use the law for years to put him behind bars, but the whole system's corrupt. If we brought him in today, he'd be on the street by morning. You want to be upset, go ahead, but justice is smiling tonight. I can't undo what's done, and if I had the chance, I wouldn't. As far as trusting me in the future, that's your choice. But keep in mind, I don't have any more dead brothers."

There wasn't much I could say. Probably in his position, after all the years of frustration trying to bring Moralli to justice, I would've done the same. We ordered more drinks and got totally canned.

The morning papers sensationalized the "Waterfront Slaughter," and two days later they followed up with horrific images of decomposed bodies found in the deep water at the end of several piers. Apparently, Moralli routinely eliminated his competition by dropping them off the piers, wrapped in chains.

* * * * *

A few days later Jackie called to say she arranged a

meeting with Bryson for next week and that her husband had returned with the endorsement of the Democratic Party. I had taken the Bryson girl to the clinic on the Island, and we agreed to meet there the next day. I hoped my suspicions about Al were wrong, but I needed to explain them to Jackie before we met with Charles Bryson.

July

Bryson lived on his dead sister's estate, which was located in a beautiful part of Staten Island called Grymes Hill, better known to the locals as Crime Hill. Many of the major Mafia bosses moved out of New York to the Island in order to protect their families from the ravages of their own profession. This migration had transformed the Island into a second Little Italy—with significantly less crime. Only on Grymes Hill could you find a Mafia boss and a district attorney living on adjoining estates, their children best of friends.

As we drove out of the ferry terminal onto the Island, Jackie insisted we stop at the clinic to check on Rachel's condition before heading to Bryson's. When we arrived, Dr. Swartz was busy with a patient, so I took Jackie on a short tour of the grounds. The gardens surrounding the pond were in full bloom, with an array of colors and fragrances that created a momentary reprieve from the harsh realities we faced. Stopping by the pond, Jackie jumped onto a swing; for the first time in days she looked relaxed. It was funny to watch her try to get the swing moving until I realized she'd probably never been on one before. It was good to hear her laugh as I pushed her higher and higher.

Shirley interrupted our tranquility as she approached along the garden path. She gave me a gentle hug and whispered in my ear, "I read about Moralli. You said you'd take care of him; God, I wish I'd been there."

Jackie stumbled as she got off the swing and joined us.

"Shirley, I'd like you to meet a friend of mine, Jackie Forsythe. We're working on the Bryson case together." Shirley pulled back slightly before tentatively offering her hand to Jackie.

"Nice to meet you, Jackie. I'm Shirley DeMotte. Your name sounds familiar. Are you someone famous?"

"No, I'm afraid not," Jackie said. "I do edit some stories for my husband, and he often gives me a byline. Maybe you've seen my name in the *Daily News*."

"That must be it," Shirley said. "I got somethin' I need to tell Joey. Do you mind if we take a walk around the pond?"

"Not at all. I'm still trying to figure out how this swing works," Jackie said.

As Shirley tugged on my arm, a nurse came over and informed us the doctor was free for a few minutes and Rachel was asking for Jackie. When we entered the clinic, Jackie followed the nurse to Rachel's room, and I headed for the doc's office. Shirley still clung to my arm and tried to pull me back.

"Joey, I need to talk to you."

"I'll come by your room later. I don't want to miss this chance to meet with the doc," I said as I entered the office.

Doctor Swartz didn't waste time on small talk. "Rachel is going through a rough time withdrawing from the drugs she was given, but I'm confident she'll recover in a few months."

"How is her physical and mental state?" I asked.

"Actually, I'm more concerned about the abuse she suffered during her abduction than her drug addiction. Currently she has no recollection of her ordeal, but when her memory returns, I'm certain she'll require therapy. I'm afraid she might need to remain here for sometime."

The doc then leaned against the front of his desk and

squinted. "Joey, I hope you realize I could lose my license for keeping Rachel here without her guardian's consent. Based on what you said about him, I'm willing to take that risk, but the sooner you get everything resolved, the better I'll feel."

"I appreciate your concern, Doc. Jackie and I plan to confront Rachel's uncle this afternoon and hope to have everything wrapped up in a few days." The doc seemed to relax, but I'm sure I sounded more confident than I actually felt.

I waited for Jackie on the veranda, and when she came through the door, she passed by without saying a word. As soon as we got in the car, she let me have it. "You'd better be right about Charles or you're going to have to deal with me. Rachel needs to be home with her uncle and around friends."

I thought it best not to respond. We drove in silence until I remembered Shirley was waiting for me in her room.

"Shit!"

"What's the matter?"

"Nothing, it's not important," I said.

We didn't say another word until we got to Bryson's estate.

The guard at the gate was expecting us, and by the time we got to the main structure, the butler stood ready at the front door. As I parked the car, I noticed an old gardener trimming back roses.

"Jackie, why don't you go on ahead? I'd like to look around the grounds before meeting Bryson."

She got out of the car without responding. As I walked toward her, she turned and backed me up against the side of the car.

"Don't take too damn long or I might just come right

out and ask Charles if he arranged for Rachel's kidnapping," she said before storming off toward the mansion.

I couldn't help but crack a smile as I watched her stride past the butler. I then turned my attention to the gardener.

He stopped trimming and stood to greet me. "You have an impressive garden. It must've taken years to create," I said.

"Twenty at least; it's the trees ya know that really give the dimension you need. Afraid I can't take much of the credit. The fella before me set the place up, and he was damn good. All I get to do is keep everything healthy and replant when necessary. But I still enjoy it."

"Then there's a chance you knew Rachel's mother. I was wondering what she was like?"

"Can't say; no one can. Mr. Bryson fired everyone soon after taking over. Strangest thing I'd ever heard. At the time I wasn't sure I wanted the job, if that's how he treated people. Can't complain though. He's been good to us."

"Mind if I walk around the grounds? I'd like to see the rest of the property."

"Makes no difference to me, but if I were you, I'd stay away from the guard dogs. They don't like strangers."

I looked the place over for a few minutes and didn't see anything unusual, just some old garden tools resting up against a shed, a few woodpiles, and some dead trees waiting for the ax. It was easy, however, to see how someone could hide in the foliage until they saw a chance to make their move. As I came around the other side of the house, the guard dogs threw themselves against their cages, baring their teeth and making a hell of a racket. I made a hasty retreat, tripped over a rotting rain barrel cover, and stepped in a mud puddle. When I got to the house, the butler insisted I remove my shoes before entering, which put me at a significant disadvantage for meeting Bryson.

Jackie and Bryson were having a drink when I entered the sitting area.

"Ah, you must be Joey Batista, the private detective Jackie has been telling me about. A remarkable fellow, she said, and if anyone can find Rachel, you can. Sadly enough, the police have given up, and I've hired several private investigators—all in vain I'm afraid."

Standing there shoeless, I needed a way to get the upper hand and decided Jackie's approach, stated in anger, might be the best way to quickly get to the truth. But first, I sensed the potential for money. "I understand there's a reward of five-thousand dollars for finding your niece. What if she's dead?"

"Of course you're right; that is a real possibility. I would still want her remains to bury with my sister."

"Five thousand doesn't seem like much from a man of your means," I said, knowing I would get a reaction.

"Good God, man. If you can find Rachel, I'll double the reward."

"Great, but is the reward for finding your niece or for finding the girl who was kidnapped?"

Sweat beaded on his forehead. "What in the world are you ranting about? I have only one niece and *she* was kidnapped."

Bryson turned pale and wavered slightly when I handed him the wire bracelet.

"You've found her? Where is she? Is she alright? My God, you've found her."

Jackie walked over to Bryson and led him to a chair. "Charles, we know most everything. We found the girl you raised as Rachel. The bracelet you're holding belongs to her brother. Why don't you tell us what happened."

Bryson still tried to pretend he didn't know what we were talking about.

"Look, Bryson, it's pretty obvious your real niece died years ago. I bet it happened the same day you fired your entire staff. Why don't you come clean and tell us the truth," I said.

Confronted with the undeniable facts, years of guilt poured out as he told his sordid story. "I didn't know about the old wells. I was only here a week when one day I couldn't find her. I thought she was hiding, playing a game. I searched frantically and finally found her at the bottom of a dried-up well. She had stepped onto a rotting cover and fell through; she was dead. There wasn't anything I could do, and all that money was going to go to strangers.

"I called the staff together and dismissed them immediately. It created quite a stir, but I paid them handsomely and they left without any real fuss. I was in a panic until I remembered my sister had once mentioned that many of the orphans at the institution where she volunteered came from the Bowery. Mothers would actually leave their babies on the doorstep because they couldn't feed them. It was then I realized that, other than my estate staff, very few people had actually seen the real Rachel. My sister had become a recluse after her husband's death.

"I went to the Bowery, found a woman with a brood of kids and paid her handsomely for one of her daughters, who resembled Rachel in age and features. God, I'm so ashamed. When I say aloud what I did, it sounds horrible."

Jackie continued to ask questions, and I didn't interfere. If my suspicions about Al proved correct, Jackie was heading for a fall of her own, and better it came from Bryson than me.

"Charles, tell me the truth. Did you hire a guy named Moralli to kidnap and kill Rachel so you could inherit the rest of the estate? I know you're having financial problems. Your donations to the orphanage have all but stopped."

"How could you suggest such a thing? I love Rachel. Now that I think about it, the only person who would benefit from Rachel's death is your husband. That's right, Al! He'd seen the real Rachel before she died and realized I had a different girl. I had no choice but to tell him everything, and he has been blackmailing me ever since."

Jackie's knees buckled as she grabbed hold of the back of a chair. "That's an accusation that's beneath you, Charles."

"It's not an accusation, it's a fact. Al needs my financial backing to finance his campaign for mayor, and when I lost most of my fortune in the stock market, he became furious. He threatened to expose what I'd done if I didn't raise the cash. I don't know for sure he had Rachel kidnapped, but he certainly had a motive. He realized I wouldn't be able to raise the amount he demanded, and he knew the details of my sister's will."

I stepped in and laid out the facts for Bryson so I could get Jackie the hell out of there. "Bryson, we found Rachel being held by this Moralli guy, who was about to kill her. Unfortunately, before we located Rachel, he'd already subjected her to powerful drugs and brutally molested her. The only good news is the goon who did these horrific things is dead."

"Where is she? Is she getting proper treatment? I insist you tell me where she is. She has been my niece for more than thirteen years, and no matter what you think about what I've done, I do love her."

I wrote down the name and location of the clinic and strongly suggested he leave Rachel in Dr. Swartz's care. I also included how to locate Rachel's real family and urged him to provide them with some form of income.

Jackie needed to get out of there, but as I walked Jackie to the door, Bryson followed, trying to find a way to ask one last question. I saved him the trouble. "As you said, Rachel is your niece. She's in good hands with Dr. Swartz, and I see no reason to change things if you've told us the truth."

Before I stepped through the door, I turned and asked Bryson a question that had been bothering me. "Why did you let Rachel keep anything from her past?"

"I didn't."

"What about the bracelet?"

"Some kid who often came by the orphanage for food gave it to her a few years back. As far as I know, she never took it off."

He was about to close the door when he asked, "What about Al?"

Jackie turned to face Bryson with renewed strength. "I'll take care of Al if he's involved in any of this."

On the ride back to the city, I told Jackie I suspected a link between Al and Moralli, and in all likelihood it was Al who hired Moralli to kill her the night we came under attack outside of the butcher shop. I went on to explain Al couldn't afford to have her background revealed during his bid for mayor and, as she'd heard, he also needed Bryson's money.

"Do you have any proof? For all we know, Bryson lied, and the Mafia could have ordered the hit on me because of Santangelo's murder. You don't know for sure," Jackie said, almost in tears.

"I know it's hard to believe, but until we can prove otherwise, I suggest you stay at my place. Al lied to me about his relationship with Bryson, and I know the Mafia has given up looking for Santangelo's killer. You said yourself Al craves power more than *anything* else."

"If he's involved in any of this, I'll kill the rotten son-of-a-bitch myself."

"If he's guilty, you can't just knock off your husband and get away with it. I suggest we take a few days to think things over. We need to find a link between them. If and when we do, then we'll deal with Al. In the meantime, I want you as far away from your husband as possible."

"We're not going to prove anything in a couple of days. Besides, any evidence against Al probably died with Moralli."

"You never know," I said.

When we found my uncle, he couldn't believe what I was asking. "Joey, I run a reputable speakeasy not a boarding house for troubled dames. Your ever-growing collection of women has taken over most of my rooms. Please, do me a favor. Don't take on any more cases. I know I need the tenants, but even you gotta admit this is getting out of hand."

Jackie had been waiting outside the office and heard everything. As soon as she came in, my uncle caved. "You didn't tell me the room was for the redhead. Of course I have a vacancy; there's one right next to me," he said as he put his arm around Jackie's waist.

"Uncle, I was thinking about the furnished apartment down the hall from my office. She's had a rough day. How about handing over the key so she can get some rest?"

It was well past midnight when Jackie finally settled into her room with a pair of my pajamas and a new toothbrush from Ma. Jackie walked me to the door and, as I was leaving, gave me a warm embrace. "I had no idea I lived with such a monster. I thought I left that world behind when I ran away from Sal. I guess I'm attracted to men with a beast inside them. Sal was just evil, Al will apparently do anything for power, and you're trying to gain control of your own demons."

Jackie somehow understood a battle raged inside me. I

desperately wanted to bring back the Joey Batista of my youth, but that Joey died when Anita vanished and was buried somewhere in the back alleyways of Europe. The Joey who survived is a cold-blooded killer who, thank God, only seems to emerge when threatened.

* * * * *

The next day, Martha oozed with excitement because she had obtained a copy of Louie Ruffalo's war records. I wanted to talk to some of the guys in his outfit, since Louie never seemed like the hero type. He followed his brother Ralph around and never stood up for himself. It didn't make sense he would give his life to save others.

According to the military documentation, Louie had saved his whole platoon from certain death. The platoon had broken through enemy lines during a heavy thunderstorm and ran into a nest of Germans. Under the cover of darkness, Louie wiped out a machine gun placement and took over their position. At dawn, when the battle raged again, he fired on the other German strong-holds and, in the confusion of all the smoke and noise, he disabled the two remaining gunnery positions before anyone knew what was happening. In the final moments of fighting, a grenade thrown by a dying soldier blew Louie to smithereens.

Martha had also located a Private Henry Long, who had survived the ordeal with a serious injury and testified to Louie's bravery. Private Long lived with his parents in Bayonne, New Jersey.

Ralph was a different story. As his parents said, the government had no record of him enlisting in the armed services. He had left home with his brother to enroll, and that's the last anyone saw of him. My only lead for locating Ralph was Private Long. Hopefully Louie had mentioned his brother's whereabouts.

Martha and I were discussing the records when Shirley barged into my office. "I need to talk to you. Right now! Don't try to brush me off again," she said.

Before Martha could react, I asked her to leave and turned to Shirley. "Look Shirley, I'm sorry about..."

"I wanna know why the hell you brought that woman to the clinic!" Shirley shouted.

"What's wrong? Like I told you, Jackie's helping me with the Bryson kid. She's close to the girl."

"Did you know *her* husband worked for Moralli?"

"I don't understand? How would you know that?"

"Joey, I told you what I did for a living. Al Forsythe was one of my clients. Whenever Moralli had legal problems, he'd send me to Forsythe, and I'd meet him at an apartment he had in the city. I'd hand over a package from Moralli, and then he'd take full advantage of my services. I don't know the exact nature of their business dealings, but I can guess. A few days after our meetings, any charges against Moralli or his men got dropped."

As chief editor of a major newspaper, Al had free access to every politician and judge in the city, and if Shirley's observation proved correct, he was Moralli's middleman. I knew there had to be a connection between the two but never suspected a working relationship.

"Shirley, up until yesterday Jackie didn't suspect her husband was involved with organized crime. Do me a favor and keep this to yourself."

"Sure, that's the least I can do for you. But, Joey, if she's really in the dark, she needs to know the type of man she's married to."

"God help Forsythe when she finds out," I said mostly to myself. Shirley gave me a strange look. "I'll explain some other time. Tell me, how's the Bryson girl doing?"

"Physically she'll be fine. Her memory of the kidnapping is coming back and Doc's concerned how she's gonna react."

"I need to take a short trip and don't want to leave Jackie alone. She has a lot of crap going on in her life right now and could use a diversion. Why don't you drop in on her and tell her you came to see me about something, and when you heard she was staying here, you thought it might be a good idea for her to visit Rachel. It'll do Jackie some good to get away, and she could probably help the girl. Jackie's in the apartment two doors down on the right."

I gave Shirley a peck on the cheek and said I'd be in touch. That didn't quite satisfy her.

"If I didn't know better, I'd say you're intimidated by former drug-addicted pro skirts, who kill their men that step out of line."

"Who wouldn't be?" I said with a smile.

"Anyway, thanks again for getting rid of Moralli. I feel a lot safer, and maybe my sister can someday have a normal life without that monster in the picture, or at least a better one, as we've discussed."

Jackie and Shirley left for the clinic shortly after having lunch with my family, and when they were gone, it didn't take Uncle Luigi more than five seconds to give me grief.

"What does this make, six or seven? All I can say is thank God she has a place to live and doesn't need a favor."

"Actually she does," I said.

"Does what? I thought you said she lived on the Island?"

"I did, but she needs a favor from Castellano."

"Great, I suppose she wants somebody whacked. Does she think all Italians are in the Mafia?"

"What kinda problem she have?" Ma asked, ignoring Luigi's comment.

I felt the blood rush to my face as I thought how to explain that Shirley's sister has a drug addiction and suffers from nymphomania. The doc told me she had kicked her drug habit, but he didn't have a way to keep her off the streets and drugs because of her illness. Shirley had once asked me if I could convince Castellano to get her sister in the high-priced end of the business, where they required the girls to be drug-free. I was sure Ma never heard of nymphomania, and I didn't feel comfortable explaining the details, nor did I want to give Luigi a chance to make any more wisecracks.

I believe Pop saw my discomfort and distracted Ma long enough for me to slip out and head for my office.

That evening, Martha and I lost track of time as we tried to determine the best way to trace the two drifters who had worked the various farms around the time of Anita's disappearance. Based on Anita's police file, we concluded it would be nearly impossible to find the drifters after so many years. The police had interviewed all the surrounding farms several miles away, and no one remembered seeing such a strange pair of hired hands. They called themselves Little Mo and Big Mo, and their names apparently fit their descriptions.

We were wrapping up for the night and about to head to Martha's place for a few drinks when Sally walked in and asked to speak to me privately.

"Sorry if I interrupted anything," she said with sarcasm. "I wanted you to hear from me that I'll be leaving soon. My father offered me a job at his bank, and I accepted. I'm going home."

"When do you plan to leave?" I asked.

"That's all you have to say? When am I leaving? You think I want to go backwards in my life? I'd hoped for more, so much more from you. It seems the harder I tried, the farther you pulled away. What are you afraid of?"

"I'm sorry Sally. The last thing I wanted was to hurt you. I'm just not ready for a serious relationship. I don't know what else to say."

"It's not work, is it?"

"No."

"Then what is it? You've surrounded yourself with beautiful women. Is that it? You're just out to have a good time? Do you have any idea how it makes me feel to see you with a new woman almost every week? To answer your question, I'll be leaving *soon*," she said as she walked away.

I wanted to go after her, but thought it best for both of us if she did leave. When I got to the fourth floor landing, Martha was waiting by her door and beckoned me to follow her.

The next morning a cab arrived to take Sally to the train station. After everyone said their goodbyes, I pulled Sally aside.

"Sally, I want you to know something. I pulled away from you because, in so many ways, you remind me of Anita. You have a way of touching people's lives, and you see things as they could be and not as they are. I didn't want to hurt you. Until I know what happened to Anita, I can't love that deeply again."

"Jesus Joey, why didn't you tell me sooner?" she said, holding my hand.

I wiped away her tears and gave her a tender kiss. "I tried."

As the cab drove away, Ma walked over and slapped me behind the head. "You may never find a girl like that again. When you gonna grow up?"

* * * * *

Henry Long lived in Bayonne, which is just across a waterway from Staten Island, along Richmond Terrace, where the clinic is located. As I drove past the clinic, I was tempted to check on Jackie, but I was more anxious to track down Henry and get the real story on Louie and Ralph Ruffalo. Henry wasn't home, but his parents directed me to a small park a few blocks down the road. I asked for a description of their son, and they said I should look for a guy in a wheelchair.

I found Henry under a weeping willow tree, with a book on his lap, watching some local kids playing a game of stickball.

"Private Long, my name's Joey Batista. I'm looking for the brother of a friend of yours, a Ralph Ruffalo. I believe you and Louie Ruffalo served in the same outfit."

The blanket covering Henry's lap caught in the wheel as he turned the wheelchair to face me. I instinctively reached for the blanket, and that's when I noticed his legs were gone from the knees down.

"You a friend of Louie's?" he asked, pretending not to notice my discomfort.

"Actually, I'm a PI, investigating a murder that took place about six years ago."

"Figures. I expected someone would show up one day. I owe Louie my life, and so do a helluva lot of other guys. But honestly, he was a real nut case. He never told me what he did, he didn't have to. He had so many nightmares none of us could get any sleep. If I had to guess, he and his brother killed someone."

I plopped down on the grass next to Henry, trying to regain my composure. For years I wanted to know what happened to Anita and now, when faced with a possible answer, I found it difficult to deal with.

"Are you okay?"

"I'll be fine. I was close to the girl who was murdered."

"Sorry," he said as he wheeled away to give me some space. As he exerted himself, Henry had difficulty breathing.

Before long I walked back to his side. "Did anyone ever report Louie to an officer?"

"And say what? Ruffalo's having nightmares. We didn't have any proof."

"I'm surprised anyone so brave could've committed murder. Just doesn't make sense."

Henry looked off into the distance before saying anything. "Ya know, Mr. PI, I've been holding this in for a long time. Louie did a heroic thing, but he was no hero. He basically committed suicide; he wanted to cash out. I think down deep he was a good guy and the guilt finally got to him."

"Did he ever mention his brother? I'd like to ask him a few questions."

"Not much, but I can tell ya one thing. If Louie made it out alive, he would have tracked his brother down himself. I know I would have."

It was hard not to follow up immediately with more questions, but it was past noon, and my stomach was loudly protesting. I suggested we continue talking over lunch at a café near the park.

"I don't know if that's such a good idea," Henry said. "Most everyone in town tries to ignore me. I guess I'm a constant reminder of the war, and people want to forget and move on."

"I told your folks I would get you something to eat, so they're not coming to wheel you home," I said as I pushed him toward the café.

I had to carry Henry up the stairs to the café and then place him into a booth. I didn't appreciate the looks we got.

Henry was used to it, but I wasn't.

"What the hell are you guys staring at? Haven't you ever seen a war hero before?"

"Joey, please. You're just gonna make things worse for me," Henry said.

No one took my challenge, so I sat down and tried to refocus on Henry. "I think you got it all wrong. Sure people want to forget about the war, but that's not the reason they're ignoring you. They don't know what to say or how to act around you. I saw it on visiting days at the hospital where I stayed after returning from the war. All you gotta do is help them feel comfortable with your physical situation."

"I wish it was that easy."

"It is, trust me."

When the food came, I went back to asking about Louie. "Do you know why Louie was so mad at his brother?"

"I heard the story a million times. I'll tell you one thing, based on what he said, his brother was a real louse."

Before he could tell me what'd happened between the brothers, one of the locals came over and joined us for lunch, and then another came. We didn't get out of there until four in the afternoon, and I still didn't know what Ralph did to Louie.

As I pushed Henry home, he reminisced about the war.

"I didn't know what I was getting into when I went over to fight with the French. The Germans overran my mother's hometown, and after that there was no stopping me. If I knew I'd be spending most of my time in a trench, covered in mud, trying to avoid a sniper's bullet, I would have waited until the Americans got into the war before joining up."

"How'd you get your injuries?" I asked as I struggled to

get his wheelchair up a homemade ramp to his front porch.

"You might say I was one of the lucky ones. The Germans first used chlorine gas at the Battle of Ypres, and I happened to be behind the line in sickbay. We knew something was wrong when the soldiers scrambled out of the trenches choking and coughing. I got a small dose, not enough to bring me home. I notice the effect more now, probably because I'm not getting any exercise."

"What about the legs?"

"That happened later, when I joined up with the Americans. We broke through enemy lines and got caught in a crossfire. I already told you what happened. That was the fight where Louie lost his life. I only lost my legs.

"What about you? How'd you make it out in one piece?" Henry asked.

"There are invisible wounds. I began as a sniper. Not along the trenches. I did my work away from the battlefield. Later I took on more difficult assignments and infiltrated the German military."

"You were a spy?"

"No, but sometimes I brought back valuable information. That's enough about me. Tell me what happened between Louie and his brother. I need to get back to the city."

"Sure, but you can forget about leaving tonight. That barge you came over on from the Island shuts down at six.

"The brothers went to enlist together, waited in line, and after Louie wrote his name, he turned to give Ralph the pen. Ralph smiled, handed it back, and said 'I'll see ya after the war, kid.'"

"Was that it? He didn't say where he was going or what he was gonna do?"

"When Louie told this story, he would stand up and reach out as if he was back in the recruiting office. 'Hey, Ralph, where ya goin?' he'd say. And then he would answer as if he was Ralph. 'To Chicago, I'm goin' to Chicago, kid. I got some friends there and couldn't bring ya along. Remember, keep your head down."

The next morning after I said good-bye to his parents, Henry came out onto the porch. "Thanks, Joey, for yesterday at the café. I think some of the old gang might come around now that they know I'm still the same person. Hell, they might even build me a ramp so I can join them for lunch."

Before leaving town, I stopped at the café and had a talk with my newfound friends. When I left, I was confident Henry would get his ramp and a special table to accommodate his wheelchair.

* * * * *

Shirley came running over to the car as I drove up to the clinic. "Oh, Joey, I'm so sorry. If I had known, I would've tried to stop her."

I attempted to open the car door, but she leaned into it with incredible strength. "Shirley, what are you talking about?"

"Didn't you read the morning paper? Jackie's been arrested for murdering her husband. I told her about his relationship with Moralli. Joey, she asked why I reacted to her the way I did when we first met. I thought she should know."

* * * * *

When I got to Jackie's apartment building, a section of sidewalk protected by wooden barriers contained a chalked outline of Al's body. The doorman recognized me and wasn't overly friendly.

"As far as I could tell, they had a good marriage until you came along. No sense going upstairs, the police have everything sealed off and guarded round the clock."

"What happened?"

"She came home, looking like the mother-of-death and a few minutes after her husband arrived the poor guy comes flying over the balcony. He landed head first, splat. Damn near hit me. The rest I'll leave to your imagination."

"Where's she now?"

"Where do you think? Downtown. Booked for murder, and if you ask me, she's gonna fry."

"I need to get to a phone fast."

"Try the drug store down the street. But if I were you, I'd stay away from her. You're just gonna get dragged in deeper. I told the police about your visits."

"Thanks, pal," I said.

"Hey, a fin only gets you information. If you wanted me to keep my mouth shut, it would've cost a hundred. I thought you said you're a PI. You should know these things."

I called Frank Galvano's office and found he was already at Police Headquarters interviewing Jackie. She had called him as soon as she got charged. I talked my way into the meeting room by pretending to be Frank's assistant. When I entered, Jackie flew into my arms.

"I didn't mean to do it, Joey. He pulled a gun as soon as he got home and I had no choice. I did it, but I was defending myself. He cornered me on the balcony and was going to throw me over. I had no choice."

I held her tight and then sat her back down. I hung back in the corner listening as Galvano continued asking questions. It didn't sound good.

Frank and I left the precinct and stopped to have a late lunch.

"I gotta be honest with you, Joey. It's pretty grim. The apartment looks like the chamber of horrors at Coney Island—knives sticking in just about every wall, and his blood splattered all over the main room and kitchen. Her story isn't believable, especially when you throw in the fact she was covered in his blood."

"That's because you don't know anything about Jackie, and you don't know why Al would want to kill her."

"Okay, you got my attention. What don't I know?"

"First, Jackie's an expert knife thrower. She would never miss unless she intended to. Second, Al tried to kill her once before. Remember the gun battle at the butcher shop? It was a hit on her, not me, ordered by Al. Third, Al was working for Moralli and was the front man paying off half the city officials so he could operate. You want more? How about this? He arranged for the Bryson girl's kidnapping and murder so Bryson would inherit her money to continue financing Al's campaign for mayor. I know none of this makes sense, but trust me, it's all true. I'll fill you in on the details later."

"Can you prove any of this?

"Probably not!"

"Shit!"

* * * * *

Jackie was headline news for the week leading up to the preliminary hearing, creating a news circus around the courthouse. The wheels of justice were in motion and grinding her to a pulp. Every reporter in town dug deep into her past, and it seemed the political machine at City Hall wanted her tried, convicted, and forgotten as quickly as possible. To make things worse, the readers of the *Daily News* practically demanded a public execution, especially after reading about her mob connections in Chicago.

Frank never had a chance at the preliminary hearing. Aside from the overwhelming evidence at the crime scene, her past association with the criminal element of Chicago and the recent stabbing death of her onetime lover, Sal Santangelo, convinced the judge to set a trial date in mid-August.

For the entire week after the hearing, Frank and I spent every waking moment trying to find some way to convince a future jury Al had reasons to want Jackie dead and she acted in self-defense. Unfortunately, any evidence indicating Al was involved with organized crime apparently died with Moralli. As far as the public was concerned, Al had been a model citizen dedicated to serving the city. To make matters worse, every aspect of the crime scene pointed to Jackie being the aggressor. There wasn't any physical evidence that Al had assaulted her; on the contrary, he had a brutal, defensive knife wound on his hand. The gun recovered at the scene didn't prove a thing since both his and Jackie's blood covered the handle. If that wasn't enough to put her away, the carving knives, cleaver, and stiletto, all embedded in the walls of the apartment, along with the overturned furniture, indicated Al desperately scrambled for his life.

We searched Jackie's apartment in hopes of finding some incriminating documents about Al's criminal activities. Jackie gave us the combination to their safe, but it didn't contain anything relative to the case. We then searched for hidden compartments in the furniture, floorboards, closets, bathrooms, and air ducts, and we even looked for a hidden door. Nothing! For a moment I thought I found something when I stepped on a loose floorboard in his closet. I got down and cleared away several shoes and some boxes. The board popped up as I put pressure on one end, but there was nothing underneath.

Not until our second pass through the apartment did we find a small safe beneath the left bottom drawer of his desk. The safe, cleverly hidden in the space between the floor and the ceiling of the apartment below, gave us some hope that it might contain the evidence we were searching for, especially since Jackie didn't know of its existence. Safecracking was one of the many skills I read about in my PI mail order course, but since I didn't have any direct experience, I had to enlist the help of a retired box cracker I knew from the neighborhood, three-fingered Malone.

"Joey, are you kiddin' me? I can't even feel my own pulse with these fingers anymore," Malone said when I asked for his help.

"Maybe you can teach me how to open the box? It doesn't look that tough to crack."

"Listen to you, the expert. Can we use explosives, maybe a little soup? How about acid?"

"Nitro's out of the question, and acid might damage any papers inside. Nope, I need to do it by touch and sound," I said.

"Good luck! Tell you what, I'll teach you the Malone touch for twenty percent of any cash in the safe; everything else you get to keep. Do we have a deal?" he asked as he extended his deformed hand.

A few days later, Frank and I were back in the apartment, and two hours into my safecracking career, the box door opened. Malone hit pay dirt and plenty of it. The safe contained forty-five thousand dollars and nothing else. No indication where the money came from or its intended use. We took the money and gave it to my uncle for safekeeping, minus the nine thousand we owed three-fingered Malone. We were no better off than we were three weeks ago, and the press hadn't let up on Jackie. The trial was less than twenty days away, and I felt useless.

* * * * *

Wallowing in self-pity and depression, the last thing I wanted was for the gang of five to corner me about Anita's case.

"Getting drunk ain't gonna help Jackie, or help find Anita's killer," Luigi said.

"Didn't you once tell me you needed to work several cases at the same time in order to look at things from a new perspective? Isn't that what you said?" Castellano asked.

Martha had her say next. "Joey, why don't you follow the lead you got from the guy in Jersey? Besides, you need to get away for a few days."

"I'm telling ya, Joey, if you don't eat something soon, your ma's gonna spoon feed ya. Take our advice and get the hell outta town fast," Pop said.

"Seems to me, Joey, the redhead wouldn't hesitate to kill a guy if she had a good reason. Are you sure she's so innocent?" Luigi asked.

The bloody image of Moralli's goon with a carving knife through his neck suddenly popped into my mind. "I don't know. She's capable of killing someone, and she had a strong motive. I hope to God she didn't do it."

Galvano finally spoke up. "Kid, get away and clear your head. You're not doing me or Jackie any good. Just be back in two weeks."

I figured they couldn't all be wrong, so the next day I hit the road heading for Chicago in my beat-up model-T flivver, but not before Pop and Uncle Luigi said good-bye one last time.

"Hey, Joey, I got a little somethin' for ya. Ya know, to

keep you safe," Luigi said as he put a long box in the front seat.

"Doesn't look like a Saint Christopher medal," I said.

"Not exactly, but in a tight spot it might be more useful."

My pop handed me a folded piece of paper. "Joey, we have a friend in Chicago who owes me a favor from the old days. If this Ralph guy is running around town, he'll know about it. Ma sends her blessing. She's inside crying and praying for your safe return. Ya better go before she gets a divine inspiration to stop you from leaving."

As I pulled into traffic, trying to avoid the masses of humanity who thought the streets belonged to them, I had only one thought and that was to avenge Anita's death.

* * * * *

When you live in one place all your life, you get used to the sounds and smells that constantly swirl around, engulfing you in their protective shield of invisibility. It's your territory, your domain. You know how to maneuver, how to survive, who to trust, and who to avoid. Leaving the city, I left all that behind, and as I transitioned onto the open road, I began to appreciate for the first time what Anita had growing up on a farm. The wind carried a cornucopia of natural smells and brought with it sounds foreign to any city. She must have felt safe, protected from the evils that lurked outside her terrain, and trusted all those around her. Someone violated that trust and that someone had to be Ralph. He was about to feel my anguish.

I knew my way around Chicago a bit from my last visit and found the Derby Club located downtown within a few hours. Pop's note said to ask for Johnny Torrio, and when I did, several oversized brutes joined me at the bar.

"What ya want with Johnny?" asked Scar Face, after he checked me for a shoulder holster.

"Ya know, a guy from outta town asking for Mr. Torrio without first checking with some of his boys can have an accident or two," said the other.

"I take it that means you two wrecking balls work for Mr. Torrio. How about telling him Joey Batista from New York has some business to discuss with him?"

"He ain't gonna discuss nothing with you. So be a nice fella and go back where ya came from before we has to show ya how things are done here in Chicago," Scar Face said after pulling back a shot of whiskey.

They both moved away from the bar, and as I turned to follow, one hit me with a right cross. The other planted a gut punch. They then grabbed me under the armpits and tossed me onto the street. The speakeasy erupted into laughter and stopped just as suddenly when I returned and tapped Scar Face on the shoulder. As he turned, still laughing, I hit him hard in the jaw with an elbow and struck my other nemesis with a fierce punch to his gut, followed by a knee to his face as he doubled over. When his head came up, I twirled him around in a chokehold, pulled his gun out of his holster, and held it to his head. As I faced the crowd, at least twenty pieces of iron pointed at the three of us, and I suspected none of them cared who the hell got shot, as long as Torrio stayed out of danger.

"Batista, if you are who you say you are, put the hardware down," said a heavy voice from the back of the room.

I didn't have a choice and prayed Pop knew what he was doing. The crowd parted as I walked to the back of the saloon and joined a lone figure at a table.

"How do I know you're telling the truth?" Torrio asked.

"My pop gave me a message for you." I handed the note to him, hoping it would be enough. After reading the message, Torrio smiled, and his eyes glazed over just enough to tell me he was remembering a different time and a different place. My pop gets the same look when he talks about the old country.

"So, Joey, what can I do for you? You need a job?"

"No, but thanks. I'm looking for someone, someone who may have killed a close friend of mine," I said.

"Castellano told me about you. You know I can't have someone come into my town and launch his own private war. What you did to Sal Santangelo tells me you're a dangerous man. Sal was a problem, not just for me, but for others as well. So I looked the other way and didn't say anything to my associates because I owe your father my life, more than once."

I didn't know what to say. I wished Castellano had prepared me for this conversation. After a brief pause, I took a chance.

"I don't really know your relationship with my family, but Pop told me he came over to this country with several of his friends and they all swore an oath to help each other. If I'm right, then you know Tom Sgarlata," I said.

"Sure, but what does this have to do with Sgarlata?"

"His daughter, Anita, disappeared several years ago, and I think one of their neighbors may have killed her," I said.

"I know about Anita. I thought she ran off with some drifter."

"Her father's dying, and on his deathbed he asked me to find the truth about what happened to her. She didn't run off. We were planning on getting married."

"Who are you looking for?" he asked.

"Ralph Ruffalo."

"Ruffalo? You're kidding, right?"

"No. Do you know where he hangs out?"

"I like you, kid. You enjoy living dangerously. Ruffalo's a respected member of our community, one of the best button men in the business. For your father's sake, leave town now, or you'll end up with a hole in your head, like so many others."

I looked at his bowtie and baby face and thought I was talking to a salesman rather that a dangerous gangster.

"Sorry, Mr. Torrio. I can't do that."

"Give me the proof you have against Ruffalo, and I'll take it to the council. If they approve, then you can avenge her death. If you can."

When I finished telling him why I suspected Ralph, I felt foolish. All I had was a hunch—at best someone else's gut feeling due to Louie's nightmares and Ralph's bizarre behavior as a kid.

"Joey, take my advice and go home. If Ralph finds out you're after him, you're a dead man."

"I'm going to find him with or without your help."

"That's your choice, but if I were you, I'd watch my back. Ralph has a lot of friends in this town."

I spent the next few days searching for Ralph, but the word was out, and no one would dare talk with me. Without Torrio's help, I had embarked on a fool's errand and had left Jackie to fend for herself. I headed back to New York, but at least I knew Ruffalo still lived in Chicago.

Once I hit the road, I had one purpose in life and that was to prove Jackie's innocence. When she got out of jail, I hoped she would join me in the search for Anita's killer. She knew her way around Chicago and had ways to get information. I sped along a dirt road, blind to my surroundings, when suddenly my car lurched forward, hit from behind. I tried to regain control as a car pulled alongside. Ralph Ruffalo looked at me with a big smile as two of his henchman fired shots at my tires. I veered to the side of the road and ran into a ditch. The car flipped several times and landed upright, with the front end on a slope, pointing up toward the road. My right side burned like hell, and my head bled where it had been hit by the tommy gun that came flying out of the box my uncle gave me before leaving for Chicago. The smell of gasoline quickly brought me to my senses, and that's when I saw Ralph and his two goons looking down into the car, laughing at my predicament.

"Hey, Joey, sorry we have to meet under such circumstances after all these years, but I can't afford to be wondering when you'll be back in town. Because I'm a nice guy, I'm gonna tell ya the truth. I have no idea what happened to Anita. She was just about the only person who was ever nice to me. I know you don't believe me, so you give me no choice. Besides, I always hated your guts. Because of you, Anita never would consider me more than a neighbor. Let him have it boys."

As he gave his little speech, I stretched through the pain in my side and grabbed the tommy gun. As they fired, I let loose with a volley that ripped through all three of them. One of their bullets had ignited the gasoline, and I had only a few seconds to pull myself out of the wreck before the car exploded. Once out, I ran like hell along the ditch and threw myself into a muddy patch of dirt just before the explosion. I looked like shit. Mud smeared my face and clothes, and blood poured from the gash in my head. As I reached the bodies, I noticed Ralph was about my size. His trousers were in good shape and his jacket was in his car. Unfortunately, I couldn't use his shirt due to the blood-stained bullet holes.

I needed to get as far away as possible before someone spotted the smoke and came along to investigate. It felt like an eternity, but I was able to dump the three bodies into the burning wreck and reignite it again with gas from a spare tank out of Ralph's car. I hit the road driving Ralph's car, wearing his slightly damaged tailored suit. I didn't like what had transpired, but if I didn't make their deaths look like an accident, there would be roadblocks set up in a few hours and, in my condition, I wouldn't make it through the first one.

* * * * *

Four days later, a little before midnight, I turned onto Market Street, parked a few buildings down, and slipped into the apartment building unseen. Rosalie, the barmaid, spotted me as I walked into the speakeasy. When she noticed my condition, she grabbed some medical supplies from behind the bar and helped me to my room.

"Joey, what happened? Are you hurt badly?"

"I think I have a few broken ribs."

She helped me out of the clothes, re-bandaged my head wound, and gently rubbed some ointment on my forearms, which had, according to her, second and possibly third degree burns. She wasn't repulsed when she saw my old scars and proceeded to tightly wrap my sides, which instantly made it less painful to breathe.

"It looks to me like you had quite an adventure. I'd hate to see the other guy," she said.

"Let's just say he's not feeling any pain."

"Your father told me you went looking for Ralph Ruffalo. Was he the one who took Anita?"

"No."

"Too bad."

"Thanks, Rosalie. How about not telling anyone I'm back? I'd like to sleep for a few days."

"I'll tell Martha to check on you when my shift starts

tomorrow. I'll bring up some food before I go home to-night. Good to have you back."

When I woke up the next day, practically everyone in the building was standing over me firing questions. Through the maze of bodies, I saw Pop notice bloodstains on the trousers that lay on the floor. He picked them up and quietly slipped out of the room. Knowing Pop, he headed for the furnace to get rid of any evidence of a crime.

August

I sat a few yards from the edge of Sgarlata's lake and stared at the skeletal remains of a hand clawing its way out of the water's surface. The developers made the gruesome discovery as they drained the lake. O'Reilly and Lieutenant Sullivan stood by their cars a few feet behind me, looking on with interest.

Gazing across the lake, their voices and the surrounding chaos gradually faded as I remembered the day my uncle and I visited Sgarlata's farm unannounced. I had run off in search of Anita, looking in all her favorite places. The tree house was empty; there was no sign of her at the beaver pond. I did, however, find some food outside the fox's den, but Anita was nowhere in sight. When I saw her clothes piled on a blanket by the fishing lake, I turned to leave. Dogpaddling, trying to stay afloat, she waved, encouraging me to join her. I had skinny dipped off the piers with the guys from my neighborhood almost daily during the hot, muggy days of August, but never with a girl around. She laughed at my dilemma and shouted that if I lived on a farm, I wouldn't be so embarrassed. Anita swam toward shore, giving me only two choices: jump in or run away, which was no choice at all if I didn't want to be teased for the next month. I took her challenge and jumped in fully clothed, undressed in the water, and threw my clothes ashore as the excitement of her girlish giggles skimmed across the surface. The softness of her touch, the tenderness of her moist lips on mine, and floating effortlessly together under the embrace of the warm sun are the memories of the lake and of Anita I will keep forever—not the gruesome scene now unfolding before me.

The coroner personally directed the assembled team, and under his watchful eye everyone took great care not to destroy any possible piece of evidence, almost as if they were at an archeological site of historic significance.

Once recovered, the skeletal structure, though small and fragile, seemed to be at the center of a powerful vortex that drew in all the surrounding sounds, light, and breathable air. As I rose to take a closer look, O'Reilly reached out and pulled me back. "Joey, best you remember Anita the way she was. There's no reason to go nearer."

I pulled away from his grasp and turned toward the lake as a second, much larger corpse emerged from the water's depths. The coroner came over and assured me the first body wasn't Anita's and that both were male skeletal remains. It would take weeks, maybe months, for the medical examiner to identify the bodies, but I knew who they were. Little Mo and Big Mo, the drifters who disap-peared shortly after Anita had vanished. The Ruffalo boys most likely killed them, thinking they had murdered Anita. The memory of their deaths drove Louie Ruffalo insane, and I hunted down and killed Ralph because I believed he'd killed Anita. I sat on the bank of the lake and wondered if I would ever put Anita to rest.

Returning late from Sgarlata's farm, O'Reilly and I went to my uncle's saloon to get some grub. O'Reilly tried to take my mind off Anita by filling me in on the gruesome details of the murders that paralyzed the residents of Staten Island and might possibly cost Sullivan his job. I was only half-listening to O'Reilly's mumblings when a crazy idea popped into my head.

"Did you ever ask Sullivan if any other young girls disappeared around the time Anita vanished?"

"What?"

"Did any other girls disappear?" I asked again.

"What's that got to do with today's murders?"

"A mass murderer just doesn't suddenly appear. Take Ralph Ruffalo. How did he end up becoming a button man? He tortured insects as a kid, then small animals, killed a couple of drifters, went to Chicago, and became a hit man. It took time to get a taste for killing."

"Are you saying whoever is terrorizing the Island also killed Anita?"

"I don't know, but it's possible. Maybe he killed a few girls and hid their bodies. Then the war came along and he enlisted. During the war he had the opportunity to kill as many people as he wanted, and not just the enemy. Who would ever know in the middle of a war if he killed and mutilated female civilians, and now he's back."

"If you ask me, you're crazy. It's just as likely Anita witnessed these two guys getting killed, got scared, ran away, and then something happened to her."

I didn't have to respond. He and I both knew Anita would have told her father if she witnessed a murder. "I'll give Sullivan a call in the morning," he said as Frank Galvano came striding into the bar and joined us.

"Joey, when are ya gonna tell us what happened in Chicago? You came back with mangled ribs, looking like hell, driving a different car, and you haven't uttered a word."

"There's not much to tell. I didn't find Ralph, but he found *me* as I drove back to New York. Thanks to the little present my uncle gave me before I left town, I survived and Ralph didn't. My car ended up in a ditch and caught fire. Since Ralph didn't need his anymore, I took it."

I wasn't in the mood for the third degree. "As far as I'm concerned, it's a dead issue, so let's leave it that way. How about giving us an update on Jackie's defense? Have you been able to link Al to Moralli? What about Jackie? How is she doing? Has she given you any useful information for her defense?"

"Nothing has changed for our side," Frank said. "I still don't have a clue how to get her out of this jam. The prosecution, on the other hand, has been digging deeper into her background. To make things worse, they developed a theory about a possible motive—you. They believe Al confronted Jackie about your relationship with her, and she killed him."

I couldn't help but crack a smile, thinking if things hadn't changed so drastically, they might be able to prove such a theory. "Have you talked to Bryson? Will he testify for Jackie?" I asked.

"He wants no part of the trial. He won't even see me."

"What about Shirley?"

"She's been great! That kid has guts, but there's no way to prove anything she says, especially with Moralli dead."

As Frank talked, I remembered a comment Shirley made when she first told me about her relationship with Al. "Have you checked out Al's apartment?"

"Joey, we did that together, remember?"

"I mean his other apartment, where he would meet Shirley."

Frank's jaw dropped.

"I guess Shirley didn't tell you everything."

* * * * *

Frank and I arrived early and waited outside the apartment building for Shirley, giving us time to discuss Jackie's defense.

"Let's say we prove a link between Moralli and Al.

How does that help Jackie?" Frank asked.

"It's another motive you can present to the jury for Al wanting Jackie out of his life. Al had hired Moralli to kill Jackie because he was worried someone would expose her past life in Chicago. Imagine what Al would do if he discovered she knew about his criminal connections.

"Okay, I'll buy that," Frank said, "but it clearly looked like she was the aggressor. I hope you realize what went on in this clandestine apartment doesn't help her case. A jealous wife is a strong motive for murder."

"If we can establish Al wasn't the saint everyone thinks, then you must prove to the jury that Jackie is an expert knife thrower. If she wanted to kill Al, he would have been dead after the first throw."

"And how am I supposed to prove that?

"Set up a demonstration."

"Give a defendant a stack of knives? You're nuts. There isn't a judge in the country who would allow a suspected murderer to handle a weapon in his courtroom."

Before I could respond, Shirley showed up, and the three of us entered the building. As I pushed open the door, an unpleasant odor of sweat intermingled with garlic wafted past us, emanating from the super, who leaned against his doorframe waiting for us to enter.

"Hey, doll, haven't seen you or your friend around lately. I was tempted to look for a new tenant."

"Listen, creep. I know the deal. The rent is paid up for a year in advance. My new friends and I are gonna spend some time together, and we don't want to be disturbed," Shirley said.

"Sure, doll, but I'm gonna have to up the rent if you're gonna use the place for more clients," he shouted as we reached the second-floor landing.

I took the key from Shirley's hand, but before I could

survey the room, the smell of cheap perfume filled my lungs, driving me back into the corridor. Shirley pushed her way past me, opened a window, then searched the bathroom for the source of the scent. She made it clear it wasn't hers when she poured the contents of an open bottle down the drain.

All the furnishings in the room paled in comparison to the bed: a small bureau, an old table with an oversized lamp, and two wooden side chairs. Clearly the room had one purpose. The only other space in the apartment was a small bathroom. I thought to myself, if Al had hidden anything in this dive, he'd have to be extremely clever.

As soon as the air cleared, Frank and I tore the place apart, searching for any written records Al may have hidden detailing the payments he made to city officials. We found a few loose floorboards, but they were impossible to lift without a crowbar. The windowsills were solid, and we didn't find anything in the bathroom. We dismantled the furniture and tore the bed apart, still nothing. By the time we finished, the place looked a wreck, and we were bushed. We took a break and sat on the floor against the wall under one of the windows.

"I can't believe Al didn't keep a record of all the payoffs he made just in case he needed to bribe someone or get protection," I said.

"The man wasn't stupid. We're just not clever enough to find it," Frank said.

"The mattress," Shirley said. "It has something inside. I know it does."

Frank and I gave each other a look. I can't say I knew for sure what he was thinking, but I couldn't get the story of the Princess and the Pea out of my head. I helped Shirley stand the mattress on its side, and we examined the seams. Sure enough, one side had a three-inch incision along the beaded edge, making it difficult to detect. I took my knife and widened the slit further and pulled out the fabric. Fifteen minutes later, the contents of the mattress littered the room. Shirley and I had fun making the mess, but in the end, the mattress was just a mattress.

I asked Shirley if she ever mentioned the condition of the mattress to Al. "That jerk just laughed it off and said it might be time for me to change professions if I had problems with lumpy mattresses."

Frank finally got off his butt, suggested we call it quits, and turned to Shirley. "If he hid anything in the mattress, he obviously moved it to a safer place. Did he ever mention any hobbies or places he liked to hang out?"

"No, we didn't spend time on small talk. Our relationship was strictly business and sex, mostly sex."

We cleaned the place the best we could and left. As I stopped to lock the apartment, Frank and Shirley went downstairs. I had trouble turning the key. I tried jiggling it, but the key still wouldn't budge. I went back inside and turned the doorknob a few times and tried again. That's when I noticed the door was solid sheet metal on the outside and oak paneling on the inside, which wasn't typical for this type of low-rent apartment. I went back in-side again and examined the paneling. After a few minutes I found a hidden mechanism under a piece of molding that flipped up. When I pushed on the metal latch, a small section of oak slid open, revealing a cavity. I sat motionless for a second, hoping I would find something, and then reached inside.

Downstairs Frank and Shirley were exchanging angry words with the super when I joined them. He apparently wanted more money, and Shirley was in the process of giving him a knee in a sensitive area when I pulled her back and paid the guy another ten bucks.

Walking away, Shirley turned her anger on me. "What the hell did you do that for? I've wanted to flatten that bum ever since I met him."

"We might need to come back, and we don't want him snooping around the apartment." At that point I handed Frank a small leather bound book.

"You found it! Where the hell was it hidden?

"I had trouble locking the door and noticed the inside of the door had wood paneling. Turns out it contained a hidden compartment."

"Why didn't I think of that? I sat there staring at the door when you guys tore into the mattress," Frank said.

"I don't understand. What made you look at the door?" Shirley asked.

"Beginner's luck, I guess." Turning toward Frank, I asked, "What's the name of the judge assigned to Jackie's case?"

"The Honorable Judge Andrew Harrington."

"That's what I thought. As you leaf through the pages, you'll find he's not so honorable. He was one of the judges taking money from Moralli. I don't think you'll have any problem convincing him to allow a small knife-throwing demonstration in his courtroom."

"I have all I need. This proves Al was crooked," Frank said with some satisfaction as he riffled through the pages.

On the way to Shirley's car, I realized the book was of little value. "Frank, you can't submit this list of payoffs as evidence in open court. Too many lives will get ruined, and we'll end up floating down the Hudson full of lead." Once he thought about it, Frank agreed.

We both turned to Shirley and asked her again if she would testify at Jackie's trial. She was understandably hesitant.

"If you're not going to use Al's records of payoffs as

evidence, how's my testimony gonna help?" she asked.

"We need to establish a link between Al and Moralli. The fact you worked for Moralli, and he routinely offered your services to Al, makes that connection," Frank said.

"I'm not so sure. If Al used other Can Houses around town, then the prosecution could argue Moralli was just another source of women to satisfy his sexual appetites. Remember, that cheap perfume didn't belong to me!" Shirley said.

Frank admitted she had a good point, and in my opinion, Shirley was more of a liability than an asset to our case. The prosecutor would tear her apart on the witness stand, given her background and sexual relationship with Al. I couldn't believe we had the evidence to prove Jackie's innocence and couldn't use it.

Our only hope now was Bryson. Somehow we had to get Bryson to testify that Al was blackmailing him.

There were still several hours of daylight left, so Frank and I traveled to the Island to pay Bryson a surprise visit. The butler apparently had orders to keep me out and tried every lie in the book. We finally pushed him aside and barged into Bryson's study, where we found him, ironically enough, reading the local paper with Jackie's picture plastered on the front page.

Bryson didn't react to our intrusion but immediately got to the point. "You're wasting your time. I'm not going to put my entire future and Rachel's at risk. There isn't anything you can say that will change my mind."

"How about if we call Rachel's real mother to the stand," I said.

"That would certainly change matters, but I took your sound advice and helped the poor family. In fact, I went so far as to relocate them to a different city," he said with a smirk.

"Bryson, you owe Jackie. We could've turned you into the authorities for hiding the death of your niece and defrauding the orphanage out of the inheritance. Is money that important to you?"

"Obviously it is or I wouldn't have fabricated such an elaborate scheme in the first place. But it's easy to make money if you know how and if you have cash to invest. What's really important is my reputation, and without that and Rachel's money, I would quickly become penniless. Not to mention, I would lose Rachel and her affection. The price you're asking me to pay is too high. I'm sorry, but I can't help you."

At that point the butler entered and politely asked us to leave before he called the police. We left without incident. I vowed somehow I'd get Bryson on the witness stand. Jackie's life depended on his testimony.

By the time we got back to the city, the nightlife was in full swing. I stopped by my uncle's place to get a few drinks to calm down after the visit with Bryson. Frank declined to join me and went to his office to continue his preparations for the trial.

I spotted Lieutenant Sullivan huddled in a corner with O'Reilly. Whatever they were discussing must have been important for him to come all this way, especially with the local press watching his every move. When they saw me, O'Reilly motioned for me to join them.

"Sullivan followed up on your hunch and uncovered some interesting new facts," O'Reilly said.

At first I didn't know what he was talking about, but then remembered the day I suggested there might be other girls who had vanished prior to Anita's disappearance.

"I went back through some old newspapers around the time of Anita's case and discovered another girl had vanished from a different part of the Island," Sullivan said.

"Why the hell didn't you know this back then?"

"Keep your voice down," O'Reilly said as he grabbed my arm and pulled me back into my seat.

"There are three different precincts on the Island, and there's little communication between us. Just the way it is," Sullivan said.

"That's not all," O'Reilly went on to say. "Five months prior to that disappearance, a young girl's body turned up in a wooded area of Tottenville, hidden in a ravine. She was mutilated like today's victims."

"I don't know how you did it, but your hunch appears to be holding up. This is the break I've been looking for," Sullivan said.

"I want in on the investigation."

"I can't do that officially, but I'll be giving O'Reilly the new case files for a few days and continue to meet with him periodically to review our progress."

"What are you going to do differently?" I asked.

"We're putting an Island-wide investigative team together to look for any connections and leads from the old cases."

"That'll just drive this guy underground if he thinks you're getting close. My guess is he entered the service sometime around 1917 to get off the Island because things were heating up back then."

"I realize that, but I need to stop these killings. We had another one last night. It should hit the papers tomorrow. I need to create some breathing space to at least uncover some suspects. Right now I have nothing. If we can figure out his identity, we can always track him down."

Sullivan handed over the two new case files to O'Reilly, who placed them on the table and shoved them toward me as they walked out.

I studied the files during the night and then dumped

them on Martha's desk in the morning.

"What's all this?" she bellowed.

"A new assignment. Look for any leads or connections between the current murders on the Island and these two older cases. I also need a list of Staten Island residents who received dishonorable discharges from the military and make sure you know why."

"What for?"

"Anita. I'll explain later." I couldn't allow myself to get sidetracked. "Jackie's trial is about to begin, and Frank still needs my help. Right now I have to find a way to get Bryson to testify for Jackie."

"Good luck. If you ask me, he's sounds like a real creep. I think you're underestimating him, but you're the boss."

* * * * *

According to Bryson, he had two reasons for not testifying at Jackie's trial: hiding the truth from Rachel and protecting his reputation. I figure I could leverage both concerns if I could find Stanley, the kid with the wire bracelet, and his family before the trial began. I could then threaten to put Rachel's real mom on the stand, giving Bryson no option but to testify. At that point it would be up to Bryson to find a logical explanation as to why he gave in to Al's blackmail threats.

I returned to the Bowery, and as expected, the family's hovel was empty. I tried to talk with a few of the folks in the area, but when I approached, they faded into their own dilapidated sanctuaries. I couldn't blame them. If I lived in such poverty, I'd be leery of strangers as well. I returned to Stanley's place again and rummaged around the rooms, hoping to find some clues to their whereabouts. All I found were some soiled clothes and Stanley's old newspapers scattered around his mattress, which struck me as odd. The first time I saw his papers, they were neatly stacked in the corner, as if they were his most prized possessions. A few of the papers actually had ripped pages; someone had torn out some pictures. It was too dark to read, so I took a couple of the papers outside. As I emerged from Stanley's dungeon, I ran into a slew of kids nearby playing Johnny-Ride-a-Pony. I guess kids are more trusting than their parents, because they freely answered my questions.

"They left in a taxi, a few days ago, all duded up. You shoulda seen them, they looked like rich folk," one of them said.

One kid pointed to the papers I held. "Stanley kept on showin' us pictures. He can't talk, so none of us understood why he was so excited. They were just some big old buildings, nothin' like I've ever seen."

"One of his sisters said they were gonna see the President. I told her she was crazy. Why would the President wanna see them?"

"They left late in the mornin'," another kid added.

When I rushed away, they were still talking about Stanley and his family and forgot all about playing their game.

I made it to Grand Central Station in time to catch the late morning train to Washington DC. It didn't take long to find a conductor who remembered helping a lady with a pack of kids.

"I'm telling ya, mister, they were all over the place. Strangest thing I ever saw. They sure looked like they had money, but they didn't act like it. One kid couldn't talk, and the others I'm sure couldn't read. The mother looked real uncomfortable, ya know, kinda nervous."

"Do you know where they went after they got to DC?"

"Sure do. She wanted directions to the Brenton Hotel. Could you imagine that? She was gonna walk, to one of the ritziest hotels in town, so she could save money, and with all them kids in tow. As it turned out, when they got off the train, a chauffeur came over. She didn't even know what he wanted and was afraid to go with him. I had to explain what his job was. Strangest thing I ever saw," he said again as he walked away, shaking his head.

I went straight to the hotel from the train station and found the whole family sitting in a hotel room not knowing what to do, too afraid to touch anything or even leave the room. Bryson had booked the hotel, probably until he could locate a suitable place for them to live, but no one had explained this to her. When I assured her she would still receive the monthly income he promised, she jumped at the chance to return home. Within hours we were all on the next train back to New York. By midnight, I had the mother and her whole brood settled at an apartment in Tony the Butcher's building.

A few days before the trial, Frank and I had our last meeting with Jackie We had a solid defense strategy, but it all hinged on her knife-throwing skills and discrediting Al.

"Joey tells me you're deadly accurate when it comes to throwing knives, kitchen knives. I want to hear it from you. How good are you?" Frank asked.

"I don't miss! Can *you* throw a carving knife from ten to fifteen feet and have it stick in a wall?" Jackie asked.

Frank looked at me, then back at Jackie. "You know, I never thought about it that way, and I would have to say it would be nearly impossible. Kitchen knives aren't made for throwing."

"That's right, and not a single knife I threw landed on the floor. Like I said, I don't miss."

"I'm going to take a chance and put you on the witness

stand to tell the jury exactly what happened that night. Then I'll ask you to demonstrate your skills."

"How can I do that in a courtroom?"

"Let me worry about the details. But I'm curious, what made you decide to practice knife throwing?" he asked.

"The warehouse where we hung out was an abandoned kitchen supply storage facility, and one day I found an old crate of knives."

Jackie explained how she got so proficient, describing some of the ways she practiced when she had time to kill, waiting in the warehouse for Sal and the gang to return from a job. As she continued talking, Frank couldn't sit still; he liked what he heard.

Two days later, Jackie's trial commenced amidst a news frenzy. The prosecution had a field day with Jackie's background, playing to the spectators' anger, which had risen almost to a mob mentality. He painted her as a Mafia whore, a Jezebel living a life of crime and debauchery. He then went on to describe Sal Santangelo's rise within the criminal world and highlighted the atrocities he performed during his career. Frank objected at every opportunity, but the impression that Jackie participated in Santangelo's life of crime was already set in the jurors' minds. By the end of the first day, the papers had her convicted and on the way to death row.

The next day, as the jury entered the courtroom, they had to walk by photographs of the crime scene, strategically placed for maximum effect. An enlarged picture of a carving knife embedded deep in one wall had a visible effect on the jurors. As other pictures circulated around the jury box, the jurors stared over at Jackie, probably envisioning her chasing Al around their apartment as he scrambled for his life. The prosecutor saved the most dramatic and damaging images for last. Holding up a picture of

Jackie covered in Al's blood, he slowly walked along the jury box, describing in minute detail a depiction of what took place in Al's home—a home where a man expects to be safe and greeted by a loving wife after coming home from a hard day of work. The prosecutor ended his dramatic, spellbinding narrative by passing around a final picture of Al splattered on the concrete outside his apartment. As the photograph silently made its way from juror to juror, he sat back down at his table without saying a word, so all could hear the emotional gasps emanating from the jury.

Frank cross-examined every one of the prosecution's witnesses and skillfully dismantled the theory Jackie killed her husband because of a love affair with me.

"Jonathan, you don't mind if I call you by your first name do you?"

"No sir."

"To remind the jury, you are the doorman for the Forsythe apartment building. Is that correct?"

"Yes sir."

"You stated to the police officer investigating this unfortunate accident everything seemed proper in the Forsythe marriage until Mr. Batista came into the picture. Is that correct?"

"Yes sir."

"Could you please tell the jury how you came to this conclusion?"

"Well, sir, as I told the police, Mr. Batista visited Mrs. Forsythe several times when Mr. Forsythe wasn't home."

"I see, so it was unusual for Mrs. Forsythe to have gentlemen visitors."

"Yes sir."

"To be honest, Jonathan, I'm not sure I believe you. The prosecutor has painted a picture of Mrs. Forsythe being a common whore and a Jezebel. She must have had many male suitors."

"No sir. Up until recently she was a very respectable lady."

"Until Mr. Batista you mean?"

"Yes sir."

"Did you know Mr. Batista is a private investigator, and he was working for the Forsythe's?"

"No sir, not at first."

"The first time you met Mr. Batista, did he ask you questions about Mrs. Forsythe and about the security at your building?"

"Yes sir."

"Jonathan, you can answer my questions with a little more detail."

"Yes sir. He wanted to know if Mrs. Forsythe had many male visitors and if I was aware they had recently been robbed."

"Did Mr. Batista ever stay the night?"

"No sir."

"Did he stay more than say three hours?"

"No sir. His visits were short."

"Short relative to what? Didn't you tell Mr. Batista that other women in the apartment building had frequent visitors and Mrs. Forsythe was the exception? So am I to assume that relative to other gentlemen callers at your establishment, Mr. Batista's visits were brief?"

"Yes sir."

Frank turned to the judge and then to the jury. "No more questions. I'm sorry, Your Honor, I do have one more. Jonathan, you stated just prior to Al Forsythe's unfortunate tumble off the balcony, you heard a scream. Is that correct?"

"Yes."

Frank turned his back to the witness stand and asked his

final question before sitting down. "In your opinion, was it a male or female who screamed?"

Jonathan leaned back against his chair and briefly closed his eyes. "It was a woman's scream. Yes, I'm quite sure. It was a long, high, shrill, desperate sound."

* * * * *

On Monday morning, Frank would have his turn to present Jackie's defense. Up until then the residents of the city viewed Al as a man of the people: editor-and-chief of one of the city's largest newspapers, a recently endorsed Democratic candidate for mayor, and a devoted, loving husband. It was Frank's job to vilify Al and convince the jury Jackie had scrambled for her life in their apartment and his death was a result of his own actions.

Sunday night Frank and I reviewed our preparations for Jackie's defense, and the only serious gap we had identified was how to discreetly introduce the judge to Al's little book that listed payoffs to half the city officials in town hall.

"I don't know," Frank said. "I can't see the judge without a representative of the DA's office present, and I can't enter it into evidence without first turning a copy over to the DA. If I do either, we've lost any leverage over the judge to allow a demonstration of Jackie's knife-throwing abilities."

Before I could respond, Uncle Luigi came up with a solution. "You know what your problem is? You're not devious enough. It's simple; it's all in how you present the information to him."

He proceeded to give us both a lesson in how to force a judge to do your bidding in open court when you had some dirt on him. It seemed to both Frank and me that Luigi's suggestion might work, so we moved on to a more sensitive issue, Shirley. We needed her testimony if we couldn't get

Bryson to testify.

"If I had any other way to make a connection between Al and Moralli, I'd use it. Besides Bryson, Shirley's our only link," Frank said.

"We have no guarantee the jury will believe her," I said. "She's a reformed drug-addicted prostitute and if the prosecutor gets wind of the fact Moralli also corrupted her sister, her testimony's useless. I say we stick to the original plan and call Bryson to the stand."

Up to this point, O'Reilly sat quietly nursing a beer. "I didn't know you weren't going to use Shirley's testimony. Won't that hurt your chances?"

"I can't take the risk," Frank said.

"I have to get back on duty. I'll catch you later, Frank. Maybe I can help."

Frank moved to follow O'Reilly, and I pulled him back into his seat. "Frank, I'll follow up with him. It just might be the booze talking. Let's stay focused on getting ready for Monday."

* * * * *

No one expected much of a defense from Frank because all the evidence indicated Jackie was the aggressor and not Al. Judge Harrington called the court to order and instructed Frank Galvano to call his first witness.

Frank called Sister Mary Magdalene Meade to the witness stand.

"Sister, would you please tell this court about your relationship with the defendant."

"I met Jacqueline about five years ago when she first arrived in the city. She came to us seeking shelter at our orphanage until she could find suitable living accommodations."

"Didn't you find that a little odd since she was a young lady at the time?"

"Not at all. After Jacqueline explained her circumstances, we felt it perfectly acceptable for us to help someone who lived most of her life on the streets without parental supervision. She was alone and unfamiliar with our city, and needed time to find a job."

"How long did she stay at the orphanage?"

"About a month. She secured a position at a newspaper and moved into a small apartment close to her work."

"Was that the last time you saw Mrs. Forsythe?"

"My goodness, no. She's been coming to the orphanage at least twice a month on a regular basis. She's quite good with the older children. She relates well with them and has helped many through some difficult times."

"Has she contributed money to your orphanage?"

"Oh, yes. She has been most generous, especially since she married Mr. Forsythe."

"Your answer seems to imply that she also made contributions before her marriage."

"That's correct. She gave us a portion of her paycheck as soon as she found employment. She has been a great benefactor and an inspiration to many of our young ladies."

"I believe the prosecutor has painted Mrs. Forsythe as a common whore, someone who associates with the criminal element. Does this describe the young woman you know?"

"Mr. Galvano, I have taken many children in off the streets, and they all have one thing in common: an uncanny ability to survive. That doesn't make them criminals or wicked. They are resourceful, use whatever they have, take advantage of every opportunity that comes along. You shouldn't judge these children by what they were, but by what they've become."

"I'm afraid you didn't answer my question. Does the description of Jacqueline Forsythe presented by the prosecutor accurately describe, in your opinion, Mrs. Forsythe?"

"No, it most certainly does not! We never ask our children about their past. We are more concerned about their future."

"Thank you, Sister. I have no more questions."

The prosecutor tried to get Sister Mary Magdalene to tell what she did know of Jackie's past, but she didn't have any additional information of importance for the prosecutor.

Frank called Charles Bryson as his next witness. "Mr. Bryson, before we begin I must tell the court that recently your niece, Rachel, whom you've raised since your sister's untimely death thirteen years ago, was recently kidnapped. Is that correct?"

"Yes."

The prosecutor objected but the judge overruled his objection when Frank explained proving Jackie's innocence hinged on this fact. During this exchange I made a point of getting Bryson's attention as I walked to the back of the courtroom where I stood next to the entrance.

"Would you please tell the court, Mr. Bryson, about your relationship with Al Forsythe?" Frank continued.

"Al and I grew up together in the same neighborhood and have stayed in close contact."

"I understand you've been making significant contributions to his future campaign for mayor."

"Yes, I have," he said, with some hesitation as we made eye contact.

Frank turned his back toward Bryson and gave me a hand signal. I opened the door to the courtroom, and a rush of children entered, scampering toward the front of the room and sat behind Jackie. I then escorted Rachel's real mother to an aisle seat next to her children. Bryson clearly got the message that we were prepared to call her as a witness if necessary.

"Over the last several years, he's been blackmailing me for large sums of money," Bryson continued.

The courtroom erupted into chaos. Reporters scrambled over each other to get pictures of Bryson, and others raced to the phones outside the courtroom to report this breaking story for their evening editions. Judge Harrington pounded his gavel to no avail and had to call a brief recess to regain control of the proceedings. He ordered both attorneys to the bench and severely reprimanded Frank for staging such theatrics.

"Sorry, Your Honor, but this information just recently became known to the defense."

"Do you have any evidence of this wild accusation besides Mr. Bryson's word?" the judge asked.

"Naturally it's difficult to collaborate since Mr. Forsythe is dead; however, Joey Batista, my private investigator working this case, has obtained Mr. Bryson's bank records and those of Al Forsythe. I intended to enter them into evidence before you called a recess. As you can see, there is a strong relationship between the two bank statements going back many years. Bryson makes a withdrawal, and Al Forsythe makes a deposit."

The judge studied the records and agreed to enter them into evidence. "I will not tolerate any more theatrics from either side. Do I make myself clear?"

At that moment the judge provided Frank with the opportunity he needed to put Luigi's suggestion into play and introduce Al's records of payoffs to government officials. "Your Honor, I do have another item that I believe will go a long way in proving my client's innocence. However, the details are so damaging to many lives I would like you to rule on its admissibility before I introduce it in open court."

The prosecutor objected and insisted on seeing the evidence as well.

"I will make the decision about what is or isn't appropriate in my courtroom and not you, counselor."

Either the judge had reached the limit of his patience, or he suspected what Frank was about to reveal.

Frank walked back to his table, picked up a duplicate of Al's book with one huge exception, and handed it to the judge. The color drained from the judge's face as he flipped through the pages.

"This is indeed highly damaging information that I can't allow you to enter as evidence without clear and independent supporting documentation."

"I tend to agree, Your Honor, but you must see how the contents of this book would help clear my client of any wrongdoing in the death of her husband. I believe, however, I can still prove her innocence without this vital evidence if Your Honor would permit a demonstration of my client's proficiency in knife throwing."

The prosecutor insisted he be able to cross-examine Jackie if the judge approved such an unusual request.

"If you agree to the demonstration, Judge, I will call the defendant as a witness on her own behalf," Frank stated.

The prosecutor turned to Frank and smugly told him he had just made a mistake and walked back to his team beaming. Frank didn't react and waited for him to turn away before reaching for the notebook he had asked the judge to review. The judge moved with lightning speed, grabbed the book, and quietly slipped it under his robes. Frank simply smiled at the judge and returned to his seat.

After recess, the trial resumed with Bryson back on the witness stand.

"Mr. Bryson, are you willing to tell this court what secret Mr. Forsythe threatened to divulge if you didn't meet his demands?" Frank asked.

"No, I'm not, but I will say it's something that occurred many years ago, and I foolishly believed if the details were revealed, my reputation and my investment business would suffer."

"Fair enough. Would you then tell us what happened recently between you and Mr. Forsythe?"

"He asked for an increased sum of money to finance his run for mayor. Just prior to this happening, I experienced a significant loss in my business holdings and could not meet his demands."

"What did Mr. Forsythe say when you refused to pay?"

"Al became furious and threatened to humiliate me in his newspaper. It was shortly after that my niece was kidnapped."

"Do you believe there is a relationship between your inability to pay and the disappearance of your niece?"

"Al was fully aware of my sister's will and understood if my niece died before age twenty-five, I would inherit the full estate."

"Are you implying Al Forsythe had your niece kidnapped and planned to murder her so you could continue making payments?"

"Yes, that is now my belief!"

Before the courtroom broke into bedlam again, the judge cancelled the hearing for the day and left the bench.

* * * * *

Frank joined my family for dinner that night. "I wish

you were there, Luigi, to see the judge's face when he opened the notebook. I thought he was going to drop dead when he realized what he was looking at. As you suggested, the only entries were the dates and amounts he received from Moralli. Stroke of genius, that's all I'm gonna say. Remind me never to match wits with you; you're too damn good," Frank said.

"Don't get too cocky. The trial's not over," Luigi said.

Frank and I gave each other a quick look. "Uncle, it sounds like you spent some time in court."

"More than I would like to admit. Ain't that right, Vito?"

Pop kept his head down and kept on eating. It felt like a good time to change the subject, so I asked Rosalie how she liked her new job running the shoe store. Pop had hired her to replace Sally.

"I wish Sally spent more time training me how to deal with salesmen. They seem more interested in getting a date than selling shoes."

"Just call me and I'll set 'em straight," Ma said.

"They'll get down to business when they see Ma standing there with her arms folded, holding a frying pan," Luigi said with a contagious, hearty laugh.

I tried to get Pop engaged in the conversation. "Pop, how's the repair business goin? Looks like you're pretty busy."

"Busy? I'm thinking of hiring some kid just to clean the shoes so I can work on them. You wouldn't believe the dirt and crap all over some of them. You'd think people would have more pride. And let me tell you somethin', these fancy shoes are damn hard to get clean, with all them eyelets and such."

His comments reminded me of the first time I met Bryson. I told the story how the butler insisted I remove my shoes before entering the house so he could clean them. Everyone got a good laugh when I described my discomfort standing in my stockings, trying to sound like a professional investigator. In mid-sentence I stopped my narrative, dashed out of the dining area to the kitchen, and called police headquarters, trying to find O'Reilly. After five minutes of confusion, O'Reilly came on the line and I explained what I needed. He wasn't happy.

"I know it's late, O'Reilly. I have the key, and Jackie gave us permission to search her apartment."

"You want everything before the trial resumes tomorrow. That means the boys will have to work through the night. That's asking a lot," O'Reilly said.

"Jackie's life's at stake. Call in some favors."

"Okay, but I hope you're onto something, or I'm gonna be in a lot of people's debt for a long time."

"Thanks. I'll see you in court tomorrow, and get there early so you and Frank can go over what you found."

* * * * *

"Mr. Bryson, yesterday you ended your testimony with a serious accusation. Could you tell us once again why you believe Al Forsythe had your niece kidnapped?" Frank asked as the trial continued.

The courtroom felt like the walls were closing in as everyone strained to hear his response. "First, let me tell you my niece has recently been returned to me thanks to the work of Joey Batista and Jacqueline Forsythe, the defendant."

This time Judge Harrington maintained control of the courtroom and Bryson continued. "On the advice of Jacqueline, I hired Mr. Batista to find my niece. It's my understanding he found her in the clutches of a gangster known as

Moralli, who had every intention of killing her. Considering the fact that Moralli never asked for ransom money and Al Forsythe was the only person aside from myself who would benefit from her death, I can only conclude he paid Moralli to kill my niece."

The prosecutor objected on the grounds of hearsay and pure speculation, and the judge upheld his objection.

After a brief cross-examination by the prosecutor, Frank called his next witness, me.

"Mr. Batista, would you explain to the jury how you and the defendant happened to find Mr. Bryson's niece."

"Believing Moralli might be involved in the murder of my close friend, I paid him a late night visit. Purely by chance I found Bryson's niece in Moralli's room, drugged and in poor physical condition. After questioning Moralli, he admitted someone hired him to eliminate the girl."

The jury leaned forward again, showing visible signs of disgust after hearing my testimony.

"Did Moralli say who hired him?" Frank asked.

"No."

"Can you explain to the court how the defendant assisted you in this dangerous mission?"

"Moralli's place can only be described as an armed fortress. I needed someone to distract his bodyguards so I could enter his room from his bedroom window without detection. Since Jackie and I were working on the Bryson case, I asked for her assistance. She agreed, so I lent her a stiletto and a gun for her protection."

"I would point out, Judge, that both Al and Jacqueline Forsythe had permits to carry a concealed gun due to their high profile in the community and the aggressive editorials they often wrote about crime in the city. This also explains why the defendant had both a stiletto and a gun on her person on the night her husband accidentally fell over the balcony of their apartment," Frank stated.

"Mr. Batista, once you found the girl, what happened next?"

"We got her out of there and to a special clinic on Staten Island. We didn't immediately notify Mr. Bryson because we suspected he might be involved in her abduction."

"Since then you received evidence that convinced you he had no part in the kidnapping. Is that correct?"

"Yes, I confided in Sergeant O'Reilly, a local homicide detective I consult with on some of my more difficult cases, and a short time later, he made a connection between the information I shared and some activities he witnessed at Moralli's hangout."

Frank Galvano called O'Reilly to the stand and as I walked back to my seat, the prosecutor slowly sunk lower in his chair.

"Sergeant O'Reilly, I understand you and some of your men kept Moralli under surveillance for a period of time. Could you explain why?"

"As Mr. Batista mentioned, we suspected Moralli or members of his gang were involved in the torture and death of a close friend."

"Isn't it unusual for you to be conducting an investigation outside the boundaries of your precinct?"

"Yes. I didn't, however, have sufficient proof to warrant an official investigation. If I did, I certainly would have gone through proper channels."

"After Mr. Batista informed you that he and the defendant rescued the Bryson girl from certain death, you recalled seeing a strange incident outside of Moralli's establishment involving Mr. Forsythe, is that correct?"

"Yes."

"Would you please elaborate?"

O'Reilly read from his notes and gave details of what he

had observed on the same night someone kidnapped the Bryson girl. O'Reilly stated he now believes he witnessed Al Forsythe delivering Rachel to Moralli in a drugged state.

Before the prosecutor could object, Frank asked the most critical question of the entire trial, and we both kept our fingers crossed that O'Reilly and his team of investigators found the evidence needed to place Al at the crime scene on the night of the kidnapping.

"Sergeant, your testimony appears to be pure speculation. Do you have any proof to back up your allegations?"

"With the permission of the defendant, we recently searched the Forsythe apartment and found several mud samples in Mr. Forsythe's closet and compared the composition of the dirt with that on the Bryson estate, where deep footprints were found outside the kidnapped girl's window. The analysis of the dirt matched exactly, even down to a unique blend of fertilizer used by the gardener. In addition, the imprints found at the scene matched a pair of Mr. Forsythe's shoes found at his apartment."

"Nice piece of detective work, Sergeant," Frank said as he entered the shoes into evidence.

O'Reilly looked straight at me and said thanks in response.

During the cross-examination, the prosecutor's line of questioning brought out even more damaging testimony against Al. I suspect Frank left this obvious area for questioning out of O'Reilly's testimony on purpose. My opinion of Frank as a trial lawyer went up a notch every time I saw him in action.

"Sergeant, I agree with my colleague. It appears on the surface you have proven Al Forsythe kidnapped the young girl in question," the prosecutor said. "Isn't it true, however, Mr. Forsythe often visited the Bryson estate, and he could have muddied his shoes on a number of occasions?"

"That's certainly possible, but not likely for two reasons. The butler doesn't allow anyone to enter the home with muddy shoes and has them removed and cleaned before guests leave. More importantly, the footsteps lead-ing away from the girl's bedroom window were much deeper than those approaching the window. This is because the kidnapper carried the girl, and the additional weight depressed his shoes deeper into the mud," O'Reilly said.

"How does that prove anything? The shoes placed in evidence look perfectly clean."

"If you look closely," continued O'Reilly as he held up one of the shoes, "there is a faint stain line on Mr. Forsythe's shoes about an inch and a quarter up the side, matching the depth of the imprints found at the scene. It's even more visible under ultraviolet light. The mud samples were underneath the eyelets, where most people fail to clean."

The prosecutor had no further questions.

Frank called his last witness, Jackie, and waited for the flashbulbs to subside before requesting a recess in order to set up his planned demonstration in the courtroom.

* * * * *

"Mrs. Forsythe, will you please tell the jury why you associated with a known Mafia boss when you were younger?" Frank asked, to the surprise of everyone.

"I didn't. Sal Santangelo just happened to be older than the rest of us street orphans, and he became our leader and protector. We had no place to live, and he found us shelter in an abandoned warehouse."

"How can that be? The prosecutor has painted Sal Santangelo as a hardened criminal, associated with the Chicago Mafia, and you as his personal whore."

"I left Chicago long before Sal became connected to the mob, and the prosecutor should know that fact, and to set the record straight, I was his girlfriend and not his whore. I believe there is a difference," Jackie said, looking straight at the jury.

"I see. Well, we shouldn't be too hard on the prosecutor. We all make honest mistakes. I'm sure he didn't intend to mislead the jury. I understand you stayed at an apartment located in Mr. Batista's building for a few days prior to the unfortunate death of your husband. Why didn't you go home during that time?"

"As Mr. Bryson mentioned, he told us he suspected my husband was somehow connected to the disappearance of his niece. I found his accusation disturbing and chose to stay away until I could decide what to do," Jackie responded.

"Did you finally go home to kill him?"

"No, I wanted to know the truth."

"Tell us what happened when you arrived home."

"Al went into a rage when he found me in the apartment, pulled out his gun, and said I was the only obstacle standing between him and the mayor's office. I tried to reason with him, but he kept backing me toward the balcony. That's when I realized what he planned to do."

"And what was that?"

"Throw me over the balcony to make my death look like a suicide."

"What happened next?"

"I still had the stiletto and gun Mr. Batista had given me, and as Al and I struggled, I raked the knife across the back of his hand. When his gun fell to the floor, I reached for mine, but he knocked it away as we fought. During the struggle Al's hand bled profusely, which is why I had his blood on my clothes and arms. I also received a small cut."

"Then what happened?"

"I ran into the kitchen and grabbed the kitchen knives. As my husband continued to come toward me, I tried to move him back by throwing the knives."

"Why didn't that stop him?"

"He knew I wouldn't kill him."

"Please continue."

"I finally had no place to go, so I ran onto the balcony and screamed. Al came charging toward me, and as he reached out, I dropped to the ground. His weight carried him over the railing. There wasn't anything I could do to save him, it happened so fast."

"I'm sorry to make you relive that night over again, but it's important the jury realize you were the one attacked."

Frank walked over to the prosecutor's table, slowly shook his head, strolled in front of the jury box, and looked each juror in the eye before asking if they believed her story. "I wouldn't!" he shouted. "Remember the pictures you saw of all those knives sticking in the walls, the blood, the overturned furniture, clearly the defendant tried to kill her husband. With each throw of a knife, Al Forsythe desperately tried to get away."

Frank turned toward Jackie. "Isn't that right, Mrs. Forsythe? Isn't that what the prosecutor wants this jury to believe?"

"Mr. Galvano, if I wanted to kill my husband, he would have died from a knife wound," Jackie said with complete confidence.

Frank once again turned toward the jury. "Did you hear that?" Do you believe her? Let's put her to the test." He strode over to a white sheet hanging from the ceiling and pulled it down, revealing a board with a circle drawn in the center. Once again the reporters scurried to get pictures.

The judge threatened to empty the courtroom and confiscate all the cameras if a similar outburst occurred again.

Frank invited members of the prosecution team to hit the bull's-eye and then some of the police officers in the courtroom. No one could get a knife to stick into the board, which was constructed of the same material as the apartment walls.

"Mrs. Forsythe, would you please demonstrate to the jury your skill with these kitchen knives? Before you touch a knife, I must warn you the judge has ordered the court security officer to shoot if you do anything other than attempt to hit the target."

As soon as the security guard placed a knife on the table, Jackie picked it up so quickly I don't believe anyone actually saw her throw it. The courtroom fell silent as the knife quivered dead center in the circle.

"Now, Mrs. Forsythe, the bailiff will release three apples tied to strings at different speeds. The apples are spaced one foot apart. I want you to slice the last apple and then the first. With the third knife, I would like you to cut the string of the remaining apple."

Once again, the knives vanished. Half of the two end apples fell to the floor, but the third apple hung from its string, silently swinging back and forth. A slight sound of triumph escaped from the prosecutor's lips just before a thin thread of the string holding the apple snapped. The prosecutor stood and asked the judge if his cross-examination could proceed in the morning.

* * * * *

That night my uncle's place overflowed with customers who wanted to get a look at Frank. Word was spreading that he might get Jackie off.

"You sure had me fooled. For a moment I thought you were going to convict your own client. How the hell did she learn to throw a knife with such accuracy?" my uncle asked.

I pulled Luigi aside and told him about Jackie's early years in Chicago.

"Let me tell you something, that one is as deadly as a black widow spider. Maybe worse," Luigi said. I couldn't disagree as the drinks continued to flow.

* * * * *

The following day the prosecutor had his last chance to win a conviction. It was the fifteenth round, and he was behind on points and he knew it. He came out swinging.

"Did you kill your lover, Sal Santangelo?"

"I'm sorry, I don't understand the question," Jackie responded.

"Oh, I think you understand. Did you kill Santangelo? He died of a knife wound to his heart."

"Are you saying I'm the only person who knows how to handle a knife? Maybe if you had conducted a proper investigation, you would have known I volunteered at the orphanage the day he died."

"If your husband tried to kill you, as you say, why didn't you just shoot him? You had a gun."

"My husband obviously was out of his mind, and I still loved him."

"Did you sleep with Joey Batista? Is that why you killed your husband, so you could be with your new lover?"

"Have we been listening to the same trial? Joey Batista and I worked together to find the Bryson girl, and we saved her life. And no, we never slept together."

"When you were with Sal Santangelo, did you ever commit a crime?"

Frank immediately protested. The judge instructed

Jackie that she didn't have to answer the question if it would incriminate her in a crime.

Jackie ignored the judge's warning, looked aggressively at the prosecutor, and answered, "Yes, I did."

"Finally an honest answer," shouted the prosecutor. "What crime did you commit?"

"I stole."

"What did you steal?"

"Books."

"Why would you steal books?"

"So I could teach myself to read and write. I knew if I was ever going to get away from Sal Santangelo and have a better life, I needed to be educated."

The next day the verdict came back. Not guilty. The jury declared Al's death an accident.

* * * * *

After the trial, Frank and I collected the ten-thousand Bryson owed me for finding Rachel, and we made arrangements to settle Al's estate on behalf of Jackie. In the meantime, Jackie lived in the apartment she had used at my uncle's.

Jackie spent considerable time at the orphanage talking to Sister Mary Magdalene, trying to figure out what to do with her life. A few times Jackie mentioned she might enter the convent, but thankfully that idea didn't last long. I knew what I wanted her to do, but didn't know if it would work. I couldn't rely on O'Reilly's advice because he has a definite bias against all women, so I turned to my uncle.

"I'm gonna say this once, kid, so listen good. If you let that woman get away, you're a fool."

Ma had a different take. "I don't know, Joey. You need to think. What about Martha? Will she be jealous? I know you two have something goin' on."

Pop took a straightforward approach. "Ask her. If she says she's not interested, you don't need to worry about other dames. If she says yes, let her work things out."

A few days later, Jackie and I went for a walk along the waterfront just before sunset. I had a sense she wanted to tell me something, and I was afraid if I didn't act, I'd never get another chance. "Jackie, I know you've been through a lot, and you're thinking about the future." Before I could say any more, she put her arms around my neck and we kissed for a long time.

"I never got a chance to properly thank you for sticking by me. I know the thought probably crossed your mind that I killed Al. If not for you and Frank, I'd be sitting in a cell," she said.

"We don't want to think about that. You should think about your future. I would like you to join me in my business. I know it's not much, but it's a good living, and it's not dull."

"A full partner?" she asked.

"Full partner."

"What about Martha? Is she the jealous type?"

"I don't think so."

"Let's go find out."

"Does that mean yes?"

"I don't know what took you so long. If you didn't pop the question soon, I planned on moving a desk into your office."

Martha had made written copies of all the important facts from the case files of the missing or murdered girls from Staten Island and had them spread out on the floor, along with her notes on each case. She didn't hear us enter the room.

"Sorry if we startled you, but I wanted you to be first to

know Jackie has accepted a full partnership in our business."

To Jackie's surprise, Martha ran over and gave her a big hug. "God, I'm so happy. Now I don't need to pass that stupid PI test."

"But you still need a gun permit," I said.

"You don't sound surprised. I thought you might be concerned," Jackie said.

"Joey and I already talked about it and I agreed. We're getting more potential clients calling every day, and I have to turn them down because he's so busy. As long as we keep our personal lives out of the office, I'm fine. Besides, I'm looking for a man to settle down with, and Joey's made it clear he's a long way from having such thoughts. Just so you know, Joey and I are good friends, and until I do find someone who wants to settle down, I want it to stay that way."

"I hope you find someone soon," Jackie said as she grabbed hold of my arm.

Martha came over, grabbed the other arm, and said she wasn't in a big hurry. I suddenly had a bad feeling in my gut, even though I was living every guy's fantasy.

I felt the need to say something to regain control of my life, but before I could react, Frank Galvano came into the office and asked for a favor.

"Why do I get the feeling I'm interrupting something interesting?" he said.

The girls dropped my arms and leaned against Martha's desk, looking like two sultry sirens.

"Remember when I told you I had a case where I might need your help? Come on, you must remember. I told you she was a real looker, and you said you had enough dames in your life," Frank said, looking at Martha and Jackie with a smile. "She didn't show up for an appointment, and she's not answering her phone. How about hopping over to her place tomorrow morning to see what's going on? She knows all about you and wants to meet you anyway. Her name is Kathryn Blair."

Frank handed me a scrap of paper with her address and left the office. I had no idea who he was talking about.

September

During the night, the last hurricane of the season made its way up the Atlantic coastline, slamming into the city. If I had any brains, I would've waited until the storm passed before heading out to find Kathryn Blair, but I owed Frank big time, and he clearly expected me to react quickly to his request.

As I stepped out of my car, a fist of swirling wind threw me back against the door. In an act of sheer determination, I gripped my coat collar, held onto my hat, and leaned into the wind as rain pummeled my head and gushed down the back of my neck. Drenched, I found myself in front of a rundown building in the low-rent district of Queens, not a great place to visit even on a nice day.

The front walls of the building's entryway, discolored in places, emitted a disturbing odor that overwhelmed my senses as I closed the door behind me. Trying to ignore the stench, I focused my attention on the one-inch square black and white tiles that lined the hall and stairwell. The white tiles had turned a brownish, putrid color, showing the effects of years of neglect. I avoided touching the banisters or sidewalls as I ascended into the building.

The steps groaned under my weight, announcing to the occupants entombed behind their triple locks and tiny peepholes that a stranger had entered their domicile.

I didn't meet anyone on the way up to Kathryn's apartment, which was probably a good thing.

The smell lessened, then changed and intensified with

every successive landing, and by the time I knocked on the door marked 302, I could taste the half-digested remnants of my breakfast. I hoped Miss Blair wouldn't answer, so I could get back to my office and tell Frank what he could do with his mystery girl. I knocked again, then tried the door-knob and gently pushed. The door opened slightly. When I leaned forward to call her name, a swarm of flies poured out through the opening, slamming into my face and body.

No one had to tell me I'd bumbled my way through the last few months, but even *I* knew the fate of Miss Blair. I sprinted down the stairs and pounded on the super's door until he answered. I got O'Reilly on the phone, then stood guard outside Kathryn's room, waiting for him to arrive.

I could hear O'Reilly's bellowing as soon as he entered the building. "Joey Batista, you better have one cold, dead body to bring me out on a shitty day like this."

As he made his way up the stairs, some of the nosier residents peered from their doorways. He shouted them back, telling them a murder investigation was in progress and to stay inside until the police took their statements. When he got to the third floor, he tossed me a rain-soaked cloth.

I followed his lead and covered my nose and mouth. He reached for the doorknob and I stepped out of the way. As I expected, O'Reilly stumbled backwards as the flies reacted to his intrusion. "Shit, I hate when that happens," he shouted as he kicked the door open. O'Reilly waited a few minutes for the flies to settle down. Looking past his shoulder, I could see Miss Blair sprawled on the floor, with some of her clothes ripped open and others discarded around her contorted body. There were no visible signs of blood.

"What do you know about her?" O'Reilly asked.

"Not much. She's a client of Frank's."

"So what are you doing here?"

"He asked me to check on her."

"Why?"

"She missed an appointment."

"That's it? Great help you are."

"Looks like she put up one hell of a struggle," I said, ignoring his sarcasm.

"I'm not so sure," he said as he bent down and inspected her fingernails.

As O'Reilly continued examining her body, I took my eyes off Miss Blair and looked around the room. It was as if the hurricane still battering the city had stormed through the apartment, overturning furniture, ripping objects off the walls, dislodging bureau drawers, and scattering their contents throughout the room.

"You might be right," I said. "If she had put up a struggle, how did the murderer have time to ransack the place? You'd think someone would've heard the commotion and called the police."

"In this neighborhood? I doubt it. Then again, a young girl living alone, crying out for help. Maybe you're right; someone might have reacted. What does that say to you?" O'Reilly asked.

"She got knocked off right away, probably by an acquaintance. Everything else, the rape, the desperate search, staged."

"Not bad for a beginner. You're right about the rape, but the killer wanted something, wanted it bad, and obviously didn't find it."

"How can you be so sure?"

"Step back and take another look, *everything's* out of place. No, the killer took his time. If he staged all this, he wouldn't have done such a thorough job, and if he found what he wanted, he would've stopped searching. My guess is he tried to get her to talk. She struggled, he tightened his grip, yanked her head back, and—snap. Once she was dead, he made it look like she was raped and ransacked the apartment to find what he wanted."

"Why are you so convinced she wasn't raped?" I asked.

"There's nothing under her fingernails. She never had a chance to put up a real fight. Most women instinctively scratch their attackers."

Just then the meat wagon arrived, and O'Reilly and I moved back into the hall.

"Why don't you go on and get outta here. You can't do any good until the boys finish with the body and check the place out. This section of Queens is out of my jurisdiction, but I know most of the guys who work homicide. I'll see to it you get a chance to nose around once they're done."

I'd never seen O'Reilly investigate a crime scene and wanted to stay, but he insisted I leave. Since I had more than a few questions for Galvano, I headed back to the office.

Frank didn't bother to greet me or even look up from his work. "So what did ya find out? It's not like Kathryn to miss an appointment."

"She's dead, murdered. Dead three, maybe four days."

Before he could ask questions, I tore into him.

"The next time you send me on a case you'd better damn well give me more details. I didn't know what the hell I was walking into."

"I didn't think she was in any real danger," he said.

"Well, I guess you were wrong. You gonna tell me now what this is all about?"

"She came to see me about her father's will. Her father died and left behind two wills dated the same day with different beneficiaries. As far as I could tell, she had a legitimate claim to his estate, as did her brother. Both wills looked authentic and legal. No one had attacked or threatened her, but to use the word terrified doesn't adequately describe her behavior. Even so, I had no reason to suspect she was in imminent danger. She acted a little paranoid, and I suggested she hire you to help sort out the situation with the wills."

"Maybe I could've done something to prevent her murder," I said.

"Hey, stop right there. You had enough going on. Besides I never officially asked you to get involved until recently, and Martha told her you were too busy to take on another case."

"I'm taking her case now. Tell me everything you know about the wills. When I get to the bottom of this estate mystery, chances are I'll find her killer."

"I can do better than that. Take my file. It contains everything you'll need to understand what was going on in her life. I have a brief to get ready for, so why don't you study the file and ask your questions tomorrow night. I'll meet you around nine at your uncle's place."

Frank's mater-of-fact reaction to the news of Miss Blair's murder initially surprised me, but it was becoming clear you didn't need to go to war to get accustomed to death, especially when you live in the confines of New York City.

* * * * *

As I entered my office, both Martha and Jackie turned toward me, each nudging the other. Jackie coaxed me to a chair and stood beside me. "We think we found a connection between all the murders that took place on Staten Island, but we're not sure." I rose to look at the reports, but Jackie gently placed her hand on my shoulder. She turned to

Martha, who leaned against her desk and motioned for Jackie to continue.

"We believe the murderer carefully selected his victims. They weren't random; he must've known them or somehow had access to their personal information. What we want to know is if you ever gave Anita an engagement ring?"

"Why?"

"All the other girls were engaged and their rings were missing," Martha said.

"We were secretly engaged, but I couldn't afford a ring. I made one out of a thin vine we found sitting by the lake on her farm. She wore it around her neck with a piece of brown twine."

"There's one more thing all the girls had in common. Was Anita a virgin?" Jackie asked.

I leaned forward, lowering my head to suppress the convulsions that gripped my stomach muscles when Ma walked into the office.

"Joey, we have a visitor. They want ya downstairs." She held the door open, waiting.

"Who is it?"

"Johnny Torrio, from Chicago. He's here to see you and the others."

As I passed Ma, I turned to face the girls. "As far as I know, she was."

I entered the dining area with Ma close behind. No one said a word. Pop looked at Ma. She turned around and went back upstairs. Once we were alone, Pop told me to take a seat. "You know Mr. Torrio. He's come all the way from Chicago to pay a debt he owes me. I once saved his life, and now he puts his at risk to save yours."

Torrio never looked in my direction, but his stoic profile reminded me of his warning not to confront Ralph Ruffalo until I had convincing proof he had killed Anita. I thought acting in self-defense would make a difference, but I soon learned nothing mattered to the Mafia except getting revenge for the death of one of their own.

Castellano spoke next. "You not only killed members of their family, you desecrated their bodies, and then drove away in Ralph's car. Don't try to explain what happened. It doesn't make any difference."

My uncle Luigi chimed in. "The Chicago council voted to put you on ice. Johnny defended your actions as best he could. His was the only dissenting vote. Johnny's arguments paled in comparison to another mob boss, Richie DeSario. Ralph wasn't just a top earner; he also protected Richie and his family."

Torrio finally spoke, not to me, but to my father. "Sorry, Vito, I did what I could. Two of Richie's boys are on their way. They have orders to make an example of your son. I did convince the council to limit the damage to Joey and spare the rest of the family."

Johnny Torrio got up to leave, but before he reached the door, I made my position clear. "Mr. Torrio, I appreciate your warning and what you've done for my family, but I would like you to take back a message from me. You tell them I will kill Richie's men, and if the council my uncle mentioned doesn't remove this death sentence, I'll come for them, and this DeSario guy will be first."

Torrio continued walking toward the door as if I didn't exist. Castellano followed and spoke to him in whispers, pointing in my direction. Torrio listened, glanced at me, nodded, and left.

I figured I had a few days before DeSario's button men made their move. Once in town, they'd probably get familiar with my routine, then snare me in a trap. Chances were good they wouldn't kill me outright, since they had orders to set an example. In an effort to dramatize my death, my experience told me they would make a fatal mistake, and, at that moment, my life would depend on my army training. I had no doubt my instincts would respond swiftly, and with deadly force.

I tried to convince everyone close to me to get out of town, but my efforts were useless. Uncle Luigi armed his entire crew, including the waitresses. I thought he went too far when he brought a small arsenal to the dinner table. Pop took a shotgun and a revolver, and Ma strapped on a thigh holster. I protested, but she quickly put me in my place.

"What? Ya think I grew up in a convent?"

I glanced over at Pop. He just shrugged. Even Martha packed some iron, and Jackie carried around more hardware than O'Reilly. The whole building, possibly the whole neighborhood, turned into an armed camp. Even Vic and Chris, who'd tried to kill me when I first returned home from the war, got involved and followed me around, watching my back. It took some convincing to get them to lay low. The hit men needed to believe they could get to me, or they would just shoot me down from a distance and leave town. I needed to draw these guys into the open.

I spent the next few days working on the Blair case, as if unaware of the danger. Martha and Jackie tried to act normally and continued to gather information to prove their theory about the Island murders. In spite of everyone's efforts, tensions remained high.

The file Frank Galvano gave me on Kathryn Blair contained meticulous notes but didn't help solve the underlying mystery. As Frank had indicated, she'd hired him several months ago concerning her father's last will and testament.

She'd also sought Frank's help on another matter. Believing she would inherit her father's estate, Kathryn had snuck into her father's bedroom before the reading of the will and removed the contents of his safe to prevent William, her half-brother, from doing the same. The day of the reading, William produced the second will naming him as beneficiary. Even though the matter was pending litigation, William had Kathryn physically removed from the family home, not realizing she had a small fortune in her possession. When he discovered what Kathryn had done, he pressed charges.

Frank had examined the wills, and all signatures looked authentic. Both were signed on the same date. The only difference were the beneficiaries. It came down to two possibilities: either the old man had a sudden change of heart, a *very* sudden change, or someone had tampered with the documents. The lawyer who read the wills agreed both sets of documents looked legitimate but couldn't explain how that was possible. He confirmed the date on the wills by producing his predecessor's appointment calendar. The witnesses, all employees of Mr. Blair, were unable to recall the exact date or the contents, since they routinely witnessed Mr. Blair signing legal documents but were never given the opportunity to read them. The old man had been bedridden for years before his death, and every day seemed like the next to the household help.

Old man Blair had made his initial fortune in the textile business and ran the local factory from his bedroom until the day he died, with the help of his plant manager, David Denton. Like many immigrants who settled in America, he was a tough man who worked hard and demanded the same from others. I could envision him getting angry and changing his will.

Kathryn Blair had insisted her father would never disinherit her and the document William had in his possession was a forgery. According to Frank's notes, with each passing visit to his office, Kathryn became more and more fearful her half-brother would kill her if she didn't return the contents of the safe and relinquish her claim to the estate. She had stolen an expensive necklace and a considerable amount of cash. As a precaution, Kathryn frequently moved and finally ended up in the dump in Queens where she was murdered.

I was leaving my office to ask Frank some additional questions when O'Reilly and I bumped into each other in the hall.

"You got a minute for an update on the Blair murder?" he asked.

I figured I could catch Galvano anytime.

"You bet. Come on into my office. I'm curious to know if your first impressions about the crime scene were correct."

"I know the investigator assigned to the case, and he filled me in on the details. We had everything right: the girl died of a broken neck, the rape never happened, and the murderer took his time tearing the place apart."

"Any leads?"

"It looks like she got bumped outta her old man's will and went downhill from there. She has a half-brother who, according to everyone who has spoken to him, is a real sleaze, but he has a solid alibi. No suspects yet. She had few if any visitors and stayed to herself. Her two neighbors on the third floor never spoke to her and didn't hear or see a damn thing."

"Any chance I can get into her place again?"

"All arranged. Here's the key, and remember, don't touch anything."

"You can trust me," I said with a straight face that didn't fool O'Reilly for a moment.

"Just don't tell me if you do. Are you watching your

back? I haven't seen any strangers hanging around. Have you?"

"Nope, but I gotta tell ya, I feel safer on the street than in this place; everyone's armed to the hilt and pretty jittery."

Once O'Reilly left, I hightailed it over to the crime scene. The weather had improved, but I couldn't say the same for the stench in the apartment. There didn't have to be a chalk outline for me to remember how Kathryn looked, sprawled on the floor like a discarded doll. As I looked around, I didn't expect to find any missed clues leading to the identity of her murderer or the money Kathryn absconded from her father's safe. My primary intent was to learn more about Kathryn Blair.

The room came furnished, so most of the items tossed around had nothing to do with her. She traveled light: one suitcase, two pairs of shoes, several changes of underclothes, two different outfits, and one picture of her and her father. The picture frame lay shattered on the floor. It didn't feel right to leave it there and have some stranger throw it away. I removed the broken glass and shoved the frame in my jacket pocket as I entered her bathroom. The bathroom looked relatively undisturbed, with a few personal items: a new container of tooth cleaner, a hair-brush, a toothbrush, and an overturned box of talcum powder that had spilled its contents onto the floor by the toilet. On the tub, a new bar of soap gave off a heavy smell of roses as it lay in a porcelain dish precariously balanced, about to fall. I bent down to move the dish when I noticed something odd about the white talcum powder on the floor by the baseboard. Some of it looked gritty, not what I expected. As I glanced up and saw an air vent above the toilet, the super came in and asked if I was the fella who found the body the other day.

"Yeah, that's right. I'm doing a little follow-up for the department," I said.

"I have something downstairs," he said, glancing over his shoulder. As he turned back, I noticed beads of sweat dripping down the side of his face. "In my place. I have something that might help ya find the guy who did this." He had scurried out and down the stairs before I could get off my knees from inspecting the powder. Given his odd behavior, I half expected to see a puddle where he had been standing.

I pulled my piece, cautiously moved down the stairs, and peered into his apartment. I dropped the gun as some big lug pulled back the hammer of the .45 he held to the head of a woman who sat bound to a wooden kitchen chair. He motioned me in, and as I crossed the threshold, a huge fist came out of nowhere. My attacker seemed to know about my prior injury; my ribs buckled under the first blow. I doubled over, and he followed up with a devastating punch to the side of my face that ripped open my cheek and loosened a few teeth. Falling to the floor, I landed a crushing kick to his knee; it didn't even faze the brute. He grabbed my leg, twisted it, picked me up by my shirt collar, and shoved my face into the wall. Before I could move, he used my kidneys as a punching bag. My legs buckled, and as I slid down the wall, he pulled out his piece, and once again I heard the click of a hammer locking in place.

"Let's do it now—pick up our buddies and get the hell out of this stinking town," he said.

His partner disagreed. "The boss said to make an example of him, so we're gonna take him back to his uncle's place and do him there." He then slit the lady's throat. As the super rushed to her side, he grabbed the man by the neck with one hand, lifted him off the floor and slowly squeezed the life out of him. I watched helplessly; the more the super struggled to free himself, the more the thug's grin widened.

"What the hell did ya do that for?" I screamed.

"We don't need no witnesses calling the coppers until we're done with ya. In a way, it's your fault," he said as he dragged both bodies through a small hallway into an adjacent room.

My attacker pulled me off the ground with one hand, and before I went unconscious, I saw brass knuckles come hurling toward my face.

I regained awareness as they dragged my wrecked body up the stairs to Luigi's place. They shoved my face against the peephole and threatened to splatter my brains through the opening if the bouncer didn't unbolt the main door. Once inside, the leader of this twosome fired shots into the ceiling and ordered everyone to place their weapons on the tables.

At the sound of gunfire, Uncle Luigi came rushing out of his office, and before he could take aim, caught a bullet in the leg.

"You must be the kid's uncle. We heard about you. You're lucky I have orders to spare the family. Drop the hardware."

The goon, who had pummeled my body, threw my limp carcass in a chair and held a knife to my throat as he stood behind me. "We're about to show you what happens when someone messes with the Chicago mob."

As he said this, he looked around the room and laughed at all those staring at him in horror. I took a chance and with both my hands, grabbed his wrist that held the chiv, swung my entire body under his arm and twisted downward as I stood up, snapping his wrist. He screamed, released the knife, and twirled around. I caught the knife and shoved the blade up under his chin, severing his spinal cord. The other thug reacted to his scream and turned to fire. As my attacker collapsed, I grabbed a gun from his shoulder holster and shoved the gun against the other guy's chest as

O'Reilly pumped two bullets into him. Turning toward O'Reilly, I fired at a drunk sitting in a dark corner. The bullet caught him dead between the eyes before he brought out a hidden gun from under his table.

With the little strength I had left, I stepped over the body lying at my feet and was heading toward my uncle when Vic and Chris shouted a warning and threw their stilettos directly at my chest. I immediately dropped to the floor and turned to see a fourth thug stumble forward with two knives protruding from his body. The flash of a fire-ax embedded in his back flew by as he fell forward onto my legs. That's when I saw Rosalie standing over him, shaking, with her hands covering her face. I tried to go to her, but my adrenaline gave out. The last thing I remember was O'Reilly trying to lift the dead weight off my legs.

When I came to, Jackie and Martha were on opposite sides of my bed, and Rosalie stood at the foot, clutching some bandages and a basin of hot water.

"Ladies, do you think you can leave for a few minutes so I can change his bandages?" she said.

Just then Ma came in with a hot bowl of soup. "Everybody out! What he needs is some hot chicken soup with my mother's special herbs," she said as she shooed Martha and Jackie from the room. Rosalie apparently had gained a higher position in the pecking order due to her nursing skills. After Ma spoon-fed me, she left, leaving us alone.

"How's my uncle?" I asked.

"He's fine. The worst patient I've ever seen. Just a flesh wound to his leg and you'd think he was about to die. I can tell you, he's not happy with you. He keeps on ranting you've been a PI for only a few months and already he's taken two bullets for you. He's telling everyone they should talk you into another profession, something less violent, like a schoolteacher. He actually has a sheet of paper on the bar where people can write suggestions."

As soon as I laughed, pain rippled through my body, and I could manage only a grin. "How bad do I look?"

"You're not as handsome as before, but the stitches make you look more menacing, so maybe everyone will stop calling you kid."

"How many ribs are broken this time?"

"Three, maybe four. Your kidneys also took a beating, but your back muscles absorbed most of the blows so I don't think there's any damage, just some bruising. You'll feel sore for a few days, but you won't really notice it. The broken ribs will see to that."

"What's that contraption you're holding?"

"Something your father made to protect your ribs. We used slivers of wood in the field hospitals, but I thought leather straps would work better and give you more flexibility. Let me help you take off your shirt so I can change the wrapping and see if this thing will fit."

The thought of lifting my arms wasn't pleasant. "I slit a few of your shirts and sewed buttons on the sides. You don't need to raise your arms," she said as she leaned closer to unbutton my shirt.

"Rosalie, I've been meaning to ask you why you moved into my old room when you agreed to take Sally's place in the shoe store. You would have more privacy if you kept your old apartment."

"There are a few reasons. As you know, I don't have a family of my own and it's nice being with people you like. Your mom's always been like a mother to me. I think I slept in your house more than my own when we were kids. My pop was always beating on my mom when he got drunk. Besides, I'm saving money, and someday I hope to have enough to go to school and become a nurse."

"Is that it?" I asked.

"What, you think every girl in this town is after you? We've known each other since we're little. You're like a brother, so don't get any ideas."

"Even a brother gets a peck on the cheek once in a while."

"I like our relationship just the way it is," she said with a sadistic smile as she tightened the brace against my ribs.

* * * * *

In a few days I felt like my old self. The leather brace my pop made worked miracles, and the swelling in my face had subsided. Uncle Luigi got around with a cane and wouldn't let me forget I owed him my life not once, but twice. I don't think he needed the cane, but he did get a lot of attention from his patrons.

"Some kinda nephew you are. If I'm gonna catch all this lead, I should get at least thirty percent of everything you make. No, that's not enough, make that fifty percent. I don't think I'll be alive much longer if I keep hanging around you. Did anyone ever tell you you're a walking disaster?"

"So you've said."

Ma and Pop took a more serious view of what recently happened and gave me some surprising advice.

"You need to finish this," Ma said as she continued setting the table.

"Joey," Pop said, "ya ma isn't happy about what happened the other night. Innocent people got killed. And she's telling you more will die unless you do something. It's the way of the old country, the only thing these people understand. They're gonna come back until you're dead and maybe the rest of us too."

Ma slammed a fist full of utensils down on the table.

"You made a threat, and if I know anyone, it's Johnny. He delivered your message! If you don't follow through, they'll think you're weak and come for you again."

I gave her a hug. "Ma, I need to give Torrio time to work things out on his end. He'll let us know if something's gonna happen."

"He might not know. You killed five of DeSario's men, counting Ralph. You think he's gonna listen to any of the others? For Torrio to come here in person to warn you, this DeSario guy must be pretty high up in the organization."

"Okay, Ma. I need another week to heal. If we don't hear anything from Chicago by then, I'll go to them."

"You'll go to them, listen to you. You're just a baby. You gotta have a plan. Go to Castellano. He can help. Talk to Luigi and Pop." During the last few months, a side of Ma I'd never seen before revealed itself. I took her advice.

Thanks to Castellano, the four bodies turned up in the city dump, and O'Reilly planted evidence at the murder scene of the super and his wife, implicating the four in their deaths. The old couple just became another in a series of unexplained homicides.

I resumed my investigation of the Blair case by returning to her apartment. My guess was the grit mixed in with the white powder was plaster. I had a hunch I would find the contents of Mr. Blair's safe hidden in the air duct—a place the killer overlooked.

I still had the key to Kathryn's apartment, and as I expected, the grit on the floor was indeed plaster that probably fell when she unscrewed the vent. Holding the vent in one hand, I peered inside and found an empty cavern. I stepped down from the toilet to take a break. My side hurt like hell and all for nothing. I gritted my teeth and was beginning to put the vent back in place when I noticed something had recently disturbed a thick layer of dust inside the air duct. Kathryn *had* hidden the money behind the vent. Who took it? The police, the killer, or did Kathryn find a new hiding place?

As I passed the super's apartment on the way out of the building, I recalled the horrors of the couple's death, both dragged into another room through a small hallway, leaving behind a trail of blood. I was reaching for the doorknob to leave that shit hole behind when images of Kathryn's room flashed through my mind. Only one small suitcase, an empty closet except for two dresses, a new bar of soap, and an untouched container of tooth cleaner. Where were the towels? There were no towels in the bathroom. I went back to the super's door, Room 101, and then walked down the hall to Room 102. Their killer had dragged their bodies into Room 102. The rooms were connected.

I took the stairs two, three at a time until I reached the third floor. I knocked on the door next to Kathryn's apartment. No answer. I leaned into the door and gave it a hard shove. The lock broke free, and I slipped inside and entered a large room with a small kitchen and another bathroom. The closet, full of clothes, lined up with the one in Kathryn's room. According to O'Reilly, everyone told the police this room was vacant, but it was the room Kathryn actually lived in. Together the two rooms matched the layout of the super's apartment, except for the closet. That's when I realized all the apartments in the building had the option of expanding into a double room simply by eliminating the back-to-back closets. I frantically tossed Kathryn's clothes onto the floor and stood staring at the back of her closet. There was only one explanation for what I saw: pocket doors. I was actually looking at the backside of the closet wall of Room 302. I went into Room 302 and examined the closet. Decorative trim bordered the back of the wall, and a similar piece of trim ran from the ceiling down to the floor in the middle of the wall. The middle trim in the closet had three small wooden knobs that rotated in one direction. With all three rotated in the same position, the two sections of wall easily slid out of the way. A small hallway now connected Rooms 302 and 301.

Kathryn entered and exited her apartment from Room 302, and whenever she left the apartment, she sealed off the hallway in 302 and converted it to a closet. When she entered Room 301, she closed the pocket doors to 302 and secured them with a simple lock she had installed. Since the super never said anything to the police, Kathryn had probably paid him on the sly for Room 301. Everyone thought she lived in Room 302, including the killer.

I walked through the hallway back into Room 301 and headed straight for the bathroom. I knew where Kathryn had hidden the money and necklace. To my surprise, the vent also contained a copy of *her* last will and testament. The deeper I got into her case, the more I felt a strange bond pulling us together, trying to point me to her murderer. That's my only explanation for reading her will. Opening the document, the witnesses' signatures jumped up at me: Frank and Martha. I had to sit down on the commode after reading the full text. I was the sole beneficiary of Kathryn's estate.

I went straight to see Galvano. "Why the hell would she leave everything to me in the event she got bumped off? If she was so sure her life was in danger, why didn't you get her police protection? None of this makes sense."

"Let me get you a drink so we can have a civil conversation. I didn't know the contents of her will until after her death. The will was her idea. She typed it out in my office and had Martha and me witness her signature. She wouldn't let us read the contents. She put them in sealed envelopes. She kept a copy for herself, and I put one in my safe. If you read the entire will, you know she wants you to do something meaningful with the estate if the court decides in her favor, something to honor her father's name."

"This is crazy. Why me? She didn't even know me."

"She read about you in the papers. I told her you could be trusted and you were the best private investigator I've ever worked with. I also saw her talking to Martha a few times." Frank opened his desk drawer and pulled out an envelope. "Maybe this will help explain. She asked me to give you this if she died and you agreed to find her murderer. As I said, I thought she was a little paranoid and overly dramatic. I was wrong."

Dear Mr. Batista,

I realize we've never met, but by now you have read a copy of my will and are wondering why I placed such a huge burden upon you. For some time now I have been concerned that my life was in danger and not just from William, my half-brother. My father would never disown me; somehow, someone tampered with his will. Please find the truth and bring my murderer to justice. I know you are the person Frank Galvano said, or you wouldn't have taken this case knowing there wasn't anyone to pay your fees.

Please don't blame Mr. Galvano. He tried to get me to go to the police after he investigated the wills. I felt helpless because I had no evidence. Who would believe me?

Good hunting,
Kathryn Blair

I put the letter down on Frank's desk and was turning to leave when the whole building shook, throwing me to the floor. For a brief second I couldn't hear and realized there had been an explosion. I ran into the hallway and down the stairs, holding my breath. Smoke and dust poured up the stairwell from the ground floor. Pop's shoe repair shop looked like a bombed-out city. I ran into the carnage shouting his name, throwing aside sheets of wood and metal.

"In here, Joey. Ma's hurt."

His voice came from behind me. I ran into the hall and across to our apartment behind the shoe store. Ma lay on the floor, bleeding from both legs. Rosalie had already tied a tourniquet around Ma's right leg and had both legs elevated to prevent shock. Pop had a few cuts and scrapes, nothing serious.

"Pop, call for help. We need to get Ma to a hospital!" He ran to the phone, but before reaching the operator, an ambulance arrived.

Rosalie wrapped a tight bandage around Ma's other leg, leaving a large spike of wood in place to be removed by a surgeon. As the medics placed Ma in the ambulance, Luigi came hobbling down the stairs covered in blood, carrying a shotgun. Martha and Jackie were right behind him, looking with horror at the wreckage. They sat Luigi down, took away his gun, and placed it out of sight just as the police arrived. Luigi had a deep gash on his head from a fall. The medics placed him with Ma in the back of the ambulance and took off with horns blaring.

Pop stood in the street and watched the ambulance leave, then came at me with a fury I've never seen before. He threw me up against a wall with ease. It happened so fast and unexpectedly I didn't know what to say.

"You created this mess, and you need to finish it. Ma warned you. I know what you can do. Castellano told me. We're gonna make sure Ma is okay, and then we leave for Chicago."

The girls stood still. When the tension broke, Jackie and

Martha went to help Rosalie clean up. Pop took Luigi's car and drove to the hospital without another word. I stood among the rubble, frozen in place, remembering another bombed-out building in another country. I'd been on reconnaissance. When I returned to the safe house I used, I found it completely obliterated—everyone inside, all of whom had risked their lives so I could complete my mission, slaughtered.

Castellano arrived and pulled me back to the present. "What the hell happened? Where's everyone? Are they hurt?" he asked frantically.

"Ma's in pretty bad shape, Luigi will be fine, and Pop's on his way to the hospital to be with them," I said.

Castellano went over to the girls to see how they were and then headed for his car.

"Tell me who my father really is," I said. "I want to know what he did before coming to America."

Castellano stopped abruptly and ran his fingers through his hair, looking down. "Now's not the time. I need to get to the hospital, and so should you."

"What I need is to know now, not later. All of you, what did you do? Why did you leave Italy together?"

"We lived in a tough neighborhood, much tougher than this place," he said, glancing at the rubble around us. "To survive you needed to stick together, have friends and, most of all, family. Your father, he was older. He did everything for us. When there was trouble, he took the blame. When there was a fight, he stepped in. When we needed something, he provided for us. Your father, he isn't a shoemaker. His father was a shoemaker. Your father is a man to be respected and feared, and your mother, well your mother was always at his side, and that's where you should be now."

"What happened? Why did you leave Italy?"

Castellano didn't want to tell me, but given the circumstances, he must've realized it was time. "One day we were jumped by some vagabonds who roamed the countryside. Torrio took a hit to the head and fell to his knees. He was about to get his throat slit when your father wrestled the knife away from his attacker and stabbed the man in the chest, then beat another to death. No one believed our story. They arrested all of us for murder. Some of our friends broke us out of jail, and we left on a boat bound for America."

"How did you manage to get away?"

"Your father's uncle was the constable. He just looked in the wrong places until the boat left. Now I'm going to the hospital. Get in."

Once Ma recovered from surgery, she insisted on going home. She wanted to be in her own bed, around family. It took a few hours of arguing, but we finally convinced her to stay in the hospital for a few days. When everyone had left her hospital room, she called me to her side. "Joey, your pop isn't gonna sit still for this. Promise me you'll protect him and listen to Castellano. He knows their world."

I tried to reassure her, but she still viewed me as the boy I was and not the man I'd become. I got into the car with Pop and Luigi, and we drove over to Castellano's without speaking.

It took a few drinks before a plan took shape. We all agreed: DeSario had to be eliminated in dramatic fashion, and soon. Castellano got the assignment to find out as much as he could about DeSario's setup and get in touch with Johnny Torrio. Luigi had spent some time in Chicago, so he had the responsibility of getting us safely out of town once we were done. He also supplied us with the necessary artillery.

When Jackie heard we were leaving for Chicago, she insisted on coming. We tried talking her out of it because there was a good chance we wouldn't get out alive. Nothing would change her mind. Knowing her exceptional ability with knives, I asked Pop to make her a special harness to hold several knives at the small of her back. The harness ended up looking like a corset, with knife handles facing down so she could easily reach under her coat, behind her back, and pull them out. Pop came up with an ingenious spring-loaded mechanism to hold the knives in place until she needed them.

As Pop worked on the harness, I tried to get her to stay and watch over Ma, but Luigi thought she would provide the perfect cover. No one, he said, would expect me to be traveling with a dame. I didn't have a chance arguing against Jackie and Luigi, so I gave up trying.

We all agreed Castellano should remain out of the picture; otherwise, a bloodbath would erupt between the cities' crime syndicates if the heads of Chicago connected us with the local Mafia. Martha and Rosalie stayed with Ma, and the rest of us hit the road. We almost made the fatal mistake of taking my car, but Jackie reminded us the car once belonged to Ralph Ruffalo. Jackie and I drove Luigi's car, and Pop and Luigi borrowed one of Castellano's. We drove in eight-hour shifts.

When we stopped traveling for the night, Luigi tried to take control, giving orders. "Okay, Jackie and I will stay in one room; Joey, you and your pop take the other. We leave again at dawn and should arrive in Chicago tomorrow night."

My uncle grabbed Jackie's hand and headed toward the room but lost his balance when she pulled back. "Since Joey and I are partners, we should be together. Besides, I feel safer with him," Jackie said.

"Safer? I'm an old man. What can I do?"

Jackie took my hand, walked over to Luigi, gave him a kiss on the forehead, took the key from him, and said, "A dirty old man can do a lot."

What happened as she closed the hotel door didn't come as a surprise to either of us. We were both attracted to each other the moment we met, and the sexual tension that had been building between us suddenly relaxed as the lock clicked into place.

She backed away from the door and turned to me. "I think you would have been safer with a dirty old man," I said as I pulled her close.

"Safety isn't something I crave, never have, never will. Do you think you can handle that?"

"Why don't we find out?"

We didn't say more. We didn't have to. Our lives had changed the moment she walked into my office in ways neither one of us could have predicted, and the future still remained uncertain as we headed toward Chicago. I carried the burden of Anita, and she bore the emotional scars of a lifetime of bad relationships. We both understood each other and simply enjoyed being together. At first I felt I was betraying Martha, but Martha had a physical need and I was simply available. With Jackie there was something else, something deeper. Both women were gorgeous, vivacious, and sexually experienced in ways most men dream about, but with Jackie, I felt an inner peace.

* * * * *

DeSario hung out at one of his speakeasies, not far from Torrio's joint. Pop wanted to let Johnny know we had arrived, but got outvoted. The less Torrio knew, the better for him.

We waited until midnight and sent Pop and my uncle in to check out the situation at the speakeasy. The news they brought back wasn't good. DeSario expected trouble and had taken precautions. There were two armed guards at every building exit, at least four more surrounding DeSario whenever he came out of his office, and according to the bartender, he even slept in the same building. It looked as though he had imprisoned himself in his own little world.

Jackie and I walked around the building to see if we could enter without going through the front entrance. Jackie said the place reminded her of the warehouse she'd hung out in during her younger days, and if that proved to be true, there wasn't another way in. The airshafts on the roof would be too narrow, and the upper windows were essentially small outlets to let out the warm air.

"Our only chance is to draw him out of the building," Jackie said.

"If he had any brains, he'd stay inside those four walls until he's sure we're no longer a threat. I think we should go in around closing time and shoot the place up," Luigi said.

Pop quickly agreed; he wanted to get back to Ma. I also liked the idea. Jackie had less of an emotional stake and came up with a more reasonable approach.

"We get him to come to us. Fewer people will get hurt, less risk for us, and we'll send a clear message to the other bosses that they're not safe," Jackie said.

"And how are we supposed to get him out of his cocoon? I don't think he would attend his own mother's funeral," Pop said.

Luigi caught on right away. "No, but he might come out for one sexy dame. I know I would."

The next night we were all set to put Jackie's plan into action. We took a couple of rooms at one of the more expensive hotels in the area. Luigi went with Jackie to the speakeasy, just to keep an eye on how things were going, and Pop and I waited back at the hotel. Jackie wore her knife contraption under a light jacket that matched her outfit, so we felt comfortable if anything went wrong, she could handle the situation.

When Luigi and Jackie returned, they gave us a detailed account of how the evening went. Jackie had sat by herself at a table close to DeSario's private corner and got his attention within minutes. As we had discussed, she played hard to get and accidentally spilled her purse so DeSario would get a good look at her hotel key.

"You shoulda seen the fool. He practically groveled at her feet. He thinks she's a high society dame who just returned to the city," Luigi said.

"He invited me to dinner tomorrow night. I'm sure he'll try to lure me to his apartment, but I'll find a way to avoid his charms," Jackie said, chuckling at me as I felt my face flush.

"I'm not sure this is such a good idea. Once you're in his club, he can do whatever he wants," I said.

"I'm not worried. He desires me because he believes I'm a few notches above his usual clientele. Part of the lure is he has to find a way to overcome my resistance. He knows where I'm staying; he'll show up here tomorrow or the following night," Jackie said.

My uncle and I waited in an adjacent hotel room, where we could hear if Jackie had visitors, and Pop stayed in Jackie's bedroom. Just as she predicted, DeSario showed up late on the third night with a couple of bodyguards in tow. Jackie had her routine set and went into her act. She opened the door a crack and cautiously peered out.

"Richie, I didn't expect you. I just got out of the tub. All I have on is my robe."

"Mind if I come in, doll?"

She opened the door a little wider so he could get a better look. "If your friends wait outside and you behave like a gentleman."

"They'll just make sure we're not disturbed, and I'll be on my best behavior. If ya know what I mean."

Once he entered the room, we left ours and walked by the bodyguards. Luigi asked for a light as he searched his pockets for a match, a cigarette loosely hanging from his lips. As one bodyguard struck a match, I pulled out my gun and held it to the other's head. Before Luigi's new friend could react, Luigi had a knife up against his throat. It didn't take us long to get them bound and gagged in our room.

I wanted to barge in, but Luigi held me back for a few minutes. Then he knocked on Jackie's door.

"What the hell do those jerks want?" DeSario shouted.

"Probably just need to use the bathroom," Jackie said.

Leaning with our ear against the door, we heard DeSario say, "Let them suffer. That's what they get paid to do." It then sounded like he grabbed Jackie and they had a small tussle.

Suddenly all hell broke loose. "Who the hell are you?" we heard DeSario demand as Pop entered from Jackie's bedroom.

I kicked in the door with my gun drawn. DeSario reached for his shoulder holster, but as we learned later, Jackie had removed his gun and placed it on a side table when she sat on his lap. Realizing the whole deal was a setup, he twirled Jackie around and used her as a shield, with an arm around her neck.

"I can guess who the hell you guys are. Either I get out of here or she's done for."

We froze. As DeSario moved, dragging Jackie toward the door, she pretended to slip, leaned back, and pushed him against the wall. When she tried to straighten up, he loosened his grip, and she turned in his arms so they were face to face. He immediately let her go, and as she backed away, she held a carving knife against his belly.

"Sorry, Richie, I'm not being a good host. These are the Batistas: Vito, Luigi, and Joey. Sounds like you've heard of them," she said.

"Look guys, I had nothing to do with that bombing. The other bosses ordered the hit, not me."

I moved toward him, backing him against the window. He took a swing, which I dodged, and as I came in to deliver a chop to his trachea, Pop shoved me out of the way and exchanged blows with him. Luigi held me back, telling me that my father needed to avenge his wife.

They were both powerful men, DeSario much younger. Even though DeSario grew up on the streets of Chicago, Pop kept on landing crushing blows to his mid-section, with an occasional uppercut. DeSario got in several solid hits, but Pop took everything that came his way. Finally DeSario had difficulty holding his guard up, and Pop moved in for the kill. He drove him back with each thrust. His powerful arms, sculptured from years of tanning leather, delivered such force we heard DeSario's ribs crack, then his jawbone. Until now I never thought of Pop as a violent man.

At this point Pop had DeSario backed up against the window. He came in low and put his entire body behind a mighty anvil of a fist that landed squarely in DeSario's chest, shattering his breastbone and sending him crashing through the window, falling six stories to the street below.

We had no time to waste. We gathered our few belongings and left the hotel through a back entrance as several police cars converged on the hotel with sirens blaring.

* * * * *

Against his better judgment, Johnny Torrio made arrangements for a sit-down with the other bosses. Pop didn't give him a choice.

"We are gonna end this now, with or without you. If you don't wanna help, then I suggest you get the hell outta town until we're done."

"Vito, in a few hours every button man in the city will be gunning for you and your family. And the police will be helping them."

"Did you tell the council what my son said he would do?"

"I did."

"Good, then either call a meeting or get outta my way. We're not leaving until these associates of yours lift the hit on my family or they're all dead."

The meeting took place the next morning at a heavily guarded location used for making hooch. The place reeked of grain alcohol, so aside from stripping us of our guns, three bodyguards also took our cigarettes and matches. I quickly removed my jacket and casually threw it across a chair, hoping they wouldn't inspect it too closely. I then unsnapped my double-breasted holster. As the guards turned toward Jackie, my uncle reached down the front of his pants and pulled out a .45, which got their attention. He kept two of them entertained by producing a derringer from under his fedora and two more from his armpits. One guard ignored his antics and patted Jackie down and felt the knife harness.

"What the hell is this?" he asked.

The other guards turned and were moving to join their buddy when Luigi called out, "What, are you a virgin or somethin'? Haven't you ever felt a corset before?"

The goon spun around, his neck muscles visibly pulsating as blood surged upward, engorging his facial features, forcing his eyes to bulge like a wild animal. He reached for

Luigi just as Jackie shouted out, "Hey, here's your chance to take a peek." She said this as she leaned against a wall, slowly undoing one, then two buttons of her blouse.

The laughter in the small hall from his fellow henchmen reached a new pitch until the double doors to the meeting room opened. "What the hell's going on out here? Send them in if they're clean so we can get this damn meeting over," Torrio said.

"I'm not done with the broad yet," the goon said as he moved back toward Jackie.

"The hell you aren't," she said as she slapped his face with one hand and reached behind her back with the other.

"Keep your hands to yourself. You already felt enough to know I'm not carrying any heat," she added with a look of disgust.

Torrio noticed Pop, Luigi, and I were about to react and barked out orders. "You two get your buddy under control, and the rest of you get in here. The council is waiting."

I grabbed my jacket, put it on, and followed the others.

The room was bare except for eight meaty, grumpy looking old men sitting around a table, each with a bottle of Canadian Scotch in front of them. Not the mental picture I had of the patriarchs of Chicago's crime families.

Torrio stood at the head of the table behind his chair, with one of his henchmen beside him. He opened the meeting.

"I bring before you members of my family." The room suddenly became alive as heads turned and whispers floated in the air. I looked over to Pop, and he signaled for me to keep still. Johnny walked over to my father and put his arm on his shoulder. "Vito Batista saved my life more than once when we struggled to survive in Sicily, and he is the husband of my sister. Luigi is his brother and my dear friend. Joey is Vito's only son, my nephew and godchild. I didn't tell you these things the last time we met because I thought Joey disobeyed my orders to follow our code of conduct and killed Ralph Ruffalo without our consent. Still, I pleaded for his life, but you all voted against me and I accepted your decision.

"We had an agreement that under no circumstances would Joey's family come to harm or get entangled in any vendetta. As I stand before you, my beloved sister lies near death due to the cowardly act of Richie DeSario, who convinced you to take action against Joey. When his attempt failed, he bombed Vito's business, nearly killing him and wounding my sister. These people have avenged this cowardly act as they should've, and I ask that the bloodshed end now. There is one more thing. This I didn't know the first time I asked you to spare Joey's life. Ralph ambushed Joey on his way back to New York. With his car and clothes ruined in the attack, he had no choice but to do what he did. He meant no disrespect to the dead."

Torrio sat down. After a few minutes of silence, the boss from the lower east side spoke. "Johnny, with all due respect, by my count we have eight brothers killed, including Sal Santangelo and his boys, by these so-called family members of yours. I say we kill them now and be done with it." Murmurs rumbled around the table.

Johnny stood once more. "There is another thing I didn't mention about my godchild. He's a highly skilled assassin, trained by the military, which is why DeSario's men failed to kill him. As I told you once before, he has sworn in my presence if he survived your attempt on his life and if we didn't call an end to the violence, he'd hunt you all down. You will notice Richie DeSario isn't with us today, and, as you know, he took exceptional precautions to protect himself."

"Christ, are we gonna let them walk outta here after

killing one of us?" shouted a red-faced barrel of a man, who slapped his meaty hands on the table and leaned forward with the fury of a raging bull.

"If you don't, he will kill all of you, and I will do nothing to stop him!" Torrio said. To reinforce his comment, I pulled out one of my army chivs from my sleeve and threw it between two of the bull's spread-eagled fingers, drawing a trickle of blood. Jackie slid out two knives from behind her back and stood ready.

The room fell silent. If we didn't leave with a truce, a massacre would ensue and everyone knew it. Torrio tipped the decision in our favor by putting his own life alongside ours. "Maybe I didn't make myself clear. You've been attacking my family; they responded as any of us would expect. If this continues, the streets of this city will run red with all our blood."

The council voted to lift the vendetta against me on the grounds I acted in self-defense, but they also made it clear Chicago was forever off-limits.

* * * * *

Pop wanted to leave as soon as possible, but I got some time alone with Johnny and learned more interesting facts about my family. When we finally arrived home, Ma greeted us with a limp and tears of joy. Martha sensed immediately Jackie and I had reached a new level in our relationship, and Rosalie spontaneously ran over and threw her arms around me. I had solved one problem in my life only to face another, as Martha and Jackie came over and joined Rosalie. Pop looked at the four of us and shook his head. Luigi, on the other hand, stood there grinning.

Ma and Pop refused to give me any more information about my uncle and godfather, other than to say when they arrived in America, Torrio chose to go in a different direction and my parents wanted to protect me from such a life. I learned later Al Capone was the one standing with Johnny Torrio, and together they truly ruled Chicago's underworld.

* * * * *

My life seemed to return to normal once again, but it was becoming difficult to define what normal truly was.

Frank Galvano hadn't made any progress on the Blair murder, and O'Reilly knew even less. Lieutenant Sullivan took seriously Martha and Jackie's theory about the murder victims scattered across Staten Island. They were convinced the murderer knew his victims and took their engagement rings as souvenirs. Martha, meanwhile, had compiled a list of eleven military personnel that fit the profile I had given her before I left for Chicago and had placed a folder on my desk with five potential new clients.

If that wasn't enough excitement to come home to, the district attorney's office had called twice, inviting me downtown for a friendly chat—invitations I chose to ignore.

October

Jackie and I entered the office together in a jovial mood, having spent the night celebrating our success in Chicago. Martha looked up briefly from the newspaper, frowned, and said, "You've got visitors."

Jackie pushed me playfully toward the office, but we collided as I stopped abruptly in the doorway. The district attorney, one of his assistants, and O'Reilly all stood to greet us. I glanced back at Martha, who still had her head buried in the paper. She should've warned us. I was also surprised to see that during our trip to Chicago, someone had transformed the office with expensive-looking furniture. Jackie barreled her way past me and headed straight for her new mahogany desk, which sat adjacent to mine at a slight angle.

"What do you think?" she said, ignoring our guests. "This was supposed to be a surprise. I didn't expect we'd have visitors this morning." She flashed one of her beautiful smiles in the DA's direction.

"Pretty nice," I said as I walked past the DA and ran my hand across the top of my desk. "I can't imagine where you found the time to do all this?"

"Martha deserves the credit. The furniture for her office should arrive any day."

The assistant DA shifted his feet, and the DA rocked back on his heels with an irritated grimace. I didn't want to push him too far, so I turned my attention to our guests. "What do you think of my new digs, gentlemen? Mr. District Attorney, take my seat. It looks comfortable, don't ya think?"

"That won't be necessary," he said as he plopped down in one of the four leather chairs positioned in a semicircle in front of the desks.

O'Reilly did the introductions. "Mr. Batista, you obviously know District Attorney Peterson."

"Yes, as you probably recall we had a little chat over the unfortunate death of Tommy Stefano."

O'Reilly cleared his throat. "This is Mr. Brown, one of his assistants. Gentlemen, I believe you both know Miss Jacqueline Forsythe."

The DA stood again and extended his hand. "I'm surprised you didn't go back to your maiden name after your husband's untimely death," he said to Jackie.

She kept her hand by her side. "I think Forsythe has a much richer sound than Smith, don't you?" Jackie moved behind her desk and pulled out the swivel chair. From that moment forward, the meeting slid downhill.

"Why are you here?" I asked the DA.

"Curiosity."

"About what?"

"You, your surroundings, your associates, and your *type* of business."

"I'm sure you know what my business is. It's painted on the office door: Private Investigator."

"Mr. Brown, remind our friend what's happened around him since the city approved his private investigator ticket."

Brown took out a thick notepad and spoke in a monotone voice.

"Tommy Stefano, shot multiple times and died in this office along with an associate of Luigi Batista, the owner of the building."

"Stop right there. We've been through this already. Stefano tried to put me on ice and you know it."

The DA nodded and waved his hand for Brown to continue.

"A gun battle that took place outside of the local butcher shop resulted in the death of six known gangsters, one with a carving knife through his neck."

The DA turned toward Jackie. "Interesting coincidence, don't you think, Miss Forsythe?" Jackie simply smiled.

"If it's your intent to blame everything that happens in this city…"

"How about we focus on the mayhem that's occurred within a block or so of this building and in which you are involved. Does that sound fair?"

Brown droned on again. "A bomb exploded on the ground floor, just under this office, seriously injuring Mrs. Batista, Joey Batista's mother. A murder occurred in Little Italy in an abandoned warehouse, and the victim, a close friend of Mr. Batista's, died a horrible death. Soon after, a crime boss, known only as Moralli, died in a gun battle on one of the piers off Front Street. We believe Moralli orchestrated the murder of Mr. Batista's friend. Two of Moralli's bodyguards were also found at the scene, full of lead."

The DA walked over to the window. "Isn't this building on Market Street, which runs into Front?" he asked as he opened the window to get a better look at the neighborhood.

"Are you insinuating I tortured a friend?"

"No," the DA said. "But you have to admit, it's an impressive coincidence that his suspected killer, this Moralli fellow, met his demise not far from here."

With a look from the DA, Brown droned on. "Joey Batista reported finding the body of a Miss Kathryn Blair in a

Queen's tenement. A short time later the building's super and his wife met a similar, although more brutal, death."

"Is that all, Mr. Brown?" the DA asked.

"No, sir. The corpses of four Chicago torpedoes turned up in our city dump, with evidence linking them to the murders of the super and his wife."

"How convenient. Is *that* all?"

"That we know of, sir."

The DA waited for Brown to put away his notepad then spoke to O'Reilly. "Sergeant, isn't this your district? What do you have to say?"

"It's a tough neighborhood. Crime happens."

"Not very original," the DA said with a weary smile.

"What I want to know, Mr. Batista, is why you went to Miss Blair's apartment in the first place. Was she a client?"

"Not really. Frank Galvano asked me to check on her."

"Ah, yes, the now famous mouthpiece, Frank Galvano."

"He simply has more talent than your average city prosecutor," I said.

The DA rocked on his heels with a little more vigor. "Mr. Brown, get a statement from Mr. Galvano. His office is next door."

I called Martha and asked her to introduce the Assistant DA to Frank. Once they left the office, the DA looked intently from me to Jackie and back again.

"Joey—I hope you don't mind if I call you Joey—I suspect we're going to be seeing a lot of each other, so why don't we drop the formalities."

"Fine with me. What should I call *you*?"

"Mr. District Attorney. Don't be fooled by my cordial visit today. If there was any way I could strip you of your license, or better yet, convict you of a crime, any crime, you would be sitting in the jug as we speak."

He passed his hand over the surface of my desk and

said, "Nice furniture," and left with O'Reilly in tow.

Jackie closed the door. "He's gonna be a problem," she said.

"The only thing he cares about is getting reelected, and we made fools of his office during your trial."

"I'm not so sure that's his only gripe. After listening to that litany, if I were him, I'd be after your ass too."

"And he doesn't even know about our recent trip to Chicago or about Ralph and his two bodyguards, not to mention Sal Santangelo and his goons."

"Thank God," she said as she reached down and pulled out a bottle of hooch from her bottom desk drawer.

"I've probably killed more people in the last year than I did in the entire war."

"You know something, Joey, O'Reilly was right. You're in a tough business in a tough town. Most of those people came after you first. You had every right to protect yourself."

"I don't know. I was different before the war. Hell, some of the guys in my old gang called me the peacemaker because I tried to settle differences without violence. I wonder what they're saying now."

"Who the hell cares what anyone thinks? We don't have time for self-pity. We've too much work to do, and besides… I don't find it attractive."

It sure didn't take her long to set me straight. "You're right, they all had it coming and we have a living to make," I said as we both downed a double shot of Scotch.

As we were about to settle back to work, Jackie unfolded a wrinkled scrap of paper and handed it to me after reading it. "O'Reilly dropped this in my wastebasket before he left. I think you better find your uncle."

I opened the door to leave the main office and found Martha reaching for the doorknob. "Sorry, I didn't mean to startle you. Did Mr. Brown get a statement from Frank?" I asked.

She pushed past me without a word, sat behind her desk, picked up the newspaper, and read it as if it held the key to the rest of her life. My experience with Martha told me to confront whatever had her so out of kilter.

"What's your problem today? You shoulda told me it was the DA waiting in the office, and now you're clamming up on me."

She stood up. "I was fine until you two came rolling in here, practically falling all over each other. Don't get me wrong, I know you're seeing both of us, but just do me one favor and don't shove it in my face."

"Hey, I'm sorry. The last thing I want is to hurt you or Jackie."

"If you ask me, you're the one that's gonna get hurt, not us."

Jackie came into the room and put her arm around Martha's shoulder. "I suggest you don't say any more, Joey, and find your uncle," she said as she walked Martha into the inner office.

It took a few hours to track Luigi down at the local barbershop, having a shave. He looked like a rabid bulldog, all foamed up with his gruff face sticking out of a blue and white-striped sheet draped over his body.

"Uncle Luigi, I've been looking all over for you."

"What, I gotta leave a trail of breadcrumbs so you can follow me around town?"

"Take it easy. I got a tip from a mutual friend today. I thought you should know about it."

"You playin' the horses now?"

"Read this." I handed him the wrinkled paper with the message, *Tell Luigi to expect a raid tonight.*

"Are you shitting me?" he said as he wiped his face

with the sheet and tore it away from his neck. "Don't I give enough money to that phony Police Benevolent Society? Wait a damn minute. Who's after you now?"

"The DA."

"Oh, Mother of God."

"Look on the bright side; at least it's not the mayor," I said, trying to lighten things up.

"Him I could deal with. You know somethin', you're a...."

"I know, a walking disaster."

"My nephew the wise guy. You think I can't come up with something new? No, well then try this on. You're becoming a real pain in my ass!"

I spent the rest of the day helping Luigi's crew prepare for the raid. His setup was impressive; it took only a few hours to convert the entire speakeasy—the bar, his office and the rooms his patrons used for gambling and other activities—into a respectable-looking social club. The raid happened as O'Reilly predicted, led by the chief of police and the DA himself, with sledgehammer in hand. I did think Luigi pushed his luck when he instructed the doorman to tell the police chief they couldn't enter without a membership card. It took about ten minutes for the boys in blue to break down the door. To say the DA was disappointed when he entered would be an understatement.

"Gentlemen," my uncle bellowed as they were all about to leave. "How about a glass of sarsaparilla on the house?" It was clear from the look he got from the DA, Luigi was now on his shit list, right below me.

The next day I showed up at the office earlier than normal and found Jackie hard at work.

"Hey, I didn't think you were such an early riser."

"Martha gave me her PI manuals to study. If you ask me, some of this stuff seems pretty basic."

"Necessary evil to get your ticket," I said as I walked around the room to get a better look at the new furnishings. "Yesterday was so crazy, I didn't really appreciate all the changes. This must have cost a pretty penny."

"I didn't think you'd mind if I used some of the money from the Bryson kidnapping case."

"What can I say? The place looks great!"

"You should know Martha and I agreed to some more improvements."

Just then Martha entered and greeted us warmly, but there was still a slight edge to her enthusiasm. She confirmed my suspicion that she wasn't quite over our squabble when she propped open the intervening office door with a red construction brick.

"Hope you don't mind. I'll be able to better hear if either of you need anything. Oh, and this wall that separates our offices makes everything feel closed in and dark, so we called someone to install two large glass panels."

"Is that all, or is there more?" I asked.

"The office is no place to display our personal lives, so we will *all* be more careful in the future," Jackie said. "I apologized to Martha, and we agreed on a peace offering."

"What kind?"

"You're taking Martha out to dinner tonight, and only dinner."

"Someplace expensive. Very expensive," Martha added.

It was painfully obvious that the dynamics among the three of us needed to change. The best way to do that would be to help Martha find a fella who was ready to settle down, and that guy wasn't me.

I waited about a half-hour and then called the three of us together to talk shop. First, I moved one of the four chairs away from the front of the desks and put the remaining ones in a circle, so we'd all be facing each other equally. Jackie caught on right away and helped with the rearrangement. "Glad to see you're a quick learner," she said.

When Martha came into the office, she smiled. We got down to business.

"Since we were gone, did anything new happen on the Blair case or the Island murders?" I asked Martha.

"You got a call this morning from Lieutenant Sullivan inviting you to a taskforce briefing about the killer stalking the Island. Apparently O'Reilly will also be attending. I took the liberty of telling the Lieutenant you'd be there. I had you both scheduled to meet with William Blair this afternoon, but I can cancel that meeting."

"Don't. Jackie can visit the Blair estate. I'll attend the briefing."

"Not a problem," Jackie said. "I'll also get an update from O'Reilly so we can go over everything tomorrow."

"Great."

Next, Martha handed me the list of residents on the Island who had received a dishonorable discharge from the military. "O'Reilly called in a few favors and got the information, but he's not sure it's complete," she said.

The list contained eleven names: four soldiers deserted under enemy fire; three used excessive force, endangering civilian lives; two performed immoral acts; and two sustained self-inflicted wounds. I recognized the last name, Andy Cognetta, a neighbor of Anita. I asked Martha to remove his name from the report before I handed the list to Lieutenant Sullivan. I wanted to talk with Cognetta myself.

"It's a good start," I said.

"Is there anything else you need?" Martha asked.

"You mentioned we had some walk-in traffic. How about recommending one or two new cases we can take on as our workload thins out?"

"That shouldn't be too difficult, but first you need to

stop taking on jobs for the police. As far as I can tell, they're not paying for your help."

Martha had a good point.

* * * * *

Before the briefing, Sullivan introduced me to the task-force leader, Nick Fuso. You didn't need to know Nick's name to guess his nationality. He wore his jet-black hair slicked back, dressed a notch above his peers, and emphasized his Mediterranean looks and muscular frame with a tight-fitting white shirt. I suspected he enjoyed being one of the few Italians on the force.

"Good to meet ya, Joey. I understand you got this team going. Nice piece of work."

"Just a hunch that paid off. Sullivan actually found the link between the current murders and the two earlier ones. Making any progress?"

"Not much. The creep has gone underground. We haven't found a body in over a month."

"Maybe he decided to hide the bodies of his new victims until the heat dies down," I said.

"So far there haven't been any new missing person reports. I suspect he's playing a waiting game to see if we come up with anything new." Nick said.

"How's he gonna know?"

"We're keeping the press informed. We have to. The public is demanding results."

"Not a bad strategy. The chances of catching him in the act are slim. Keep him scared, and eventually you'll get a break."

O'Reilly came over as Nick and Sullivan walked away to begin the meeting. "I understand you took care of business in Chicago. I wasn't sure you guys would return in one piece," he said.

"Let's say we got lucky. I haven't seen you around since our little meeting with the DA. What's been happening?"

"The bastard's on my back. He thinks you're a danger to the general public and, more importantly, to his chances for re-election. He wants me to find some excuse to pull your ticket."

"He looked mad the other night when he showed up at my uncle's joint with half the police force."

"I'm glad you found my message in the wastebasket. He suspects I tipped you off, and that's why I haven't been hanging around. You'd better watch yourself."

"What can he do as long as I don't stray too far over the line?"

"You'd be surprised. Tell Luigi the next time the DA plans a raid, I might not know about it."

I handed Lieutenant Sullivan the list of dishonorable discharges from the service when he rejoined us. Sullivan showed particular interest in those who used excessive force and said he'd have someone follow up.

"How'd you get this information? This stuff is highly classified."

"I can't give away my sources."

He smiled and put the paper in his inside jacket pocket. "I'll keep you in mind the next time I need access to confidential records," he said as he walked away.

O'Reilly and I paid more attention to Nick's report as he began giving details about the girls murdered several years before the current string of mutilations.

"We have some new information about Deborah Simonette. As you know, she disappeared in June of 1913. At the time, she was seventeen. We recently discovered she had a history of running away, and we now suspect she had a drug problem. Her parents refused to confirm our suspicions, but based on recent interviews with some of her close friends, we're fairly confident this information is correct."

Someone asked why this fact just now surfaced. "Her friends also used drugs at the time and didn't want to admit it," Nick said.

He went on to discuss Gloria Vitale, the young girl found in a ravine in a sparsely populated area of Staten Island. The murderer struck on a night that she had attended an evening church meeting. Not feeling well, she'd left before the service ended. The initial speculation was someone from the meeting had offered her a ride home, but everyone could account for their whereabouts that evening. No new leads had turned up since Gloria's death.

Fuso talked next about Anita. Ralph Ruffalo's name came up several times as the primary suspect, but Nick couldn't rule out Anita might have fallen prey to today's killer.

* * * * *

I returned to the city in time to get ready for dinner with Martha. When she opened the door to her apartment, I stuttered my first few words. She had on a chic flapper dress with a red satin sash around her waist that was unconventional but effective in revealing her sculptured figure. A red velvet cloche hat, worn slightly to the side, framed her face, which when combined with her dress, gave her an impish appearance.

"You want to come in for a drink before we leave?" she asked.

"I better not. We may never make it to the restaurant."

"That would be my choice, not yours," she said as she

joined me in the hallway and locked her door.

Martha had picked a family-owned French restaurant, and in the fine tradition of European dining, we enjoyed a leisurely meal with succulent meats basted in a rich wine-flavored sauce. As the evening progressed, a small jazz band appeared and Martha insisted on dancing. I pretended I didn't know how.

"Why don't we just watch? Dancing isn't something you learn growing up in my neighborhood."

"Well, it's time you learn," she said grabbing my hand and dragging me onto the dance floor.

Little did she realize the army had instructed me in all the latest dance moves even before I learned how to rappel down a steep mountainside. Working behind enemy lines, infiltrating the upper military ranks, required social as well as combat skills.

Martha seemed pleased as we cleared the dance area to the delight of the other dancers, who watched as we glided effortlessly across the floor.

"You're full of surprises. Where did you learn to dance like that?"

"In the army."

"Do you expect me to believe that?"

"It's the truth."

In between dances, I learned more about Martha and the struggles she overcame growing up in an overcrowded tenement section of the city riddled with crime and corruption. In many ways our lives had followed similar paths. She'd also lost a loved one. Her loss was more recent than mine, yet she found the strength to move on. As she talked about him, she sensed what I was thinking.

"I know what happened to my fiancé. He died in France near a farmhouse. A farm girl wrote a letter after the war and told me where her family had buried him. She said she was sorry for my loss and Carl died calling out my name. I can't imagine how it would feel not knowing what happened to him."

As she spoke, distant memories of Anita came rushing back from the first time we met to our last goodbye. "In a couple of days Anita's house is going to be demolished. There are a few things I would like to get, but I'm not sure I can face going back again."

"I know everyone deals with their grief differently, but it's okay to remember, to keep something. I wouldn't want all the things I cherished to vanish when I die."

I needed to change the subject, so I grabbed Martha's hand and returned to the dance floor. We danced and drank until the lights went out.

The next morning the rays of sun rising above the city skyline pierced the bedroom window and moved over my face, waking me from a sound sleep. As I tried to shield my eyes, Martha stirred next to me. At first I felt confused, but then the reality of the situation struck me as hard as a gut punch.

I found my clothes scattered around the room, intermingled with Martha's. I dressed and walked over to the window, watching the clouds slowly move across the sun, spreading its gloom over the city.

I don't know how long I'd been standing there when Martha came to my side and tenderly passed her hand over my shoulder and back. Tears rolled down her face. Neither of us could remember what had happened the night before.

"I'm sorry, Joey. I had no intention for this to happen."

"I know."

"Are you thinking of Anita?"

"No, about us and Jackie. This situation is confusing at times. I know it's my fault. I'm letting Anita's memory control my life."

"Is it because of grief or guilt?"

I turned to her in anger, but as she looked up with her puffy red eyes and put her arms around my neck, I understood I felt both.

"When we turned eighteen, she wanted to get married and had already received her father's blessing and a promise to give us half-interest in the farm. I had always assumed we would live in the city. She refused to leave her father alone to run the farm. We argued, and when I left, she was standing on her porch crying. That was the last time I saw her. If I wasn't so selfish, she might be alive today."

"And she might not. Every decision we make impacts us and those around us, but so do the decisions of others. What we did here last night will have consequences. If we didn't get drunk and had simply said goodnight, we wouldn't be standing here together, but who's to say for sure?"

"Martha, I know you're trying to help, but I don't understand what you're saying."

"You can't go through life blaming yourself for everything that goes wrong because you made a particular choice. Life doesn't revolve around you alone. Decisions made by others also affect our lives. You know, it was Jackie who suggested we have dinner together. She must have known this might happen."

"You're saying even if we had gotten married, Anita might still have disappeared."

"That's right."

* * * * *

That morning we entered the office at different times to avoid any discomfort. I immediately got the three of us together in our circle and asked Jackie to fill us in on her meeting with William Blair.

"Are we all on good terms?" Jackie asked before updating us.

"Yes, but it cost him dearly," Martha answered. "You should have him take you dancing sometime. I think you'd be amazed."

"I'll do that."

"I thought we agreed to keep our workplace professional," I said.

Jackie furrowed her brow as she looked at me and then glanced down at her notes. "I can sum up the whole visit with William Blair by saying the guy is a pompous ass. He recognized me from the papers and seemed more interested in knowing if I killed my husband than finding out what happened to his sister. He does, however, have an alibi for the time of Kathryn's death. He threw a party celebrating his inheritance, which when you think about it, is gruesome. In essence, he celebrated his father's death."

"Can he prove he never left the party?"

"I checked with the staff, and they all remembered seeing him several times during the evening, but no one could say for sure he never left. The Blair mansion is huge, so it's possible he could've slipped out for a short time."

"Did you ask about the two wills?"

"He believes Kathryn and the lawyer were in cahoots and somehow made a false will. According to William, after their mother died, the old man wanted nothing to do with Kathryn; she wasn't his blood. William accused her of knowing the estate would be tied up in court, which is why she stole the cash and left the mansion."

"Sounds like a motive for murder," I said.

"He's certainly mad enough about the money."

"Anything else?"

"He hired a private investigator to track Kathryn's movements from the time she left the mansion to when she died. He's still searching for the money."

"I expect we'll be hearing from his PI before long," Martha said.

"If the guy's any good at his job," Jackie said. "Next, I paid a visit to the textile mill the elder Blair enjoyed running and talked to the plant manager, a David Denton. He couldn't tell me much about the family other than the old man kept a tight rein on things. He insisted on signing all documents of any significance."

"Who's running the business now? Is William Blair taking an active role?" I asked.

"That's the strange thing. Blair could care less. He's fixated on finding what Kathryn stole. That's the part I don't understand. The old man left behind millions, so why is he concerned about a few thousand?"

"What about the cops? Do they have any leads on her murder?"

"According to O'Reilly, they believe the killer was right-handed and at least six inches taller than Kathryn."

"How could they know that?"

"From the angle and tilt of her broken neck.

"Witnesses?"

"None that will talk."

I ran out of questions but then remembered the picture I found in her apartment showing Kathryn standing next to her father, wearing a necklace.

"Did Frank get the necklace appraised?"

"He didn't think it such a good idea with her brother, and potentially a killer, still searching for the money. As you know, she had close to sixty thousand dollars and the necklace looks expensive."

For being an amateur, I thought Jackie had done a great job. "Are you sure you haven't finished reading those PI books? You gathered some good information." She gave me an inviting smile; I made a mental note to compliment her more often.

"This David Denton fellow probably had more contact with the old man than the kids. I think we should delve a little deeper and pay Denton another visit," I said.

"Let's not forget about William Blair," Jackie added. "As you pointed out, his alibi for the night Kathryn died isn't airtight, and I didn't buy his comment about her relationship with the old man. Kathryn's father obviously bought that necklace, and she cared enough for him to keep the picture."

I turned my attention to Martha, hoping Jackie wouldn't catch any subtle clues to last night's mishap. My face flushed as Martha swept aside a strand of hair and launched into her report. Fortunately, Jackie dropped her notepad, which gave me time to regain my composure.

"Did you come up with a couple of new clients for us to evaluate?"

"I talked to an older gentleman who insists the Mafia is following him. He would like us to find out what they want."

"If it's the Mafia, he would already know what they wanted," I said.

"I agree, but he's truly scared. The next case sounds a little more interesting. One of the dockworkers, a George Kowalski, turned up dead last week with a bailing hook through his neck. His daughter, Sadie, said you two were friends."

Before I could answer, Jackie jumped in. "I say we look into the old guy's case. We already have one murder investigation going on, and we're helping Sullivan with his situation. Besides, we don't want to draw more attention from the DA."

I was inclined to look into George Kowalski's death.

I'd known him as far back as I could remember. He always worked with a smile. One day I asked why he looked so happy all the time, even in the sweltering heat of summer. He said *because I live here in America and have a job.* I reluctantly agreed with Jackie, but hoped the cops would soon track down Mr. Kowalski's killer.

Jackie grabbed her coat and headed out to track down the old man with the Mafia complex. Martha stood by the door with my hat and coat.

"Are you going to Anita's house?" she asked.

"They're going to auction off the contents of the farmhouse tomorrow, and I'm gonna grab a few items Anita would want me to have."

"I know it will be difficult, but it's the right thing to do."

As she handed me my hat, I pulled her close. "Thanks for not spilling the beans to Jackie about last night."

"Why would I? Besides, she knows."

"How?"

"She's a woman," she said as she gently pushed me away.

* * * * *

I stood motionless with my hand on the doorknob, remembering the first time Anita had asked me into her bedroom.

"Don't be silly, Joey. My dad's not going to get angry if he finds us together in my room. He trusts me, and besides, he knows we have over a hundred acres where we can do anything we want. Come on, I have something to show you."

I turned the knob, knowing exactly how everything would look. On her bureau would sit a heart-shaped stone. I found it in a creek bed and had given it to her the day we promised to marry. I inscribed on the rock's surface, *Joey and Anita Forever.* Next to the rock would be a hand-held mirror and a brush set, along with a matching comb. It belonged to her grandmother and then her mother. She said someday she would give the set to her daughter. Under the bed would be an old shoebox filled with trinkets we'd found on the days we searched for buried treasure. Every time we dug up an Indian arrowhead, she would make up a story about how the arrowhead ended up where we found it.

When I gathered strength to enter, I took these items and quickly left the house. Before leaving the farm, though, I hiked over to the creek and replaced the rock exactly where I'd picked it up so long ago. It belonged in the creek, just like Anita belonged to the farm.

Next, I drove to Andy Cognetta's farm, Anita's neighbor who had received a dishonorable discharge from the army. When I got there, he was unloading a wagon full of hay. He didn't stop working when he saw me.

"How's the leg?" I asked.

"I get by. What brings you around, as if I didn't know? Heard you stopped by Ralph's place not long ago asking about his whereabouts, and a short time later his folks were burying him."

"I guess he became a big-time gangster in Chicago. I hear it's a pretty tough town."

"What do you want?" he asked again as he hoisted a load of hay up to the loft over the barn.

"Ralph's mom told me you were wounded in the war. Just came over to see how you're doing."

"I can read the papers. They say you've become quite the PI. My guess is you know how I got my bum leg."

I didn't feel the need to answer him. He knew someday

someone would show up knowing he shot himself in the leg to get out of the army.

After securing the rope, he hobbled down from the wagon. “It’s about Anita, isn’t it?”

“Why else would I be here?”

“Ya know, I never liked you because Anita wouldn’t give me or any of the other guys a second look, but I’m gonna give you some advice anyway. Let her go. I saw what it did to her father. Just let her go.”

He looked more sad than afraid, which made me feel his warning was sincere. “I’ll never stop until I know what happened to her. I came by to see if there’s anything new you can tell me about her disappearance.”

“And if I don’t, what are ya gonna do? Tell everyone I’m a coward and not the war hero they think I am? I really don’t care anymore. Living with what I did is a hell of a punishment for a few minutes of poor judgment.”

Looking at him I could see part of myself. We both lived in pain for what the war did to us. My nightmares were different than his, but nightmares nonetheless. “No, this is the last time I’ll ever come by unless my invest-tigation leads me back. I’m not going to judge what you did, and I wouldn’t want you to judge me. I know what it was like over there.”

For the first time, he made eye contact. “There *is* one thing. Anita was scared before she disappeared,” he said looking down again, kicking up some dirt.

“How do you know?”

“Ralph, Louie, and I were fishing one day by the lake when Anita came running over and said the two drifters her father hired came into the barn when she was cleaning out the stalls. The big guy closed the barn doors, shutting out most of the light. They didn’t say anything, but she could hear their heavy boots crushing the hay as they came toward her. Luckily, the stall she hid in had a loose board that she could push out and swing sideways, and that's how she got out."

"Why didn't she tell her father?"

"She was afraid of what he would do to them. She wasn't even sure they knew she was in the barn."

"Did you tell the police?"

"Ralph told me to keep my mouth shut and I did. You knew Ralph—crazy as a wounded bat and sadistic as hell. A few weeks after Anita disappeared, the drifters vanished. It didn't take a genius to know Ralph took care of things. I wasn't surprised the other day when they pulled two skeletons from the bottom of the lake."

"Do you think Ralph might have killed Anita and gotten rid of the drifters to throw suspicion on them?"

"It's possible, but I doubt it. We all grew up together and felt protective of Anita, even Ralph."

"Any strangers around during that time?"

"Nah, we didn't get many visitors, just the usual. You know, the preacher, old Doc Swanson when needed, and a patrol car snooping around every so often. That's about it."

We talked for a few more minutes. I left convinced he had nothing to do with Anita's disappearance.

* * * * *

That night I showed Ma the stuff I recovered from Anita's room and offered her Anita's hairbrush, mirror, and comb. To my surprise, she refused to accept them.

Before we could finish talking, my uncle barged into the kitchen and demanded to know where I'd been all day.

"I don't need to let you know my every move," I said, irritated at his attitude.

"Look, I'm the one getting shot at, having my building

blown up and raided by the DA. How am I supposed to know what's gonna happen next if you don't tell me what you're doin'?"

"Do what you always tell me. 'Be prepared for anything.'"

He leaned forward with clenched fists and then waved his arms about. "What's this I hear that O'Reilly might not be able to tip me off the next time there's a raid on my place. How the hell am I gonna stay in business?" he said, then stormed out yelling all the way up to his joint about what an ungrateful little squirt I've become.

I turned to Ma for moral support, but she added to my frustration.

"This PI business, it's dangerous. Maybe working in the same building where you live is not such a good idea."

It felt like the whole family was turning against me.

* * * * *

As Jackie and I entered the Blair estate, a security guard waved for us to pull over next to a towering hedge that lined the gravel drive.

"You need to stay to the side. An ambulance is on the way."

"What happened?" I asked.

"There's been a hunting accident."

Two police cars arrived, followed by an ambulance. We left the car and walked the remaining distance. Five massive, marble stone steps led up to a veranda that ran the full length of the house. Before I could use the knocker, the huge brass door opened noiselessly, and a butler ushered us into a sitting room, where Mrs. Blair lay on a sofa, crying uncontrollably. Jackie went to her side, and I turned to the butler.

"Are you a doctor?" he asked.

"No, we had business with William. My partner will do what she can to help. What's Mrs. Blair's name?"

"Laura."

"And yours?"

"Joseph, sir."

"Joseph, you didn't say what happened."

"They were hunting quail, and one of the guns fell and fired. I don't think he's going to make it."

"Who?"

"Mr. Blair."

"Did anyone see the accident?"

"Only Mrs. Blair. They were alone."

"Why don't you wet a small cloth with cold water. We'll try to comfort Laura until the doc arrives."

Jackie had already taken every precaution to prevent shock and applied the cloth to Laura's forehead.

"The ambulance has arrived, and your doctor will be here shortly to give you something to sleep. Laura, listen to me," Jackie said. "You need to try to calm down. Put your hand on your stomach, take deeper breaths, and breathe out slowly."

The doctor stormed in, and Jackie stepped aside. We walked over to a terrace window, looked out across a field, and watched as two attendants carried William's lifeless body out of the woods on a stretcher.

"She's putting on an act and a bad one at that," Jackie said. "She'd better hope the doc gives her something to knock her out before the police question her."

"You think she killed him?"

"That or she really didn't love him."

"She could have married him for his money. She does looks older than I expected. I had the impression William was younger than his sister, yet Mrs. Blair looks older than

Kathryn," I said.

"My guess is she has at least eight years on him."

Before I could get back to the butler, the police ushered us into a room with the domestic help. Once they realized we had arrived after the shooting, they politely asked us to leave.

We sat in the car, trying to make sense of the bizarre events in the case.

"Maybe everything is as it seems," Jackie said. "William didn't kill his sister, this was an accident, and the father made a new will."

"Then who killed Kathryn?"

Jackie thought for a moment. "Someone who knew about the money she stole. Sixty thousand is a great motive for murder."

"It's possible, but I'm not ready to jump to any conclusions. There are too many unanswered questions: How can two wills exist without the lawyer knowing about them? What do we know about Laura other than she probably just shot her husband? Where does David Denton fit into the picture? What kind of relationship did old man Blair actually have with his kids?"

"There's only one way to get the real story on the family," Jackie said.

"Yeah, and what's that?"

"Ask the butler."

Having a female partner, although unconventional, certainly has benefits. "Good idea. He's yours. That leaves the question of the wills, and the lawyer should have the answer to that one."

"Hey, this is fun. I don't really mean fun, it's interesting," Jackie said. We would've continued discussing the case, but a cop came over and moved us along.

By the time we got back to the office and filled Martha

in on the latest developments, it was late afternoon. I took the rest of the day off, leaving Jackie and Martha working together to set up appointments and figure out how to gather more information about the Blairs.

A few days later, Jackie and I finally caught up with David Denton, the Blair textile plant manager. He seemed pleased to see us—or at least Jackie—again. Denton basically repeated what he'd already told her, but our visit gave me a chance to delve a little deeper. I felt Denton might not be a casual observer in this affair, since he was so heavily involved in the family business.

"How many times a month did you have to get the old man's signature to keep this place running?" I asked.

"I would go there once a week, sometimes twice."

"Did he ever turn the responsibility over to you or William before he died?"

"Nah, the old man kept tight control over the business until his last breath. If he was going to turn things over to anyone in the family, it would've been Kathryn. She knew more about the business than William."

"How are you managing to keep the place running? It appears the estate will be tied up in the courts for some time, sorting out the two wills."

"The judge gave me the authority to draw on a line of credit that was in place at the time of Mr. Blair's death. Unfortunately, the factory's expenses exceed its income this time of the year, and the credit is about to run out."

"I would think the textile business would be fairly steady during the year," I said.

"That's what you'd think, but the reality is most everyone waits for the holiday sales."

"What's going to happen if you run out of money?" Jackie asked.

"I'll have to shut down and let everyone go. It's a

shame. It really is a profitable business," Denton said.

"I'm sure my associate told you Miss Blair hired us to investigate her murder."

"She did, but I don't understand how that's possible."

"Let's just call it woman's intuition. What's important is Kathryn gave us a sizable retainer, and I'm willing to use some of that money to keep the factory open until the legal issues are resolved."

"Why?"

"I think Kathryn would have wanted it that way. How about going over your monthly expenses to see how much it would cost."

We spent the next half-hour looking at the factory's books. The business definitely had a seasonal swing, which is probably why the old man kept so much money in his private safe. Denton did mention Mr. Blair didn't trust the banking system.

"I'd like you to keep our little deal quiet until we figure out who killed Kathryn. In the meantime, you can work directly with my secretary when you need cash," I told Denton.

* * * * *

District Attorney Peterson finally got his day of glory when he caught my uncle unprepared, with his joint in full swing and booze flowing like tap water. The DA gave orders to wreck the place, and his men did a thorough job with fire axes and sledgehammers. By the time they were through, not a single glass remained whole nor a table on which to put the shattered pieces. As the DA left, he flipped a nickel at Luigi and told him to buy himself a sarsaparilla.

The next day Luigi got a summons to appear in court on bootlegging and racketeering charges. Forsythe's little black book of civil servants he bribed gave us a persuasive argument to convince the judge to throw the case out on a technicality. The outcome of the trial incensed the DA, and he redoubled his efforts to monitor my activities.

If having the DA on my back wasn't enough, my uncle blamed me for bringing a pox on his house and for turning him into a common apartment super.

"What am I supposed to do all day?" he asked over dinner after the trial. "Walk around in a dirty undershirt and drink beer sitting on the front stoop like the rest of the supers in this damn town?"

"Luigi," Ma said. "I can manage the tenants, and there are plenty of tradesmen around the neighborhood if the building has any problems. You should go and open another business."

"Yeah, like what?"

"You can always help me," Pop said.

Luigi shot out of his chair so fast he bumped the table, spilling the wine glasses. "Sure, why not? You still need someone to clean the shit off the shoes so you won't dirty your hands?"

Luigi was turning to leave when Ma stopped him with an angry tirade. "Luigi, you leave this table now, you'll never share a meal with us again. Is that what you want?"

I reached him before he could react, put my arm around his shoulder, and led him into the hall. "Uncle Luigi, I'm sorry for everything. I promise I'll make it up to you somehow. Don't let this break us up. We're family. Nothing else matters."

He gave me a gentle embrace and returned to the table.

Pop poured more wine, and we tried again.

"Ma had a good suggestion, Uncle Luigi. She can take care of the tenants. You need to get back into the speakeasy business," I said.

"The DA will just shut me down again. Besides, I don't have the dough to open a new place."

"Work for Castellano," I said. "He has several joints around town, and they never get raided. Convince him he could use you to oversee all his saloons, so he can concentrate on other matters."

"I'll think about it," Luigi said, and that was the end of the discussion.

Since Jackie and Martha didn't make it to dinner, I helped Ma clean up.

"What did you decide to do with Anita's hairbrush set?" Ma asked.

"I don't know yet. Right now it's in a box under my bed."

"You should keep it and give it to your daughter if you have one someday."

"Don't you think my future wife would have a problem with that?"

"If she does, you shouldn't marry her. We all lose people we love, and over time we move on, but we should never forget."

"Someone else told me the same thing."

"I wear a locket that belonged to my grandmother and inside are pictures of her parents. I want you to take it and put it in this box with Anita's stuff."

"Ma, I can't take this now."

"You need this locket more than I do. Someday you give it to your daughter and tell her about your family and then give her Anita's hairbrush and tell her how much you loved each other. But Joey, first you need to get married, and to do that you need to put Anita in the past."

I did what she suggested, and when I placed the locket in Anita's box, I felt her presence and a sense she also wanted me to move on with my life.

* * * * *

Over the next few days, information about the Blair family trickled in from various sources. Jackie met with the butler, and Martha had dinner a few times with David Denton. Between the two of them, a picture emerged that didn't seem to support prior statements made by Kathryn or her brother, William.

"The butler has a low opinion of Laura Blair. He has such strong feelings, his eye began to twitch five minutes into our conversation," Jackie said.

"Why?"

"He believes Laura seduced William into marrying him, but when the old man died, she cut him off completely. They've slept in separate bedrooms and even ate at different times."

"How long did they know each other?"

"A little over nine months, married for six," Jackie said.

"How did they meet?"

"According to the butler, she was a secretary at the law firm the family used and came to the house to take dictation for old man Blair from time to time."

"Did you ask about the shooting? Was Laura an experienced hunter?"

"William liked to quail hunt on the estate and somehow convinced Laura to join him. It was only the second time they went out to practice when the accident occurred."

"Anything else?"

"Get this. Neither Kathryn nor William were direct descendents of the Blair line."

"How's that possible?" I asked.

"Simple. His wife was married twice before and had a child with each husband."

"Then William lied to us about his relationship with his

father, which means he could've lied about how the old man felt about Kathryn. Any other bombshells you want to drop to make this case even more confusing?"

"That's about it, other than the fact the butler and maid were let go a few days after the shooting."

"Nice bit of snooping," I said. "We now have a connection between Laura and the law firm. Based on the butler's observations about the sudden change in Laura's behavior toward William, I'll bet the accidental shooting wasn't an accident and another man's involved."

"Are you going to investigate the shooting?" Martha asked.

"No. I think we need to stay focused on the wills and why Kathryn was murdered."

"The obvious motive is the loot she stole from the house. I've met a few people who would kill for sixty grand, not to mention that necklace," Martha said.

"Maybe. Did you get anything out of Denton?"

"A couple of nice meals," she said with a suggestive look at Jackie I'm sure I wasn't supposed to catch.

"I'm glad you had a nice time, but I'm more interested in information that could help us find Kathryn's killer, and not your personal life," I said, a little irritated.

"Oh, sorry. Then you might be interested in knowing the lawyer who drew up the 'wills' isn't the current Blair attorney, as I'm sure you assumed. That man died in an auto accident less than seven months ago, and his younger associate took over the account."

"That would explain why the family lawyer didn't know about a second will," Jackie said.

"Not necessarily. Denton's theory is the lawyer is up to his neck in whatever's going on," Martha said.

It was getting late, and I offered to take them both to dinner so we could continue the conversation. To my surprise, they turned me down.

"I have a date tonight," Martha said.

"Who?"

"I thought you weren't interested in my personal life."

I could feel my face burning again. "I don't think Denton can add any more to our investigation."

"If you must know, I'm going out with Anthony Brown, the assistant district attorney."

And with that she left the room. I looked over to Jackie.

"Sorry, I'm busy tonight. I'm meeting with our new client, the one who thinks he's being followed by the Mafia."

"I'll come along."

Jackie returned to her desk before responding. "Actually, if you don't mind, I'd like to see if I can handle this case on my own."

"Sure, I understand," I said, but I really didn't.

* * * * *

The first chance I got, I dumped everything I knew about the Blair case into Frank Galvano's lap, and he shoved it right back.

"You don't have a thing. It's all circumstantial evidence, if that."

"Frank, how can you say that? Even a ten-year-old could put this puzzle together. Laura Blair and the new lawyer planned this whole mess months ago, and now three people are dead."

"Look, you're too emotionally involved, and I know it's my fault. You need to forget Kathryn reached out from the grave and asked you to find her killer. You don't have any hard evidence. Besides, your theory doesn't make any sense."

"How can you say that?"

Frank looked at me as he would a lost puppy. "Have a seat and I'll explain.

"Let's assume you're right. Then where the hell did the second will come from? The will naming Kathryn as sole beneficiary is dated the same day as the one naming William as beneficiary. Why would Laura kill William before her so-called accomplice, the lawyer, proved Kathryn's will was bogus? As it stands right now, Kathryn's estate could get everything since the will naming her as beneficiary was the one in the lawyer's safe. There's one more thing you're overlooking. If the lawyer is involved with Laura and everything that's happened is part of some complex plan, why does a second will even exist? You'd think the lawyer would have destroyed the will naming Kathryn as beneficiary."

I didn't say anything, put the chair back, and left his office. I slammed the door, more out of frustration than anger, and headed downstairs for dinner. Frank was right. I let myself get too emotionally tied up with Kathryn. She asked for my help before she was murdered, and I wasn't there for her. Aside from feeling frustrated, I also felt incomepetent.

To make matters worse, dinnertime was routinely turning into a shouting match between my uncle and me. He still blamed me for his run of bad luck. Seeing Ma limping around, trying to be her old self but getting depressed when she couldn't do everything she wanted, didn't help matters, and all Pop could do was swear about his bombed-out shop. Martha hardly joined us anymore, and Jackie would take a plate of food up to the office to continue studying for her upcoming PI exam. That's what she said, but I think she was just getting away from all the tension. I felt like I was living inside a pressure cooker, waiting for the lid to blow. It finally did, and all it took was an innocent question.

"Uncle Luigi, how are things goin'?"

"What, you being a wise guy? How do you think it's goin? It's the shits. I spent all these years building up my business, taking care of my customers, and you destroy it all in less than a year."

"So, what now? You're blaming me again because you got busted for running an illegal business. It was gonna happen sooner or later. Your problem is you didn't have any back-up plans."

"I wouldn't need no back-up plans if the DA wasn't on your ass. You draw trouble like shit draws flies. Look around ya, Joey. Everyone's busted up but you."

"You think I don't know what went on back in Italy? Torrio told me everything. If I'm trouble, it's because I got your blood running through my veins."

That's when Pop jumped into the argument. "What did Torrio tell you?"

"He told me plenty—enough to know how you could beat a guy to death and not show any signs of regret."

"Joey!" Ma shouted.

"Hey, don't worry. I have blood all over these hands, and it doesn't bother me either. Why you looking so shocked, Ma? Remember, you didn't grow up in a convent."

Ma caught me with a wicked backhand across the face before Pop reached me, saving me from a sound trashing. I had sense enough to leave the room.

No one ever apologized. It was as if the conversation never took place, and that was fine with me. I apparently scratched the surface of a family secret, and I wasn't sure it was in anyone's best interest for me to know more. I did my best to concentrate on work and let any family issues resolve themselves.

* * * * *

It was clear from my meeting with Frank Galvano that our next priority in the Blair case was to question the new family lawyer, Gregory Johnson. Unable to get an appointment after several attempts, Jackie and I barged in unannounced. Mr. Johnson's secretary, who looked like she should be modeling clothes rather than sitting behind a desk, took her job seriously and refused to give us access to her boss. Frustrated, we simply walked into his office.

"And who might you be?"

"We have a few questions about Kathryn Blair's murder," I said.

"Are you with the police?

"Private investigators."

"I already gave a statement to the police."

"You'll talk to us now or I'll turn over to the police what we've uncovered."

"Is that supposed to be a threat?"

"We don't make idle threats. How long did Laura Blair work for you before marrying William Blair?"

Johnson leaned forward on his desk. "What the hell does that have to do with Kathryn's murder? I demand to know who hired you, Mr.…."

"Batista, Joey Batista, and this is my partner, Jacqueline Forsythe. It has plenty to do with Kathryn, and it's none of your business who hired us. I'm putting you on notice, pal. Once I prove the will you executed naming William Blair as sole beneficiary is a fake, you and your girlfriend, Laura, are going away for a long time."

"What are you talking about? The will in my safe named Kathryn Blair as the sole beneficiary. Somehow William produced a second will duly signed by my predecessor and properly witnessed. I have no idea how any of this is possible. For a private investigator, you have your facts mixed up."

Jackie stepped in, trying to see if she could rattle his confidence. "I don't think it will be too difficult to prove you and Laura were more intimate than you'd like people to believe, and how about Kathryn? Did you also have a relationship with her? Maybe you were covering both bases."

"This whole conversation is absurd. I didn't draw up either will and just to get you two out of here, Laura and I never had anything other than a professional relationship, and Kathryn Blair was a client and nothing more. I suggest you leave before *I* call the police."

"Call a lawyer instead. In case you haven't noticed, three people are dead, and they are all linked to this office," I said as we walked out.

Leaving the building, I said to Jackie, "That conversation went well."

Jackie frowned. "If you ask me, he has a point. We don't have a clue what's going on in this case."

"We do now."

"What are you talking about? He just confused the hell out of me."

"Look at it this way. Either he's lying or he's telling the truth."

"How does that help?"

"If he's lying and he and Laura are involved, then he will have to prove Kathryn's will is a fake. If he's telling the truth, then there must be a third will. The original will."

"How did you come to *that* conclusion?"

"Laura, as the secretary, typed the original will, so she knew its contents. William probably agreed to marry her if she would somehow change the will. The old man dies and who gets the estate? Kathryn. The question is who changed the will again and how?"

"The lawyer," Jackie said.

"How would making Kathryn the beneficiary help him?"

"Just as I suggested, he and Kathryn were planning to get married."

"So you think he double-crossed Laura?"

"Why not?"

"To get his hands on any money, he would have to kill both William and Laura. Too complicated."

"Okay, but explain again why you think there's a third will."

"If William's will is phony, so is Kathryn's because Laura would have destroyed it if Kathryn was the original heir," I said as we got into the car.

Jackie didn't say anything on the ride back to the office but turned toward me after I parked the car. "So what do we do now?"

"Hey, don't forget I'm new at this business too. I guess we keep on digging for information, react to whatever happens, and hope we get lucky."

November

A few nights later I made the mistake of joining O'Reilly at his new watering hole when he was with a few of his police buddies. I should've walked out as soon as I saw the crowd surrounding him. Living under a saloon all my life, I knew when a wop drinks with more than one Irishman, one of three things happen: you'll find yourself in a drinking contest that you have no prayer of winning; in a brawl where you'll be on the losing end; or both, in which case you'll probably wake up in the hospital.

Around midnight the drinking got serious as we switched to chugging Guinness Stout boilermakers. O'Reilly glanced my way as he lowered his glass and nodded toward the door. That was all the encouragement I needed. A few more rounds of drinks and I would be trading insults with some of New York's toughest cops, and O'Reilly and I both knew how that would end. I stood as straight as I could, threw some money on the table, and weaved my way to the exit followed by the sounds of hearty laughter and a few slurs about Italians who can't hold their liquor.

Once outside, it didn't take long to sober up as a glacial wind blasted me with rain and sleet. Hunched over, I sunk deeper into my army coat and tightened my scarf as I trudged along Front Street. Clutching my coat collar with one hand and shielding my eyes with the other, I leaned farther into the wind and turned onto Market Street. About two blocks from my apartment, I noticed a dark shadow wedged between concrete stairs and the edge of a storefront. I reached over and gave the guy a gentle shove.

"Gino, that you?"

"Who wants to know?"

"Me, Joey Batista. What ya doin' out here? Don't you have a place to hole up? You need to get indoors."

"A couple of bums took my bedroll and kicked me out of my shelter. I'll be okay. I got me a pint."

When I straightened up, I saw my reflection in the store window, with warm clothes clinging to my body. Just a few minutes ago I thought I would freeze to death, and here sat Gino with ice clinging to his beard and nothing on but a pair of overalls and a light jacket. I unbuttoned my coat and shrugged it off my shoulders. In a few minutes I'd be home; Gino needed it more than I did.

With my arms entangled in the coat behind me, I felt a sudden presence. Before I could react, a thin wire encircled my scarf and pulled me back against an unknown attacker. I struggled to free myself, but the more I resisted, the faster the wire cut through the scarf. Gasping for air, about to pass out, I heard my old drill sergeant shouting in my ear, *Batista, how many time do I have to tell you? Thrust yourself back away from the pressure, not against it.*

With what strength I had left, I heaved backwards pushing us both through the store window. As glass fragments rained down upon us, the pressure around my neck lessoned, giving me the chance to pull one arm up enough to slip a few fingers under the scarf. This gave me the leverage needed to roll over, smashing his body into the ragged glass held in place by the vertical edge of the window frame. The pressure on my neck vanished as more glass fragments rained down upon us. I hurled forward, using my arms as a shield, and landed on the ground just as a shard of glass fell from the top of the window frame, severing the assailant's carotid. I knew he'd be dead in a matter of seconds.

The wind and rain swirling around us turned the blood squirting from his neck into a red mist. I covered his wound with the palm of my right hand, trying to stop the shower of blood from drenching me as I rifled through his coat pockets. All I found was a folded piece of paper. As I opened it, the writing bled blackish red.

It took a few seconds for the meaning of the quickly fading words to sink in. When they did, I sprinted as fast as I could. Nothing would stop me, nothing, not even the pain from my numerous cuts. The stairs flew by in a blur as I took three at a time to Jackie's apartment. What to do? Knock, shoot, yell, maybe all three? Suddenly I faced a giant with a bowie knife in his huge grip. He raised the knife and moved toward me. I had difficulty holding my gun steady. Before I could get off a shot, his back arched violently, then he bent forward, swayed, and fell with a deep groan, hitting the floor.

As I looked up from the brute, I saw Jackie standing by her dining table with blood gushing from her nose, holding a bloodied carving knife. We moved toward each other and embraced. As we separated, I attempted to stop her bleeding, but the more I tried, the more blood covered her face.

"Joey, stop. Oh my God!" she gasped.

That's when I realized the extra blood was my own. Suddenly my legs felt wobbly and my vision blurred. Just before losing consciousness, I heard Uncle Luigi's gruff voice.

"What the hell's goin' on now?"

Two days later I woke in a hospital room with my wrist and face bandaged and the DA standing over me. "Doc says you're okay to leave, so we're taking you in." Next thing I knew, I was sitting in an interrogation room with O'Reilly leaning against a wall and the DA straddling the back of a chair across from me. He pushed a pack of butts across the table.

"Not my brand," I said, sliding them back with my good hand.

He took his time lighting up, then blew smoke in my face.

"How'd ya get all those cuts? The doc told me you're pretty lucky; a little deeper slice across that wrist and you would've bled to death."

"Sorry to disappoint you."

"There's always next time. You gonna tell us why you killed that fella?"

"I don't know who you're talking about."

"The guy they removed from a storefront window, not far from your place. He had cuts like yours and a severed neck."

"Are you telling me I'm the only person you could find in this city with a few scratches?"

The DA took a swat at a fly.

"No, but the trail of blood leading to your office was a unique clue."

"I want to see my lawyer."

O'Reilly pushed away from the wall and pulled up a chair, mimicking the DA. For some reason I felt like I'd been through this charade before. "Tell us what happened. It'll go a lot easier on ya," he said.

I watched O'Reilly, looking for some sign, anything that would tell me how to respond. He took a cigarette from the pack on the table, lit up, shook one free. "*No*, I forgot, not your brand," he said, handing the pack back to the DA. The message couldn't be clearer: keep my mouth shut.

"I want to see my lawyer."

The door opened, and a guard let Frank Galvano and Gino into the room. The DA slumped forward, putting his head on his hands, which gripped the back of his chair, then stood to face Frank.

"We've been waiting for you. Who's this fellow?"

"He's a local who hangs out around the neighborhood. I have to move him along every now and then," O'Reilly said before Frank could answer.

"Are we inviting bums off the street now during murder investigations?" shouted the DA.

Frank shoved a court order for my immediate release into the DA's hand. "He's a witness to what happened the other night and just made an official statement. He saw the guy fall through the store window stone drunk. Joey tried to help and got cut up pretty bad for his efforts."

"So why the hell did Batista run away?"

"What would you do if you lived a few doors down the street and your wrist was slit open?" Frank asked.

The DA turned to O'Reilly. "Get this bum out of here and double check his story. And find someone to take Batista's statement."

I rose to talk to Frank, but the DA shoved me back. If Frank wasn't present, I think he would've lost control. His hands closed into fists and his face flushed. "Where do you think you're going? I'm not done with you," he said as he leaned forward, inches from my face. "One of these days, Batista, your luck is gonna run out, and when it does, I'm gonna bury your ass so deep into the justice system the only way you'll get out is in a box."

"For that to happen, you gotta be around, and the way I see it, you're doing such a lousy job protecting the citizens of this precinct, you'll be pounding the pavement in a few months."

He shoved the table, hitting me in the chest, and headed for the door. "Stay put until we get a full statement, and you better pray I don't connect you to any more dead bodies," he said as he pushed past Frank.

Once in his car, Frank explained how Gino got me off the hook. "After you took off, Gino poured whiskey down the guy's throat and put the bottle in his pocket."

I turned to Gino. "I don't know what to say. How can I repay you?"

"How about a bottle of whiskey?"

We paid for a month's lodging at one of the better flophouses, after we got Gino a new bedroll, some warm clothes, and a supply of liquor. On the ride back to Luigi's brownstone, I tried to get Frank to tell me why the DA didn't know about the dead guy in Jackie's apartment, but he wouldn't give. As he dropped me off in front of the building to go find a parking spot, he leaned across the seat. "Everyone's waiting for you inside. All I can say is you're damn lucky you have friends and connections."

As soon as I entered the main living area, Ma smothered me with kisses and Pop gave me a rare embrace. Even Uncle Luigi showed a little emotion. Rosalie inspected my bandage and walked me over to a chair.

"You need to take it easy. You've lost a lot of blood," she said.

"Don't worry, I've had enough transfusions to satisfy a vampire."

"Thanks to Luigi. We thought they were gonna drain him dry," Ma said.

Before I could thank him, Luigi just brushed it off. "I got more than enough for both of us. Just do me a favor and wait a few weeks before you get shot up or somethin' so I can build up a fresh supply."

Ma didn't appreciate his sense of humor and wanted to

know who tried to kill Jackie and me.

"We don't know yet. Neither person had any identification, but I'm sure it has something to do with one of the cases we're working."

"So why did the DA arrest you when this man attacked you?" she asked.

"The DA has it out for me. Don't worry, I can handle him."

I think Luigi hated the DA more than me. "I'm gonna get that son-of-a-bitch. He's messin' with the wrong family."

"He's untouchable," Pop said.

"That's what you think. He's up for reelection, and I control this ward. The other ward bosses will follow my lead on this one. They all hate his guts."

"You might not have the control you think. Remember, women can vote now," I said.

Luigi looked at me as if I was crazy. "Women ain't gonna vote, and if they do, they'll vote the way their men tell them."

Ma didn't say anything, but from the way she looked at Luigi, I'd bet against him on that one.

"He has one thing goin' for him: he's honest," I said. "All I need is to convince him we're on the same side."

"What makes you think he's honest? He's just as crooked as every other politician in this town," Luigi said.

"He's wasn't on Forsythe's payoff list."

"That's chump change to him. He gets a cut from every speakeasy in town. The Feds, the DA, and the beat cops all get theirs right off the top, just part of doing business."

My uncle's point made me realize how naive I was about the inner workings of City Hall. I decided to take the DA's warning more seriously.

* * * * *

Jackie insisted I stay with her for a few days until I fully recovered, but Ma had other ideas.

"I think I can care for my son."

"We know that, but someone tried to kill both of us. It's best we stick together," Jackie said.

Ma wasn't about to give in, but thanks to Luigi she finally relented.

"I'll post a few boys on the fourth floor; they'll be safe. You got a business to run and need to make sure that leg of yours doesn't get re-infected."

"My leg's fine!"

"Then quit limping around bellyaching all day about how you can't do this and you can't do that."

Jackie and I slipped out of the room as Ma shifted her ire to my uncle.

The doctor ordered complete bed rest, so we stayed indoors and spent most of our time reviewing where we stood on the various cases and trying to figure out who hired those goons to bump us off.

"I talked to O'Reilly when you were laid up in the hospital, and he thinks they were brought in from out of town, professionals."

"I guess we got lucky, but before we speculate on who tried to kill us, I want to know something. How come the DA didn't ask about that ugly brute in your apartment?"

"The cops never came to my place."

"How's that possible? The DA said the cops followed the trail of blood and it should've led to your door."

"After Rosalie stopped the bleeding, we moved you outside our office so the ambulance attendants or the cops wouldn't see the mess in my apartment."

"What about the blood in the hallway?"

"Your uncle had some of his men clean the hall and replace the stained carpet in my place."

"I guess he also took care of the dead body?"

"No, you have Castellano to thank for that."

For some time it had become painfully obvious that if I didn't have the support of family and friends around me, I'd probably be dead or in the can. I knew someday they might not be there, and if Jackie and I were going to survive in the PI business, we'd better learn from our mistakes.

"Tell me what happened before I arrived. How did the guy get in your room?"

Jackie looked away as if disgusted with herself for making such a stupid blunder. "I'd already gone to bed and was about to fall asleep when I heard a noise. It took me a few seconds to realize someone was knocking on my door. I thought it was you. When I released the lock, the door swung open, sending me flying across the room into a table with a bloodied nose."

"That proved to be a fatal mistake for your attacker."

"True, but I was dazed long enough for him to pull out the biggest chiv I'd ever seen."

"You're lucky you had your knives nearby."

"I had a bad feeling after leaving the lawyer's office and have been wearing your father's harness ever since. Before going to bed, I laid it on the table. If you hadn't fired those shots at my door when you did, I think he would have reached me before I had time to react. He turned when you burst in, and that's when I drove a carving knife between his shoulder blades."

"You're one tough dame, but from now on I want you to also carry your gun."

We turned our attention to figuring out who wanted us dead. The list of potential candidates mirrored the DA's litany of accusations. After looking at all the possibilities, we agreed that whoever killed Kathryn Blair was probably getting nervous and wanted us out of the way. It seemed too much of a coincidence that the attack came so soon after leaving the lawyer's office. Our second choice was someone from Chicago. We certainly made dangerous enemies on our last trip. I called Castellano the next morning and asked him to check out that angle.

We spent two days and nights together, but not the way I'd envisioned. Jackie insisted I get plenty of rest and waited until I fell asleep before coming to bed. Both nights I woke out of a deep sleep in a cold sweat. On the second night, Jackie didn't believe my explanation.

"You don't have a fever, and your cuts are healing nicely. So don't give me any more bull. Tell me why you're having nightmares."

"I think most guys who made it home from the front lines have nightmares. Don't worry about it."

"How often do you have them?"

"I can't predict when they're gonna happen. Usually they last for a few days, then might not occur again for weeks or months."

"Is it always the same nightmare?"

"No, I went on numerous missions."

"Did you ever share your war experiences with anyone?"

"The army docs in Switzerland tried to get me to open up, but I wasn't ready."

"Maybe it's time. I'm a good listener."

"It's not pleasant."

"I've had some rough times. I don't think you'll shock me," she said.

"I guess not. I already told you I joined a special unit, but didn't tell you why. To be honest, after Anita's disappearance, I felt I had nothing to come home to."

"I understand. Go on."

"It was near the end of the war, and we had to eliminate one of Germany's greatest strategists before a major offensive, but he never left his fortified headquarters or allowed anyone into his inner circle he hadn't personally known for years. We tried to come up with a plan for over a month without success."

"Who was he?"

"You wouldn't know him. The Germans kept him under wraps and well protected."

"Did you ever get to him?"

"We were running out of time when I came up with a crazy scheme. The chances of success weren't high, but we had to act. There was only one way to get into the castle. I had to become a high-value prisoner. The plan was simple. Get caught with details about an imminent invasion with only one piece of information missing—where the landing would take place!"

"That's insane. They would torture you to get the location."

"That was the idea. When they believed I was near death, I would agree to give up the details only to the general."

"Wouldn't he be suspicious?"

"That was one of the many pitfalls of the plan, but if I could hold out long enough, we figured he'd do anything to get that last bit of information as the date of the invasion neared."

"Is that how you got all these scars?"

"Most of them. The electric shock treatments were the worst. All the nerves in my body felt like they'd burst into flame at the same time, consuming every ounce of my flesh."

"How in the world did you expect to do anything in

such a state, even if you got close to the general?"

"Everyone in our unit was considered expendable, and part of our ongoing training consisted of withstanding excruciating pain. The enemy didn't inflict all of these scars. The army conditioned us to keep a reserve of energy to take advantage of any sudden opportunity. I had prepared for two years between missions for such an assignment."

"That's not possible."

"Everything's possible, because the mind has complete control over our bodies and how we respond to our surroundings. We know from experience that fire burns, skin bleeds when cut, and if our air supply gets cut off for a few minutes, we die. But it doesn't have to work that way. I've seen skin burn from a piece of ice because the person believed he was being touched with a hot metal rod, and I've walked across burning coals without getting a blister. It can be done."

"Is that how you made it to my apartment? You blocked out the pain from your wounds?"

"Even without the training, nothing would have stopped me from reaching you."

Jackie's eyes glistened as she reached for my hand and held tight.

"What happened after they tortured you?"

"I agreed as planned to give up the location of the invasion to the general and only him. Two of my torturers brought me into the general's office and threw me into a soft leather chair. The general didn't even bother to look up from his desk, just gave the order to leave us alone. It was the last order he ever gave."

"What did you do?"

"As soon as the guards turned to leave, I was on my feet and tapped one on the shoulder. When he turned, I drove the bridge of his nose up into his skull, grabbed the bayonet from his belt, sliced his partner's throat, and skewered the general as he stood in horror. I don't think I'll ever forget the look on his face."

"How did you get out of the castle?"

"Let's save that for another night," I said as I reached for her.

"Is this going to be like the Arabian Nights?" she asked with a playful smile.

"I don't have that many nightmares, but now I wish I did."

"Maybe this nightmare will stop. The war's over, the general's dead, and they didn't break your spirit."

I didn't respond, but I did feel a sense of relief after talking about what'd happened in that dungeon.

The next day I went back to my apartment to rest, and when I awoke alone, I felt a churning in the pit of my stomach—a feeling I hadn't experienced since Anita's disappearance.

Upon entering the office for the first time in nearly a week, I caught David Denton blowing Martha a goodbye kiss. They had just finished reviewing some bills that needed to be paid. Martha greeted me more formally than I anticipated, but then again she'd made it clear from the outset our relationship would only last until she found Mr. Right. Whether that was Denton or the assistant DA, I didn't know.

In stark contrast, when I entered the inner office, Jackie gave me one of her knockout smiles. Vivid memories of the last few days generated thoughts that definitely didn't help my concentration.

We settled into our own routines, as if nothing unusual had taken place between us, which seemed odd until I realized violence, bizarre happenings and revelations about our personal lives were becoming commonplace. A truly dynamic and unpredictable workplace had turned into a regimental routine of new heights of excitement, followed by sharp drops in adrenaline. Little did I know a new cycle had already been set into motion.

Jackie was giving me an update on the old man who thought the Mafia had marked him for death when Martha opened the door and leaned against the doorframe, silent and motionless except for the blood draining from her face, leaving behind a ghostly mask. I stumbled over the waste-basket as I came from behind my desk. She waved me away and gingerly moved to one of the chairs.

"I just spoke with Lieutenant Sullivan. Shirley was found murdered this morning on the clinic grounds," she said. "I'm sorry, Joey. I didn't expect anything like this to happen to someone we know."

Rage and guilt forged a renewed feeling of vengeance that had been simmering below the surface for years. I couldn't believe the lunatic roaming the Island, killing innocent woman, had snatched another person from my life.

"Did Sullivan give any details?"

"No, only that he doesn't think it's the serial killer."

Once I regained control, I realized Shirley didn't fit the pattern. I sat down and was reaching for the phone when Jackie let out a small shriek. As I turned toward her, she brought her hand up to cover her mouth and then wiped away tears.

"I just remembered, Shirley called and said she needed to talk to you, but then said she'd call back later."

"When? Why didn't you tell me?" I shouted as I slammed down the receiver.

"You were in the hospital. She didn't sound scared or concerned. I offered to go to her, but she said it wasn't necessary. When the DA took you from the hospital, all hell broke out around this place. In the excitement I forgot about her call."

"You forgot! She's *dead* because you forgot."

"Please don't say that, Joey. I can't live with that guilt."

"You're going to have to. How can I trust you as a partner if you can't do something as simple as give me a message?"

She stood rigid, looking down at me with pain and anguish in her eyes. "Didn't you hear what I just told you? And don't talk to me about trust. What about you two? Did *you* forget to tell me something? You think I don't know you slept together and then lied about it? You never needed me as a partner in the first place. Martha does all the real work. I don't know why you even asked me to join you."

As I stood, she moved back. All I could think about was that Shirley was dead because I wasn't there when she called for my help. "It's simple. You needed a job after killing your husband, and I felt sorry for you."

Before I could say anything else, she picked up her purse and stormed out, slamming the door behind her. Martha and I sat in silence, staring at the closed door.

"Go after her, Joey. You didn't mean what you said."

I wanted to. I wanted to take back every word, but having a female partner in this business was insane and dangerous for us both.

"Maybe later. The way I'm feeling, I'll just make things worse. Besides, this is no business for a woman," I said.

"Jackie can take care of herself."

"I thought the same about Shirley."

* * * * *

O'Reilly and I met Sullivan at the clinic. Shirley's murder had taken place by the swings, near the pond. Sullivan showed no emotion as he went through the crime scene.

"The victim probably knew her attacker. The knife wound entered the abdomen just below the navel. It appears whoever killed her enjoyed what he was doing. The coroner's guess is he held her close as he shoved the blade deeper and deeper into the initial wound, to the point the attacker's hand actually penetrated the stomach. He probably held her close, looked into her eyes, and watched her die with each upward thrust of the blade."

"You're sure it's not the same guy who killed all the other girls?" I asked.

"Nothing fits. She's older, obviously not a virgin, wasn't walking a lonely street at night. No, this guy wanted her dead and took a risk. My guess is there was a sense of urgency, or he would've waited for a better opportunity," Sullivan said.

O'Reilly asked if they found any evidence that would be useful.

"No one heard or saw anything. Everyone was sleeping. There's no sign of a struggle; it hasn't rained in several days, so the ground didn't reveal any footprints."

"Has Shirley's sister been able to help?" I asked.

"The doc has her sedated, so we haven't gotten a statement yet," Sullivan replied.

After O'Reilly and Sullivan left, I paid the doc a visit.

"Naturally the girls are disturbed; Shirley had a great rapport with them. Somehow she understood what each and every one of them were experiencing and could relate to their emotional and physical pain," he said.

I never told the doc or Maria about Shirley's real background. Of course she related to the girls. She had done it all and somehow found the courage to pull herself out of her own personal hell.

"How's her sister?"

"The only reason she's still here was Shirley's influence. I'm afraid she'll leave as soon as the sedatives wear off."

"You mind if I stay with her? I'd like to be there when she wakes up."

"Sure, but be warned. She's beyond help."

It took a few hours for Debbie to wake. As she pulled herself up into a sitting position, I sat next to her on the bed.

"My sister?" she murmured.

"She's gone, Debbie."

Debbie put her arms around me and cried on my shoulder. It was difficult to find the words to comfort her, so I held her gently and let the grief rack her body. When she pulled away, I wiped away her tears and a few of my own.

"She liked you," Debbie said.

"I know, and I felt the same about her. She had great courage and strength, and ultimately made something of her life."

"And look what it got her," she said bitterly.

"That's one way to look at it. On the other hand, she found peace with herself and a way to help others. That's more than most people will ever find."

"Not me. I'm going back to what I know."

"Why don't you take a few days to think things over? You could stay here and continue your treatment."

"I don't need *treatment*. Since when is enjoying sex a sickness? It's my profession, and I'm good at it."

"I'm not going to argue with you. It was only a suggestion. Your sister once asked me to do her a fav…"

"I don't want you looking after me."

"That wasn't the favor. I can get you a job uptown, but you have to stay off the dope. Can you do that?"

"I'm clean, and if that's what it takes to work the high-end, I'll stay that way."

"Then it's a deal. I'll need a few days to make arrangements."

"Please hurry. Even the groundskeeper is looking good to me. You wouldn't want to stay a little longer, would you?"

"I think you know the answer to that. But I do have a few questions."

"All I know is what I was told."

"Let's give it a try. Did Shirley ever have arguments with members of the staff or any of the patients?"

"Not that I know of."

"Was she seeing anyone?

"Are you kidding? She didn't have a life outside of this place."

"Anything stand out about the girls' parents? Did she have any problems with one or more of them?"

"I don't think Shirley ever met the parents, except over lunch on visitation days."

"Anything unusual happen lately, anything at all?"

Debbie brushed away a few more tears. "No, not really, every day is the same around this place."

"You hesitated. What crossed your mind?"

"She recently spent a lot of time in the basement."

"Why?"

"I don't know. Putting away some old folders, I guess. You know, records of girls who finished their treatment or who just decided to leave. That's where I'll end up, a few pieces of paper in a folder hidden away in the basement of an old building."

I couldn't think of anything else to ask and was moving to leave when she clutched my arm. "You'll come back for me."

"In a few days, I promise."

* * * * *

The following day I entered the office, hoping to find Jackie hard at work.

"She's gone," Martha said.

"You mean she's not coming to work today?"

"No, I mean she's gone, moved out of her apartment. I told you to go after her. What were you thinking? Even when I'm angry I don't say anything nearly as hurtful. What's going on, Joey? I know you care for her."

"I didn't think she would leave."

"God, you have a lot to learn about women."

I walked over to Martha, and we held each other for the briefest of moments, then I backed away. "I care for both of you. I'm just feeling overwhelmed with everything that's been happening. My family's disintegrating, the DA's constantly on my back, and every time I turn a corner, I think someone's waiting to pounce, or I'll find another dead body."

"Jackie will come around. She knows what you're going through and realizes Shirley's death was a shock. In the meantime, you need to get back to work and concentrate on solving crimes."

"Maybe I should go to her," I said.

"You missed your chance to do that last night. As I said, get back to work, give Jackie some time, then get in touch with her. Hopefully by then you'll know what to say."

As usual, Martha made a lot of sense. I had to contact Castellano to make arrangements for Shirley's sister, get back on the Blair case, and make sure Sullivan kept me in the loop as he investigated Shirley's death. Before I called Castellano, Martha asked me to have dinner that evening. We both knew our close personal relationship was over, but sometimes you just need to be with a friend. I suppose she's been there a few times herself and sensed my need.

I chose the restaurant, one specializing in northern Italian cuisine. Martha looked as beautiful as ever and seemed to be more at ease and confident than I'd seen her.

"I'm finally enjoying my job. I like digging up information that will help with your investigations."

"You're good at it," I said.

"Thanks. I don't think you've ever complimented me before."

"I should have. Without you and Jackie, I'd still be trying to solve my first few cases."

"I don't buy that, but I'm making useful contacts in the DA's office and at the police station, thanks to O'Reilly."

"Sounds like you're getting your wish and meeting more people."

"I am," she said with a subtle smile.

As we continued to talk, I realized we had experienced a complete reversal of attitudes toward life. When we first met, I was full of energy and anticipation toward my new career, and she needed to get out of a rut.

The evening passed quickly. As I walked her to her room, she blocked the entrance to her apartment and gave me a gentle goodnight kiss. I turned to leave when she reconsidered and asked me in for a drink.

"No thanks, I've got things to think about. Looks like Jackie and I are going our separate ways."

"We all are," Martha said. "I have a chance for a real relationship with someone who wants the same things I do. You do too; you just don't realize it yet. Hopefully, it won't be too late when you do."

She slowly closed the door, and as I walked downstairs to the third floor and passed Jackie's apartment, I felt a familiar emptiness.

That night I broke into the stash of liquor I salvaged

from Uncle Luigi's bar on the day of the big raid. I spent the weekend in my room completely balled up, canned to the gills, feeling sorry for myself. When I finally pulled myself together, I had knocked off two bottles of whiskey and had a colossal headache to show for my efforts.

* * * * *

I kept my promise to Debbie, picked her up at the clinic, and had her stay in Jackie's old room. Before long an elderly woman accompanied by two perfect male specimens came and whisked her away without any prior notice. I tried to get some details out of Castellano, but he wouldn't divulge Debbie's whereabouts. To make matters worse, Ma grew attached to Debbie, and when she realized what I had arranged with Castellano, she refused to talk to me. That is, until she had to deliver bad news.

"Your uncle's moving out."

I couldn't believe what I was hearing. "Why would he do that?"

"He's working for Castellano and needs to be closer to the action. That's what he said."

"What's gonna happen to the apartment building?"

"The second floor will get fixed up, your pop's closing down his shoe store and is just gonna repair shoes, and I'll keep the tenants happy."

"What about Rosalie?"

"She's gonna become a nurse. She'll continue to live with us and pay us back after she graduates."

"I can give her money for school."

"That's something your pop wants to do. Now go see your uncle."

I ran upstairs to find Luigi. He looked up from packing as I burst into his office.

"Why didn't you tell me?"

"Look, Joey, things have changed, and we have to accept that. A lesson you still need to learn."

"What's that supposed to mean?"

"You know damn well what it means, and you better get your shit together before you lose everything. As far as Castellano is concerned, I'm only gonna run a few speakeasies and that's it. Just like you suggested and nothing else. I'm no fool."

Before I could say any more, he shoved me out of the office.

I barged back in. "What about my jack?"

"What dough?"

"Don't give me that malarkey. You know what I'm talking about. You've got over a hundred grand of my money in your safe."

"Oh that. Where you gonna put it, under your mattress? I'll keep it in the safe. Just come by when you need some."

"Don't get too attached to it," I said.

"Too late for that. I was hoping for a loan sometime soon."

"What for?"

"Castellano might be willing to sell me a joint in a few months."

"I need to give most of that money back to the Blair estate."

"What the hell for?"

"I'm thinking of dropping the case. With Jackie gone and Shirley's murder, I have too much going on."

"You made me a promise and I'm holdin' ya to it. You said you'd pay me back for all that's happened, and I'm calling in the debt. No one knows you have the dough. Drop the case if you have to, but keep the jack."

"I can't do that."

"Then swallow your damn pride and get Jackie back. Just have the dough ready when I need it. Now get outta here before I forget you're my nephew."

* * * * *

With the speakeasy closed down and Uncle Luigi gone, O'Reilly and I spent more time at his new hangout, a small restaurant down along the piers known for its fried oysters and fresh eel. I meant to ask him why he chose such a dive. The place filled each night with old men, who sat around scarred tables crusted over with remnants of past meals, smoking tar-flavored stogies that smelled worse than the bilge tanks on an old tugboat. The only positive thing about the place was that the patrons hardly ever missed the spittoons.

I found O'Reilly in the back shooting the bull with the same bunch as the other night. As soon as I came over, he asked his drinking partners to move on.

"Sorry guys, my friend and I have some stuff to talk over. I don't think he came by to challenge us to a drinking contest."

I sat down to a chorus of laughter, and from the grin on O'Reilly's face, he looked half-plastered. The stuff they served was real rotgut, locally brewed and not the Canadian whiskey my uncle had sold.

Before long we argued again over Shirley's death, and the more we drank, the meaner we became.

"I don't know how you can be so damn sure all these murders aren't connected," I said.

"Why should I think that, just because they happened on the Island? Give me a break."

"And here I thought you were a good homicide detective. Do I need to spell everything out for you?"

"I wish you would, Joey boy. Maybe if you heard yourself, you'd shut up about your stupid theory and get working on helping us find the real killer."

"This guy is a sadistic animal; he takes his time and enjoys watching people die. He held Shirley close to him and watched the life drain from her eyes as he slowly sliced through her insides. With each thrust of the knife, he smothered her screams by burying her head into his coat."

"How many times I gotta tell ya nothing fits," said O'Reilly. "So this guy enjoyed what he did. I'll give you that, but that's where the similarities end. I'm telling you, Nick Fuso doesn't think the crimes are related, and he's running the taskforce. Unless Sullivan bucks him, our hands are tied."

"Have you heard Fuso's theories?" I asked. "She opened the gate to the clinic in the dead of night to let in an old John, even though she's been off the streets for years."

"It's possible, but I agree not probable."

"What's the other one? Oh yeah, the Moralli theory. One of his boys decides to make an example of Shirley for leaving the business two to three years after the fact."

"Maybe they just found out where she went," O'Reilly said in Nick's defense.

"Let's not forget the random killer theory. Some bloodthirsty nutcase sees Shirley walking the grounds in the middle of the night, hops the fence, and kills her," I said with some disgust.

O'Reilly's neck turned red, so I moved my chair back. Usually bad things happen when his color changes. "Shit, what the hell do you expect me to do? The only reason we have our fingers in this case is because Sullivan's doing me a favor and I'm doing you one. I know you have a good gut for this business, but Nick has a point. Why the hell would the killer we've been after change his methods and kill

Shirley? Tell me that!" O'Reilly knocked into another patron as he got up.

"I don't know," I said, downing my last drink of the evening.

"Exactly!" O'Reilly said as he meandered between the tables to leave.

"Maybe if we knew the answer, we'd find our killer," I yelled after him.

As I got up, Martha entered the restaurant, came to the back section, and sat down. "I've been worried about you, thought you might need some company."

We talked for a little bit before I finally got around to asking the question I'd been holding back for several days. "Have you heard anything from Jackie?"

"We had dinner the other night. She's fine."

I had to contain my anger. "You know I've been worried about her. Why didn't you tell me?"

"She wanted it that way. I think she's as stubborn as you." Martha took a drink out of my hand, downed it, and pushed her chair back. "If I were you, I'd stop by the orphanage and say hello to Sister Mary. I'm sure she'd be glad to see you."

What an idiot I'd been. Of course Jackie would go back to the orphanage; that's where she felt most wanted.

Before heading to my apartment, I stopped in the office and rummaged through Jackie's desk for the case file on the guy who believed the Mafia had it in for him. I thought I could use the case as an excuse for visiting Jackie at the orphanage. The folder was in her top right-hand drawer along with a draft for fifty dollars from a Donato Cafiero. No wonder she wanted to take the case; from the look of his signature, the guy had to be at least ninety. He shouldn't have to worry about the Mafia at his age. As I flipped through the pages, my eyes began to lose focus as the booze I'd consumed hit me. I closed the folder, locked up the office, and flopped into my sack.

When I returned the next morning, I continued looking through Cafiero's case file. As I got to the last page, I found a loose piece of paper. It contained the message Jackie wrote down from her phone conversation with Shirley: *Joey, Shirley called and said she might have some information about the killings on the Island. She wants you to come by when you get out of the hospital. Jackie*

More than likely Jackie had gotten interrupted after taking the message and closed the file on the slip of paper. I finally had the proof I needed to tie Shirley's murder to the other cases, but I had to know what happened to make Jackie forget to pass on such an important message.

Before leaving for the Island, I asked Martha if anything unusual happened during my stay in the hospital that might have distracted Jackie.

"It's hard to say. We all had to help clean up your blood, rush you to the hospital, remove the dead body in Jackie's room, and, on top of all that, the DA had you arrested for murder. No, I would say things were fairly normal."

At first I thought some of my uncle's sarcasm had rubbed off, but she always had a cutting wit. "That's it? No one got shot or demanded we take on another case? Just another typical day?" I asked again, adding a bit of my own humor.

"You might check with Frank. After we found out the DA had taken you downtown, Frank rushed in to see Jackie and, soon after, she left the office."

Frank confirmed what I'd suspected. He had asked Jackie to check with the local bums who hung around the streets to see if anyone had witnessed my attack the night I shot my way into Jackie's apartment. He figured it didn't make sense my assailant was drunk, since O'Reilly thought it was a professional hit. Frank reasoned someone tried to make it look that way, someone who knew me.

Jackie found Gino, got him to talk to Frank, and, in all the excitement, forgot about Shirley's call. What a complete fool I'd been. Jackie had everything a guy could want in a dame: street sense, fearlessness, intelligence, and looks. For the first time I realized how much she meant to me and that I couldn't live without her.

I called the orphanage several times, but each time the phone went dead when I asked for Jackie. It was becoming obvious she was going to make me work to get her back. After four calls, I gave up and refocused back on Shirley's murder. I called both O'Reilly and Sullivan and told them about Shirley's phone message, and they agreed to meet me at the clinic.

I left the office early for the meeting and swung over to the orphanage, hoping to get a few minutes with Jackie to apologize in person. Unfortunately, I couldn't get past two burly nuns who clearly had orders to keep me away. They did, however, agree to give her a package that contained Donato Cafiero's case folder, a brief update on the Blair case, and a personal note of contrition.

I arrived at the clinic a few minutes late and found O'Reilly, Sullivan, and Nick Fuso having coffee with Doctor Swartz.

"Have any of your patients come forward with additional information?" Nick asked.

"At the beginning of each session, I ask the girls if they've thought of anything new that might be useful to your investigation. So far nothing."

"Your patients are locked in their rooms at night, is that correct?" O'Reilly asked.

"Only staff members have complete freedom to walk the

grounds at night," the doc said.

"Do all the staff members have a key to the front gate?" I asked.

"They do."

"So, Shirley could have let someone onto the grounds the night she was murdered," Sullivan said.

"It's certainly possible, but not likely. After lockdown, it would have to be an extreme emergency to allow anyone onto the premises."

"Shirley's sister mentioned Shirley spent some time in the basement prior to her death. Do you know why?" I asked.

"Probably storing old folders, but there could be other reasons. Aside from patient records, we keep decorations down there we might use during holidays and other celebrations. If a patient leaves behind any belongings, we also store them in the basement."

Once in the basement, Nick asked to see Jackie's note. "Why the hell didn't she give you this message immediately?" he said as he handed it back.

Sullivan stepped in and took charge. "Questions like that are not what we need right now," he said to Nick as he turned to me. "Okay, Joey, you've had some time to think this through. Tell us your theory of what happened."

Nick didn't like Sullivan asking for my opinion, but wisely kept quiet. "Shirley spent all her time at the clinic," I said. "There can be only one logical explanation: she read something in the papers about the killings that triggered a memory from her past or indicated to her that the clinic was connected in some way to one or more of the murdered girls."

"So you think she came down here looking for information about a former patient?" Sullivan asked.

"That's right, and from the briefing Nick gave the other

day, I would say Shirley searched for a folder on Deborah Simonette, since she had a drug problem. As you recall, she was one of the killer's early victims, and her life story, along with the other victims', had been plastered recently in all the major papers."

Nick turned to the cabinets. "Deborah Simonette…her parents certainly had the dough to afford this place."

I spent time checking the clinic's files during my investigation into Angelo Castellano's death and knew the clinic's filing system. Sure enough, Simonette was a former patient, and her folder was empty.

O'Reilly looked baffled. "How the hell did the killer know Shirley made a connection between Simonette and the clinic?" No one had a good answer, but somehow the killer had known.

"Batista," Sullivan said. "I want everyone who had access to Jackie Forsythe's note or heard her conversation with Shirley in my office at one o'clock sharp tomorrow afternoon."

Another dead end. No one knew anything.

Jackie came to the meeting, made her statement, and left without saying a word to me. I caught up to her in the hallway before she left the police station. I grabbed her arm and turned her around.

"Did you get my letter?"

"I did," she said with little emotion.

"Are you coming back?"

"Why should I? Nothing has changed. You don't have real feelings for anyone. Although your letter was nice, it didn't go far enough. When you grow up and can put the past behind you, I'll consider it. Until then, I'm not living in Anita's shadow any longer," she said, then walked away.

I don't know how much O'Reilly overheard, but it was enough. "Why don't you and I call it a day and get a few drinks?" he suggested.

I don't remember much after that.

* * * * *

I would have preferred working with Nick on Shirley's murder investigation, but he didn't want my help, and I needed to solve the Blair case. Helping Uncle Luigi get back into the speakeasy business would go a long way toward repairing the rift developing within our family. To do that, I had to justify keeping Kathryn's money and necklace so I could lend Luigi the money he needed to buy his new saloon.

Unfortunately, nothing seemed to be coming together on the case. Jackie's theory that Laura Blair and Johnson, the new lawyer, had an affair before she married William didn't pan out. I didn't have a clue how to unravel the Blair mysteries: Who killed Kathryn and why? If there was a third will, where was it? How involved was the lawyer or was he just a pawn in a complex chess game? And if that wasn't enough, David Denton kept coming around asking for money to pay the factory bills. I must have been nuts to think I could solve Kathryn's case in just a few weeks.

I found it depressing to be at work, sitting in my office next to Jackie's empty desk and staring at the wall separating Martha and myself. Thank God Jackie had a bottle of whiskey stashed in the bottom drawer.

One day I reached for the bottle as Martha came into my inner sanctum, looking as radiant as ever. Every time I saw her it reminded me of what a fool I'd become. How the hell did I screw up so badly to end up this lonely?

"I finished going through all the Blair invoices for the last year," Martha said. "My guess is Denton will borrow ten grand of Kathryn's money before the business turns around. His vendors are ordering more merchandise as the holiday season gets into full swing. By the end of January he'll have enough to pay back the bank's line of credit, and we should receive the ten grand sometime the following month."

I needed to talk. "This Denton guy, you think he's a good manager?"

"I'm not sure, but he seems to know the business," she said as she sat down.

"Why didn't the old man turn over the day-to-day running of the factory to him, especially when death came knocking?"

"David didn't take it personally. Running the business gave Mr. Blair a reason to go on fighting, to stay alive. It's a shame though. I could tell from how much his signature changed on the invoices that his pain increased with each passing week, especially near the end."

As Martha went back to work, I suddenly had an image of my uncle behaving the same way—a cantankerous old man, still trying to run his saloon on the day he drew his last breath, barely able to scribble his own name.

I froze in mid-thought and must've yelled for Martha, because she came running in with a worried look. "Get me all the factory invoices from last year," I said.

Martha hesitated. "Quick, get them and put them in stacks on my desk by month, right up to the time of old man Blair's death."

When the invoices were in neat piles, a critical piece of the Blair puzzle leapt off the desk.

"I can't believe it," I said.

"Believe what? I checked the invoices several times and even called some of the vendors to make sure everything's legit," Martha said, shifting her weight and folding her arms across her chest.

"Relax, I'm not questioning your work. Get Kathryn's folder. I need the date the wills were executed and I want to see the signatures again."

It seemed to take Martha eons to return. "The wills are dated March fifteenth," she said.

"When did the old man die?"

"I think sometime in late July."

"You just found the key to solving this case."

"I did?"

"Yes." I impulsively hugged her and to my delight, she responded and put her arms around my neck as we enjoyed the sweetness of each others' touch.

I reluctantly released her and apologized. "I shouldn't have done that. It won't happen again."

She ran her fingers through her hair and pushed down on her skirt to smooth out the wrinkles. "No need to apologize. Just tell me how any of this tells you who killed Kathryn."

"It doesn't, but it explains everything else."

I picked up the invoices and marched over to Frank's office with Martha in tow.

Frank didn't appreciate our intrusion. Ever since Jackie's trial, he'd been swamped with work and had even put an ad in the local paper for a partner.

"I'll give you one minute," he said, looking at his pocket watch.

I put the two stacks of invoices on his desk and pointed to the signatures without a word. He looked from one to the other, picked up two invoices, one from March and one from June, placed them back in the pile, stood up, and came around his desk to shake my hand.

"Will someone tell me what's going on?" Martha said.

Frank retrieved a photo of the will Kathryn had given him. "Look closely at the signature. It's not the same as these in the March pile, but it should be."

"Why?" Martha asked.

"Because the dates on the two wills are the same, therefore, the signatures should be identical to the one on this early March invoice. See how the old man's signatures on the invoices deteriorate as time goes on? The signatures on the June invoices are barely legible," he said.

"When I began my investigation, Frank had mentioned he'd examined the wills and all the signatures looked authentic, which implied they were the same," I said.

"But old man Blair's signature is slightly different on the two wills," Martha said with a smile of understanding.

"My guess," Frank said, "is he signed four; maybe five copies of the will at the same time in March. One went to William Blair, one the old man kept, and the rest went into the lawyer's safe. Someone removed the copies from the safe shortly after he signed the originals and somehow tricked the old man into signing a new will with Kathryn as beneficiary a few weeks later. "

"Why did you tell Joey the signatures looked authentic?" Martha asked.

"I did notice a slight change, but I assumed it was because he signed the papers lying down and had trouble controlling his hand."

"Kathryn didn't have access to the documents, so who made the switch?" Martha asked.

"That's right, she probably wasn't even present," Frank said. "In my opinion, there are only three possibilities: the lawyer, his assistant lawyer, or his secretary, Laura. We can rule out the original lawyer since he's dead and Laura, since she had nothing to gain if Kathryn inherited the estate. That leaves the assistant lawyer. He probably reasoned that as Kathryn's lawyer, he would have control of her assets and could easily swindle some money."

Frank looked pretty pleased with himself. I think his recent success and notoriety were affecting his judgment. I have to admit, I enjoyed throwing out another explanation, especially after he'd practically tossed me out of his office the last time we met.

"That was my first reaction, but it's too simplistic," I said.

"Many crimes are, since they're spontaneous. Someone gets an idea or urge and acts," Frank said.

"I don't think this was a crime of passion or opportunity. It took planning. Let's assume the assistant lawyer had nothing to do with any of this," I said.

Frank simply dismissed my suggestion with a wave of his hand. "Then nothing fits."

I suggested he take a seat and listen to another possibility. "There are a few pieces of information we uncovered that, if true, present a different picture," I said.

"Like what?"

"That neither William nor Kathryn are Blair's biological children. They were his wife's from two previous marriages. William led us to believe he was a direct descendent and the old man cut Kathryn out of the will because she wasn't."

"So he lied," Frank said.

"He did, but most lies have some truth to them. Suppose the old man cut both William and Kathryn out of his will," I said.

Frank's look of skepticism suddenly changed. "Are you suggesting there's a third will?"

"That's what I believe."

"For that to be true, the wills would have to be changed twice and probably by two different people," Martha said.

"That's right. I believe Laura made a play for William, told him what his father was planning, and they made a deal. She altered the documents just as Frank suggested, but William's name was on the bottom copy, not Kathryn's."

"Who did the old man really leave his fortune to?" Martha asked.

"We may never know. Chances are the original was destroyed," Frank said.

"I'm not so sure," I said. "The old man seemed to be a stickler for details, so my guess is he asked for a copy, just like William kept a copy of the altered version."

"Wouldn't the original lawyer eventually notice the change in the will?" Martha asked.

"I think that's why he had an unfortunate accident soon after the signing of the original will."

"They killed the lawyer?" Martha said, more as a statement than a question.

"That's my guess."

Frank's interest piqued. "Who changed the will the second time naming Kathryn as beneficiary and why? I don't believe she would do anything so devious."

"There was only one person with easy access to the lawyer's office after Laura quit and married William, and that would be her replacement. I'll bet the new secretary was hired the end of March or early April."

Frank reached for the phone. "We need to get O'Reilly over here and get him interested enough that he'll follow up and find out who our mystery girl is."

"I know who she is," Martha said. "She used to work for David Denton as his secretary. Her name is Evelyn Jones."

Frank stared at Martha, put the phone down, then retrieved the two wills again, along with some other documents he had. "Denton's a witness on both wills and was Kathryn's beneficiary before she made out her new will naming Joey. They were secretly married before the old man died. How do you know Denton?" he asked Martha.

Martha looked pale, and I caught her before she collapsed and gently placed her in a chair. "She's been dating Denton," I said to Frank.

"Joey, I'm sorry. He's been asking so many questions about your business. If you have any leads on Kathryn's murder. How much money she paid you. God, I've been such a fool," Martha said.

Before I could say anything to reassure her, O'Reilly knocked on the door and entered. "I had a hunch I'd find you here. I've got to bring you in, Joey."

"What for?"

"The murder of Evelyn Jones. I'm afraid it's gonna be tough getting out of this one. This Jones dame filled a harassment complaint against you a few weeks ago, and they found your stiletto, the one you once lent Jackie, at the crime scene."

"Who the hell is Evelyn Jones?" Frank asked.

"I just told you," Martha said. "She's the secretary who took Laura's place."

* * * * *

I was front-page news once again. The DA went on record, standing on the steps of City Hall, declaring he had apprehended a rogue private investigator known for taking justice into his own hands.

District Attorney Peterson smelled blood and took off his holier-than-thou façade and got dirty during my interrogation. "Joey, we've been at this for almost three days. It's late, and I'm exhausted, so I want you to meet my personal bodyguard, Timothy O'Toole. His friends call him Red, and not because of the color of his hair."

Red's face looked like it had been rearranged more than once, and I suspected he had a few parts missing upstairs from being hit so many times. As a kid I used to watch guys like him fight in the back alleys for two cents a ticket. They were big and strong but didn't know the first thing about fighting other than to hit and hit hard when they got the chance.

"When am I going to see my lawyer?"

"Funny, that's what everyone asks," the DA said with a sinister grin.

"Where's O'Reilly? Shouldn't the arresting officer be present?"

"What do ya know, a smart private dick. It just so happens he's working on another homicide. Regrettably, no one else is available to assist me," the DA said as he blew smoke in my face and smashed the butt into a filthy ashtray.

"Red, I'm going out for another smoke. When I come back, I want a confession from our friend. Remember, Red, don't touch his face."

"Okay, boss."

"Wait, you know I didn't kill Evelyn Jones," I said to the DA before he could close the door.

"Well, that's what Red is here to find out. I'm finished talking, Joey, and I'm tired of having your friends lying to get you out of a jam. I have an election coming up, and you're a big story, a real big story. In my town, you'd be better off keeping a low profile."

As soon as the door closed, Red tossed the table aside and stood in front of me with a big, toothless grin. Fortunately, my hands were cuffed by a length of chain behind my back and not to the chair. I was on my feet and spun out of the way before his shoe hit the chair. Splinters flew in different directions as I jumped over the table, now lodged at an angle in the corner. By the time he lifted the table and threw it across the room, I had slipped my legs through the loop of chain cuffed to my hands. I was still limited in what I could do, but at least I had my hands in front of me and about six inches of chain I could use to my advantage.

Red grabbed my shirt and hurled me against the opposite wall. In less than two strides, he was on me again and about to smash his massive fist into my face.

"Not the face. Remember what the boss said."

"Oh yeah, I forgot," Red said.

He put me down gently then wrapped his arms around my waist in a crushing bear hug, lifting me several inches off the ground. His foul breath choked off my air as he roared to gather more strength. In an effort to get away from the stench, I shoved the chain across his open mouth and pushed his head back hard against the brick wall. The pressure on my spine continued to increase. Out of desperation, I raked the chain across the back of his mouth, slicing open the edges deep into his cheeks. His screams were deafening as he dropped me to the floor, trying to stop the bleeding by shoving his fist into the bloody opening.

Anticipating another onslaught from the brute, I picked up a split piece of wood from a leg of the chair and held it against the palm of my hand. If he came at me again, I intended to thrust the sharp point into a meaty part of his flesh.

As I stood poised to defend myself, the interrogation room door flew opened. A crowd rushed in past the DA, who stood in the opening holding onto the doorknob. Jackie and Martha got the key from the DA, freed my hands, and led me into the hall and out to a waiting car as Pop and Luigi held Red at bay.

It wasn't until the following day I got the full story on how they got the charges dropped. During the ride back home, however, I did pick up on the fact that Jackie had somehow found the real killer. No matter how hard I tried to get more details, everyone insisted I get some rest. I had to finally agree. I was bushed after such a long interrogation. Besides, what really mattered was that Jackie was back, or so I hoped.

December

Frank strutted about with his thumbs tucked behind his suspenders, leaned against his desk, and stared at me. I sat back and prepared myself for a lengthy explanation. Frank had a captive audience, and like any lawyer, took full advantage of the opportunity.

"Martha and I were both in a state of shock when O'Reilly came into my office and arrested you for the murder of Evelyn Jones. But it didn't take long for Martha to react. She went straight to the orphanage where Jackie was staying, and within two hours, they were both sitting in this office giving me the third degree."

"What about?"

"The Blair case, of course. They wanted to know everything I had on Kathryn and if I thought your theory about a third will had merit."

Frank sat behind his desk and took his time packing his pipe with a sweet-smelling tobacco.

"Frank, I don't have all day."

"Don't worry, I'm getting to the good part. The girls and I jabbered back and forth for several hours and finally agreed there must be a third will. We didn't understand its significance until Jackie pointed out all the Blairs were dead, as well as two people from their legal firm."

"I never looked at it that way, but she's right," I said.

"Precisely, and what do you think everyone involved in the case is looking to find?"

"Damn, how could I be so stupid?" I said. "We all

thought the money Kathryn stole had been the motive for her murder. The reality is no one could find old man Blair's copy of the original will. They assumed Kathryn had taken it."

"Exactly! Frank said, pointing at me with his pipe. "Our discussion raised another interesting question. Why didn't Kathryn go to her husband, David Denton? Her father was dead; why continue to keep their marriage a secret?"

"I don't believe this," I said. "Kathryn must have found the original will and realized Denton modified the document and married her for the inheritance. She was hiding from her brother and Denton."

Frank walked over to his window and put both his arms on the sides of the frame. It appeared he was looking out the window, but I believe he was remembering a beautiful young lady sitting in his office asking for help. I waited, steeped in my own thoughts.

Frank wiped his face on his outstretched arm and sat back at his desk. "Next, we made a list of all the remaining players in this bizarre case. We ruled out the butler and maid, since they had nothing to gain. That left Denton, because of his relationships with Kathryn and Evelyn Jones. We then added everyone else associated with the lawyer's office."

"So, Johnson, Laura Blair, and Denton are suspects," I said.

"Martha told us you didn't find any evidence Laura and Johnson ever had a romantic relationship, so the logical conclusion was Laura acted on her own and changed the duplicate copies of the original will, naming William as beneficiary."

"You think Laura and William killed the old lawyer, because he would've realized the original will had been modified," I said.

"Logically it fits."

"But we're back to the same old question. Why would Laura kill William Blair before Johnson could prove Kathryn's will was invalid?"

"Only one explanation. William's death was indeed an accident," Frank said.

I lit a cigarette, and Frank relit his pipe. "Isn't it still possible Johnson is somehow mixed up in this mess? Just because I couldn't prove he was involved with Laura shouldn't eliminate him as a suspect in any of the murders."

Frank looked pensive for a few seconds. "It's certainly possible, but we can't prove any of these theories without possessing all three wills. The good news is O'Reilly did get the department to reopen the investigation into the old lawyer's death."

It was my turn to pace the room. "Let's make sure we're in agreement about the wills. Old man Blair decides to disinherit both his stepchildren for whatever reason and dictates a will naming some unknown person or persons as beneficiaries. Laura, the lawyer's secretary at the time, sees an opportunity, makes a play for Blair's son, William, and tells him his stepfather is going to cut him out of the will. She then lays out a plan to modify the contents naming William as sole heir on the duplicate copies of the will. She knows from experience no one ever looks at all the copies as they sign the documents since they assume they're all the same. Let's call the modified copies Will Number Two, and the original top copy, Will Number One. Are we in agreement so far?" I asked

"Let's not forget Johnson, the assistant lawyer at the time, could have come up with the plan and used Laura," Frank said.

"That's a detail we can figure out later. The main point is the original lawyer ended up dead because he would eventually discover the change in the will. William and Laura or Laura and Johnson killed him. In either case, he was murdered."

Frank puffed furiously on his pipe. "So, what's Kathryn's real involvement in this whole mess? How did she end up with a will naming her sole beneficiary?" he asked.

"What you're really asking about is Will Number Three! When Laura leaves her job to marry William, that's when Denton sees his opportunity. Who knows how long he schemed to get Kathryn to secretly marry him, convincing her that her stepfather would never approve? He must have been devastated when he realized old man Blair disinherited both William *and* Kathryn. I wouldn't be surprised if the old man found out about the marriage and made sure Denton was a witness to Will Number One."

"Denton gets Johnson to hire his secretary, Evelyn Jones, after Laura leaves and somehow convinces her to change the copies of the will in Johnson's safe, creating Will Number Three, naming Kathryn as beneficiary," Frank said as he puffed on a dead pipe. "If you ask me, this is where everything breaks down. What incentive did Evelyn Jones have to get involved in this whole mess?"

"Leverage," I said.

"Explain!"

"Look at everything from Evelyn Jones' point of view. For Denton to really get his hands on the estate, he has to bump off Kathryn, and in order to keep Evelyn's mouth shut, he agrees to marry her once everything is finalized."

"Okay, I'll buy that," Frank said. "But how did Denton get original signatures on the third will?

"Old man Blair trusted Denton to run his business and signed most documents he put in front of him without asking too many questions, especially as his health deteriorated. The maid and butler never read anything they witnessed, and all Denton had to do was forge the dead lawyer's signature."

"If old man Blair trusted Denton to basically run his business, why would he object to him marrying his daughter?" Frank asked.

"Because he was an employee and didn't come from money."

"So you believe Denton killed Kathryn. It's interesting how you came to that conclusion, because until Jackie proved Denton killed Evelyn Jones, we all assumed William had killed Kathryn," Frank stated.

"Are you telling me Denton confessed to killing Kathryn?"

"We'll get to that later. Go on, I'm fascinated with your reasoning ability," Frank said.

"It all fits together. With Kathryn out of the way, Denton inherits the estate. Remember, he doesn't know Kathryn made a new will naming me as her beneficiary. Denton got greedy and decided his mistress and accomplice, Evelyn Jones, was too much of a liability and tried to frame me for her murder, which gets her out of the picture and stops me from snooping around."

As Frank filled his pipe again, it was my turn to look out the window at the mass of humanity below, but rather than being impressed with the amazing amount of commerce taking place, I wondered about all the evil lurking in the shadows of a city this size.

I turned to Frank and took the match from his hand. "I'm glad we finally agree on most aspects of the Blair case, but what I really want to know is how did you prove Denton killed Evelyn Jones?"

"That's another story entirely, and I have a client coming in a few minutes. I suggest you get Jackie to tell you how she accomplished that feat. All I'm gonna say right now is you're one lucky SOB. If I were you, I'd keep those two broads happy."

"It's not always easy."

"Try harder," Frank said as he ushered me out.

I was about to go back and insist on the details when Jackie came out of our office into the hallway.

"Jackie, where you going?"

"To thank your parents for the use of their spare bedroom, then back to the orphanage."

"Why?"

"That's where I live and work now."

"Looks like you're working two jobs. Isn't that one of our case folders you're holding?"

"I'm worried you won't have time to follow up on the Cafiero case."

"I don't. That's why I need you as my partner. About the other day...I was out of line. Can we go inside and talk things over?"

She turned away, and for a moment I thought she was going to walk down the stairs. Instead, she opened the office door and entered. I followed, and as I passed Martha, I gave her the sign to take a walk.

Jackie sat in the chair in front of my desk, and I almost made the mistake of sitting behind it. Instead, I sat next to her, forcing her to shift around so we faced each other.

"You did get the note I left at the orphanage?"

"Yes. As I said, it was nice, but doesn't change things."

"I was hoping it would. I meant every word."

"Look, Joey…"

"No, please don't say anything. What happened with Martha after I took her out to dinner was unexpected. We got drunk and it happened. We both felt terrible, and that's why we didn't say anything. I didn't lie. I just didn't tell you about it. I hope you can understand why."

"Martha already explained everything, including turning her down for a drink the other night. Your relationship with Martha isn't the issue. You said some terrible things, and I lashed back with the first thoughts that came to mind. The truth is I've spent enough time in my life with men who wanted me around for all the wrong reasons. I need something more now. I thought you were different, but you're like all the rest."

"I'm not! You must know that. Shirley's murder came out of nowhere. I wasn't thinking straight, and for a moment I thought whoever killed her also killed Anita, and that he was targeting people in my life. I know it sounds ridiculous, but that's what was going through my mind. I asked you to be my partner because you understand the type of people we have to deal with in this crazy business and because I cared for you. Now after being separated these last few weeks, I realize I love you."

Jackie reached for my hand. I stood and pulled her up toward me. "I never thought I would ever tell another woman I loved her," I whispered as we held each other.

She gently pushed me away, and I saw the sparkle return to her eyes. "Maybe there's hope for you yet. I'll tell you one thing—I'm not going to mention to Martha you said that because now that Denton's out of the picture, she might try to get her claws into you again."

Jackie walked over to the door, turned, and said, "I could use some help moving my things back, if my apartment's still available."

"The rent's paid up for the next three months."

"Were you that sure?"

"Just hopeful."

* * * * *

Jackie insisted I see Evelyn Jones' crime scene before explaining how she and O'Reilly gathered the evidence needed to spring me from jail. O'Reilly came along, since the police were still working the scene.

"To be honest, Joey," O'Reilly said, "I thought you were headed for the chair. Before I hauled you in, the DA had you tried, sentenced, and buried."

"Makes me wonder how many innocent bastards he's put away over the years."

Jackie nailed the DA's real motivation. "He wants to be reelected, maybe run for mayor someday. To do that in this town, he needs the newspaper editors behind him, and the only way to gain their backing is to show you can generate sensational headlines. It's all about increasing circulation, which translates into money," she said as we entered the office.

Except for the bloodstains, everything looked the same as when Jackie and I had first barged into Evelyn's office without an appointment to see her boss, Johnson, about Kathryn Blair's murder.

"We think she came around the desk when Denton entered; they exchanged a few words; he then slit her throat from behind with your stiletto," O'Reilly said.

As I listened to O'Reilly's description of how Evelyn slowly and painfully died, it reminded me of Lieutenant Sullivan's unemotional description of Shirley's slaughter. In war, death is an everyday occurrence, and you come to accept it as normal. As O'Reilly went through all the gruesome details, I finally realized New York City was a war zone.

"Every gang member in this city owns a stiletto. How did the DA know it was my chiv?"

"It was evidence in Jackie's trial. Don't you remember you gave Jackie your stiletto and a handgun before she went back to her husband? They had a picture of the knife in the court documents," O'Reilly said

"You didn't help yourself by not being able to produce an alibi for the night of the murder. Evelyn was working late and your only defense was you went to bed early," Jackie added.

"To make matters worse, Evelyn Jones filed a complaint against the both of you for harassment," O'Reilly said.

"I know all of this. When is somebody going to tell me how the hell you guys got me out of this mess?"

"We got lucky," Jackie said. "Look around the room. Do you see anything unusual?"

I stepped back to the door, trying to avoid the large bloodstain in the carpet where Evelyn fell to the floor. The main part of the room opened to my left and looked fairly comfortable, with several nice chairs and a long, redwood magazine rack under two bay windows. The door to Johnson's inner office was directly opposite where I stood. A few cabinets were scattered against the walls and were easily accessible to Evelyn. Behind Evelyn's desk, in the corner, stood a sturdy cardboard box with some packing material sticking out of the top. Denton must have entered soon after she had unpacked a new piece of office equipment.

"The area behind her desk looks more crowded than I remember. I would say she was testing out this piece of equipment. What is it?" I asked Jackie.

"A Dictaphone. It records sounds. They've been around for a few years with little success, but recently professional offices have been purchasing them for leaving messages and dictation. I had one when I worked for my husband."

"Are you telling me there's a recording of the murder taking place?"

"That's right," O'Reilly said. "The damnedest thing I ever heard."

"How'd you know it was Denton?" I asked.

"The sound quality is poor, but she called him David when he entered," O'Reilly said.

"How's that prove anything? There could be several Davids in her life."

"True, and to get the judge to drop the case against you, we had to find the actual killer. I tried to get a search warrant for Denton's apartment, but the judge wanted more evidence. That's when your partner here came to your rescue," O'Reilly said as he ushered us into Johnson's office so his boys could get back to work.

"I was tempted to go over to Denton's place and confront him," Jackie said, "but realized it wouldn't accomplish anything other than give him enough warning to dispose of any evidence that might still exist."

"So what did you do?"

"I went back to our office to talk things over with Martha. During our conversation, Martha commented she was surprised the private investigator William Blair had hired to find the money Kathryn had stolen hadn't come snooping around. I agreed, especially when you were the one who found Kathryn's body. That's when I realized he was probably following up on other leads, leads that might help us."

"How'd you find this guy?"

"Like I once said: if you want to know anything about a wealthy family, ask the butler. The PI's name is Buddy Creso. He has an office downtown by the ferry terminal. At first he didn't want any more to do with the Blairs. Laura had him thrown off the estate when he tried to collect his fee. When I told him we'd pick up the tab, he dumped everything he had, which wasn't much, but it was enough.

He'd discovered Kathryn and Denton had secretly gotten married, so he tailed Denton, thinking he would lead him to Kathryn and the money. After Kathryn's murder, he continued shadowing Denton and also Johnson the lawyer. His log book showed Denton entering and leaving this building on the night of Evelyn's murder."

"With that, I got a search warrant, and we found traces of Evelyn's blood type on one of Denton's socks," O'Reilly said. "Oh, and get this, Denton not only admitted killing Kathryn, but also told Evelyn if he didn't find where old man Blair hid the original will, he might not get a dime of the estate."

I picked up one of the wax drums on Evelyn's desk. "Hard to believe I owe my freedom to one of these weird contraptions."

* * * * *

Once Jackie got back into the routine of work, even some of my family issues seemed to fade away. Ma had recovered fully from her injuries, Pop's shoe repair business had taken off once he purchased a Goodyear Lockstitching Sewing Machine for resoling shoes, and Uncle Luigi had a job he seemed to relish, which certainly made the mood around the dinner table more enjoyable.

"Hey, Pop. When you gonna hire some help?" I asked.

"Soon, but no more females."

Martha jumped on that one. "You got somethin' against women working?"

"They can work all they want, just not in my shop. All they want to do is change things. I'm not selling shoes anymore, so I don't need a female's touch."

"How about Gino? Maybe we should help him out. What do ya think, Pop?" I asked.

"What do I think? I think you're nuts. He's a bum. I don't need that kind of problem."

"I'll tell you one thing, he's smart, and he got me out of a jam. Pouring whiskey over that guy who tried to kill me was a clever move," I said.

"That's not saying much. We all got you out of a jam this year," Uncle Luigi said as he raised his glass to make a toast. "To Joey, may next year be prosperous and less dangerous for all of us."

The wine flowed freely that night. We had a good time, and in a moment of weakness, Pop agreed to give Gino a try.

* * * * *

Jackie passed her PI test on the first try. When she was gone for the day taking the exam, I had her name added to the main door of our office, *Joey Batista & Jacqueline Forsythe - Private Investigators.*

To celebrate, I booked La Cucina Restaurant for the entire night. Just about everyone from the neighborhood came, including Mr. Castellano and his family. Even someone from the DA's office was there, thanks to Martha. It didn't take her long to get over Denton and shift her attention to the assistant DA.

I asked Lieutenant Sullivan and O'Reilly to stick around after the party so we could discuss how Nick Fuso's taskforce was doing tracking down the Island killer. I was especially interested if the investigation into Shirley's murder had provided any new leads.

"Has Nick confirmed the Simonette girl received treatment at the clinic?" I asked Sullivan.

"The parents still insist their daughter didn't have a drug problem, but Nick got confirmation from Maria

Taglio, who used to run the clinic. She remembered the girl."

"Great, that should give Nick some new leads to follow."

"I'm afraid not. Nick believes it's just a coincidence and that Shirley's death and the girl's murders have nothing to do with each other. He's still focusing his attention on the last four victims."

"What do you think?"

"Me? I think Nick's off base and so does O'Reilly, but we can't figure out how everything ties together."

Jackie had enough. "I don't believe what I'm hearing. You guys are ignoring what Shirley discovered. She's dead because she realized Simonette had been a patient at the clinic."

"How did the killer know Shirley made that discovery?" Sullivan asked.

"I think that's Jackie's point," I said. "Answer that question and we have our killer. Shirley was streetwise and wouldn't have made such a statement if she wasn't sure."

"It's Nick's case, and I'm not going to interfere. If there's a link between the murders, he'll eventually find it," Sullivan said.

The booze I consumed during the party had loosened my tongue. "Yeah, and how many more young women have to die before he does? It might be Nick's case, but it's your job."

"What do you want me to do? Yank him off the investigation?"

"No, but you should give him a shove in the right direction."

O'Reilly ordered more drinks. When they arrived, I explained how Frank Galvano, Jackie, and Martha cracked the Blair case by simply sitting around throwing out ideas, and suggested we use the same technique. We scheduled a meeting for mid-week and Sullivan agreed to drag Nick along.

* * * * *

Martha continued getting walk-in traffic, everything from lost dogs, unfaithful husbands, blackmail, and even two unsolved murder cases. She let us know what she thought about how we were running the business after she turned away six cases.

"I don't mean to keep harping on the same topic, but how the hell are we gonna stay in business if you guys don't take on some new cases?" she said as she threw down four folders on each of our desks.

She had every right to be angry, but we still had three open investigations and that, in my opinion, was enough. "We need to close out the cases we have," I said, pushing the folders aside.

"What does it take to close out a case? We know who killed Kathryn Blair, case closed. That old man who sees a shadow around every corner isn't paying you jack, and I hate to say it, but Shirley's murder isn't our case. It's an active police investigation."

Jackie came around her desk and got Martha to sit down. "The Blair case isn't closed because we haven't found the original will."

Martha fired back. "I still don't see how that impacts us. You can't be doing the police department's job, especially for free."

"That's true," I said. "But right now we have close to sixty thousand dollars and a valuable necklace that belongs to the rightful heir of the Blair estate. If we can locate the original will, then we can return the money minus a fee, a rather large fee."

"You're wasting your time. Laura isn't going to let you near the estate, and besides, she probably already found where the old man hid the will and destroyed it. I know that's what I'd do."

"O'Reilly's working on getting a warrant, and when he does, we'll have a chance to look around the estate," I said.

"I still don't see how that justifies not taking on new clients," Martha said as she stood to leave.

I grabbed her hand, and we all sat in our familiar circle. "You're right. We could take on some new cases. The truth is I have a chance to finally know what happened to Anita by helping find Shirley's killer. I don't want to add other distractions."

The look in her eyes changed from anger to compassion. "All you had to do was tell me what you were thinking. Most of the more interesting cases can wait until January."

As she went back to her desk, Jackie and I looked at each other and smiled. We knew she'd be back if we didn't make progress soon.

As it turned out, the next day I found the original Blair will without leaving the building. Frank Galvano and I planned to visit Kathryn Blair's gravesite to pay our final respects, since her murderer was now behind bars. I asked Pop to build a watertight box to hold the picture frame I had found in the room the day I discovered her body. I sat at my desk with the box Pop made and the picture frame, along with a new piece of glass covering. When I removed the backing on the frame, I found the original will behind the picture. I looked at the picture again, and it truly felt like they were both smiling at me.

All along, I'd thought the picture belonged to Kathryn, but it must have been the old man's. She probably took it with her when her brother forced out of the mansion.

The Blair estate belonged to the butler. The old man

explained in his will why he disinherited his stepchildren. William was a lazy good-for-nothing, and he knew Kathryn had eloped without his blessing.

* * * * *

When Nick Fuso entered the room and saw Jackie and Martha seated with the rest of us, he stopped in midstride.

"What are they doing here?" he asked.

Sullivan jumped in before I could react. "I suggest we get to work. Joey, why don't you explain why we're here?"

"As you all know, I believe the key to finding the Island killer is to understand why he went out of his way to kill Shirley."

"Do I have to waste my time listening to this crap? There's no hard evidence to support his statement," Nick said.

"If you want to keep your job, you will," Sullivan said.

I continued, "With this assumption in mind, I want us to ask questions, and whoever has an answer, throw it out. Martha, take notes and feel free to participate. I'll begin. What do all the murdered girls have in common?"

When Nick didn't respond, Sullivan answered for him. "They were all young, between sixteen and twenty-five, and all virgins."

"Except Shirley," Nick said with some sarcasm.

"Did they put up a struggle?" Jackie asked.

No one answered. Sullivan turned again to Nick.

"No," Nick said.

"How can you tell?" Martha asked.

"No bruises or other physical evidence that they resisted."

"When did the murders take place, during the day, at night, or both?" I asked.

"Based on the reports I've read, they all took place sometime after sunset," O'Reilly answered.

"Is it true the murders stopped during the war?" O'Reilly asked.

"There's a two-year gap. It looks like our boy joined the military," Sullivan said.

"What were the girls doing before they got killed? Were they alone?" Martha asked.

"As far as we can tell, all the girls were out walking alone, either going or coming home from a party or some other social gathering," Nick said.

"That would imply the killer planned when he was going to kill the girls, since most social events are scheduled out in time," O'Reilly said, thinking aloud.

"At least one girl left a church meeting early because she felt sick," Nick said.

"That would imply the killer drives around looking for young girls walking alone at night," Sullivan said.

"But these aren't random killings. The girls have some things in common, and they didn't put up a fight. I think he knew them," Jackie said.

"That's highly unlikely," Nick countered.

Even before Nick finished his statement, Jackie strode toward him with her fiery red hair flailing in all directions. The only sounds in the room at that moment were the echo of her shoes striking the tile floor and the air rushing from her flared nostrils.

"Unlikely, but true. Maybe you should take your blinders off and open your mind."

Nick was about to get up. "Let her speak," Sullivan ordered.

"This guy knew the girls, *all* of them. They trusted him enough to get into his car or allow him to approach at night. The girls were from different parts of the Island, so he must have spent considerable time in each area, and we can assume it's not unusual for him to be traveling at night in his car."

Hearing Jackie state all the critical clues together caused me to recall my conversation with Andy Cognetta. "I interviewed a neighbor of Anita, and he mentioned that the only visitors to the farms were the local priest, a doc when needed, and a patrol officer making his rounds."

"That's exactly what I believe," Jackie said. "This killer is either a priest or a cop who worked the more isolated parts of the Island before the war and now works near the ferry terminal in Tompkinsville."

"Jesus," O'Reilly said.

Sullivan put on his coat and headed for the door. "Let's go, Nick. We got some old records to go through."

"You're not buying this crap? Do you really think a psycho cop or a priest is on the loose killing these girls?"

"Until you come up with a better idea, we're going with this one."

"Wait a minute. How does Shirley's murder fit into the picture?" Nick asked.

"There's only one logical explanation," Sullivan said. "Shirley found the Simonette file and probably called the person who brought her to the clinic. And my guess is he's our boy!"

As Sullivan held the door for Nick, it suddenly felt like everything moved in slow motion: the waiter placing a plate on a customer's table, the door closing in infinitesimally small increments as Sullivan's coat trailed through the opening. I rushed toward the door, throwing a table to the side. Sullivan and Nick reentered to see what the commotion was about.

"Joey, what's going on?" O'Reilly said as he spun me around.

"I know who the killer is."

"That's impossible," Nick said.

"Let's hear him out," Sullivan said. "Let's have it, Joey."

Part of me wanted to leave and find the bastard myself. All I needed was a few minutes alone with the creep and I would know if he killed Anita. It was too late for that now.

"Jackie's right, the last few murders occurred near the ferry terminal, so our killer currently works in Tompkinsville, close to the clinic. I believe Shirley recognized his name in the Simonette file and called him."

"Who the hell is it?" Sullivan practically shouted.

"He's a cop. The same cop who helped in the search for Anita. I met him again the first day I came to the clinic to investigate Vincent Taglio's death. Sergeant James Rafferty is your killer."

* * * * *

The girls wanted to come along, but I convinced them to stay with my parents and Uncle Luigi. There was no telling what this nut would do, especially if he got away and realized I was involved.

By the time we got to the Island and checked the police roster at the station, it was past midnight. Rafferty had the night off and, as I had suspected, he'd had the night shift when Shirley was murdered. Sullivan felt he had enough circumstantial evidence to make a move that night.

He called in three police cars to block off Rafferty's street. We parked four houses down and made our way to Rafferty's place. Sullivan and Nick knocked on the front door as O'Reilly and I went around back. It was pitch dark and, as in childhood nightmares, objects looked larger than life, every sound became amplified, and the smells emanating from the earth filled the air with impending doom. When we turned the corner around the house, the odor of decaying garbage overwhelmed our senses, causing us to turn away and cover our faces. The hairs on my neck suddenly stiffened, and I knew instantly something was wrong. It was a familiar feeling that had saved my life more times than I would like to remember during the war.

"O'Reilly, something's not right. This is too easy. I think we're doing exactly what Rafferty wants. From the smell of that garbage, he hasn't lived here in weeks. I'm going back around front. Be careful," I said.

I was making my way along the side of the house when I heard a loud crash followed by the sound of a shotgun blast. As I rounded the front of the house, I saw Nick's lifeless body, covered in blood, sprawled halfway down the porch stairs. Sullivan was crouched by the right side of the doorframe, about ready to fire into the doorway. My screams froze his movements. I ran past Nick's body, grabbed Sullivan's arm, and yanked him off the porch in a flying leap just as the house exploded into a fiery inferno.

I got to my feet, feeling a little wobbly, and knelt down by Sullivan's side. He had a fractured leg and a dislocated shoulder. This time I was fortunate and had only a nasty gash on my forehead from some flying debris. I apparently looked worse than I felt.

"You okay?" Sullivan asked.

"I'm fine."

"You sure?"

"Just a head wound. Don't move until *you* get medical attention. I'm going to check on O'Reilly," I said.

O'Reilly looked like shit but was uninjured. The explosion had thrown him down, into a mud hole.

Before Sullivan left the scene in an ambulance, he put O'Reilly in charge and made his intentions clear. "Find that dirty bastard and end this thing tonight."

O'Reilly didn't waste any time. He put blockades at all exits off the Island and ordered every passenger on any ferryboat that had already left the Island checked for identification.

"How did you know the house was gonna blow?" O'Reilly asked when we were alone.

"That booby-trap is straight out of the army's espionage manual. Set up a dummy safe house, draw in the enemy, and blow it to hell. My guess is Rafferty had special training similar to mine."

"How did he know?" O'Reilly asked me.

"As soon as he killed Shirley, his time was running out, and he knew it."

"You're telling me he's gonna be hard to catch?"

"You'll catch him only if he slips up. I guarantee you he has a way off this Island."

"What do ya mean, if he slips up?" O'Reilly asked.

A storm cloud opened up and drenched us in a matter of seconds. We both looked like hell; blood encrusted my hair and face, and O'Reilly, encased in mud, smelt like he had just emerged from a grave.

"I suggest we see if Doc Swartz will put us up at the clinic. We can't do much more tonight, and I'll explain what I meant after we clean up." O'Reilly agreed.

* * * * *

Sullivan got O'Reilly officially assigned to the case and put him in charge of Nick's taskforce. It didn't take long to verify Rafferty fit the profile we had pieced together the night Nick got himself killed.

After going door to door around the neighborhood, we discovered Rafferty had moved a few houses down the block on the opposite side of the street. Just as I thought, he'd had a front-row view to all the action that took place that night, and I was sure he'd hung around to watch his handiwork. He probably dreamed of the day someone would set off his booby trap and anxiously anticipated the explosion. I was right, once he killed Shirley he knew it was just a matter of time before he became a suspect, so he set a trap that also destroyed any evidence that might have been in the house.

O'Reilly didn't think Rafferty made it off the Island, and if he had, he didn't believe he would be stupid enough to hang around waiting to get even with me. I knew differently and enlisted the help of Castellano and my uncle.

"Castellano has men stationed all over Market Street," Uncle Luigi said.

"Good, now I need you to stay with Ma and Pop until this is over."

"They won't like it."

"They'll get used to it."

"What makes you so sure this guy's gonna come after you or someone close to you?"

"He recognized me the first day we met at the clinic and knows I've been working with Nick's taskforce to track down Anita's killer. I won't stop looking for him until one of us is dead, and he knows it."

"If I were him, I'd get the hell out of town and worry about you some other time, on my own terms," Luigi said.

"That would be logical, but this guy is deranged. He was a sniper in the war, which tells me he enjoys playing cat and mouse."

"I get it. He kills someone close to you to get even and the games begin," Uncle Luigi said.

"Something like that, and given how much he enjoys killing women, my guess is that he'll go after Jackie, Martha, or Ma."

"That sick bastard."

The next three days passed uneventfully. We ran the office as usual, and the girls stayed with me at night. They were both armed, and Jackie wore her knife harness around the clock. By the third day I couldn't help but wonder if O'Reilly was right and I simply had an overactive imagination. Two nights later we got a call from Maria Taglio.

"Joey, Rafferty says to tell you he's here at the restaurant. He wants you to come over. I'm scared, Joey."

"Don't do anything to upset him. I'm coming."

When I told my uncle, he wanted to tag along and bring some of Castellano's boys.

"No, I need you here. It might be a trick to draw us away. Maria could be dead by the time I get to the restaurant."

There was no stopping Jackie or Martha from joining me. When we arrived at the restaurant, I gave them the job of backing me up, but only as a last resort.

"I'm going in the front door. You guys go around back. And try to get in without making too much noise," I said.

"Don't worry, I know how to jimmy a lock," Jackie said.

"Let's not end up dead heroes. Just distract him if I get in a jam. He'll have a gun, and I'm sure he's damn good with it."

Jackie headed around back. Martha hesitated long enough for me to see tears forming in her eyes.

"Don't worry. I'll be okay," I said.

"He's gonna kill you the moment you walk in that door."

"I don't think so. His ego's too big. He needs to know who's better."

The front door opened with ease. The place looked more like an English pub than an Italian restaurant. Thick, dark rafters crisscrossed the ceiling, held in place by sturdy weather-beaten posts interspersed among the numerous dining tables. A highly polished redwood bar meandered along the right wall, now used by the wait staff to minimize the number of trips back to the kitchen. Every chandelier in the room shone brightly, making it difficult to see far into the restaurant. Maria sat at a back table with her hands tied behind her back, and Rafferty held a gun to her head. I got to within fifteen feet when Rafferty put his hand up.

"Far enough. Put your gun on the floor and kick it over here," he said.

I did as told. "If you had any brains, you'd be half way to Chicago by now," I said.

"How did you know where I was heading next?"

"Chicago's a perfect place for a low-life to hide. Why hang around here and take the risk?"

"I seem to remember some dumb kid pestering me years ago who wouldn't give up looking for his girlfriend. Amazing how a small pain in the ass can grow into a big one," he said as he stood behind Maria and put a knife to her throat and pointed his gun at me.

In a few seconds, both Maria and I would be dead.

"So that's it. You shoot me, kill Maria, and you're home-free."

"You're close. I shoot you, have a little fun with Maria, and then I'm home-free."

"I'm disappointed," I said as I flipped open my stiletto. "Your army records indicated you're an expert in hand-to-hand combat. So am I."

Rafferty pointed his knife at me, "You think you can take me with that toothpick?"

"Actually I was thinking about using something a little more to your liking," I said as I reached my left hand behind my back and pulled out the bowie knife that had belonged to the hatchet man Jackie killed in her apartment.

Rafferty was impressed, but then he noticed a break in my concentration as my eyes shifted to his left. He turned, fired, and hit Jackie, sending her smashing back against a wall. The knife in her hand fell to the floor as she slid down, leaving behind a trail of blood.

Everything happened in a split second. My stiletto missed its mark but did enough damage to prevent Rafferty from getting off a second shot. He dropped his gun when the blade penetrated his back above the right shoulder blade. As I dove for my gun, two shots rang out, striking the post next to Rafferty. Martha wasn't a great shot, but she got close enough that Rafferty overturned several tables for protection. Maria took advantage of the opportunity to lunge out of her chair and scramble on the floor toward me as I fired a barrage of bullets in Rafferty's direction to give her and Martha some cover.

Suddenly an eerie silence engulfed the restaurant. I quickly glanced over at the girls and saw Jackie keeping a bead on Rafferty's position as Martha tried to stop the bleeding from her side.

"Rafferty!" I shouted. "Looks like we have a stand-off and you're running out of time. The cops will be here any minute."

Maria whispered in my ear that Rafferty had two sticks of dynamite tucked in his waistband around his back.

"Not necessarily," he said with an unnatural laugh.

The sparks from the fuse flying through the air indicated we had less than ten seconds to find better protection. I pulled Maria up and ran, dragging her forward as she stumbled. There wasn't time to reach the end of the bar.

Two feet from the bar, I grabbed her waist with one arm, outstretched my other, and hurled us over the top of the bar as the dynamite exploded. The concussion from the blast obliterated the mirrors hanging on the wall, and one of the chandeliers fell, shattering on the countertop. We both had numerous cuts, but nothing life-threatening.

Jackie fired several shots, keeping Rafferty pinned down, but I could tell she was weakening as her shots lost their accuracy. Martha was still working on her wound.

I had to act. We wouldn't survive another blast, and if he threw his last stick of dynamite in Jackie and Martha's direction, they wouldn't have a chance.

"Hey Joey, you still kicking?"

"At least until I get to put a bullet through that deranged head of yours."

"Sorry pal, but I don't think that's gonna happen."

As he spoke, I walked up to his position and pointed my gun at the back of his head. He turned to heave his last stick of dynamite.

"You got two seconds to pull that fuse before I pump you full of lead," I said.

Rafferty stood, grinned, and tossed the dynamite at my chest, "You do it," he said.

As I fumbled with the rapidly burning fuse, he ran into the kitchen of the restaurant. Before following, I called out to Martha.

"We're okay. I stopped the bleeding. Go get the bastard," she shouted back.

Maria went to be with the girls as I pushed open the kitchen door. The lights were out, and I could hear Rafferty fumbling around, trying to find a back exit. I was familiar with the layout of the kitchen and silently made my way to the back door and waited. When he got to within a few feet, I cocked my gun.

Rafferty ran for the light coming through the kitchen doors, back into the main part of the restaurant. I was right behind him when he suddenly stopped and raised his arms. Martha stood five feet in front of him with her gun pointed at his chest. I shoved Rafferty against a wall and put my gun under his chin. He still held his hands over his head and faced me with a sinister smile.

"You have nothing on me. There's no hard evidence connecting me to any of those murders. I made sure of that when the house blew. I'm going to walk, move out of this town, and then someday you're going to lose everyone you care about. One by one."

I backed away and aimed my .45 at his gut. "Did you kill Anita?"

Sweat beaded on his forehead. He didn't know what I was gonna do and neither did I. "You're the detective. Isn't that your job to find out?" he said as he slowly lowered his arms behind his head.

I grabbed his shirt collar and yanked him forward, accidently tearing open his collar. He saw the recognition in my eyes and dropped his hands behind his neck, but he wasn't fast enough. I put my three remaining bullets into his stomach at close range. He staggered then slid to the floor. I tossed aside my gun, leaned over his heaving body, and pulled out my bowie knife. Both Jackie and Martha yelled at me to stop, but I remained focused on only one thing as my vision blurred from tears I'd held back for years. Martha rushed to my side and reached for my arm as I ripped open Rafferty's shirt and cut the brown twine he had around his neck. I fell to my knees and watched him die, clutching in my hand the rings he took from each of his victims. Suddenly I was back with Anita, sitting on the bank of the stream that flowed into the lake, making a ring out of a small vine. I took some packing twine out of my pocket, strung the twine through the ring, and tied it around Anita's neck. "I'll never take it off, Joey. I promise."

"You killed him in cold blood," Martha said, bringing me back to the present.

I reached behind Rafferty's head and pulled a knife from a sheath he had behind his neck.

Martha pried open my other hand and immediately understood the meaning of what she saw. "Anita and her father can be at rest now, and so will you."

It took O'Reilly two hours to arrive and secure the scene. In the meantime I had taken Rafferty's gun and fired two shots into one of the overturned tables to ensure the DA couldn't accuse me of killing Sergeant Rafferty out of revenge. I then called a local physician, who arrived within minutes and patched up Jackie's side. She had received a wound just above the right hipbone. Once O'Reilly finished questioning us, we got her back to the apartment building, where Ma took complete control over her life for the next few days.

As Jackie recovered, I visited the cemetery where we buried Anita's father and placed her box of trinkets containing her grandmother's hairbrush, comb, and mirror atop his coffin. Before the gravediggers replaced the dirt, I laid her homemade necklace and engagement ring alongside the box. I didn't need them to remember her.

On the way home, I had to complete one last wish for Anita's father. I went to see Sister Mary Magdalene Meade at the orphanage and turned over all the proceeds from Mr. Sgarlata's farm.

When I got home, I gave Ma back her locket.

* * * * *

The new editor of the *Daily News* called shortly after the

story broke about the death of the "Island Homicidal Cop." He wanted an exclusive interview based on the contract I had signed with Jackie's deceased husband, Al Forsythe. I reminded the editor that based on the contract, he owed me back pay and made it clear the paper needed to pay up if they wanted the story.

Once again Jackie and I were front-page news, and with this recent notoriety came a deluge of new clients looking to secure our services.

As usual Martha did the initial interviews and compiled a list for our review. With all the press coverage, we briefly contemplated hiring another partner.

"What am I supposed to do with all these people? Everyone has a sob story that would tear your heart out," Martha said.

"Maybe it's time to expand," Jackie suggested. "We could rent a larger office and hire two or three associates."

"If we did, I would be spending most of my time managing and less time investigating. I've only been in the business a year," I said.

As Jackie and I debated how to solve our problem, Martha brought us back to the present. "I'm sorry, but I've got a room full of people who want answers now."

Jackie and I joined in the effort to get preliminary information and told each potential client we would get back in touch during the first week of January. At that time, we would either take their case or refer them to a reputable detective agency.

This strategy worked fine for a few days, until Sadie Kowalski showed up. "Joey Batista, do you remember what you said to me at my father's funeral? Well, it's been months and I haven't heard from you. The cops have all but given up on finding my father's murderer."

"I'm sorry, Sadie."

"It looks to me like you're taking on new clients. What about your *friends*? Jesus, Joey, we grew up together. My father was a good man and didn't deserve to die with a bailing hook through his neck."

"We'll get right on it. I swear we'll find who killed your father."

Both Jackie and Martha stood side by side with their arms folded, looking disappointed. Jackie stepped forward, put her arm around Sadie's shoulder, and ushered her out, saying we would begin to investigate her father's death during the second week in January. "Joey has another commitment until then," she said as she closed the door.

"What commitment?" I asked.

"A vacation. We rented a cabin in the Adirondacks so the four of us could get away."

"Four of us?"

"I wasn't sure about David Denton, so I also dated Assistant DA Brown at the same time," Martha said with a sparkle in her eye.

"What's his name again?" I asked.

"Anthony."

We agreed to leave two days after Christmas.

* * * * *

The media frenzy that followed the news story about the death of the Island Killer disrupted any possibility of a normal holiday celebration, and that didn't set well with Ma.

"Joey, you gotta get outta this detective business. Look at us: Luigi, your beloved uncle, shot and without his bar; your partner also got shot, thank God she's gonna be okay; your secretary falls in love with a murderer; Pop's store gets blown to pieces; and I end up in the hospital."

"Ma, I know it's been a tough year, but you gotta remember, I'm still learning this business. Besides, we have a lot to be grateful for."

"What? Are you making a joke?"

"I'm serious. Let's go around the table. Uncle Luigi, you go first."

"Me, I'm alive, and no thanks to you."

"Hey, quite fooling around and give it to us straight. How are things going?"

"Give me a minute to think. Let's see, I still own this building and the rents have increased now that the second floor is usable for tenants. Working for Castellano, I'm learning more about running a speakeasy and how to set up a joint to avoid a raid. I think pretty soon I'll have my own place again. Ain't that right, Joey?"

"Don't push it, Uncle. I'm working on getting you that loan you asked for. What about you, Martha?"

"God, I'm so lucky I found out about Denton. Do you believe I picked him over an assistant DA? My job is incredibly interesting. I actually helped stop a mass murderer!"

"What about it, Pops? Are you still angry?" I asked.

"Nah, I like the repair business. It's a hell of a lot easier than making shoes, and factory shoes need new leather every two or three months. At five bits for each repair, we'll soon be able to move to Grymes Hill."

"Jackie?"

She got up from her chair and bent over to give me a kiss on the cheek. "Aside from a pain in my side, I think life is good. I finally have a family to be with and a man who appreciates my not-so-tender side."

"Okay, Ma. The moment of truth," I said.

She couldn't help but smile. "Your pop is much happier, which makes me happy."

"Is that it? What about managing this building? How does it make you feel?" I asked.

"More useful."

"Good! Now let's all enjoy this food and be thankful we have each other and celebrate the holidays the way we have always done—with family, friends, and some good Italian wine."

* * * * *

The four of us met in the office, about to leave on our vacation, when Joseph, the Blair butler, entered unannounced.

"Sorry, sir. I was hoping we could have a word, if it's not too inconvenient."

"We have a train to catch, but we can talk for a few minutes. You don't mind if my partner joins us."

"Of course not, sir."

Martha and her date left for the train station to pick up the tickets in case we ran late. I was curious as to why Joseph showed up, and there was still the issue of the cash and necklace that now technically belonged to him.

"Joseph, I'm afraid we don't know your last name," I said.

"Stewart, sir."

"Well, Mr. Stewart, now that you're a multimillionaire, I suggest you drop the 'sir'."

"Yes I know, but it's a difficult habit to break."

"Have you decided what you're going to do now that you're rich?"

Without hesitation he said, "I'm going to marry the maid and then hire a butler."

Jackie and I broke out in laughter, and Joseph chimed right in. It was probably the first time he'd cracked a smile in years.

"What can we do for you?" I asked.

"Well sir, I want to thank you for all you did in bringing Kathryn's murderer to justice and for finding the missing will. But most of all, I want to make sure you were properly compensated."

"That won't be necessary. Kathryn paid us handsomely before she died."

"I see. Then I won't delay you any longer."

"There is the issue of the money and necklace Kathryn stole from the estate," I said.

"Kathryn would never steal from her father. The items she took belonged to Kathryn, part of her dowry left to her by her mother."

"Are you saying all that money belongs to her estate?"

"That's correct, sir. There was considerable more cash in the safe that she didn't take. My understanding is Kathryn left everything to you, in the event she was killed and if you found her murderer. It's unfortunate that no one has located these items."

"You never know. They might show up someday," I said.

* * * * *

As soon as we arrived at the cabin, a blizzard hit, forcing us to stay inside the whole week. We had plenty of food, as well as wood for the fireplace, along with a few good books and, of course, each other.

You know how it goes. When you're having fun, time seems to pass too quickly, and Jackie never did give me enough time to finish Zane Grey's latest book.

* * * * *

I was surprised to find Martha wasn't at her desk when I arrived at the office later than usual on the first day back. Entering the inner office, I expected to see Jackie, but instead found Castellano sitting behind my desk.

"I didn't think you'd mind if I gave the girls the morning off," he said while lighting a cigar.

"Joey," he continued. "Take a seat. We need to talk."

I sat in one of the leather chairs in front of my desk and crossed my legs, trying to look relaxed. "It must be serious," I said.

"I hear that Sadie Kowalski hired you to find her father's killer."

"I intend to begin today."

"I own this waterfront, and if you're gonna nose around my docks, you need to see me first. You should know this."

"I would think you would want to know what happened," I said.

We stood at the same time as Castellano snuffed out his cigar on my new mahogany desk. Standing inches away, he gave me a warning.

"I would risk my life for your family, but this is business. Stay away from this case unless *I* ask you to get involved."

"I can't do that Mr. Castellano. I made a promise to Sadie."

"Break it!" he said as he silently closed the door behind him.

Jackie and Martha walked in the office shortly after Castellano left.

"What was that all about?" Jackie asked.

"Just a gentle warning about investigating the Kowalski murder."

"He didn't seem gentle when he told us to leave the office. You sure he didn't *order* you to stay off the case?"

Martha asked.

I recalled my uncle's warning about Castellano: *"You give him a finger, he'll take an arm. Give him an arm, and he'll take your soul."*

"He did, so we'll move cautiously. Martha, contact O'Reilly and get everything he has on the murder. Jackie, you need to wrap up the Cafiero case. I want all our energy focused on finding who killed Sadie's father. He was a friend of mine."

The girls left the room, and I found myself gazing out the window, wondering how my life and the lives of those around me would change during my second year as a PI.

About the Authors

Tom and Judy Viola were both raised on Staten Island, New York. They met in high school and have been married for forty years.

Tom has degrees in physics, engineering physics, and electrical engineering and also has an executive MBA. He retired from Hewlett Packard after thirty years of service.

Judy has a BS degree and is a registered nurse specializing in emergency medicine. She is also a former middle school teacher.

This is their first novel, and they are currently working on *The Gumshoe Chronicles – 1921* and a science fiction novel.

LaVergne, TN USA
05 May 2010
181567LV00002B/2/P